Meadow's Keep

Also by Shanon Grey

Book One: The GATEKEEPERS Series
The Shoppe of Spells

Pennyroyal Christmas
~A Ruthorford Holiday Story~

Meadow's Keep

THE GATEKEEPERS – Book Two

Shanon Grey

Meadow's Keep

Copyright © 2013, Shanon Grey
Print ISBN-13: 978-1484939352
Print ISBN-10: 1484939352
Digital ISBN: 9781301844364
Cover Art Design by Crossroads Publishing House, LLC

Trade Paperback release, May 2013
Digital Release, May 2013

Crossroads Publishing House, LLC
PO Box 723
Emporia, VA 23847

Crossroads Publishing House
http://www.crossroadspublishinghouse.com/

www.CrossroadsPublishingHouse.com

Acknowledgements

I want to thank so many people who encouraged me to do this book. If I have forgotten someone, please forgive me, you are there in the heart of the book.

First and foremost, I want to thank my family, who always believes in me, yet isn't afraid to make a comment, suggestion, or an edit. They take endless hours reading and rereading my manuscripts, until I'm sure they could quote it by rote. You are my mainstay, my reason for being. I love you all so very much.

I want to thank my publisher, Crossroads Publishing House, for continuing to love my stories and for helping me get them to the public.

I want to thank Linda and Judy for being the kind of best friends a writer needs.

I want to thank Pam for being a genius and for pushing when I needed that extra push, as well as all the Pearls for having my back, no matter what.

I want to thank Tara for encouraging me and being willing to spend her lunch hours plotting or rehashing a scene.

I want to thank Ruthy and Doris for being the kind of women I have always aspired to be. They keep me on my toes and thinking ~ ever striving to do my best.

I want to thank Doug for inspiring me to add my poem, heart, to Meadow's Keep.

And I want to thank my readers and fans for your cards, and messages of encouragement. You are t work to produce the very best stories I can. ⊤

Dedication

There are those that are fortunate to have never witnessed violence to themselves or someone else. That number is fewer than I'd like to admit. For others, violence comes swift and unexpected, at least in the beginning. Then, for many reasons, that violence is endured until the victim gets help or dies.

One of the obstacles, often ill perceived, is that they feel they have no options and no place to go. But that isn't so. There are real places, similar to my fictional Safe Harbor, ready and willing to offer a haven, safe from those that would cause them harm. It is to those places and the incredible people that dedicate their lives to helping the victims of domestic violence that this book is dedicated. In a perfect world, places like Safe Harbor wouldn't be necessary. Until that time, let us commend the people that dedicate their time and money helping those in need.

For more information, RAINN (Rape, Abuse, and Incest Nation Network) is a good place to begin. Here's the link: http://www.rainn.org/

On their site is listed the following hotline: National Sexual Assault Hotline | **1.800.656.HOPE(4673)** | Free. Confidential. 24/7

Safe Harbor

The doors we close

Bear the Weight

Of silent cries and hasty goodbyes

As we disappear into the night

Shrouded—protected by the dark

Seeking shelter—a comforting hand

To wipe the tears

And heal the wounds

From tortures left unseen

To all but a few—us

~Shanon Grey~

Prologue

Jasmine Monroe hauled the suitcase out from under the bed and, using both hands, hoisted the reinforced leather case onto the mattress. With swift movements, she flipped the latches on either side of the handle. Sweat beaded and slid down the cleavage between her breasts. She twisted her shoulders and pulled the damp T-shirt away from her body, fanning it.

She threw back the lid. Inside lay a tangled mass of chains and locks, some open, some closed. She grabbed a large lock and cursed when it resisted her tug, captured by the weight of the chaos around it. Holding the closed padlock in her right hand, she narrowed her eyes, focusing on the mechanism. She heard a crackle as the current moved from her body. The shackle slipped out of the lock and twisted to the side. She upended the lock to allow the chains to fall back into the suitcase and tossed the lock on the bed.

Jasmine thrust her hand back into the mass of chains. Using the back of her left forearm, she wiped the sweat away from her upper lip. *Ah, gotcha!* She twisted through the chains and yanked several times. The $1,400.00 military-grade titanium padlock moved a few inches, then stopped, still attached to two heavy-duty links of metal. As before, she held the padlock and concentrated. Nothing happened. She pressed her lips together. Her obsidian eyes narrowed. As her other hand moved forward, she resisted the urge and pulled it back. No, she had to be able to do it single-handed. She felt the energy build and move into her hand. With a loud pop, the padlock's shackle gave way. She yanked it free of the chains and, turning around, slid down the side of the bed to the floor, tears streaming down her cheeks.

Her gaze drifted down. Through the blur of tears, she could still see the scar on her wrist. Never again would some son of a bitch chain her to anything. Never again would another person have control over her body.

Chapter One

The peregrine falcon broke from its handler's arm and soared above the crowd, its screech piercing the air as it circled. It swooped down. Jasmine thrust her arm up in defense. Staring into the eyes of the diving predator, her world tilted. Her vision skewed and she was looking down upon her own upraised arm. The falcon thrust its wings, caught the air and descended onto the cashmere-covered perch. Jasmine blinked again and stared into the face of the bird, its head tilted as if studying her.

The crowd turned. Jenn sat rigid next to her, not moving a muscle.

Jasmine stared at the feathered predator, which blinked long looks back at her.

"Well, aren't you a pretty thing," she trilled in a soothing tone, not sure which of them she was comforting.

"Just be still, miss." The trainer approached, his voice shaky. He was watching her arm.

"I'm fine," she commented and looked from him, seeing the long, thick glove encasing his hand and arm, to the bird balancing gingerly on her thin arm. She felt no pain from the talons. She shifted her full attention back to the bird.

"Maybe if you give me a glove for my other arm, she'll transfer." Jasmine lifted her other arm out toward the handler, never letting her eyes move from the bird.

An assistant slid off a glove, handed it to a handler, who eased it onto Jasmine's outstretched arm. She moved her arms closer, close enough for the bird to step across. She was concerned that the talons might catch in the sweater and tether the bird, frightening her. Jasmine stared at the bird. As if in silent communication, the predator stepped over to the gloved arm and proceeded to groom its beak on the glove. A single thread of yarn remained attached to the longer back talon. She moved her arm away. The thread didn't budge. She slipped her arm inside the sweater until she could grasp the thread with her fingers. She looked at it with an intensity only Jenn caught. The thread disintegrated, not harming the bird. A faint whiff of burnt wool touched her nostrils.

"Time to go home, I'm afraid," she cooed and turned the bird over to the handler. The bird looked back at her before hopping onto the perch of the man's gloved arm. Jasmine nodded.

The handler moved away with the bird as the crowd burst into applause, thinking Jasmine to be a shill, planted as part of the show. She smiled, stood, and picking up her drink, stepped into the midway.

Handing Jenn her drink, Jasmine pulled off the heavy glove as the handler rushed over, now free of the falcon. Jasmine smiled and handed him the glove.

"Are you hurt?" he asked, his eyes scanning her arm.

She let her smile reassured him. "Not at all. She's very gentle."

"Not normally. Bryn doesn't like humans very much. A hunter killed her mate. She wasn't thriving when we found her." Still not convinced she was unharmed, he stared at her arm until she pushed up her sleeve, revealing smooth, unmarred skin.

"I'm sorry about her mate. But, she was extremely careful with me."

He handed her his card, hesitating before he spoke. "Well, if you have any problems or questions, you can call me. My cell number is the second one."

She flashed her dark eyes. He blanched, then flushed. Now certain it wasn't a come on, she rewarded him with a genuine smile. "Thanks," she said and took the card.

She and Jenn walked a good ways down the midway before Jenn spoke. She seemed to be pondering something. "What was that?" She asked the question quietly, not with the agitation that Jasmine could feel pouring off the smaller woman.

"I have no idea."

Jasmine stopped when Jenn did, turned and faced her. She lifted her shoulders. "I really don't have any idea what took place back there."

Jenn turned back and took a step forward.

"Except...." Jasmine added.

Jenn turned back and waited.

"For an instant," she took a deep breath, "when she was in flight, our eyes met and we seemed to connect."

"How?"

"I'm not sure." Jasmine frowned, thinking back. "It wasn't even communication. Or...maybe it was. I've never felt anything like it. I didn't call her, if that's what you're asking."

Jenn shook her head. "She came right to you. It seemed to be the most natural thing. When you raised your arm, I thought...." She took another step and turned again, started to say something, thought better of it, and started to turn. "Never mind." She was silent for a couple of steps, then spoke, "Maybe this wasn't a good idea." Jenn's assessing eyes studied her. Jasmine had come to Safe Harbor, Jenn's pride and joy, not abused by a family member, but kidnapped and attacked by a madman. As Jasmine healed, their friendship grew.

Jasmine put her arm around her short friend, giving her a quick hug and making Jenn's blonde curls bounce. "Are you kidding? I can't tell you the last time I went to a state fair."

Jenn laughed, a bubbly tumble of merriment that often escaped her lips. Jenn had a joy for living that Jasmine had seldom seen in anyone and especially not in someone who faced such tragedy every day. That laughter was infectious—and healing—as so many women and children could attest.

"I'm so glad you were willing to go with me. This escapade usually falls to Morgan, but I can't see Dorian sending her up to Virginia when she's so close to delivery."

"Not likely," Jasmine agreed. "He's become an absolute lunatic when it concerns Morgan and the baby." She laughed. She never thought she would see the day Dory would lose his cool. Morgan's appearance in his life had done just that.

Jenn interrupted her thoughts as she pointed to a sign. "Hey, let's go there."

Jasmine turned. *The Mysteries of Eryk Vreeland* blazed in 3-D graphics. "You want to go to a magic show?" Jasmine raised a brow.

"Why not?" Jenn laughed. "It might be fun." She took off in that direction.

Jasmine shook her head, smiled, and followed, dumping what remained of her sweet tea in the large trash bin outside the building.

They came to a stop at the poster outside of the auditorium. Neither spoke. They were held spellbound by a pair of emerald green eyes—all that could be seen of the face—staring at them. The green was facetted, like Morgan's—a trait specific to *some* of the descendants of the founding families from Ruthorford. Not a trait Jasmine shared, her own eyes black as coal. A shiver ran up Jasmine's spine. She looked at Jenn.

"You first," Jenn gave a nod toward the door.

"You sure you want to do this?" Jasmine asked. This didn't bode well. A member of a founding family in a magician's act? Highly unlikely. However, being a member of a founding family herself, Jasmine knew her obligations to Ruthorford, Georgia and Abbott House, the foundation started by the original family. No matter where she was living, Jasmine's ties to Ruthorford were strong. She took a steadying breath.

At Jenn's positive nod, Jasmine stepped through the door.

Dim lights cast shadows across the auditorium. A black curtain hung in deep folds in front of the stage. Jasmine led Jenn halfway down and stopped, letting Jenn go in first. They took the two seats next to the aisle. Although the auditorium was mostly empty, Jasmine had no intention of being hemmed in by people. They waited as more people filed in. Surprisingly, it filled quickly.

Music began and an announcer stepped out from between the curtains, proclaiming the amazing feats they were about to see were like no other. At the end he touted, "…with eyes that read the soul. Are you brave enough to let him read yours?"

Jasmine and Jenn looked at one another.

The music died as the curtains parted. Eryk Vreeland appeared in the middle of the stage out of nowhere. The audience resounded in loud gasps. Vreeland turned his head and looked directly at Jasmine—or, so it seemed.

Jasmine and Jenn clasped hands and squeezed. On stage stood the spitting image of Dorian Drake, Morgan's husband. With a white, billowy shirt tucked into tight black pants, he looked every bit the pirate. His black hair, longer than

Dorian's, brushed his collar. Lithe, well-formed muscles bulged beneath the tight fit of his pants as he moved. He was downright gorgeous.

He began talking, letting his gaze linger on them. Then, just as Jasmine began to feel uncomfortable, he turned his attention toward the full audience. The voice was different, still sexy, but with a European accent. Jasmine wondered if the accent was real. She studied the man on stage. There was something else she couldn't quite put her finger on. He was Dorian, yet not.

She smiled. Dorian. Her first love. Actually, her only love to date. Her ill-fated love. They had been too alike. She felt the sizzle in her fingertips and looked down as the tiny fibers of the sweater danced on end. Yes, they were definitely alike—only no one knew it but her, and, even then, only for the last year.

Applause brought her attention back to the stage. As the show progressed, she relaxed. He was definitely talented. Definitely a showman. With great drama, he bisected his beautiful assistant, the shrill scream of the saw filling the auditorium. Gasps rose as blood sprayed across the stage. Having donned a lab coat, now spattered with red, the magician wiped his brow, pulled the saw back, and separated the apparatus. With eyes glued to the stage, no one made a sound until his assistant wiggled her feet. Then, the audience burst into applause. He pushed the pieces back together, unlatched it, and helped the lovely woman, obviously unharmed, step from the contraption.

Later, he performed Houdini's Metamorphosis. He stepped into a large black cage, pulled the door closed with a loud clink and, with a flick of his hand, held onto the bars as the cage lifted and swung out over first few rows of the audience. With another wave of his hand, it rose higher, swaying in suspension. He yelled a corny, "Abra-ka-dabra" and a loud pop sounded as smoke filled the cage. To squeals of delight, the smoke cleared to show the beautiful assistant had replaced him in the suspended cage. Spotlights panned over the audience, back and forth, until finally, they stopped, converging on a single spot in the back. From one of the very back rows, the magician rose and bowed. The crowd went wild.

As he loped down the aisle toward the stage, he passed Jasmine's seat. The hair on her arm stood on end. He stopped, turned, and looked from her to Jenn, studying them, a look of consternation on his brow.

He spun back toward the stage and jogged down the aisle. People were throwing roses on stage. As he stepped onto the front of the stage, he turned toward the audience, lifted his hand and a rose froze in midair, suspended. He flicked his fingers and the rose exploded into a sparkling ball of energy, which he sent out over the audience. A collective gasp rose from the people. The ball hovered, swaying gently back and forth, then suddenly flew toward Jasmine. Without thinking, she raised her hand and the ball of energy careened back onstage, over his head, where it exploded into a shower of rose pedals. For barely an instant, his mouth hung open, then he looked at his audience and took bows to the standing applause.

Jasmine grabbed Jenn's hand and pulled her into the aisle. Ducking, they made their way toward the exit, hidden by the standing crowd. Outside, they stopped, turned and started talking over one another.

"Did you see that? Did you see his eyes?" they asked one another.

"What did you do?" Jenn grabbed Jasmine's arm.

They went silent, staring at one another, each weighing what they'd just seen.

Jasmine pulled the phone out of her pocket and started pacing, running through the numbers on the phone. She looked at her watch and dialed one.

A hoarse male voice answered the phone. "This better be good."

Jasmine laughed in spite of the situation. "And a fine 'how are you,' old man."

"Jasmine?" The voice sounded genuinely stunned.

"Yeah, Bask, it's me." A flicker of a smile touched her lips and was gone. "We have a situation."

Without hesitation, he was firing questions. "Location? How many? Will one team do?"

"Whoa!" She waited to get his attention. "It's not that kind of situation. I'm at the Virginia State Fair. There's a magician here. Eryk Vreeland. Except," she hesitated and took a deep breath, "he's Dorian with Morgan's eyes."

She listened to the silence and pondered what to say next.

Her exasperation showed as she rolled her eyes and snapped into the phone, "No, I haven't been drinking. Geez, Bask…." Her voice grew louder as she argued into the phone.

Grabbing the phone, Jenn said, "She's not kidding, Mr. Bask. This is Jennifer Davis. This man looks exactly, and I do mean exactly, like Dorian. Except, as Jasmine just told you, he has Morgan's very green and very *different* eyes." She handed the phone back to Jasmine.

Jasmine listened and burst out laughing. "And just how do you expect me to get a sample of his DNA, you old pervert?"

Jenn tugged at her arm. Jasmine turned to see the man in question striding toward them.

"Yeah, yeah. I'll think of something. Gotta go." She disconnected. God, was Bask gonna be pissed. He expected deference from everyone, no exception. He was, after all, *the* foundation.

Jasmine slipped the phone into her pocket. "Look, Jenn, it's the magician," she announced loudly, pointed at the man fast approaching them, and tried to look thrilled.

"Wow!" Jenn gushed. "You are fabulous. We were just discussing your act."

"I bet you were." He looked from one to the other.

His accent was gone. Jasmine placed his speech pattern from somewhere slightly north of Virginia. Jasmine raised one arched black eyebrow. "And here I was swooning over the European theme," she taunted him.

His brilliant green eyes scanned back and forth, finally stopping on Jasmine. "You." He reached out to grab her arm and jerked his hand back as the electricity arced between them.

"Damn!" He rubbed his hand down his thigh then looked at it. "What gives?"

"Better watch out or you might get stung." Her eyes flashed a warning. So much for the idea of DNA gathering. Didn't look like she was getting anywhere near him. That jolt had gone both ways, except, given what she'd experienced in the auditorium, she'd pretty much anticipated it and could hide her reaction.

"You almost ruined my act," he declared.

They both knew he was referring to what had happened earlier. "No, I didn't. I thought you were attacking me." In truth, Jasmine hadn't thought, she'd reacted. It had stunned her as much as it had him. Maybe more. Trying for a more diplomatic tactic, she worked at dampening her energy and stuck out her hand. "Hi. I'm Jasmine Monroe." Her black eyes sparkled.

He hesitated, narrowing his eyes as he looked from her hand to his, lifted the corner of his lip in a hint of a smile and grasped her slender hand in his larger one. A current flowed from both at the same time and slammed into their hands. His eyes darkened—the green facets beginning to swirl—and locked onto her obsidian orbs.

A loud pop had Jenn staring at their clasped hands. Without thinking, she grabbed their arms to pull them apart. The current burst through her, flinging her backward onto her butt as it broke the connection. For the briefest second, Jasmine stared at him as a sense of loss coursed through her and was gone.

"Are you all right?" Jasmine, knelt, fighting to keep the vibration out of her voice. Her entire being was on fire. The memory of the current flowing through her was vivid. Their heartbeats had matched, beat as one. She looked at the man kneeling beside her. His pupils were still dilated, but the green was returning to normal.

"I am so sorry…I don't understand," he said quietly. He reached out to offer Jenn a hand up. Jenn studied it, made a face, waved it away, and struggled to her feet.

Dusting off her jeans and not looking at the man in front of her, Jenn commented, "Must be a storm nearby."

Jasmine took the cue, looking to the sky. "We better get going before it hits." She turned to the magician. "Interesting show."

Eryk ran his hand across the back of his neck, dazed. "Yeah. Wasn't it?" He looked at the cloudless sky.

"Nice meeting you," Jasmine called over her shoulder as she pulled Jenn along with her. She didn't know how long it would be before he followed them. As soon as they rounded a curve, they took off for the parking area.

"What was that all about," Jenn asked, out of breath. "And that zapping thing. What…?"

"I don't know. I dampened my energy, but it didn't seem to matter. On the other hand—literally, I might add—I got his DNA."

"How?"

"When you grabbed us and we came apart, I scratched him. Any way to bag and tag this?" she asked and held up her hand, a twinkle in her black eyes.

Jenn laughed and shook her head. "Whatever you do, don't wash it?"

As they climbed into the car, Jenn reached over the console, into the back seat and grabbed a box of plastic bags, pulled one out and handed it to Jasmine.

Jasmine took the bag and held it up. "You're joking, right?"

"Nope. It's the best we can do until we get you home."

With her right hand in the baggy, Jasmine dialed Bask. Her fingers trembled as she punched the code. She'd felt an undeniable pull toward the magician and wondered if it was because of the similarity to Dorian. The height, the build, the hair, even to the warmth of his voice. They were all Dorian. But, those eyes definitely were *not* Dorian. She'd seen those eyes before—a *blended* trait—in Morgan, Morgan's birth mother, and in Kayla's daughter, Meadow.

All women. Thinking back, Jasmine couldn't recall having seen that particular trait in a man.

A heaviness settled over her. Her parents were both descendants and she, therefore, should have had the eye trait. She had the birthmark, or what was left of it after the attack, but not the green eyes. Which explained why she and Dorian had never matched. God knows, they'd tried.

Bask's brusque questions interrupted her reverie. "Yes, it's in a bag...and still attached to my arm, thank you very much."

She glanced at Jenn and shook her head. "Bask," she chided, "you have no sense of humor. Love you." She hung up, knowing she was one of the few people to actually get away with such offbeat behavior around the head of Abbott House. She'd been doing it since she could remember and getting away with it just as long. Not that she didn't respect him. She did. He was, after all, the head of the protectors of the founding families.

"He's going to have someone meet us at Safe Harbor," she said to Jenn.

She looked down at her hand resting on her lap, inside the baggy. Her fingers still tingled from the contact with the magician. The memory of his heartbeat, syncing with hers, and the heat that was pooling low in her gut, caused a tingling of a very different sort.

Was this what Dorian and Morgan felt?

Poor Morgan, pulled into Ruthorford without any foreknowledge, except that she'd been given up for adoption, never told, and suddenly had to claim an inheritance and a legacy, no questions asked.

When Morgan had arrived, Jasmine knew instantly that she was Dorian's match. At first, it hurt. But, as she'd discussed with Dr. Browne, her therapist at Safe Harbor, she wasn't sure if it really hurt, or if it was just that she'd felt it was supposed to hurt. Either way, it had left her being catty to Morgan, behavior she regretted and had since begged Morgan's forgiveness. Morgan, ever gracious, repeatedly gave Jasmine the assurances she needed, and encouraged their friendship. Which was good—because, right now, Jasmine could use some sisterly advice from another descendant.

Jenn reached over and patted Jasmine's arm as she drove the SUV through the gates at the entrance to Safe Harbor, following the drive around to the helicopter pad Abbott

House had had installed. A helicopter was there, its blades almost stopped. Several men stood talking, one of them Dr. Yancy, Jenn's uncle, whose medical bag sat on the ground at his feet.

Suddenly, Jasmine's gut did a somersault. Before, she'd felt foolish. Now, watching the building brouhaha, she knew something was coming. Maybe it was the remnant of the energy she still felt in her body. Even after the long ride home, her body hummed. She had an incredible urge to go back and find him again. To touch him. To feel the current.

She shook it off as Dr. Yancy pulled open the door. His gray eyes studied hers, concern etching the already deep lines by his eyes.

"I'm fine," she reassured him before he could ask.

He didn't say anything, but continued to watch her eyes as he reached for her bagged hand.

She dropped her gaze. He was busy wrapping tape around the baggy and her arm.

Secure in that he'd preserved the evidence, he helped her out of the SUV, holding onto her arm at the elbow. She felt like an idiot, her hand sticking out in front of her, encased in a baggy, as she made her way into the building.

Meadow, Kayla's fourteen-year-old daughter flew down the steps to meet her. A true blend, she combined Kayla's Native American beauty with the green-eyed traits of her father, to create a gorgeous, albeit tiny, young woman. Still young for her years, she reminded Jasmine of a young filly, all legs and energy. Seeing her as a cross between the legendary faerie folk and a Creek maiden, Jasmine smiled at her impish friend.

Meadow's eyes widened in horror. "What happened? Did it hurt? I'm learning my healing abilities with Morgan's help. Can I help you, Dr. Yancy? I won't get in the way, I promise." The words rushed out in a single stream.

"Whoa," Dr. Yancy chuckled. "First of all, she isn't hurt, so your abilities aren't required for the moment." He smiled at his young protégé. "We need to get some evidence from her hands, so we're protecting them."

Meadow studied the hand. "Evidence? Like a crime scene. I love forensics shows. Can I help?"

"Not this time, sweetings," Dr. Yancy said, repressing a laugh. "With all that energy flowing around you, we could blow it away." He then added, after seeing her dejected look, "I'll tell you all about when we're done."

"And I might have a scratch or two," Jasmine interjected. "You could keep me from scarring."

"Okay. Just call me." With that, she bounded up the stairs and past her mother. Kayla, standing at the top of the steps, just shook her head.

Kayla turned to Jenn. "I have the information you asked for. It's in your office."

"Thanks, Kayla. I'll come get it while Uncle Mike sees to Jasmine."

Jasmine looked at Jenn. She'd heard Jenn talking on her cell phone while she'd talked to Bask but hadn't paid too much attention. Now she was curious.

Jenn offered a smile to Jasmine. "You go on. I'll catch up with you later."

Jasmine nodded. Nothing she could do about it now. She was at the mercy of Dr. Yancy, who pulling her down the hall toward his office. He led her straight into an exam room, with one of the men from the helicopter following, carrying his medical bag and another case.

The doctor made her sit in a chair and wheeled an instrument table in front of her. He took a covering the other man handed him from the case and placed it over the table, then rested her hand carefully on top of the covering. He placed a thin container under her fingertips before he carefully removed the baggy, making sure her fingertips remained over the container. He resealed the baggy, once it was off her hand, and set it aside.

Jasmine watched as he took some sort of pick—it reminded her of a dental tool—from a sealed bag, and proceeded to give her a makeshift manicure, scraping underneath each nail. To be on the safe side, he clipped her nails onto the bed of another container.

"Good thing I don't wear acrylic nails," she laughed.

Yancy's head popped up, suddenly aware of the liberties he was taking with her nails. He stopped, his color heightening. "I'm…" he stuttered.

She flashed him one of her radiant smiles, known to bring the mightiest of men to their knees.

His color heightened some more.

She let him off the hook with a laugh. "After all this time, you should know when I'm teasing you."

He took a deep breath and grimaced. "I know how you women are about your nails and I just lopped yours off without thinking."

"You could at least file them now," she wiggled her fingers. He was sealing the containers, having moved them safely away from her antics.

"I draw the line at scraping and clipping," he tossed back. "Now, if you want me to paint…," he let the words trail off as he smiled back at her.

"No thanks, Doc," she countered and put her hands under her legs. "You've done enough damage for one day."

Dr. Yancy reached up and tousled her short black hair, ruffling the soft straight wisps that gave her a pixie-ish look— a rather tall, gorgeous pixie—but still a mysterious creature of the imagination. Realizing what he'd done, he pulled back his hand.

"It's okay, Doc," she laughed. "My hair needed fluffing."

"I...I,"

Jasmine leaned over and kissed his handsome, weathered cheek. This was the man who'd rushed to her bedside in the hospital, where they had taken her after Dorian had found her chained to that timber in an abandoned mine. There wasn't a part of her battered body this gentle man hadn't examined and treated, reassuring her all the while that she would be okay. With his kind ministrations and those of Dr. Browne, Jasmine felt she was close to being okay, now. The nightmares were gone, her body healed, and she'd begun to be her flirtatious self once more.

All of her life, she'd loved to tease—always in a friendly, fun-loving way. She'd been born with an overabundance of self-confidence, fostered by her parents. Unfortunately, her parents had been killed in a skiing accident when she was twelve. Teresa, her cousin, had taken over the task of raising her and Jasmine had grown up in the Abbott Bed & Breakfast, where she never lacked for attention, either by the guests of the B & B or the townsfolk of Ruthorford. She'd rarely, if ever, gone back to the estate where she'd been raised, although it sat just on the edge of town. Abbott House, or Bask, more specifically, took care of its upkeep. Abbott House had also taken care of her heritance, which, when she came of age, had enabled her to buy the building that housed her boutique and upstairs apartment on Main Street across from The Shoppe of Spells. Her personality, strong and bold, proved a perfect match for her sense of fashion and her boutique had thrived.

Maybe it was time to think about....

"You went far away for a moment, young lady," Dr. Yancy said, watching her.

"Wool gathering," she tried to smile. They were alone in the room. When had the other man left?

"You want to tell me what's going on?"

She took a deep breath. Better to show than tell. She held out her hand, the one he'd just cleaned and clipped. She turned it over, palm up, and stared into the center of the palm. The energy moved through her body and gathered in her hand. Sparks started zipping between her fingers. Then a ball of energy formed, floating just above the palm of her hand.

She looked up to see his eyes widen in amazement. As her eyes met his, the ball flew up and burst against the ceiling with a loud pop.

"I haven't got that down, yet," she flushed.

"When? How?"

She smiled. His gray hair stood on end. She absently reached up and ran her fingers through her own. Soft spikes fell back in place.

"It started shortly after the attack. I've been working with it."

"Have you told anyone? Called Dorian?"

"No." She looked down at her hand.

"Why not?" he asked. "Of all people, he could help you."

Jasmine shrugged. "He's busy with the shop, Morgan, and the baby…."

"But this is something. I don't think we've ever had a wom—"

He stopped, scooting back, when she raised her hand. When he realized his reaction, he flushed. "Sorry."

"See," she said quietly. "I frightened you. You know I would never hurt you." She was quiet for a second. "But I have thought about it. Not you," she amended quickly. "But wondering, if I'd had this ability when Rob kidnapped me, would I have?" Her own eyes narrowed as she looked into the good doctor's sympathetic gray ones. "Damn straight I would have," she said through clenched teeth and forced herself to take a calming breath. Changing the subject, she stated, "I know what you were going to say, that I'm an oddity. The only people that have had this ability are our men."

"You don't know that. There could be people out there...."

She raised one perfectly arched eyebrow at him.

"Does Dr. Browne know?" he asked.

Jasmine shook her head. "She's not one of us. I don't know just what I can or can't tell her."

"I'm not *one of you*," he said softly.

Her gaze shot up. "You are, too."

"Not really. There are those of us who help you...who protect you. But we are not like you."

"The *Protectors*," she whispered. "Sounds like some sort of cheesy television show. I'll think about telling her," she conceded, "after I ask Bask, which will be after I tell him."

"He doesn't know?"

Jasmine shook her head. "You know. And Jenn knows because I knocked her on her ass at the fairgrounds." She laughed. "Oh, and that Eryk Vreeland knows, because he's like Dorian in more than just looks. He's different, too. He has Morgan's eyes."

"What the hell...?" he ran his hands through his steely mass of hair.

Jasmine smiled at the older man. He really wasn't old. He was thin but muscular, had steel gray hair, matching eyes, and a weathered look. She'd known him all of her life. She'd known him when Teresa had loved him but left him for Bill Ruthorford. She suspected her cousin still loved him. That was a topic best left alone.

"That's what the DNA's for. Bask is trying to identify him," Yancy commented.

A soft knock interrupted them.

"Come in," Dr. Yancy called.

Jenn opened the door, carrying a sheaf of papers. "Busy?"

"Done," Dr. Yancy closed his medical bag.

"Stay," Jenn commented as she walked past him. She spread the papers out across the exam table. "Kayla's good. I'll give her that. I'm sure Bask can get more, but we have a very good start."

Jasmine and Yancy stepped over to the table. Jenn strew copies of newspaper articles across the top of the table. Eryk Vreeland smiled back at them in black and white.

"And?" Jasmine asked, lifting a sheet with Eryk's picture on it. Just looking at him made her blood race.

"Let's see. Born August 22,—Dorian's birthday is September 25—of course, those things can be altered—to Martha and Donald Vreeland."

"As in Vreeland Enterprises?" the doctor questioned.

Jenn scanned the papers. "Yep. The very same."

Jasmine looked from one to the other. Yancy spoke. "One of the twenty-five richest men in the world."

"Then, what's his son doing as a sideshow magician?" Jasmine set down the picture, reached over and shifted through several more sheets. This didn't make any sense. She stopped. In a disturbed way, it did. "Are you sure he's Donald Vreeland's son?"

"I'll have to verify with Bask, but everything points that way," Jenn said. "Apparently, the State Fair sideshow thing is a charity deal he does once a year. He's been known to perform in Vegas and has done several TV shows."

"I've never heard of him," Jasmine said.

"I have," Dr. Yancy said. "In fact, I went to one of his shows in New York about four years ago. He's amazing." He scratched his head, "I don't know why I didn't notice the similarity. I was at a convention. He was doing this show in Madison Square Garden. Come to think of it, it was for charity, also. The seats were expensive, but it was sold out. He did a magic show in the round. It was incredible."

Jasmine nodded. "Of course he did. He has nothing to hide. I'll bet a whole bunch of his magic is the real deal."

They looked at her. Jasmine lifted her hand and sparks flew from her fingertips. "If he's like Dorian, he's been practicing most of his life. Plus, with Morgan's eye trait, there's no telling…." She let the words trail off.

Jenn commented. "Rich little boy with weird abilities. Wanna make book that the Vreeland's aren't his real parents?"

Jasmine picked up another article and looked at it. "I don't know. He looks a lot like his Dad." She handed Jenn the paper. Donald Vreeland was on stage with his son, handing him an oversized check, made out to some children's hospital, for half of a million dollars.

"…and Morgan looked just like her adoptive parents," Jenn interjected.

Jasmine studied the picture of father and son. There was something about the stance of the father. And his look. He didn't look comfortable. It reminded her of Dr. Yancy's look earlier, when she'd displayed her ability. Plus, the two men were separated by one huge check.

****

Jasmine kicked back the covers. The room was stifling. She lay there in the dark, feeling the perspiration on her skin between her breasts. The lightweight T-shirt clung to her body like a wet bandage. She pulled it away from her chest and fanned it up and down. The cooler air made her nipples harden. A tingle went through her body and her thoughts sought the green-eyed wizard who'd sent sensations pooling in her gut earlier that day.

A roll of thunder brought her to a sitting position. It was awfully late in the season for a thunderstorm. She rose from the crumpled bed, walked over to the window, and pulled it open, letting the warm breeze move over her body. She was on the third floor of Safe Harbor where Jenn and the live-in staff had quarters. Right now, that was Jenn, Dr. Yancy, Kayla's cousin John, the security specialist, and herself. It was the only area that didn't have rails on the windows, being high enough that there was minimal risk of a break-in. There were enough security measures around this place that the president would feel safe.

Lightning outlined the clouds in the distance. She could smell the ozone in the air. As if in response, the hair on her arms and the nape of her neck stood on end. She stepped back and closed the window. Since she had no idea how her new abilities responded to lightning, she decided to play it on the safe side and move away from temptation. Something else to ask Dorian about when she got up the nerve.

Her phone buzzed and danced across the top of the bedside table. She'd forgotten to take it off vibrate after the show. She glanced at the clock. It was past one in the morning. Who in the hell...Bask showed on the display. She grabbed the phone.

"Miss me?" she said throatily.

"Yes, immensely," he retorted. "Are you awake?"

"I am now." She wasn't about to give him the satisfaction of knowing he hadn't awakened her.

"Sorry," he said and almost sounded contrite—but not quite.

"What's up?"

"We have a match," he said without preamble.

"Let me guess. Dorian."

"Yes. How'd—"

"You didn't see him."

"I saw the picture with his father."

She was over the quipping. "How much of a match?"

"It looks like they could be twins."

Jasmine sat down on the bed. Even though she'd suspected, it still hit hard. Dorian's twin.

"You there?"

"I'm here," she said quietly.

"The DNA is strange…."

Her choke of laughter stopped him, "You think?"

"Jasmine, let me finish," his voice became clipped as it always did when he was annoyed. "We have a damn good match. I mean *match*. Except in eye color and some other alleles. But you know as well as I do that identical twins aren't completely identical, especially with Ruthorford's descendancy thrown in. Hell," he sighed through the phone, "I don't know all that mumbo jumbo. What I do know is that he's Dorian's twin, but with the green-eye trait."

"Now what?"

"I want you to—"

"Whoa. Stop right there," she interrupted. "I don't want to do anything you're suggesting."

"You haven't heard me yet."

"I don't care." She stood and started pacing back and forth, her long legs crossing the room in four strides, turning and moving back to the bed.

"Jasmine." It was a command.

"I'm not healed." She grimaced. That really was low.

"Bullshit."

She sank down onto the bed. A crash sounded outside the window. The phone crackled.

"What was that?"

"Electrical storm."

"You need to go?"

"I should be okay, I'm on my cell." Then she thought about earlier and wasn't sure at all. Wait. Why had he just asked that?

"Yancy called me," he answered her unasked question.

"Son of a…" she mumbled.

"Some of us are loyal to Abbott House." He tried to sound stern.

"Okay." She fell back across the bed and stared at the plaster swirls in the ceiling. "What do you want me to do?"

Chapter Two

Eryk walked through the rehearsal with his mind preoccupied by the vixen that had totally flummoxed him the day before. It wasn't until his assistant yelled that he even realized how distracted he was.

"Hey, you big lug, you wanna get me outta here?" Brandy shouted.

He reached over and unstrapped the case where she lay for the trick they had perfected over a year ago.

"I'm sorry. My mind's not on this," he apologized.

"You think?" She groaned as she sat up and wiggled her shoulders.

He took her hand and helped her down, offering her an appeasing grin.

"It's that girl from the audience. The one with the cat eyes," she said as she watched him.

"You could see her eyes?"

"Boy, are you gone. The spot followed you down the aisle, stopped when you stopped to stare at her. She's a beauty, all right." She stretched out her leg and moved her foot in circles. "Are we done? I'd like to get these shoes off for a couple of hours before the show."

"Sure. I'm sorry, Brandy."

She'd already walked toward the side of the stage, waving a hand back over her shoulder.

As he put the props in order, he let his mind wander back to Jasmine. What was it about her? Besides the fact that she was drop dead gorgeous with that short crop of shiny black hair framing a perfect face. Eyes, black as coal, with a slight upward tilt, gave her an exotic look that went straight to his loins. And her mouth, the bottom lip a little fuller than the top, begged to be nipped.

He felt the blood pound in his veins and ran his hand through his hair, changing his focus—remembering her outside where he'd followed her. Then, taking her hand in his. The shock—the current running from her to him and back again. He could have stood there forever, holding onto her hand and feeling the rhythm of the energy shift and match, until their hearts beat as one. Unfortunately, it stopped when they'd knocked that other poor girl on her ass.

Was she like him? A freak of nature. She hadn't seemed shocked—now that was an appropriate word—by the encounter. He was, though, mentally and physically. He'd lived with his abilities all his thirty-one years, working with them, figuring them out, and disguising them so as not to embarrass his folks.

Shit. He remembered they were coming tonight to make an appearance, acknowledge his existence, and make another donation. His poor parents, born to wealth, raised in wealth, and strapped with an aberration of a son. His mom blamed it on her late pregnancy and overcompensated by feeling sorry for him. But only in private. She barely acknowledged him in public. Only when his dad forced her to attend these events. She just couldn't get her mind around the fact that her son, a Vreeland, was a performer. A magician, for heaven's sake.

They had enough money for him to hide comfortably out of sight. Why should he display himself in public? Even the charity contributions didn't help matters. They could, and did, write checks for much more. Why did he have to embarrass them? If it were left up to her, he's be ensconced somewhere on one of their estates, never to come to the big house where someone might see him.

His father—well, good ol' dad had avoided him and the issue for as long as he could remember. He'd set up a trust fund the day Eryk was born and money flowed freely into it. Eryk was now a wealthy man. He didn't have to work, if he didn't want to—his dad had made sure of that. Plus, he'd had the best education money could buy, all privately done, of course.

It was one of those tutors who taught Eryk the basics of magic, giving Eryk a way out. Eryk would be forever grateful and had proven as much, setting up his mentor and friend, Jonathan Latham, with an early retirement in the Catskills, where he visited whenever he could.

Jon had proven to be a loyal friend as well. He was one of the few people that knew and accepted Eryk in his entirety. Jon also helped him research and perfect his act, making sure his true "magic" was hidden well enough to fool even Brandy. Hell, Jon made it to more shows than his own father did. Only when the publicity put Vreeland Enterprises in the society pages for another contribution, did Donald Vreeland publicly acknowledge his son.

In private, Donald Vreeland stayed as far away from his freak of a son as possible. He couldn't seem to be around Eryk and look at him without a scotch in his hand. That spoke volumes, because Donald Vreeland rarely drank.

Frustration built until Eryk spun around, held out his hand toward the table, and the water bottle flew from the table into his outstretched hand. The sound of slow clapping made him drop the bottle.

Still in his agitated state, he spun toward the door of the auditorium, slowly closed his eyes and opened them. The intruder came into view in a myriad of vibrant colors. The aura spiked out from the colors as pulsing energy. He knew it was *her*.

He blinked once more and his vision returned to normal. He watched as she moved down the aisle. He'd never seen a woman with such fluid elegance. A camel colored cashmere poncho, belted at the waist, topped a black pair of pants. His breath caught. The wide neck of the soft material had slipped, revealing a bare shoulder, and his eyes dropped to her chest and the gentle movement of her breasts. His gut tightened.

Jasmine stopped a few steps from the stage, eyeing the man who stood alone in front of her. Even relaxed, with muscles that draped comfortably over his frame, he stood with the grace and energy of a panther, watchful and ready to spring.

She could make out the emerald green eyes easily from where she stood. Like Morgan's, she suspected they shimmered in the dark. His black hair, more unruly than before, was thick and wavy, enhancing that air of a rebel, a buccaneer.

She tilted her head, studying him. He was the same height as Dorian, but leaner, harder than Dorian. His face looked the same, yet different. Was it the eyes that made the difference? He had the same chiseled features, but this man's seemed more pronounced. Then... there was the pull. She could feel it from where she stood. She'd never felt that around Dorian.

They stood scrutinizing one another for several moments, neither wanting to be the first to speak, each weighing what was going on.

Knowing she had an advantage, Jasmine spoke first. "Mr. Vreeland, I'd like to talk with you, if you don't mind."

Her voice was hypnotic and flowed around him. He started to speak and his voice cracked. He cleared his throat. Then, he spoke in his performer's voice, accent and all. "The next show doesn't start for several hours." He let the words capture her. As he'd intended, it held her mesmerized. "I have some time." He stopped on the top step and held out his hand.

Jasmine took a step back, her eyes hardening. "You can drop the act. I'd prefer to talk outside…if that's okay?"

Eryk caught a glimpse of panic before she artfully concealed it. He put his hand down by his side. "Sure. We could grab a bite," he said, the accent gone. "I'm starved."

She smiled, almost.

He bounded down the stairs, two at a time, until he was beside her, careful not to touch her. They walked out of the building in the same fashion, each aware that the other's energy was pulsing just below the surface.

He led her to a stand, bought two barbeques, fries, and two drinks, turned and walked over to a picnic bench set away from the few people milling around.

"This okay?" He straddled the bench and set the food out, placing the fries between them.

Jasmine sat on the bench across from him. She unwrapped the barbeque, took a bite, closed her eyes, and moaned. "Wow," she mumbled, chewed and swallowed. "This is great barbeque."

"Old family recipe," he commented and held up a fry.

Jasmine took it without touching his fingers, bit, and looked into his green eyes.

She didn't stare or look down as most people did, he noticed. It was as if she'd seen eyes like his before.

He studied her. The cool breeze ruffled her short hair, making it feather around her face. The sun glinted off her gold spiral earrings. She smiled. Perfect white teeth surrounded by a lush mouth. *God.* He felt his groin tighten. It was going to be damn near impossible to be around her without a hard-on.

"Mr. Vreeland," Jasmine said, setting her sandwich down and wiping her hands on a napkin. "As I told you yesterday, my name is Jasmine Monroe. I'm from Ruthorford, Georgia. I have someone I want you to meet."

"Okay," he said and looked around.

"He's in Ruthorford."

His eyes narrowed. "Sorry," he said wearily. "We're running through the weekend."

"That's fine," she said, ignoring the coolness in his voice. He probably thought her to be some sort of stalker. "I wouldn't ask this if it wasn't important." She tilted her head and looked at him, reading him, then reached down, and pulling her purse up beside her, drew out a photo and held it out to him.

Careful not to touch her, he took the picture. As he studied it, a crease formed above his brow and he looked up at her. "What the hell?"

He looked back at the picture. A man and a woman stood side by side, arms around each other's waist. Her other hand rested atop her large, pregnant belly. They smiled from ear to ear. The man was the spitting image of him, except for the eyes. Yet, his eyes stared back at him—from the woman's beautiful face.

"That's Dorian Drake and his wife, Morgan."

He laughed. "I've heard we've all got doppelgangers, but this takes the cake." He started to hand the picture back. She shook her head.

"Keep it. He's not a doppelganger. He's your brother."

"I don't have any brothers...or sisters, for that matter." She lifted one beautifully arched eyebrow.

"Hey, look at the eyes," he pointed to Dorian's image.

"Hey, look at the woman," she challenged.

"He married his sister?"

"Of course not. It's complicated. That's why I want you to come to Ruthorford. Meet Dorian. Talk with Bask."

"Who the hell is Bask?"

Jasmine laughed. "Now, *that's* a good question."

He watched her. She was light itself. When she laughed, she laughed with her whole being. He longed to run his hands over the fluttering black hair, to see if it was as soft as it looked. He wanted to put his lips over hers and feel her warmth. He watched her smile die.

Jasmine saw his eyes change; she saw the lust in them. For a second, she panicked. Gathering her reserve, she pulled her purse to her and started to stand. "I need to go. Someone will be in touch." She didn't look at him.

He blinked, scanned her through his "filter," and watched her aura change. The energy had pulled close around her, almost protective. He blinked again.

"I'm sorry. Somehow, I've frightened you. I didn't mean to," he said softly and started to reach for her hand.

She drew back. "It's okay. I really do have to go." She turned to walk away.

"Stop." He spoke low, barely audible. "Don't go." It was a command. He pushed his thoughts at her slightly. "I just want to talk."

Jasmine stopped. She could tell something was happening. Where she'd wanted to run before, she now wanted to stay. She fought it, then turned and looked at him, anger in her eyes.

"We'll sit here and talk." He'd stopped pushing when he saw her waver. "Please."

She narrowed her eyes at him, but moved back to the bench. "Don't think I don't know what you're doing." She sat, a defiant look on her face.

"Why'd you want to run?"

"That's none…" She looked at him. He wasn't being forceful. He really seemed to want to know. She decided to be honest, sort of. "Look. You make me nervous."

He immediately looked down.

"Not your eyes. I am very used to eyes like yours. It's no big deal where I come from."

"Seriously?"

She nodded. "Seriously." Was that hope she heard in his voice?

"So, why do I make you nervous?" he asked and smiled a little.

He had the tiniest chip in one of his front teeth. When he smiled, it made him look mischievous, young, and beguiling. She couldn't help returning his smile.

"I have a narrow comfort zone. I don't like to touch people or have them touch me." Okay, she wasn't exactly lying. She shuddered, thinking of Rob. Damn, that memory snuck in at the damnedest times.

He saw the slight movement of her shoulders. "Throwing off ghosts," he asked. Something was bothering her. That thread led to the pulled-in aura. Bad time with a man, would be his guess. "Okay," he said and held up his hands. "I will try my best NOT to touch you. But I must admit, in terms of fair disclosure, touching you is something I very much would like to do."

He watched her pull inward again. Although her body didn't actually move, it was as though armor went around her.

"I said 'like to' not 'would.'"

He could see she was trying to relax.

"Let's talk about this Ruthorford." He pushed her drink toward her, encouraging her to stay.

"Okay." She took a small sip. "Ruthorford is a small town in the mountains of Georgia. Many of its inhabitants are descendants of the founding families. I'm one of them. My suspicion is that you and Dorian are, too."

"This Dorian, he's not from there?"

"No. He was born in Washington, DC, but he became the ward of Mel and Thom Kilraven and grew up in Ruthorford."

"And his wife?"

Jasmine took a deep breath. Talk about complicated. Yet, this was still the easy part. "Morgan is the natural daughter of Mel and Thom, but was adopted by Becky and Talbot Briscoe and raised in Virginia." She glanced around. "Not too far from here, actually."

He started to open his mouth to let the questions pour forth, thought better of it, and closed his mouth again.

Jasmine laughed. "Yep, now you're getting the hang of it."

He seemed to ponder something before he spoke. "I have a small plane at the airport. We could fly down after the show closes. Brandy, that's my assistant, can go on with the show and I'll catch up later."

He saw panic flicker in her eyes before she looked down.

She ran her finger around the rim of her cup. "You fly down. We'll have a car meet you. I'll go in the Abbott House plane."

Something really spooked her. He tried to make it light. "You do understand I'll be flying the plane?" he said, letting a teasing note tinge his statement.

She blushed, but stood firm. "I'll meet you there." *Geez.* It's not like he could fly a plane and attack her at the same time. Maybe she needed a few more sessions with Dr. Browne, after all.

He shrugged.

Deciding a change of subject was needed, Eryk held up his hands. He looked around and, when he saw no one nearby, let the sparks fly from one hand to the other. "What do you know about this?"

Jasmine lifted her hands. He watched as a more delicate, finer thread of current moved from the tips of her long fingers to the tips on her other hand. "Family trait," she said and put her hands down in her lap.

"What else can you do?"

A glint showed in her eyes. "I'm not a dog. I don't do tricks." It came out more clipped than she'd intended.

"Whoa. I didn't mean to imply…," he frowned as the words died.

"Sorry. I might as well tell you. Not many people know I can do that. It's new to me," she said, then realized she'd confided in this complete stranger something she couldn't bring herself to tell her therapist.

Nervous, Jasmine reached over, took a sip of the soft drink, and realized all the ice had melted. It wasn't particularly warm out. She looked down into the cup. Not a single piece of ice remained. She looked up, sensing a feeling of warmth around her. She had an urge to heighten her own senses, something she'd tried but hadn't been able to do successfully. She could dampen her energy a little to keep from shocking someone, but that took a lot effort. She knew

Morgan and Dorian could heighten their perception of their surroundings, but she couldn't quite get the hang of it, and was too embarrassed to ask. Suddenly, she wanted very much to learn all sorts of things.

He watched, then as if reading her mind, he spoke softly, "Close your eyes. Let your other senses open. Feel your surroundings."

With only momentary hesitation, she did as he suggested. Immediately, she felt the warmth. Like a shell surrounding them—a protective barrier of energy. She could reach beyond it, but sensed others couldn't penetrate it. She pushed and felt her energy brush against his.

She opened her eyes and looked at him. "Thank you."

Her voice was quiet. Soft, a like a caress. Of course, to put the barrier up, he had to be open, so he was more sensitive to her projections. He took a deep breath and dampened his energy. The barrier dropped, taking hers with it.

Jasmine felt the change immediately The safety of their cozy cocoon was gone. Feeling raw and open, she rubbed her hands up and down her arms. "You've been doing that."

He nodded.

"Not to be trite but, what else can *you* do?"

"Unlike you," he said and laughed, "I specialize in tricks."

"Eryk…Eryk!"

Eryk stood, looking around. "Over here," he called.

A gangly teenage boy raced from the auditorium, his face beet red.

Eryk moved toward him. Jasmine followed.

"It's Pops! He's pinned his arm in a gear."

Eryk turned to Jasmine. "Call 911," he ordered and took off running after the boy.

Jasmine pulled out her phone and hit the numbers while running, hoping not to lose them. When the operator came on, she gave the location and running closer, saw the crowd. "It's a ride next to the Ferris Wheel. Man has his arm caught."

She stepped closer and saw Eryk move in toward the workings of some sort of contraption. Parts lay on the ground. An older man, the color drained from his face, was on his side. His arm, up to his elbow, was inside a piece of equipment.

Eryk knelt next to him. He moved his hands over the gears. He pulled back and placed a hand on the old man's shoulder and said something. The man nodded and seemed to relax. Eryk turned to her.

"I need your help."

She stepped forward, shoving her phone into her pocket.

"When we touched before, my power surged. I need you to do that now."

She swallowed, but nodded. To get close enough to Eryk, she had to step across the man, straddling his body.

"Wait 'til I'm ready, Bobby," he directed the young boy. "When I say, I want you to pull Pops toward you. Okay?"

Bobby, tears streaming, wiped the back of a greasy hand across his face and nodded. He grabbed the old man's legs and watched them slip. Wiping the grease from his hands on his own pants, he grabbed hold.

"Not 'til I tell you."

Bobby nodded again and planted his feet.

Eryk, never touching the equipment, moved his hand near the surface of the machinery. Jasmine saw small sparks fly between metal and hand. His hand stopped. Without looking back, he stretched his other hand out behind him. Jasmine swallowed once and clasped her hand around his wrist. His hand immediately latched onto her wrist. She edged closer to Eryk, their bodies almost touching. She felt the kick of energy and current flowed back and forth. Her own heart beat in her ears. Then, she heard two beats. The current leapt. Their heartbeats synchronized into one strong beat. She imagined her energy flowing into him and closed her eyes.

"Now, Bobby," Eryk hissed.

She heard the machinery groan but was afraid to look. Instead, she concentrated on the flow of current.

A siren screamed in the distance, coming closer. She focused on the heartbeat.

"It's okay," Eryk's whisper caressed her ear. She opened her eyes. He was standing next to her.

The old man, Pops, was lying on the ground. He was pale, but color was coming back into his face. His arm looked bruised, but there wasn't a lot of blood. Several people tended him.

Eryk, holding her hand, pulled her away from the crowd. They moved into the recesses, under the trees, their hearts still hammering a quick staccato beat. He turned to her, looked into her eyes and murmured, "I'm sorry," just before his mouth crushed down on hers. She stiffened. Still clasping her hand between their bodies, he let his other hand caress her neck, tilting her head up to meet his.

His warm lips moved over hers. His tongue touched the seam of her lips and she felt her lips part in response. As though dissociated from herself, Jasmine felt her body relax as his warmth filled her. The panic and desire that warred within her subsided. Unable to resist, she leaned into him, feeling their clasped hands against her chest.

He lifted his head and watched as her obsidian eyes opened and looked into his.

"I...I," he stopped. There was nothing to say. He couldn't any more explain to her the need that had overcome him than—

"Mr. Vreeland," a man interrupted.

They moved apart. As soon as their hands separated, she felt cold, bereft.

The EMT moved in and questioned Eryk about what happened. She watched Eryk do his thing, pushing a suggestion, and the EMT thanked him and returned to Pops.

"Did you do that, the push thing, with me—just now?"

He looked at her for a long moment. "No." He started to step toward her and stopped. "That was just us."

"Thank you."

He smiled. "Any time."

"No. I mean for not pushing the suggestion."

"I wouldn't." With that, he turned back toward the crowd, which was parting to let the gurney through. He walked over to the man they called Pops, put his hand on the older man's shoulder, and spoke. Pops forced a smile.

Eryk walked back over to her. "I have to get ready for the show." He studied her face. His voice but a whisper, he said, "Stay."

"I can't." Watching his face, she added. "I have to get back."

He reached in his pocket and pulled out a card, took a pen and wrote. "It's my cell phone. Call me. I'll meet you whenever or wherever you want. And, I promise to behave, if you want to fly with me."

She arched an eyebrow at him, but took the card.

"At least think about it."

"I will."

****

Eryk Vreeland gave the performance of his life. Whether it was the excess energy coursing through his body or the memory of the enthralling woman fixed in the back of his brain, he had no idea. But, every step was precise, every illusion perfect. Except...they weren't all illusions. He used his natural abilities and forged them with professional techniques to elevate the performance one step above plausible. He wished she'd stayed.

At the end, the crowd was on its feet. The applause was almost deafening. He waited until it calmed down and brought his father on stage. They had performed this act many times. Only this time, Eryk looked at his father differently. He saw the hesitancy as they moved closer together. He saw how Donald wouldn't meet his eyes. He accepted the small check and, with a puff of smoke, the check appeared huge—a wall between them.

His parents didn't wait to see him after the show. By the time he was done, their limousine had long since left the fairgrounds.

Chapter Three

Fog had rolled in, filling the dips in the road with cloud-like wisps, slowing Jasmine's drive back and giving her more time to think about what had just happened. After agreeing to Bask's request to go see the magician, she'd convinced herself that she was going back to see Eryk for Ruthorford, Abbott House...even Dorian. Maybe even Eryk, himself. Not for her. Of course, she'd been intrigued by the magician. She'd never met anyone like him and, coming from Ruthorford, that was saying something. She decided that she'd study him, like some specimen, something unique to Ruthorford.

Yet, as soon as she'd laid eyes on him standing on that stage, she'd felt the pull. The attraction. She hadn't felt it with anyone in Ruthorford, including Dorian. She'd always thought that was because she'd lacked something. She didn't have descendants' traits. At least not the traditional ones. But neither did Eryk.

When his mouth had crushed down on hers, she didn't fry him—the reaction she was sure would happen to any man who laid hands, or lips, on her. Instead, she melted into him as his energy filled her, compelling her to respond. Jasmine's fingers brushed her lips, aware of the tingle his memory brought.

Damn! She slammed her hand against the steering wheel, felt her energy surge, and nearly drove off the road when the car alarm went off, the short, sharp BBBMMM, BBBMMM, BBBMMM filling the car. She pulled onto the shoulder just as her headlights started blinking. Frantic, she flipped switches and pushed buttons, to no avail. In an act of desperation, she turned off the engine and found herself plunged into the dead black of night. Except for her hands, where tiny arcs of static fizzled around her fingertips.

Jasmine took several deep breaths and tried to dampen her energy, watching her hands. The arcs disappeared and she sat in total darkness, afraid to touch anything around her. A car whooshed passed her. "This is stupid," she said aloud, grabbed the key and turned it. The SUV started right up, no beeping, no flashing, nothing. Another breath and she pulled back onto the road.

In the next small town, Jasmine pulled through the Burger Bite drive-thru, ordered a cheeseburger, fries, and a milkshake and pulled into the only vacant parking space. She nibbled a fry, watching teenagers enter and leave the small burger joint, stopping to talk with other teens they passed. Obviously, this was the only hangout in the small town and business was booming. *Not bad!* She took a big bite of her cheeseburger and enjoyed the flavors.

Under normal circumstances, her diet was much more controlled. However, about a half-hour after she left the fairgrounds, her stomach had started growling and she'd wanted to eat—right then. She'd pushed it away. Then, after the car acted up, she caved and started scouting the highway for some place to get food.

The heavy meal did its job in calming her, so when she did call Bask, she felt more in control. As was his habit, the old man fired question after question at her. She left out her part in the emergency—and the kiss, of course. Bask wanted Eryk in Ruthorford as soon as he was able to make the trip.

He offered the plane and, when she said Eryk had his own, Bask assumed she would be riding with him and went on to the next topic. Then, something or someone distracted him and, with a quick "talk to you later," he was gone. Looks like she was riding with Eryk, after all. She wasn't sure if the butterflies were because of Eryk, flying, or both.

It was late when she pulled up to the gates of Safe Harbor, the place she'd called home for the last year. She moved forward and stopped, watching the gates open. Easing through, she stopped and looked in the rearview mirror until they had closed behind her. Funny, it had become second nature to her, making sure those gates were closed securely.

Jasmine pulled into her parking spot and stretched as she got out of the vehicle. Her muscles ached as if she'd just competed in a triathlon. She twisted to release the tightening muscles in her back. She felt rumpled. God, she hoped she saw no one until after she'd had a nice, long, hot shower and put on some fresh clothes.

She unlocked the front door and eased it open. Jenn, for a change, was not on the ready for anyone entering the house. Of course, with the amount of security in and around the compound, she didn't need to be. She usually was, nevertheless. Jasmine walked across the foyer toward the wide steps that led one level up. There the huge lounge/waiting area with a large screen television sat empty.

As she approached the stairs, she glanced to her right. A soft light glowed under Dr. Browne's door. She walked to the door and tapped.

"Come in," Dr. Browne's muffled voice called through the door.

Jasmine turned the knob, pushed open the door a crack, allowing her to peek around the door. Dr. Browne sat at her desk, hunched over, her reading glasses perched on her nose, scanning a file. As Jasmine pushed the door open further, Dr. Browne raised her eyes to look over the upper edges of the glasses and, seeing Jasmine, sat back and pulled off the half-glasses.

Like Jasmine, Dr. Browne looked disheveled, not uncommon for the doctor, and tired—a rarity. The low light from the desk lamp softened the dark circles under her eyes, but they were there, nevertheless.

"You're here awfully late," Jasmine looked at her watch. It was after ten.

Dr. Browne's eyes shifted to the small clock on her desk. She refused to have one displayed where a patient could see her mark time, or do it themselves. "Dr. Yancy called me in. A late arrival."

"Anything I can do?" She had inventories of clothing for new arrivals. Best to get them out of the clothes they wore in and get them freshened up as fast as possible.

"Jenn took care of it. How was your evening?" She angled her head to one side as if to study Jasmine.

Jasmine shifted on her feet, suddenly self-conscious. She flushed.

"Want to talk about it?"

"It's late."

"I don't have any plans. Do you?" She rose from her desk, walked over to a credenza and pulled out two china cups. "How about you share some tea with me? I could use some."

Jasmine tried to look relaxed. "I can do that."

Dr. Browne leaned over and flipped a wall switch. Small spotlights cast a soft light on the credenza, as well as a small table and chairs nearby. She put several small scoops of loose tea in a ball, closed it and set it in the delicate pot. Picking up the electric kettle always ready with hot water, she poured the water over the tea ball.

Watching her reminded Jasmine of the many times she'd enjoyed a similar tea ritual in Ruthorford. Mel and Thom had specialized in herbal teas—among other things. She and Dorian had sat up late many a night, drinking tea and talking.

Dr. Browne carried the tray with the pot, cups, and two biscotti over to the table and set it down, easing her bulk into the chair opposite Jasmine. Not until the tea was poured into the cups and she was stirring in honey, did Dr. Browne speak.

"It's been a rather enlightening day," she took a sip of the steaming liquid and set the cup down.

Jasmine ran her hand through her short hair. Sometimes, when her energy was up, the tips would rise to meet her fingers before she even touched it. "How so?" she asked, trying to act nonchalant.

"First, Dr. Yancy came to see me. Later, it was Jenn. Then, I got a call from Bask."

Jasmine took another sip, felt the blood drain from her face, and took several quieting breaths.

"They care a great deal about you."

"I care about them. So, what did they say?" Jasmine slowly stirred the liquid in the cup.

Instead of speaking, Dr. Browne reached over and took Jasmine's other hand, lifted it and turned it palm up.

Jasmine fought the urge to pull back. The touch was feather-light. She watched Dr. Browne study her slender hand. Gently, Dr. Browne returned it to the tabletop.

"Doesn't that constitute a betrayal of confidence?" Jasmine asked, knowing why Dr. Browne was studying her hand and imagining the conversations about her.

"Not when it's doctor to doctor. And," she looked into Jasmine's eyes, "when it has your best interest at heart." The

doctor took another sip of tea. She was so good at drawing
time out. "Jenn came to me after you left and explained that
Bask had sent you back to talk to that man at the fair. Then
Bask called me about thirty minutes ago, after he talked with
you. Believe it or not, he's also concerned about you."

Jasmine smiled. For all his gruffness, Bask had a kind
heart. Having known him all her life, she'd seen both sides.
Sure, she chided him like crazy, but she felt certain he knew
she adored him. His was not an easy job—an avocation,
really—being in charge of Abbott House and looking out for
the founding families. That was a conversation she'd liked to
have overheard—him talking to Dr. Browne.

Jasmine sat back, moved her head back and sideways,
stretching her neck, trying to relax the tightness that had
returned to her shoulders. She took a deep breath and let it
out. Slowly, she raised her hand, held her fingers and thumb
to form a C, concentrated and made the energy leap between
her fingers and thumb. Carefully, she turned her hand palm
up and flattened it out. A ball of energy formed and danced
lightly above her palm. She blew on it. With a poof, it
disappeared.

Dr. Browne sat immobile, applied her best therapist look,
and appeared as though she saw people do that all the time.
After a moment, she let out a laugh. Self-conscious, Jasmine
slipped her hand off the table into her lap. Dr. Browne shook
her head slightly and smiled. "Wow. That was something."
The therapist was good at her job and her own smile had
Jasmine relaxing, until she smiled back.

Yet, inside Jasmine's mind raced. That little
demonstration was effortless—nothing compared to what it
would have taken yesterday. After what had transpired at the
fairground with Eryk today, she felt as though she was twice
as strong.

Her thoughts turned to Eryk and the reason she was stronger—their shared connection. When he'd clasped her wrist, she'd felt the power flow both ways, not just from her. Yet, it was her added strength that enabled him to manipulate that machinery. She wasn't sure exactly what he'd done, but when it moved, the man's arm had slipped free. Then, Eryk had pulled her away from the crowd and kissed her. As if thinking about the kiss gave it life, her blood raced and she felt the heat move through her body. Feeling the doctor's eyes on her, she felt the blush crawl up her neck to warm her cheeks.

"What's that for?" Dr. Browne was watching her.

"Nothing."

Dr. Browne lifted a single brow. She was the only person Jasmine knew that could do it as well as she could.

"He kissed me," she blurted out. Maybe if she said it out loud, the power of it would dissipate.

"Who kissed you?"

"Eryk."

"The magician?"

Jasmine nodded, watching, looking for some sign of judgment. There was none.

"And he did this why?" Dr. Browne drew out the words.

Jasmine smirked and shot the doctor her most arrogant look. Seeing that she wasn't buying it, Jasmine said, "Okay, it was after we joined our energies to free a man's arm. The energy was flowing strong between us. It was almost like being on too much caffeine. He pulled me aside and kissed me."

"Are you okay with this? How did you react?"

Jasmine remembered the initial panic, then the warmth.

"Well, I didn't fry him." Her sarcasm died almost before it was out of her mouth. "At first, I was startled. Frightened. Then...I suppose I kissed him back."

Dr. Browne smiled. She really smiled—to the point where the edge of her gums showed. Her eyes twinkled. She reached over and patted the hand resting on the table. "There is much we need to work on. You know that. But, you didn't panic."

Hearing that, Jasmine decided, to be fair, she needed to divulge one more thing. "Dr. Browne, there's a reason I'm okay about what happened. Not perfect, mind you, but okay." She took a deep breath, not sure if this information would set her back in the good doctor's eyes. "I've been practicing."

"At kissing?"

Jasmine choked out a laugh. "Here? No. At using my ability...to break locks."

"I see. And are you successful?" When she'd first seen Jasmine, nearly a year ago, Jasmine's arm was in a sling, her face bruised and swollen and her spirit all but broken. Her kidnapper had chained her hands to a mine timber and repeatedly raped and beaten her. Dr. Browne swallowed, remembering the injuries the poor girl had sustained. But, she'd proven resilient, even from the first. She'd known Jasmine would heal and deal with what had happened.

"Yes. Very. I've bought many different kinds of locks and secured them to chains. I haven't acquired one yet that I can't open."

"And this is done how?"

Jasmine wiggled her fingers and her smile disappeared. "Too bad I didn't have this ability before I was kidnapped."

"Does that bother you?"

"Sure. I mean it did. But then I realized I might have killed him. It really wasn't his fault. His mind was altered...," she stopped not knowing how much the doctor knew or which story she'd been told.

"Do you think it was the trauma that enabled your abilities?"

Jasmine shrugged. She'd thought about it a lot over the last year. Her ability seemed to appear about a month after the kidnapping. At first, she was setting off electronics or would get shocked just touching things. In a similar, but much smaller way, to what happened in the car. Back then, she'd thought it was static electricity. When she fried a rather expensive computer and ruined a security circuit board, Jasmine realized she was the problem. Why hadn't she thought about that tonight, before she got in her car. Maybe she could have grounded herself.

Having grown up around Dorian and Thom, both of whom had the ability to manipulate energy, Jasmine was familiar with the concept. In Ruthorford, or at least at The Shoppe of Spells, these abilities were treated as normal. She'd been around on many occasions when Dorian and Thom had started throwing balls of energy at one another—until Mel would run them outside. She was grateful she'd been allowed to hang around during Dorian's lessons. She'd tried to apply the lessons she remembered to her own burgeoning abilities, with a little success. She felt she was learning by mishap. Tired of trying to reinvent the wheel, she planned to corner Dorian and ask him about a million questions.

She couldn't wait to show Dorian. He would be so shocked. She laughed.

At Dr. Browne's frown, Jasmine pulled her wandering mind back to Dr. Browne's question. "I think, Dr. Browne, that, over the years, I repressed my abilities. I didn't think I was supposed to have them—therefore, I didn't. I don't know of any other woman, who's a descendant, who carries this trait." Then, thinking of Eryk, she added, "I sure don't know another man like Eryk."

"Almost like he was made for you," Dr. Browne commented, almost under her breath.

Jasmine set down the cup. Still unsure just how vetted Dr. Browne was on Ruthorford's secrets, she gave her a noncommittal smile. Dr. Browne's statement was far closer to the truth than the good doctor realized and something she hadn't considered. Jasmine knew there would be little else she'd be thinking about tonight.

If Browne saw her consternation, she ignored it and changed the subject. "Bask wants to make sure you are okay with flying down in the magician's plane."

"I wasn't, but then I figured he couldn't do much while flying the plane. Honestly, I'm more worried about our combined abilities screwing up the electronics of the plane."

"Bask said to tell you he'd have no problem sending a plane for you."

Jasmine lips curved in a smile. Yep, underneath that exterior, Bask was a softy. "I'll think about it and let him know."

"It's okay, either way," Dr. Browne said and held up the pot of tea. "Warm-up?"

"No, I think I'll call it a night." Jasmine pushed back the chair and stood. "Thanks for the tea and the chat."

"My pleasure. You know I'm here for you, any time."

"I know. I figure it's time you move on to more urgent needs."

The doctor's eyes looked over at her desk. "Yes," her voice saddened, "we got a couple today."

"Is there anything I can do?" Jasmine asked.

"Not at the moment." The doctor's voice had quieted. She walked back over to her desk and sat down.

As Jasmine neared the door, the doctor called to her, "As I said…any time."

"You, too."

The doctor spoke softly. "Yes. Well, maybe when you get back I can get you to serve as a sounding board for some of the intakes. Sometimes they share more with someone who's been through it."

In Jasmine's mind, there was no way the one attack from Rob would equal the years of abuse some of these families went through. "You know I'll do whatever I can," she said and meant it. On occasion, when outfitting the women and children, they would talk. She'd listen. Sometimes just a sympathetic ear, with no fear of recrimination, helped fill the void.

Chapter Four

Jasmine managed to escape Jenn's questions when Jenn was called away to take a phone call. The owner of Safe Harbor had cornered her in her room. In that respect, Jenn was like Bask. They would fire a volley of questions, knowing that you'd be so overwhelmed you'd divulge more than you realized. It wasn't that she didn't want to share her experience with her friend. Of all people, besides Dorian and Morgan, Jenn would have understood the most. However, being a person of normal abilities, there were things that Jenn couldn't understand. Morgan was the one person Jasmine wanted to talk to.

Morgan had come to Ruthorford barely aware of her abilities. It wasn't until she'd come in contact with Dorian that those abilities had evolved, as had their attraction to one another. Jasmine remembered Morgan telling her after the wedding, "It was like trying to stop a freight train."

Jasmine finally understood. Since leaving the fairgrounds, Eryk kept popping into her thoughts—into her being. She could feel him, as if he was standing in front of her. His imagined touch was almost as powerful as the real thing. Her breath hitched. Her body ached.

She went to the mini-fridge in her room, took out a can of ginger ale, and rubbed the cold metal against her forehead. Then against her lips. The tingle reminded her of the sensation she'd felt the instant Eryk's lips.... She popped the lid and took a deep swallow, letting it burn down her throat. Was she really ready to be in a plane for hours with this man?

Jasmine went to her laptop and started it up. She checked her messages and emails—nothing significant. The Crosstown Gazette, a weekly newspaper shared between Ruthorford and her sister town in Virginia, Adams Grove, detailed some of the goings on in Ruthorford, while emails from Teresa supplied the rest. According to Teresa, Morgan was getting closer to her due date and had Dorian redecorating the nursery—for the second time. Jasmine laughed. He was such a wimp. She could just imagine what their little girl was going to look like. Eighty-five percent of the babies born to blends were girls with green eyes. Very special green eyes. Jasmine glanced into the mirror over the table at her very dark eyes. Unless the baby ended up with traits like hers. Jasmine was supposed to have the green eyes, since her parents were blends. What had happened? She felt her energy rise and mentally tamped it down. This was her third computer.

She read on. Miss Grace had entered a national pie contest and had made the finals. She and her sister were going to Atlanta to participate in the contest. Miss Grace and Miss Alice were from a founding family. Neither had married. They lived in the family home on some acreage at the end of town near her old home and bestowed the favors of their pies and goodies on the townsfolk. No one made pies like Miss Grace. In fact, even Teresa—who was famous for her baked goods at the bed and breakfast she and her husband, Bill, owned—served Miss Grace's pies on Sunday. Jasmine felt her mouth start to water. She could do with a slice of apple pie.

Her shop was doing well. Reading that, Jasmine felt a twinge of homesickness. She loved her boutique and missed the fast pace of the fashion industry. With her approval, the girls she had managing it had added a couple of new designer labels to the boutique and it was a huge success. They'd sent some pictures of their changes and Jasmine was thrilled. Even the slightly Goth jewelry, with its chunky darkness, set off the clothes beautifully. Jasmine made a mental note to let them know she'd be coming in, when she knew the date.

She sent Teresa a quick email, sending her love to everyone and telling her that she planned a visit soon and would send updates as soon as possible.

Then, she googled Eryk Vreeland. Page after page popped up—images of him from various shows, ranging from state fairs to over-the-top charity functions. Several showed him with his father. The resemblance was uncanny. But, the older man looked staid, his smile forced. She guessed theirs wasn't a close relationship. Neither man looked particularly comfortable with the other. She clicked on some more. The society pages showed him in picture after picture with a beautiful woman hanging onto his arm. She studied the pictures. He definitely looked comfortable there. Each time it was a different woman. Nowhere did she read of any long-term relationship. She smiled. No, that was not good. She chided herself. She wanted him in a long-term relationship—with someone else. Yet, that thought made her stop smiling.

After reading a bunch of articles about Eryk Vreeland's good works, she shut down the computer. Either the man was a blessed saint, or he was good at covering his tracks. There was no mention of the type of thing she'd witnessed today. From what she'd seen, it didn't look like he resisted using his abilities. How come no one ever noticed or wrote about it? With him being wealthy, from a highly placed social family, as well as a celebrity in his own right, the paparazzi should have had a field day.

Flying to Georgia should give her plenty of time to get to know him—to feel him out—just so she'd know how best to approach him about Ruthorford's secrets. Even with her resolve wavering each time she thought about their trip together, Jasmine was determined to call him first thing in the morning and make arrangements.

****

The morning proved too busy for Jasmine to give a thought to contacting Eryk. She was just finishing up her egg and bagel—she was still amazed at her craving for protein—when Jenn came into the dining room. She got some coffee, came over, and sat down across from Jasmine.

"I'm going to need your help," she stated.

"Sure. Dr. Browne said you'd taken in some clients last night."

"Yes," Jenn said, stirring too much sugar into her coffee, "I did. But, they aren't it. I just got a call from the police department. They picked up a girl last night for soliciting. Apparently, she didn't do a very good job of it. They took her to the precinct. She said she was nineteen. They don't believe her. Her ID's fake. During the body search—you remember Lieutenant Meyers—well, she was subbing on homicide last night, and the lone female, so she got called in to do the search. She found some injuries, old as well as new. Looks like the girl's taken some pretty severe beatings, expertly done, maybe by her pimp. They told her if she would agree to come here, they'd look at reducing the charges. She finally agreed."

Jasmine saw the strain on Jenn's face. All her wards, as Jenn called them, were special, but the young ones bothered Jenn the most. "You know I'll do anything I can." She pushed the untouched half of her breakfast across the table. "If you'll eat something."

Jenn picked up the bagel and took a bite, chewed, and swallowed. Jasmine doubted her friend knew she'd eaten anything. Jenn set the bagel down and frowned at it, as if seeing it for the first time. She grabbed her coffee. "What's on it?"

"Cream cheese and jelly."

Jenn shivered and made a face. She pulled the bagel apart and, taking Jasmine's knife off her plate, scraped off the spread. She took another bite and continued. "Well, Sonya called me a little while ago. They ran a missing persons on her. Nothing. When Sonya asked about her family, the girl freaked out. I think that's where the old injuries came from. So, my guess is that the poor thing went from an abusive relationship at home to an abusive relationship on the streets."

"What do you want me to do?"

"This time I want you at intake. Show your style. I have a feeling she'll respond. Then, we'll play it by ear. Maybe you could strut your stuff right after she gets here."

Jasmine smiled. *Strutting her stuff* was one thing she knew how to do. She was already mentally going through her wardrobe. "I guess we want to entice her to stay, not run."

Jenn laughed. "You got it. I have Dr. Browne on call."

"God, does that woman ever leave? She was here late last night."

"I know. I really like her. I think she'll work out well."

"Yeah, me too." Jasmine thought of the tea. "Any hints on the girl's looks?"

"Oh yeah," Jenn reached into her pocket and pulled out a folded piece of paper, the faxed mug shot.

She was a pretty thing. Round face. Too much make-up. Jasmine guessed her age between sixteen and eighteen. She hoped for the girl's sake it was eighteen. "Vitals?"

"Five-six, one ten. Slim."

"Between a four and five dress size. I have an idea."

Jenn rose. "Whatever you can do, just do it."

Jasmine looked at Jenn's posture. The vitality that poured from her was gone. "You all right?"

"Just tired. It's been a long week."

Jasmine reached out and placed her hand on Jenn's arm. "You're our mainsail. You need to take care of yourself." With that, she gave a little push and a pulse of energy.

Jenn's eyes flew open.

"Too much?" Jasmine gave a half-smile. She still had a lot of practicing to do.

Jenn laughed. "A bit." She shook her curls. "Funny thing, I do feel better." She reached over and hugged her. "Thanks."

****

There was a light knock on Jenn's office door just before it burst open. Jasmine, wearing black capris, an open-drape white cardigan over an azure blue silk shell, and canvas ankle-laced platforms the exact color of the shell, strode into the room. Her hair, softly spiked, moved when she walked. Silver earrings hung down her long neck. She looked every bit the fashion diva and presented the air of a runway model. She carried a hanger slung over her shoulder, on it a tone on tone ivory embroidered top with open cutwork sleeves and a Queen Anne neckline. She stopped in front of Jenn, whose eyes had opened wide.

"I'm so sorry to interrupt." Her deep southern accent sounded not in the least contrived. "Marsha has dropped out. She has that appointment for the audition you talked her into doing. Now I have no one to wear this Nina Ricci top in our fashion show."

Sonya made a sound in her throat.

Jasmine pinned the detective with her black eyes, made even darker outlined with coal. She sighed. "I'm sorry, Sonya, I just don't have it in your size this time. You did wear that gold lamé at the Christmas bash to perfection."

The young girl's eyes flew to the plus size woman standing near the window. The sun glinted off her caramel colored skin. The woman stance shifted, one of a model. Her suit lines changed at the movement and, other than the shoulder holster bulging under the jacket, she looked like she could easily carry off a lamé dress. The light in the girl's eyes heightened.

"You!" Jasmine twirled and stepped in front of the young girl, who flinched, her eyes once again hooded in fear, as she looked beseechingly at the tall beauty standing in front of her. It took everything Jasmine had not to drop the garment on the floor and enfold the young girl in protective arms. Instead, she swung the top in front of her and, tilting her head, studied the top, then the girl. "Well...I suppose...," her voice drawled, dripping southern honey with each exaggerated syllable.

Jenn coughed, interrupting. "I'm sorry. But Lily—it is Lily," Jenn asked, directing her question to the young girl in the chair, "isn't it?" When Lily nodded, she looked up at Jasmine. "Lily hasn't decided if she wants to avail herself of our facilities."

A small voice spoke. "Well, if I could help...." Lily stared at Jasmine.

Jasmine looked her up and down. "I don't know. This is a 5-ish."

The girl smiled for the first time. Perfect white teeth graced her mouth, except for a chip which had broken off the side of one of her front teeth. *A little porcelain...*, Jasmine couldn't help thinking. "I'm a five," Lily said, her large brown eyes widening, almost too big for her heart-shaped face.

"Well, you do have that perfect neck," Jasmine purred, hiding the horror she felt when she saw the deep purple bruise peeking out above the line of her deeply cut t-shirt. She wanted to kill the son-of-a-bitch who'd done that to Lily with her bare hands and made a mental note to talk to Dr. Browne about that—someday.

Jenn interrupted. "Lily, this is Jasmine. She came to us a year ago and has graciously agreed to stay and help me out. She owns an upscale boutique in her hometown and provides these gorgeous pieces for our women. We have impromptu fashion shows," she added, trying to cover the ruse. *Well, what the hell, a fashion show might just be the ticket.* Jenn jotted a note on her desk blotter. "Unfortunately, it's in-house only."

"I...I," Lily stammered, eyes darting to Sonya, tears springing to her eyes. "I don't want to go home...I can't." She looked at the lieutenant again. "I'm afraid they'll make me go home."

Jasmine knelt in front of her, crumpling the expensive top without a second thought. She took her hand. "Lily...listen to me," she looked into the frightened hazel eyes, "I promise you, if you don't want to go home, you won't."

She saw Sonya take a step forward and held up a hand. Sonya stopped.

"You must be honest with us." She tried to use her own little push. "How old are you?"

"Seventeen," she whimpered.

Jasmine saw Sonya roll her eyes.

The young girl looked from one to the other. "But I'll be eighteen next month. Honest."

Jenn spoke. "You can stay for now." She turned to Jasmine. "I'll call Bask."

Jenn looked at Sonya.

Sonya cleared her throat and forced a cough. Her voice, when she spoke, sounded hoarse. "I've got this terrible cold. I'm having the worst time hearing. A ringing in the ears. It's a real nuisance. How old did you tell me you were?"

Lily looked down. "Eighteen," she mumbled.

"Yep, that's what it says on the paperwork. I have to get back to the precinct. Young lady, if you would please sign these papers, I can get out of here."

Jenn held out a pen. Lily looked as Jasmine, who took the pen and handed it to Lily, and nodded. The young woman scrawled a name, probably fake, across the paper.

Jasmine leaned back on her heels as every adult in the room gave a silent sigh of relief.

By the time Jenn escorted Lily to her initial meeting with Dr. Browne, the girl looked completely different—and much younger. Her brown hair fell in soft waves to her shoulders; her face was devoid of make-up, except for a light lipstick. She was wearing a new pair of jeans and that $800 shirt that Jasmine had lured her with. Jasmine didn't have the heart to take it away.

Jasmine smiled as they walked past, encouraging her. Lily smiled her broken-tooth smile as she passed.

Chapter Five

Jenn whipped the SUV in front of the general aviation building and pulled to a stop. She turned to Jasmine, pushed up her sunglasses and stared at her friend with a worried look etching her pretty forehead.

Jasmine smiled. "I'm fine. Honest." Truth was, her stomach was doing somersaults.

"I may not have any 'special' abilities," Jenn air-quoted, "but you don't look fine. I can still arrange for Bask—"

Jasmine held up her hand to stop Jenn. They both noticed the tremor. Jasmine dropped her hand down into her lap. Her smile was one of resignation. "It wouldn't matter," she shook her head and said, "which plane I got on. I don't like flying."

Jenn turned around and slumped back in her seat. "Well, I'll be damned," she murmured. She turned back to Jasmine. "You? I don't believe it. You are the most confident woman I know. Even...," she hesitated a second, softened her voice, "...even after all you went through...you were so strong...you never broke...." She shook her head.

Jasmine laughed. "Yeah, I can face death, pure evil—nothing. Put me on a plane and I quake with fear."

"Speaking of planes," Jenn nodded toward the building, "here comes your pilot now. Still not too late."

Jasmine barely heard the last of Jenn's comment. She had swung her attention toward the tall man walking toward them. Sunlight glinted off his wavy black hair. Dark jeans hugged the muscles of his strong legs. He'd pushed the sleeves up on the black sweater he wore, revealing tightly muscled forearms. He strode toward them, smiling. As he neared, he lifted his sunglasses. Jasmine heard her own intake of breath as she stared into those green crystalline eyes.

"Holy…," Jenn whispered.

"You got it," Jasmine said back and reached for the door handle.

He was there in an instant, pulling open the door. "Pre-flight's all done. We can leave any time you're ready." He turned as Jenn walked around the vehicle. "Last time I saw you, you were dusting dirt off your…." He glanced at her hips.

"Yeah, I know." Laughter tumbled out. She looked at his outstretched hand, up to his eyes, and stuck out her hand. "I'm game if you are."

"I like you." He laughed and took her hand. Nothing happened.

"There." Jenn smiled, as if she'd accomplished something. "Jenn Davis."

"Eryk Vreeland," he responded and returned her firm handshake.

He turned to Jasmine as she stepped out of the car, his gaze lingering on her lithe form, before moving to her face. They stared at one another, caught in some sort of trance.

Jenn turned, walked back to the rear of the SUV, and pulled up the lift gate. She saw the two of them awkwardly smile at one another and follow her. A tiny flicker of hope built in her chest.

Eryk let out a whistle as he scanned the four suitcases lined up in the rear of the vehicle. "Good thing my plane can handle luggage for six," he said. He reached in and took the two largest cases.

"Hey, fashion's my passion," Jasmine defended and grabbed the other two.

"And your job," Jenn added, closed the rear gate, and took one of the two suitcases Jasmine held.

"I have to make some change-outs from the store while I'm there," Jasmine added.

"She has this great boutique in Ruthorford," Jenn said to Eryk. "She supplies the clothes for our clientele when they first come to Safe Harbor. Gives them a sense of change—and well-being."

They followed him through the building and out the back. A small jet sat near the hangar. He walked over, set one suitcase down, grabbed a lever, twisted and backed away to let the stairs ease down.

Jasmine swallowed and looked at the small jet. *Magic* was scrolled across the tail of the plane in vibrant green, nestled amid the black that slanted in a slash across the back half of the plane. It was a beautiful plane, as planes went.

Eryk shifted his sight, letting the auras of the two women whirl around them. Jenn's was vibrant and danced about her, just as he suspected it would. Jasmine's, on the other hand, was snug next to her, like armor, like he'd seen it at the fairgrounds. It was also a little more opaque, shadowy, than her friends. He'd seen that before, too—on a war veteran. Except the veteran's wasn't shielding him, trying to keep others out, as Jasmine's did. He made a mental note to keep tabs on her aura.

He blinked, returned everything to normal, walked toward the tail of the plane, and opened a space for the luggage. "Set those down. I'll take care of them. Go on, have a look inside."

Jenn moved up the steps into the small cabin, turned and waited for Jasmine. When she didn't follow, Jenn stuck her head back out. "You coming?"

"I'll get there," Jasmine hissed. She glanced over at Eryk, hoping he hadn't heard.

"Honey...," Jenn started and stopped at the wave of Jasmine's hand. She watched as the tall beauty took one step at a time, hunched over and entered the cabin.

"Not much room," she whispered as Jenn plopped down in one of four comfortable seats.

"Nice," Jenn cooed and messed with a fold-away table.

Jasmine moved as Eryk crouched inside. "Small, but very efficient."

Jenn stood. "You'll call me when you land?"

Jasmine nodded, trying to smile.

"She'll be fine," Eryk reassured Jenn, seeing the frown. "I'll take good care of her. I promise."

Jenn bounced down the small stairway and turned back. "Happy flying," she called and waved. She turned and, without a backward glance, headed back to the building.

Eryk reached over, grabbed a strap and pulled the stairs up. With one swift motion, he locked the airstairs in place. "We have facilities in the back." He nodded toward the rear.

Jasmine didn't turn but chided, "Well, if you gotta go, go now, 'cause *I'm* not flying this baby while you go potty."

He laughed and stepped over and down, settling into his seat in the cockpit. He pointed to the seat next to him. "Come on."

"I'm not a pilot!" Her voice was shrill. She swallowed.

His voice became soft, modulated. "I know. But, I think you'll like it from up here." He patted the co-pilot's seat. "Don't worry, I solo all the time."

God, she hadn't asked just how many hours of airtime he had. What if he was new? She felt her hands start to tremble.

He held out his hand for her, but she pulled hers back in close to her body. He moved his arm back and waited until she had gotten into the seat, not an easy feat. At one point, she'd grabbed his shoulder as she stepped over the console. He could see tiny beads of sweat on her upper lip. Her pupils were dilated.

"Fly much?" he asked off-handedly.

She shook her head as he reached over her and fastened her harness, careful to make minimal contact with her body. She was scooching back into the seat away from him. He pretended not to notice, finished, and reached for a headset, handing it to her. "We can talk better with these," he said as she took it.

She adjusted the headset, all the while watching him move switches and talk into his. He turned a knob and the engine on her side started to whine. Then, he turned the knob next to it and the second engine came to life. The whine built to a high-pitched scream. She was grateful for the earphones. Faintly, she heard a feminine voice recite some sort of data. The plane started to move. Jasmine gripped the edge of her seat.

Eryk noticed the tightness in her body but was too busy to do anything about it—yet. He taxied to the end of the runway and revved the engines. The Phenom 100 moved down the runway. In no time, the sleek jet was up and gaining altitude. He smiled. He loved his plane. He banked slightly to the left and kept climbing. A quick glance showed him Jasmine's face had gone ashen and her knuckles were white where she gripped the seat. Her chest rose and fell quickly.

He reached over and touched her shoulder. She flinched, her eyes huge. He sent a mental push to calm her and saw her battle it. He added his voice through the headset. "Relax, it's a beautiful day. Enjoy the flight." Her shoulder softened under his hand and she smiled a tremulous smile before she turned to look out the window.

In that instant, his vision changed, shifted, and he was seeing unlike he'd ever seen before, which was saying something, since his eyes allowed him to see all sorts of nuances he knew other people didn't see. However, this was different—and he sure as hell couldn't fly a plane this way—not yet, anyway. He realized his hand still rested on Jasmine's shoulder. He yanked it away and blinked. His vision returned to normal. *What the hell?* She seemed to be in a daze, staring out the side window toward the receding earth.

"Jasmine," he spoke softly into the headset, not wanting to startle her.

She turned her head slightly, but, her eyes remained focused out the window, as though she couldn't pull them away from whatever it was she was watching.

"Jasmine," he said again, louder.

She blinked several times, looked at him, and blushed.

"What was that?" he asked.

Jasmine looked him in the eyes. "I'm not sure. I'm okay now." She offered a small smile.

"We'll be cruising at about 31,000 feet. It'll be like walking on the clouds," he said, his voice soft, suggestive.

She knew what he was doing. She let him. Her anxieties about flying seemed to have existed forever, as far back as she could remember, anyway. Until this time, she'd always sucked it up and done what she had to do, refusing any help.

The Abbott House plane was large enough that she could sit back in the cabin, listening to loud music, popping gum, and get through it. She hadn't even mentioned it to Dr. Browne. It seemed of little consequence, since she didn't see why she should fly when there were perfectly good roads on which to travel. This small jet was something else. It felt like there was no plane.

For a few moments earlier, in fact, when she'd looked out the window, it had been like she hadn't been in the plane at all. Out of nowhere, she was flying—without the plane, above the trees. She could see the ground, vegetation, buildings. Hell, she saw a mouse scurrying to get away from a grass snake. And, she could see so far. It was amazing. Plus, she wasn't afraid. Then he'd called her name, pulling her back. She didn't want to let go. He'd called again, with a command she couldn't ignore. In an instance, she was back in the plane and all her senses got tangled. Her anxiety level shot up.

Jasmine reached up and wiped the moisture from her upper lip. *What's happening to me?*

"Tell me about your hometown," he interrupted her thoughts.

"Ruthorford?" Jasmine let her mind conjure up a picture of her hometown. "It's a small, southern town in the mountains of northern Georgia. Well, the low mountains. It's just a little way from Atlanta. We don't have the hustle and bustle of Atlanta. Yet, we aren't far from it."

"However," she said, turning toward him, "Ruthorford is set off by itself. It's almost surrounded by water. You cross a bridge to get in and a bridge to get out. Most of the inhabitants can trace their families back to the original settlement, either Native American or Scot."

She glanced back out the window, but kept talking. "We have the main town, which is encircled by farms. It's very pretty. The town is very Victorian, its buildings old and quaint. A median runs down Main Street—its fountain is almost always shooting water."

"Is there someplace I can stay? A motel?" He looked over at her and flashed her a smile. "Unless you want me to stay with you," he added, only half teasing.

"Abbott Bed and Breakfast sits near the end of town. That's where you'll be staying," she retorted, then let her voice soften. "My cousin, Teresa, owns it. Wait until you see it. She—the inn, not my cousin—is a true painted lady, with wide porches and gables."

She became more animated as she talked, her eyes twinkling. "The lawn behind the bed and breakfast slopes down to the water with trees all around to cool the tables. The weeping willow is my favorite spot. You can dine under its branches. It's like hiding behind a veil where you can watch the other people. I used to do my homework under that tree."

"Tell me about your shop," he asked, wanting her to continue. He liked hearing the sound of her voice.

"Fashion Flair? I have two girls running it for me. Bonnie and Claire—the twins. I jokingly called them Bonnie and Clyde growing up and it stuck." She laughed, a full, throaty laugh.

He couldn't help but smile at her. Her black eyes looked into his. It went straight to his gut.

"They used to get into so much trouble," she chortled. "We weren't sure they'd make it to their teens. But, they did." She took a breath. "And, they grew into gorgeous, gracious girls. They are perfect for my shop. They've added a young, kind of funky touch. They've brought in some younger clientele, while keeping the others. I'm really proud of them."

"And...The Shoppe of Spells?" He watched as something moved across her eyes and was gone. He couldn't tell what.

She took a breath. "The Shoppe of Spells has been a part of Ruthorford from almost the beginning. It has a reputation for being rather...," she paused, "...eclectic." She seemed pleased with her choice of words. "I think I'll let you see for yourself."

"Oh," she said as an afterthought, "Ruthorford is privately owned. By the Abbott House."

He frowned. He'd never heard of a town being privately owned.

"But, I thought you had property there?"

"I do. I'm part of Abbott House." With that, she turned away to look out the window at the clouds.

It wasn't long before they began their descent. Her least favorite part. He motioned for her to look out of the window. Jasmine had no desire to watch the ground rushing up at her. However, she knew this place. It was home. She pointed, wanting him to see it as it first donned its fall colors. She shifted her gaze down and smiled as she was rewarded with the show of trees, tipped in gold and orange, standing at attention along the waterways that encircled Ruthorford. They flew over the town and headed further south toward the small airport. She listened as he talked to voices over the headset. Then, ahead, she saw the runway. Unable to resist, she grabbed the seat.

It was a smooth landing.

"You can take your death-grip off the seat now," he laughed. "We're on the ground."

"Sorry," she whispered and flexed her fingers from the cramping.

A young man ran out as they taxied toward the building and waited for them. He pointed to a spot and Eryk parked the plane and shut it down. Eryk reached over, unfastened her harness, and held out his hand to steady her as she stepped over the console and back up into the body of the plane. One thing he'd not liked in the small plane was the lack of hand-holds, but now, having the black-eyed beauty placing her long fingers in his, he wasn't so sure.

A small current ran between them. Her eyes flew to his. He said nothing, just watched her and felt the pulse change. Desire followed. He watched her eyes grow even darker, if that was possible. Then the look took on something he didn't like. Was it fear? Of him? His eyes? He gently squeezed her hand and smiled. "Let's get this show on the road." He tried to sound light, carefree.

When the airstairs lowered, the young man was waiting, all excited. "You've got a car waiting for you," he smiled. "It's a fully equipped Range Rover." His excitement was palpable.

"Bask," Jasmine commented to Eryk.

"Why don't you bring it around so we can get the luggage?" He smiled at the teenager.

"You mean it?" He was almost hopping.

"Sure. You work here, right?"

"Yes, sir." He saluted and ran off.

Jasmine followed Eryk down the stairs and smiled at him as he closed and latched the stairway. "You just made that kid very happy."

"You don't mind, do you?"

"Not at all. It's not my car. I think I'll go freshen up before we get started," she turned and walked toward the small building.

Eryk stopped what he was doing and watched her. She moved with incredible grace and the she filled out a pair of jeans was a pleasure to behold. He felt the blood rush to his groin. "Down, boy," he half groaned.

He blinked, letting his vision shift so he could see her aura. It was a little less tight than it had been before the flight, but she was still encased in one hell of a protective wrapper. Returning his vision to normal, he pondered the woman that was haunting his dreams while he unloaded the bags, and then watched as the kid raced the vehicle, a bit too fast, toward his jet.

****

Jasmine finished washing her hands, dried them and dug the small phone out of her jeans pocket. She applied a light swipe of lipstick as she waited for Jenn to answer.

"On the ground, again?" Jenn piped up.

"Yep. At the airport. Bask left us a Range Rover. Think I'll give him a little tour on our way in."

"Everything *hunky* dory?" Jenn let her voice linger on the hunky.

"Oh, yeah. I'm fine," she affirmed, "and so is he. How's Lily?"

"Skittish. Didn't want to join us for dinner. Meadow changed her mind. They're in your wardrobe room, now."

"Well, Meadow's sweet nature could warm anyone."

Jenn laughed. "The lasagna helped. And Meadow's constant chatter about your designer clothes. They didn't wait for desert."

"I'm glad. There's something about that girl that went straight to my heart."

"I know. Mine, too." Jenn said, sounding more subdued. "Call me tonight."

"Will do. Bye," she responded and shoved the phone in her pocket.

Eryk wasn't at the Rover when she went out. She climbed into the driver's seat and started the engine, as he walked out of the building and moved toward her. She definitely liked the way he moved.

"Nice ride," he said, climbing in beside her and fastening his seat belt.

"Abbott House," she said simply.

"This Abbott House...," he started to say, shut his mouth, and gripped the hand bar as she swerved onto the small road.

"You can relax," Jasmine quipped, "we're on the ground." She hit a button and the sunroof slid back as she slowed to a comfortable speed.

Trees lined the road, displaying their colors in vibrant coats of gold, orange and red. Jasmine realized she was more than a little happy that he would be seeing Ruthorford at its best. Black painted fences snugged the curve of rolling pastures where horses grazed. High upon a hill a red barn with white trim proclaimed its southern heritage.

They passed more farms and crossed several bridges before the country road widened into a four lane highway.

Within minutes, he found himself in a bustling center of commerce—divided highways, concrete walkways, lights. He'd gone from country back roads to major shopping in no time.

Jasmine pulled into a parking lot. "Just need to run in here for a moment. Be right back."

"Is this Ruthorford?"

"Oh, no." She darted into the store.

Eryk got out of the car and stretched. Going from cockpit to car left his muscles cramping. He started to follow her into the large electronics store when something caught his eye and he walked around the side of the building instead. Old tombstones stood upright in a small area fenced off by black wrought iron fencing. The asphalt of the shopping center stopped abruptly at the ornate gate, turning into a small gravel drive that barely accommodated one car. It wound through the tiny cemetery and then led back to the gate.

"Oh, there you are," Jasmine called and walked over to join him.

He nodded toward the cemetery. "What gives?"

She shrugged. "In Georgia, cemeteries are grandfathered. You don't move the cemetery. You build around it."

"But it's small," he commented.

"I've seen smaller—stuck right in the middle of a development. One or two graves, fenced in. They don't do this where you're from?"

"You know...I don't know," he said and turned back toward the car.

"Well, we better get back on the road. I want you to see Ruthorford before it gets dark."

She took him into town by way of her favorite route, across the bridge near the Abbott Bed and Breakfast. She smiled as they passed the small chapel next to the grand inn. Pots of orange and purple blossoms lined the steps leading to the wrap-around porch of the Abbott Bed and Breakfast. The summer white rockers had been replaced with black ones, one of the little seasonal touches Teresa liked to do. She could almost see Teresa standing on the porch, waving, as she used to do when Jasmine would come home from college. Right now, the porch was empty. "That's where you'll be staying. We'll drive through town and come back."

They passed the tiny Victorian post office. Brenda, the postmistress since forever, had already decorated the front in fall colors. She slowed to a crawl as they passed The Shoppe of Spells, the afternoon light twinkling off the bottles and stones that decorated the front windows. Jasmine pointed out her shop directly opposite, across the median. In the middle of the median the fountain's water shot up, its spray wetting the pots of chrysanthemums encircling it.

Two older women were walking down the sidewalk in front of her shop. She waved. They waved back, stopped, and stared, long after the SUV had passed.

"An interesting pair," Eryk turned back to her, having turned in his seat to watch them lean into one another, talking and gesturing with their hands.

Jasmine glanced up into the rear view mirror and smiled. They were still pointing and talking. She could almost hear them. "That's Miss Grace and Miss Alice. They're sisters. They've been around forever. No one makes pies like Miss Grace. You'll get a taste, I'm sure, at the bed and breakfast. And news of your arrival will soon be all over town."

"Gossips?"

"More like the top of the phone tree," she laughed.

They passed more shops and came to where the median narrowed. There, Jasmine stopped to swing the car into a U-turn and head back down the other side to the inn.

"Where's your house?"

She hesitated a fraction of a second before she pointed past him, toward the far end of town. "A little ways that way. But, I live above my shop."

Jasmine pulled in front of the bed and breakfast and was just coming around the front of the vehicle when Teresa came running down the steps, her arms wide. "It's so good to see you," Teresa called and pulled Jasmine into a tight hug.

Eryk watched the shorter woman wrap Jasmine in a warm embrace. Shorter and more muscular, she resembled Jenn more than Jasmine, down to the bouncing waves of hair, streaked with white.

Jasmine, laughing, hugged her back, and inhaled. Teresa smelled of herbs and fresh bread. She closed her eyes, embracing the memory. The scents of home.

Allowing one last squeeze, she stepped back. "Teresa, I'd like you to meet Eryk Vreeland."

Although she'd been forewarned of his resemblance to Dorian, all Teresa could say was, "Oh, my." When Eryk offered a smile and his hand, she stepped past it and put her arms around him. "You're family." She hugged him and spoke softly, warmly. "Welcome home."

His hug was tentative. This woman seemed convinced that he was something he wasn't so sure about. Yet, he could sense her sincerity. Well, two could play at this game. When she stepped back, he smiled and looked deep into her eyes, studying her reaction. His eyes didn't bother her in the slightest.

"Wow! And I thought Dorian was handsome." She patted him on the arm and placed herself between the two of them. Linking arms, she led them back up the steps. "We'll get your bags later. Come on in. I want Bill to meet you. Then I'll get you settled in."

Eryk glanced back down the road toward The Shoppe of Spells, almost compelled. No one was about. His eyes wandered across the median, taking in the splendor of the town. It really was beautiful. Norman Rockwell beautiful. He turned his attention back to the two women on his left.

Although the weather had begun its cool-down, it was still warm enough that guests of the inn were moving out onto the wrap-around front porch, taking in the view and enjoying the cool breeze. Several smiled at them as they passed. Ever the gracious hostess, Teresa smiled and said hello, pausing briefly to announce that her cousin has come home for a visit and if they needed anything, just ask at the desk.

"You go on," someone called. "We can find our way around. Besides, you've always got everything so taken care of, we don't need a thing."

Teresa glanced back. "Why, thank you Miss Jill. We'll see you at dinner."

Eryk opened one of the beautiful double doors, the Victorian wood arching gracefully around a large pane of glass. They stepped into the huge foyer/lobby. Scents of herbs and baked goods wafted from the dining area.

A tall man stepped through the door, wiping his hands on an apron. "Well, that about takes care of the late lunch crowd," he beamed.

"Not quite yet," Teresa pulled them over.

"Jasmine," his deep voice resonated as he pulled her into a bear hug, lifting her off the floor.

She laughed, hugging tight around his neck. "Bill, you old coot, I've missed your hugs."

He laughed, put her down and turned to Eryk, extending his large hand, laughter still in his eyes. "Bill Ruthorford."

Eryk took it and felt a surge. However, this one he couldn't place. "Eryk Vreeland. Pleased to meet you." It took everything he had not to pull his hand away. Out of the corner of his eye he saw Jasmine studying the older man, a small frown passing fleetingly over her eyes before it was gone. *This is Teresa's husband?* He hoped his astonishment couldn't be read in his expression.

"Have you two eaten? Of course not," he said and led them into the dining room. "Let's sit over here." He led them over to a table overlooking the side garden and held the chair for his wife, while Eryk pulled out Jasmine's. "I'll be right back." He headed into the kitchen.

He'd barely passed through the doors when Jasmine spoke, "Teresa, why didn't you call me? What's wrong with Bill?"

Teresa's shoulders visibly sagged. "I don't know. He says he's fine, but he lost thirty pounds and looks like he's aged thirty years." She unfolded her napkin and placed it in her lap. "You know he won't go to Mike Yancy."

"There are other doctors," Jasmine insisted.

"Not for us. You know that."

Jasmine looked down, then up, brightening. "Morgan and Dorian...," she began and was cut off by the wave of Teresa's hand.

"He won't let Morgan do anything because of the baby and Dorian doesn't have the healing power." She smiled and patted Jasmine's hand, trying to reassure her. "Miss Alice and Miss Grace have been giving him some of their concoctions. It seems to be helping. He's not as tired." She stopped speaking and plastered a smile on her face as Bill reappeared through the doors with a pitcher of iced tea.

Eryk blinked and allowed his vision to shift. The man's aura was mottled. The entire thing had a lavender glow. Nothing he'd ever seen before. The other colors spiked in jagged arcs. There were definite breaks in the energy.

Jasmine touched his hand and he felt the tingle. He blinked and looked at her. She frowned. He tried to smile at her, but the smile didn't reach his eyes. He placed his hand over hers and squeezed, allowing a small about of energy pass between them. He heard her intake of breath and watched her eyes sparkle.

"You could...," she started. He gave her hand another squeeze and gave an almost imperceptible nod, hoping she caught his motion.

"What a beautiful inn," he directed his attention to Teresa. Teresa was looking at his hand over Jasmine's. He gave one last squeeze and put his napkin in his lap.

"Yes," Teresa said, not skipping a beat. "It's one of the oldest structures here. It was built by the Abbott family to hide away one of the daughters thought to be not quite right in the head." She smiled at Bill as filled the glasses and sat down.

"Lunch will be but a moment." He took a deep breath and placed his own napkin in his lap with a flourish. "Now, isn't this something. Me sitting down to a meal with my two favorite women." His smile was warm and encompassing.

Eryk could tell Teresa had reached under the table and taken Bill's hand.

"I was just telling Eryk about this old place," Teresa said.

"Hedy's hideaway?" Bill laughed.

Teresa hit him in the arm, "Bill. That's not funny." She was laughing, nevertheless.

She turned back to Eryk. "Helen Abbott, nicknamed Hedy for some reason," she shrugged, "was one of the first to have green eyes." Then she looked at Eryk directly. "…and the visions."

Eryk frowned.

Jasmine piped up. "We haven't had a lot of time for conversation."

"Oh," Teresa said, shrugged again, and continued, "rather than have her institutionalized—back then that was like condemning someone to hell—Mr. Abbott built this house for her. Sent her here with servants and here she remained for the rest of her life. Quite happy, I'm told."

"I thought you said it was privately owned?" he looked at Jasmine.

Bill spoke up. "It is. Abbott bought all the surrounding lands, once he got approval by the tribal counsel. It gets complicated, but everything goes back to the Abbott House in Atlanta. It's the foundation that holds everything. I am sure you will hear from Bask, if you haven't already."

"I got an email from a Kristoff Bask about flying Jasmine down. A very assertive personality, even in writing," Eryk said.

"That's the one," Bill said enthusiastically. At that moment, several young women appeared carrying trays. Plates were placed in front of them. Grilled pork chops in a wine demi-glaze, sugar peas, grilled zucchini, and herbed potatoes. Fresh yeast rolls were passed around and Eryk found his mouth watering. The tea glasses were refilled and everyone dug in, silent except for murmurs of appreciation. When Eryk rolled his eyes and groaned, Bill laughed, "Now, that's a real compliment."

As they finished off thin slices of several types of pie, Jasmine rose. "I hate to do this, but I want to check on the girls." When Eryk started to rise, she gently rushed him back down. "You. Stay. Teresa will show you your room. Freshen up. I'm come back for you and we'll head over to Dorian and Morgan's." She stepped around and kissed Teresa and Bill each on the cheek and waved over her shoulder as she walked out of the room.

Teresa watched Eryk's gaze follow Jasmine and smiled.

****

Eryk stood on the balcony, the French doors thrown wide. He'd taken a shower and changed, then stepped onto the balcony, not sure what he'd expected. At soon as he stepped out, Jasmine's description came to mind, as did her enthusiasm. If anything, she'd understated its magnificence.

A lush green lawn stretched down to a winding creek. Trees dotted the lawn, each one encircled by colorful plants. Wrought iron tables graced the lawn and couples dined in the cool afternoon air. The weeping willow she'd described was beyond anything he could have imagined. Green limbs spread away from the huge trunk, its many stems thinning and dipping, moving gently in the breeze, like green gossamer tresses.

Jasmine knocked lightly on the door. She opened it when he called, "Come in."

He turned as she walked into the suite. She'd thrown on a black cowl neck sweater over black jeans, tucked into black boots. Her hair softly framed her perfect features and her lips were touched with a hint of red. She smiled and his breath caught. She was stunning.

She stopped. Their eyes locked and it felt like a charge moved through the room. Trying to ignore it, she looked away, around the room. It was one of the Inn's biggest and best, other than the bridal suite. In fact, she liked this one best. It had a Scottish feel to it—heavy mahogany, highly polished, plaid fabrics with paisley. It fit his personality to a tee. Unable to stop herself, she let her eyes move back to him. He leaned against the wooden balcony, something she would never do, his hands resting on the rail, his legs slightly parted. The breeze ruffled his black hair and it looked as though his green eyes sparked.

As though nothing could stop them, they moved toward one another. When they were but a foot apart, he raised his hands and gently framed her face. The surge between them was immediate. "We're no longer in the air," his deep voice whispered as he brushed her lips with his. He heard her intake of breath and waited until her lips parted slightly in invitation. Then he claimed her mouth. For an instant, she was his. His mouth moved over hers and their tongues danced. Then, just as suddenly, she pushed away, staring wild-eyed.

He frowned.

"We better go," she said a little breathless and turned away. She continued to move away until the energy between them subsided. Without looking back, she pulled open the door and walked down the hall.

Eryk followed her.

They waved at Teresa as they passed through the lobby and out. The afternoon was lengthening and shadows played across the median. They strolled down the sidewalk toward her shop, stopped, but did not enter. They crossed the median, moved around the fountain, up to The Shoppe of Spells.

It rose like a gothic mistress, beckoning. She grabbed the doorknob, pushed open the door, and stepped aside, letting him walk past her. Nothing like its outward face, the shop was bright and airy and smelled of herbs, with a floral undertone. Glass shelves displayed soaps and lotions. A door under the stairs opened.

"What can I do—" Dorian's words died in his throat.

Although forewarned, they stood immobile, facing each other, seeing *themselves*. Other than Dorian's ice-blue eyes and the few pounds difference in weight, it was like looking into a mirror. Neither spoke.

Jasmine stepped forward, breaking the silence. "Dory!" She threw herself into his arms.

He grabbed her and twirled her around. "Jas," he laughed, set her down, held her at arms' length. "You look gorgeous, as usual," he said. "Morgan's in the garden."

"I'll get her. Dorian, Eryk—Eryk, Dorian," she said as she made her way out the back door screen door, letting it slam behind her. Better they get over the shock without her. It was hard enough seeing the two of them together. Having to watch them dance around each other was more than she wanted to handle at the moment.

Jasmine stopped on the stoop. Meesha, Dorian's Border Collie, leapt up and raced toward her, tail wagging. She leaned down to brush the soft fur, letting her eyes rest on the woman kneeling in the garden. Morgan's faceted green eyes locked on Jasmine's obsidian ones.

The redhead broke into a wide grin. "Well, don't just stand there. Help me up," she laughed cradling the large stomach of a late term pregnancy.

Jasmine bounded off the steps and ran to her, gently taking her arm and hoisting her to her feet, not letting go until she was steady. "What are you having," Jasmine grunted, "a whale?"

"Some days it feels like it," Morgan groaned. She flung her arms around Jasmine. "Oh, to be lean and mean again," she laughed.

Jasmine hugged, stepped back, leaned over and stroked the round belly. She cooed a loving comment and planted a kiss, only to feel a foot against her mouth. "I just got kicked," she exclaimed, thrilled.

"Welcome to my world," Morgan said and pushed on her stomach, rearranging the offending limb. "Inside?" She glanced at the building.

Jasmine nodded. She was glad she and Morgan had not only made their peace but become friends along the way. Something deep inside her told her Dorian and Eryk would need the both of them.

"Let's give them a moment, then."

Jasmine looked around the garden. Even for fall, it was lush and full. Morgan's magical touch had brought it back to the opulence Morgan's birth mother, Melissa, had enjoyed. It was a shame Morgan never got to know Melissa—they were so much alike. Unfortunately, Melissa and Thomas Kilraven had died in a plane crash a little over a year before—which was what had brought Morgan to Rutherford in the first place. Jasmine wondered if Morgan would be married to Dorian had they not died. Jasmine forced herself to stop musing. History didn't change.

Morgan led Jasmine toward the beautiful cottage nestled at the back of the garden. The Dutch door stood open. Jasmine loved the cottage and was thrilled that little had changed in it over the last year. Herbs were hanging from the beams in the great room, drying, their fragrance scenting the air. Crystals and stones rested on window sills and the mantel, sparkling. French doors led to the back bedroom and bath. The woven rug rested in its special place in front of those French doors.

An involuntary shudder passed through Jasmine. "Any activity?" she asked, letting her gaze linger on the old woven rug.

Morgan's gaze followed hers to the rug and she shook her head. "Nothing. Which is making Dorian a very happy man." Her hands went protectively to her stomach. "Let me go pee and we'll go check on the boys." She waddled the walk of a very pregnant woman through the bedroom to the bathroom.

Jasmine pushed down a twinge of jealousy and called toward the back. "When you have some time, I need to talk with you."

Morgan appeared, pulling down her shirt over her pregnancy pants. "I will be so glad NOT to have to use every facility within reach," she laughed. "Want to talk now?"

"No. But soon."

"Okay. Let's go see how the boys are getting along."

They walked back through the garden, arm in arm. Morgan stopped right before they reached the steps. She turned to Jasmine. "How are you doing?"

"Good," Jasmine commented and dropped her arm.

Morgan took her hand. A small, controlled current went from Morgan to Jasmine, almost a challenge. Jasmine laughed. "No fair. I don't want to risk the babies."

Morgan's eyes widened. "How did you know?"

Jasmine put her arm around Morgan's shoulder. "Have you looked in a mirror lately?"

Morgan rolled her eyes. "Not if I can help it."

"Sweetie, you are way too big for that to be housing just one little Drake. I mean...I know Dorian is special and all...but really."

"Well, there's my lady love," Dorian's voice carried through the screen door. He stepped out on the porch to help her into the house.

"You know, I expect this treatment to continue after the babies are born," she leaned on his arm and stepped into the kitchen. Her gaze turned from the face of her husband to the man now standing on the other side of the kitchen table. She stopped in her tracks, which left Jasmine on the other side of the open door.

Jasmine made a small sound in her throat.

"Oh," Morgan blushed and stepped forward, extending her hand. "I know I shouldn't be surprised, but I am." She was looking at the spitting image of her husband, except for the brilliant green eyes—her eyes. He was a little leaner than Dorian and seemed a bit more fashion conscious, judging from the jeans and sweater he wore. She felt the energy pouring off of him.

Eryk moved toward Morgan. Other than Jasmine, before him stood the most beautiful woman he'd ever seen. Heavy auburn tresses curled about her shoulders. Just slightly shorter than Jasmine, she glowed with happiness. He'd heard the term, peaches and cream complexion, but had never seen it. And, with those brilliant green eyes, his eyes, she was breathtaking. He stared at her, blinked, and held her hand while viewing her aura. He'd never done it with a pregnant woman before and he found himself staring at the two separate auras emanating from the roundness of her body.

"All well?" she asked.

He realized he was still holding her hand and let it drop as heat crept up his neck. He quickly blinked and, in that instant, saw her do the same. He smiled into matching eyes. "All's perfect."

"Same here," she returned. "Come on, sit down."

Dorian set mugs on the table, a large pot of tea, and some scones. "Help yourselves," he said and left the room. He returned carrying a large folder, set it down on the table, and settled in the chair next to his wife.

"Bask?" Jasmine asked.

"Of course," Dorian opened the folder.

Eryk sat quietly, watching the three others around the table. He seemed compelled by Morgan's eyes to look deep into them. They were the same eyes he saw in the mirror every morning. Is this what other people felt looking into his?

She was talking with Jasmine, who was pouring tea into mugs and handing them out. They fell into a camaraderie he's never felt with anyone and he found himself actually hoping there might be a place for him with these people. Dorian's ice-blue eyes watched Morgan as if trying to anticipate what she might want before she spoke. Their silent communication was evident when their eyes would meet and a nod, a smile, or a touch would follow.

Dorian pulled some papers out of the folder. "Here are the results of the DNA tests." He handed Eryk the results.

Eryk frowned. "How?" He looked around the table.

Jasmine cheeks turned pink and she looked down when he frowned at her. She took a breath and confronted him. "The day we met and knocked Jenn on her ass—" She stopped at Morgan's laugh.

"Jenn told me about that." Morgan patted Jasmine's hand. "Apparently, you guys delivered quite a jolt."

Jasmine's face only became more inflamed.

"It's okay, Jas," Dorian said and laid his hand on hers, "it takes time to learn to control it."

As Eryk watched the intimate gesture he found himself feeling something new to him—jealousy.

Jasmine smiled at Dorian before pulling her hand back and turning to Eryk. "I scratched you when we pulled apart."

He held up his hand, showing a faint red line down the side. "I know. I'll probably have a scar," he teased.

"Don't worry, she's not rabid," Dorian offered.

"Are you sure?" Eryk quipped back, pulled the papers out and leafed through them. Lab reports. A glance showed numerous matches between he and Dorian. Yet, they'd done this without his permission. "I don't remember signing any releases," he said without looking up.

Silence fell around the table until Dorian spoke his voice tight. "So, sue us."

Eryk snorted and looked at the three people watching him. He slowly shook his head, trying to tamp down the hurt he felt by his "parents'" betrayal. "Ironically, it's not you all I want to go after."

Dorian leaned forward. "Believe it or not, I know how you feel." He waited until he had Eryk's full attention before he continued. "There is so much you don't understand. About Ruthorford. Us. Yourself. But know this—we've got your back."

"Ooh," Morgan hissed, sucked in her breath, and put her hand on her side.

Dorian's attention shifted in an instant.

Morgan rolled her eyes. "Braxton-Hicks. Nothing more. I've got another month."

Jasmine's eyes riveted on her stomach. "You sure? It looked like your whole stomach tightened."

"It did. Whew," she smiled. Her cheeks were flushed.

Eryk started to rise. "Maybe we should let you rest."

Morgan waved him back down. "No. But, I am hungry and I don't feel like traipsing over to the B & B. Why don't you boys go over and get us something to eat?"

Dorian didn't move. "I don't want to leave—"

Jasmine interrupted, "What do I look like, Jell-O?"

Dorian looked at Eryk and, in very similar, fluid movements, both men rose.

With a frown, Dorian stared at his wife. "I'm fine," she assured him and waved them away. "And don't hurry," Morgan called after them.

Dorian blew her a kiss as he closed the door.

"There. That's better. Too much testosterone was filling this space," Morgan said and rubbed her stomach in a circular motion. "Wow, they are very alike, aren't they? Especially given the fact that they were raised completely apart." She turned to Jasmine. "Now, tell me what's going on with you two."

Jasmine didn't hesitate. "I don't know. This attraction is unreal. It's like I have no choice when I'm around him. And when I'm not—"

"—you're in agony until you're back with him." Morgan finished the statement.

"Yes."

"Have you…?"

"Oh, no. I just met him."

Meesha's bark had Morgan pushing back her chair.

"I'll get it," Jasmine rose, walked over to the back door, and let the Border Collie in. Meesha gave a quick lick to Jasmine's hand before settling down at Morgan's feet. Jasmine returned to her chair, ruffling Meesha's fur as she passed.

"Don't let her fool you. She's still Dorian's baby," Morgan said. "Let's get back to Eryk. Are you all right? I mean…after what happened with…," her words trailed off.

"You mean with Rob. Morgan, I thought you and I were done with the uncomfortable moments and inappropriate guilt. I'm fine," she added, maybe a little too emphatically. "Okay," she amended, "I'm working on it. I have to admit this thing with Eryk makes me a little nervous. I've never felt anything like it."

"Jasmine, it's okay to take your time. Remember, I'm here if you need me." She hesitated only a fraction before continuing. "I can tell you he's very healthy and very strong, both physically and mentally." A twinkled sparked in her green eyes. "Very healthy," she emphasized.

"Oh." Jasmine's brow furrowed. "Oooh!"

"Well, they are twins."

"So, how do I fight this attraction?" Jasmine blurted out.

"Do you really want to fight it?"

"I don't know if I'm ready. I mean, what if I can't. I mean, what if I…"

"Jasmine, stop that. Talk to him. Tell him what happened. If he's one of us and he is, he's not going to do anything to hurt you and I'm sure he won't rush you, especially if you tell him."

"I don't know if I can," she said it in almost a whisper.

Morgan grasped the hand resting on the table. "You didn't do anything wrong. In fact, you probably saved my life. You were attacked by a madman. Period."

Jasmine looked at her, tears welling. "I know," she said in a whisper. "I'm much stronger. I feel like I can handle just about any situation. At least I did, until I met Eryk."

"Then talk to him. Or not. I know you won't let anyone push you until you're ready."

"Never," Jasmine hissed, almost too emphatically.

Morgan squeezed her hand. "Now, let me show you the nursery while I can still get up the steps."

They went upstairs, Jasmine insisting on following behind her, just in case.

"Well, don't get mad if I fall and squish you," Morgan said.

Their laughter drifted out an open window into the street below.

"It's so nice to have Jasmine home," Miss Alice whispered to her sister as they walked toward the B & B, each carrying several pies.

Chapter Six

"Now, isn't this just double the pleasure," Teresa trilled as the two Adonises walked into the lobby of the B & B. Both men blushed like little boys. Unable to resist, she rose on tiptoe and loudly kissed each one on the cheek. "You know you might as well just march up and down Main Street for a while and get it over with. In the meantime, why don't you boys grab a table out in the sunroom while I fix up a basket of goodies." She propelled them toward the dining room before heading through the swinging door into the kitchen.

Heads turned and stared as Dorian led the way out to the sunroom overlooking the back lawn that Eryk had admired from his room. As they took a table by the window, a young waitress stepped up to the table.

"Tea?" she looked from one to the other and back again. "Dorian?"

Dorian lifted his hand. "Hi, Sandra. This is Eryk." He didn't expound. He wasn't ready to declare him a relative, just yet, which was stupid, given the fact that they looked exactly alike, except for those eyes. He was staring at Morgan's eyes, in his own face. Damn, it was weird.

He remembered his own twins nestled snug in Morgan's belly and hoped he would remember this moment, so he could relay it to them, when they hated looking like one another, which he'd been told to expect. He prayed that didn't happen. Thoughts of his and Eryk's separation and not knowing his own brother slammed into him and he studied the man across from him. Well, he couldn't get that back, but he could do his damnedest to make sure it didn't happen to his children. It was up to him and Morgan to make sure it didn't.

Dorian snapped out of his reverie to watch Eryk flash Sandra a smile. Her gaze riveted on his face and she seemed unable to move. "It's nice to meet you," he said, throwing in the stage accent for good measure.

Sandra giggled, turned, walked a few steps, looked back and giggled again.

"Can you package that?" Dorian asked, laughing.

Without missing a beat, Eryk laughed. "I have."

"I guess you have, at that. Nice touch, the accent."

"Quelque chose que je pris sur le continent." Eryk replied in French, translating after eyeing Dorian's expression. I said, 'Something I picked up on the continent.'"

"O-kay," Dorian raised a brow.

Eryk started fiddling with the edge of his napkin. "I had a lot of time on my hands growing up and an ear for languages."

Dorian just nodded. Sandra returned, set down two teas, flashed Eryk a smile and left.

"I suppose you do, too," Eryk said and took a sip of tea.

"What?"

"Have an ear for languages."

"I don't know." He thought for a moment. "Maybe," he added, thinking of how he and John would switch back and forth into Musckogean. It worked great when they were away from Ruthorford. Not many people knew the Creek language.

"Can we talk about Jasmine?" Eryk asked.

Dorian stopped the glass in midair. "Sure." He tried to sound nonchalant, but his eyes narrowed. "I've known Jasmine all of her life." Dorian voice lowered in timbre as he said the last, like a warning.

"Lucky guy."

Dorian's eyes narrowed to slits.

"I have a question," Eryk said. "Something happened to her. She's got one hell of a barrier up."

"Yeah? A barrier? I wouldn't know."

"You can't read auras? See barriers?"

"Not a bit."

Eryk studied his twin. It had to be an eye thing, then. He'd known he had the ability but wasn't sure, until now, just how. As a toddler, he'd fallen down, skinned his knee, and begun crying. As the tears filled his eyes, he tried to blink them away. His governess was running toward him and burst into an explosion of color right before his eyes. He closed his eyes tight and rubbed them and, when he opened them again, she was back to the drab woman she'd been before. From then on, he would entertain himself turning it off and on. One day, he did it on his governess and the beautiful colors had been replaced by a swampy gray-green. She committed suicide the next week. It took him a long time to use it again—until he was older and realized what he'd done hadn't had anything to do with her committing suicide.

"Well, *little* brother," Eryk said, implying his majority since their birth certificates gave him the distinction of being older, "I guess you can't see the aura of your babies."

"No."

"Well, they look great." Eryk said, wanting to assure the man sitting across from him.

Dorian smiled, grateful. "Thanks, *big* brother."

Eryk's expression changed. He looked down, moving the napkin. "I guess you can't see Bill's aura either?"

Dorian shook his head. "No."

"He's sick. Even Jasmine noticed it," Eryk said.

"I know he's sick. It doesn't take special vision to see that. Morgan wanted to give him a boost of energy but he wouldn't let her." Dorian started to say more and decided against it.

"I'm guessing Morgan and Jasmine think I can help him," Eryk said. "I've never done anything quite like that but I'd be willing to try."

"I know when Morgan does it, it's draining," Dorian started and stopped, saying instead, "Thank you. That would mean a lot. Bill is Ruthorford. Papa Ruthorford."

"I'll do what I can."

They fell silent. "So, you grew up a Vreeland?" Dorian prodded.

Eryk shrugged. "Yes. But I'd rather talk about Jasmine." There was more to Jasmine than she, or anyone else, was sharing. Eryk wanted to know everything he could about her since she was getting under his skin. Deep under his skin. "What gives with her?" he asked, trying to sound casual.

"That's something she's gonna have to tell you, herself. Ask her." He looked at Eryk and narrowed his eyes. "But know this. You be careful with her. Because if you aren't, and she gets hurt, you'll have more than me to deal with, you'll have Ruthorford."

The air crackled between them. Teresa walked over carrying two baskets, set them on the table behind her and turned to them. They weren't breaking eye contact. She felt her own hair start to lift. "Shit," she murmured and placed one of her hands on each shoulder.

The air immediately shifted. They each took a deep breath and turned, as if noticing her for the first time.

"Do I have to tell you two to take it outside," she hissed under her breath.

"No, ma'am," they said in unison.

She plastered a big smile on her face. "Good. Now, I've got enough food for an army in these baskets. Plus, Miss Grace insisted I send Jasmine an apple pie. This ought to keep you two out of trouble for a little while." She shook her head. "You'd think you two grew up together."

Eryk stood and reached for his wallet.

Teresa's brow furrowed. "Don't you dare."

He caught Dorian's slight head movement and leaned over and planted a kiss on her cheek instead. "Can I, at least, tip Sandra?" He laid a five on the table.

"That you can do. Stay out of trouble, you two. I don't want stress causing those babies to arrive early."

They each grabbed a basket and headed toward the front door, heads turning as they went past.

****

The tinkle of the bell over the door was the only warning Morgan and Jasmine had that the men were back. That and the fact that a ball of energy flew across the shop and burst over a shelf of antique bottles, nearly toppling them. Morgan put her hand on her hips and looked at them with green eyes flashing.

"Sorry," Dorian said, turned and locked the door, flipping the closed sign over. "It's a beautiful night," he said, hoping to change the subject.

Eryk said nothing but burst out laughing as he watched the interplay between the two of them. If ever there was a perfect picture of a gorgeous green-eyed witch, it stood before him in the stature of Morgana Drake. Jasmine stood behind her doing everything she could to keep from laughing, including biting that plump bottom lip of hers. Eryk's eyes lingered on that sight a little too long and he felt his groin tighten. Jasmine swung away, opening and closing the cabinets, grabbing plates and putting them on the table.

"I can see you two have been getting to know one another," Morgan said, trying to sound stern.

The guys started at once, talking right over each other. Dorian won out. "He can see the aura and still has my energy control. Probably just as strong. He's been using it in his act for years. He can also push and weave a barrier. I bet he can see the Gulatega." Dorian sounded like a kid with a Christmas toy.

Morgan just shook her head and rolled her eyes, taking Dorian's basket and setting it on the counter.

Eryk set his next to it.

"The Guly-whats-it?" he asked.

Everyone went silent.

"Thanks sweetie, for easing him right on in…." Morgan patted Dorian on the cheek. "…kinda like you did with me."

Dorian tried to think of something, anything in his defense. "It's not every day one gets a twin brother."

Jasmine laughed. "He's not a dog."

Meesha barked, easing the tension.

Morgan set the last container on the table. "Let's eat. I work much better when these guys are full and sleeping." Her hand made slow circles around her protruding belly.

As they ate, Eryk told them about his act and how he'd met Jasmine, including the burst of energy that had come flying back at him.

"So." Dorian looked at Jasmine and popped a piece of herb biscuit in his mouth. "How long have you been able to do the energy thing?"

Jasmine shrugged.

Morgan spoke up. "I noticed it when we stopped by Safe Harbor last year."

"Could you do it before the attack?" Dorian asked before he realized what he'd said.

"Attack?" Eryk didn't miss a thing.

"Sorry, Jas," Dorian said.

Jasmine carefully laid her napkin in her lap and raised her black eyes to look into Eryk's green ones. "It's okay, Dory. He was bound to find out sooner or later. She rested her hands on the table. Morgan reached over and patted one, nodding encouragement. "About a year ago, shortly after Morgan came to Ruthorford, Rob showed up."

"Rob was an ex-boyfriend of mine...or so I thought," Morgan interjected.

"He showed up in Ruthorford, staying at the B & B. He was handsome and very charming. Being a bit jealous of the new girl in town," Jasmine looked over at Morgan and smiled, "I had dinner with him at the B & B, hoping...no, knowing...it would get back to Morgan. But, he spent more time talking about Morgan than anything else, so I let it drop. Anyway," she said and took a deep breath, "I went on vacation later that week and who should I run into but Rob. He wined and dined me." She gave another half-hearted shrug. "I suppose I let him think that, because I was from Ruthorford, I had abilities similar to Morgan's." Her face took on a reddish cast. "I...I was just plain jealous." She stopped, took a sip of tea and continued, "I remember having a drink with him in the hotel bar. That's the last thing I remember until I came to and found myself shackled in a mine in North

Carolina. He had become a madman." Her voice cracked and tears shimmered in her eyes.

"Don't," Eryk said, not only seeing her pain, but feeling it as well. The green in his eyes took on a slow swirling pattern.

Jasmine sent Dorian a silent plea, then lowered her gaze, remaining silent.

Dorian took a deep breath and picked up the story. "There is much about us you don't know," he said to Eryk. "I'll give you the short version. There are places, this town included, that rest on some sort of energy site. These sites can be activated by people like us…and some others," he added, thinking of Ian, "to open a dimensional portal. There are small creatures, Gulatega—cat-like creatures—that slip through. They can cause Altzheimer's-ish symptoms. People like Morgan—and probably you—can see them. With the help of someone like me—or Jasmine, possibly—you can open the portal and send them back."

Eryk looked to each person at the table, waiting for someone to laugh, to let him in on the sick joke. No one did. Jasmine's head was bowed, tears dropping from her eyes onto her lap. He wanted nothing more than to stop all this, take her in his arms, and banish the horror he felt emanating from her. Ignoring the fact that he wanted to throw down his napkin and say, "This is bullshit," he studied the girl next to him and opted for: "We don't have to go on."

Jasmine never looked up. "Yes, we do." Her voice was barely above a whisper.

Dorian took the hand Morgan offered before he continued. "Eryk, this isn't bullshit. It may sound like it, but trust me, what I'm telling you is as real as…," he stopped, thought for a moment, and added, "your abilities." When he knew he had Eryk's attention, he continued. "Ian, a very bad man," he started and changed his statement when he felt a squeeze from Morgan. "That's not entirely accurate. We aren't sure about that. Ian came from Scotland with the idea that he was a throwback to 'visitors' from the other plane. He married Kayla—but that's another story," Dorian amended, not ready to go into that yet.

"He's the only one we've ever seen like that...." Dorian stopped, something nagging at his mind, but when he couldn't grasp it, he shook his head, and continued. "He believed that, if he didn't get through the portal, he would die. He convinced Morgan and me that he would. Anyway, he'd hired Rob, a physicist, to help him figure out a way open the portal. But Rob's mind was affected by the creatures and he thought Morgan...then Jasmine...," his voice broke.

Jasmine looked up, her eyes now dry. "I know it's confusing. It's also complicated. There are crystals and gems that help direct energy, or so we think. Rob was obsessed with those. That's why he took me to the mine. I quickly realized he was crazy, and I didn't want him going after Morgan, so I let him think that I could help him. When it didn't work, he went over the edge, and raped and beat me." She hesitated. "Repeatedly."

"Son of a...." Sparks flew from Eryk's fingers.

Jasmine reached over and grabbed his hand, bleeding off some of his energy into herself. A small gasp escaped her lips. When he tried to pull away, she held tight. "Dory found me. Jenn brought me to Safe Harbor to recover and I found a life there. The end." She finished a bit too quickly and flashed a half-smile at him.

The end. His anger flared. "What happened to—"

Morgan spoke. "Rob had a complete breakdown and, although better, is in a special hospital. He has no memory of what happened."

"Or he's not owning up to it," Dorian ground out through clinched teeth.

Morgan ignored him. "Dorian and I helped Ian, the man who started the mess, get through the portal."

"And the creatures?"

"There hasn't been any activity since he went through. At least we haven't seen any."

Eryk turned to Jasmine. "I am so sorry."

Her smile was tremulous. "Me, too. But hey, I got this." She lifted her hand and bands of energy leapt between her fingers.

He took her hand. At first, she felt the tingle, then the energy dissipated as he brought it to his mouth and kissed her fingers. "So you did."

Dorian and Morgan looked from the couple sitting across from them to one another, a wealth of meaning passing between them.

"That's some story," Eryk said and held onto Jasmine's hand when she tried to pull away. "I've no doubt about the attack—"

"Jasmine," Morgan interrupted and stood, using the table for leverage, "why don't you show Eryk the cottage while Dorian and I clean up." She watched Jasmine until she saw Jasmine's understanding nod. "Then we can have pie and coffee." Dorian was on his feet, steadying his wife.

The moment Jasmine opened the back door, Meesha dashed out, leaping from the stoop to the middle of the path. With a happy yap, she was off, racing around the garden beds and finally disappearing around the side of the building.

"If I eat another bite today…." Eryk laughed.

"Just think of it as your good will effort," Jasmine said. "Besides, you haven't tasted Miss Grace's pie yet."

The moon hung heavy in the evening sky, casting streams of light across the garden and the cottage.

Eryk stopped and looked around him. His eyes adjusted to the lower night light instantly. "It's lovely."

"Ummm-hmm," Jasmine hummed and stepped on the path that led from the shop to the cottage. The gazebo, which stood across from the cottage, glowed bright white in the moonlight. So many memories came rushing at her. She felt like she'd been gone forever.

They approached the cottage. Its diamond-shaped panes on the window overlooking the garden gave it a quaint, European flavor. One almost expected a thatched roof. Late blooming vines encircled the windows, where beams of moonlight caught the facets of carefully placed stones. Bits of colored light sparkled from inside.

"It's almost magical." Eryk followed her as she stepped inside.

"You have no idea," Jasmine said and closed the bottom of the Dutch door, letting moonlight shine through the upper half.

This is how she wanted Eryk to see the cottage—like some faerie-built dwelling set amidst the human world. She led him past the stone fireplace to a spot in front of the open French doors and stepped into a braided rug, stopping as he stepped on it as well. Facing him, she held out her hands.

A slight frown creased his brow, but he took her hands in his and felt a slight tremble move through his body. He barely saw the room as he watched her, his eyes riveted on the lines of her slender neck. When Eryk looked up into her obsidian eyes, he thought he might drown.

"I've never done this before," she said, her voice slightly deeper, a lover's whisper.

Before he could comment or pull her to him, he felt the energy pulse from her to him. Instantly, he responded, sending back a matching pulse. The intake of her breath let him know his eyes had begun to glow. Like his eyes, the stones in the room sparked to life. The rug beneath their feet took on a glow, as well. He could hear a pulsing sound, then a hum. Between them, light shot up from the rug, spiking between them and through them, sending energy up his entire body.

Jasmine closed her eyes. Eryk watched and, as it had begun, the hum, the glow, and the energy, began to dissipate until they were once again standing in an ordinary room on an ordinary rug. Except, his body still thrummed from the power coursing through him and he stepped into her. Her lips were parted, her eyes closed, and he watched the tip of her tongue moisten her bottom lip. That was his undoing. Even knowing what he'd just learned about her, he couldn't seem to stop himself. Like a magnet, she drew him.

He brought his mouth down on hers. For an instant, he felt her stiffen and he let his lips softly rest against hers, his breath mingling with hers. He felt the tension ease from her body and she leaned, ever so slightly, into him, letting his mouth take hers. In the next instant, she jerked back, as if shocked.

His voice, when he spoke, was so husky, so deep, he almost didn't recognize it. "I won't hurt you. Ever. I won't do anything you don't want me to. I promise you."

She nodded. Before she could answer, a shrill whistle pierced the night and Meesha barked in response.

"Well," Jasmine said, trying to sound casual, "now you've seen the cottage." Without looking back, she headed for the Dutch door.

"What's in there?" Eryk nodded back toward the French doors.

"The bedroom and bath."

"Ahhh," he looked back longingly but followed her, slightly chiding himself.

"So, you want to tell me just what happened?"

"That was the portal. If there had been any Gulatega out and about, they would have gone back through. They are drawn to it," she hesitated for adding, "just like they are drawn to those that can see them."

"Now you tell me." Eryk stepped outside and waited for her to reattach the door halves. He looked toward the shop and could see Dorian and Morgan moving around in the kitchen, Meesha at their feet. Dorian placed her food bowl on the floor and she gave a quick tail wag before concentrating on business. As Jasmine stepped past him onto the path, he took her hand, and they walked through the garden to the shop, their fingers entwined, a slight pulse moving between them. She released his hand as they stepped into the kitchen.

"Looks like you've got your stand-ins," Jasmine announced and took a seat at the kitchen table. "We can open the portal."

Morgan placed warm apple pie in front of Jasmine and Eryk and straightened, her hand immediately going to the small of her back. "That's not...." She let the words die off when Jasmine arched a single brow at her. "Well, not entirely. Bask did mention...." Again, she let the words trail off.

Jasmine looked at Eryk. "There are several of these spots around the world. Most of them are safeguarded by couples." She felt her face redden as she said the words. "People that can control the portal," she amended. "With Morgan pregnant, Bask—who I'm sure you will meet soon—wants to make sure this one is covered. When Melissa and Thom died—" She stopped suddenly, her eyes shifting to Dorian. "Oh, Dory—"

He waved a hand, taking a gulp of air. "My parents—sponsors—were killed suddenly last year. It left the portal unguarded. That's why Bask brought Morgan down. We matched."

"Matched?" Eryk looked from Dorian to Morgan, then to Jasmine.

It took a moment for Dorian to find the right words. "Two people with matching traits, like Morgan and myself or you and Jasmine." He studied his twin. "Hell, you seem to carry all the traits. You might match with Morgan—or me for that matter—we need to try that out. Hell, you might be able to do it by yourself."

Eryk frowned. He wasn't thrilled with the idea of being "matched" with anyone but Jasmine. And he sure as hell didn't want to do it by himself.

"It takes a matched pair and—until you and Jasmine—it was always a woman with the green-eye trait and someone like me, with the power of the earth—to control the Gulatega and the portals." Dorian grabbed a container of ice cream from the freezer as he spoke and brought it to the table, hefting the scoop into the air like a flag. "Anyone?" They all smiled and he dished heaping scoops of vanilla on top of the hot apple pie.

All eyes turned to Eryk as he took a bite.

"I've gone to heaven," Eryk exclaimed.

"Miss Grace is absolutely the best pie maker in the world," Jasmine exclaimed.

"I think I'm in love," he moaned. "Wonder if she'll marry me?"

"Stand in line." Dorian laughed.

The foursome sat with pie and coffee until they'd finished off both the pan and the pot. As tempting as it was, Morgan refrained from the caffeine, drinking milk instead. They talked about the need for a couple to be available near the portal, since that seemed to keep the creatures at bay. Those that were loose were drawn to the person who could see them. Then, they could be sent back.

It was agreed that when Morgan went into labor, with Eryk's and the Abbott House's airplanes readily available, Jasmine and Eryk could be in Ruthorford and ready to take over within a few hours.

Eryk found himself agreeing to something he still wasn't sure was real.

By the time Jasmine and Eryk walked through the lobby of the B & B, the lights had been turned down low with a sign on the desk read, "Ring Bell for Service." They walked up the stairs to his room and he slipped in his key.

"This is the first time *I've* been walked to my door." He smiled at her, his skin forming little crinkles next to his eyes. "Want to come in?"

Jasmine immediately took a step back. "No. I want to go visit my apartment. It's been so long."

He didn't push, as much as his body ached for the closeness of her. "Then, I'll see you tomorrow." He stood there for a second. "Isn't this where my date gives me a kiss?"

A laugh erupted from her and she stepped forward and planted a kiss on his cheek.

"Not what I had in mind, but I guess it will have to do."

She turned and strolled down the corridor, waving her fingers over her shoulder.

****

Jasmine jogged down the dim stairs as she'd done for years. Growing up in the Abbott Bed and Breakfast, she knew this building like she did her own face. Smiling, she let her fingers trail down the banister as it curved toward the lobby. She slowed as she reached the open lobby with its ornate furnishings, glancing back toward the dining room. There, silhouetted against the moonlit window sat a lone figure, hunched over, absently stirring what looked like a cup of tea.

"Want company?"

Teresa jumped, startled out of her reverie. She waved her over. "I heard you come in. I didn't expect you to come down so soon."

Not commenting, Jasmine pulled out the chair across from her cousin and sat down, letting her gaze linger out the window over the backdrop of the grand weeping willow dipping its feathery limbs into the shimmering water. "I guess we take for granted just how beautiful it is here."

"I know I do," Teresa said. "Sometimes, all I can think of is how far it is down to the water...toting a tray."

Jasmine heard the deep sigh. "You okay?" she asked, letting the love and concern tint her question.

"Yes...no...I don't know." Teresa picked up the spoon and stirred her tea again. The moonlight caught the silver's gleam, sending a glimmer with each stir. "You want a cup?"

Jasmine shook her head, "I couldn't put one drop in my mouth without exploding. I forgot how much food was involved in everything we do here."

She watched Teresa study her cup. "Is there anything I can do?" Jasmine knew Teresa was worrying about Bill.

Teresa shrugged as though her shoulders had grown heavy under the weight of her worry. She looked over at her cousin, the girl she'd raised as her own. "I didn't want to worry you."

"You're my family."

Teresa tried to smile at her. "Yes. We are." Then, taking a deep breath, she continued, "So, being family, I will ask you to intervene. Talk to Bill. Make him see reason. If he won't see Mike Yancy, make him see someone."

Jasmine heard Teresa's voice hitch and saw the glimmer of tears in her eyes. She reached across the table and covered the thin hand with her own. "Of course I will. I promise." She hesitated for a moment, thought about Eryk and how she should ask him first, then decided to hell with it and spoke. "Eryk has Morgan's abilities...plus Dorian's. Let me ask Bill to let him try a healing push. I know he wouldn't let Morgan, her being pregnant and all. Maybe he'll let Eryk."

Teresa nodded. "Anything," she said. "Anything at all."

Jasmine rose. "I'll talk to him first thing in the morning. I'm headed over to my apartment now. I want to see it."

"It's clean. There are some things in the fridge. I tried to keep it ready in case you showed up."

"I figured you would. Call me if you need me." She leaned over and kissed the top of Teresa's head. "Promise?"

Teresa reached up and patted her hand. "I promise," she said quietly then turned back to her cup.

Jasmine stopped once as she opened the front door to leave, glancing back at the woman she loved like a mother—the woman everyone loved. There was something about her. She wore a mantle of caring. Her. Dorian. Bonnie and Claire. the Misses, Grace and Alice. Everyone that came within her sphere was the better for it.

And Bill. Jasmine didn't know the real story about them, except that Teresa had taken Bill under her wing as well when he'd returned to Ruthorford all those years ago. It had been quite a scandal for a while. After all, Teresa and Mike Yancy had been dating for three years. Even though he wasn't a descendant, everyone expected them to marry. They were the perfect couple. Love showed from their eyes so strongly you could feel it.

Then, Bill came back, having left Ruthorford right after high school to make his fortune—or, just get away. He swept Teresa off her feet. Suddenly, she and Mike were no more and she and Bill were married.

It was right after they got married that Jasmine's parents died and she went to live with them. Bill was big, burly and lovable. He was also a recluse. He lived in his kitchen most of the time. They worked hard at making a family for her, giving her a "normal" life. But, from what Jasmine saw, it was a façade. She knew they loved each other. As she got older, she realized that the love they shared was different. Definitely not the love Jasmine had seen between Teresa and Mike. She'd asked Teresa about it once. Teresa became vehement—the only time she'd seen her really angry—telling Jasmine it was none of her business. So, Jasmine never asked again.

Jasmine stepped down the stone steps and stopped, taking her fill of Main Street as it stretched before her in the night. The fountain was off. The street was lit by the low burning street lamps, giving the visage of a time gone by. A few lights shone from the shops. A light from the second story above The Shoppe of Spells showed that Dorian and Morgan had retired for the night. A soft light filtered from her apartment above The Fashion Flair, as well. She headed down the street, letting its familiarity hug her. Even after her attack, she felt safe here. Ruthorford would never let anything happen to her.

She unlatched the wooden gate and stepped into the narrow alley that led from Main Street to the back of her shop where her car was parked. A light beamed down from the upper landing. She made her way up the stairs and put the key in the lock. *Home.* It had been too long. She twisted the knob and stopped as the screech of an owl pierced the night. That was something else she hadn't heard in a long time, the sound of Ruthorford's Snowy Owls. She stilled, waiting. It was comforting to know they were about, even if the activity of the portal was reportedly nil.

Legend was that the Snowy Owls flew en masse, warning the inhabitants that the creatures were roaming. She'd only seen them swarm once, and that was right after Melissa and Thom had died. Not having the ability to see the Gulatega, even with her enhanced abilities, she had to rely on someone like Eryk or an animal—like the Snowy Owl—to warn her. They'd flown nightly after the deaths, until Morgan arrived. Once she joined with Dorian, the owls quieted. Still, she listened for the cacophony of birdcalls. None came.

A motion in the air made her turn. Suddenly, she was watching the ground speed past, the detail precise. A mouse scurried far below. Just as quickly, the image was gone and she fell against the door, which swung open, propelling her into the apartment. Unable to gain her balance, she careened across the room, falling over an ill-placed chair. A screech of her own carried into the night as she landed on her wrist.

On his balcony, Eryk heard a sound. Another owl screaming in the night? He listened. His hearing had always been enhanced. More of a curse than a blessing, he heard everything. And, unless he consciously tuned it down, everything at a high decibel level. Jasmine's voice was one of the few that didn't completely grate on him. Thinking about it, he realized he'd had less issues with his hearing since he'd arrived in this small town.

A pain shot through his wrist. *What the hell?* He looked down at the wrist he'd just pulled away from the railing. It looked fine. *Jasmine.* It was more of a feeling than a thought.

He took off running, leaving his room door open and leaping the last four steps into the lobby. He stopped, looking down Main Street. Two lights shone out of upper story windows. One over The Shoppe of Spells and a very faint one directly across from it. He ran around the side of the B & B to the small lane that ran behind the shops. He saw the SUV they'd driven and headed that way. He looked up and saw the door hung open above what he assumed was her shop. He didn't care. At this point, he'd rather apologize than be wrong. Taking the stairs two at a time, he bounded up, calling her name. He heard a faint whimper, then a curse.

His vision allowed him to see into the dark space. She was on the floor, leaning against the couch in the dark. A chair lay on its side, nearby. He saw a faint line of light coming from under a closed door. Jasmine moaned and held her wrist.

"Jasmine," he called softly, not wanting to scare her.

"Eryk?" She let out a soft moan.

He was by her side in an instant, kneeling, taking her arm in his hands. She winced. He blinked and looked at the wrist. The energy spiked at an angle, but with no irregular spikes. "It's out of its socket. Hang on." He let the energy flow through his arms into his hands, warming her joint, then he moved it quickly, snapping it into place.

"Shit!" she cursed. "Why is it my joints keep coming apart?" She moaned the question.

He immediately scanned the rest of her. She looked fine. "That's the only one," he told her.

Jasmine pushed back her bangs with her free hand and struggled to get up. When she reached the level of the couch, she collapsed into the soft cushions. Shaking her head, she looked at him. "When I was in the mine, my shoulder became dislocated. Dorian had to put it back in. Not the greatest feeling in the world."

"I bet not," he said and sat down next to her.

"What are you doing here?" She looked at him. His beautiful eyes glowed, the light moving. He blinked and it stabilized into a steady, albeit unusual, green. He turned from her stare. "You might want more lights on in the future," he said. "Just a suggestion."

"Thanks, Sherlock. You didn't answer my question."

"I heard you."

Her eyes widened. "I screamed that loud?"

"Probably not. I have hyperacusis...a sensitivity to sound," he explained when she furrowed her brow.

"I can see where that might come in handy."

"When it's not painful," he amended.

"Oh...I'm sorry." She softened her voice.

"You don't have to do that. For some reason, your voice doesn't bother me. In fact, nothing has bothered me since I arrived in this town. I still hear everything, it just doesn't hurt." He reached over her and turned on the lamp on the table. "Your turn."

"What do you mean?"

"What really happened?" He smiled at her.

She started to shrug and decided what the hell. "It was like the plane...or the fair...suddenly I was seeing from the air. I became disoriented and leaned on the door, which, unfortunately, I'd already opened. Hence...," she held up her wrist.

In response, he took it gently and moved it to his lips.

Teasing, she pointed a finger to her pouting lips. "Ouch," she pouted.

He smiled into her eyes right before he let his mouth cover hers.

Bad idea, she thought as she melted into his kiss.

****

Across the street, things weren't quite so agreeable.

"Why didn't YOU tell him?" Morgan spun around on the small bench, wielding the hairbrush like a pointer, or a sword, depending on one's perspective.

"Be careful with that thing," Dorian taunted her.

Morgan narrowed her eyes.

"Look, I thought you were going to talk with Jasmine." He took the brush out of her hands and started brushing her long red hair.

Morgan relaxed into the soothing strokes of the brush. "Dorian, Jasmine and I haven't been all that close," she sighed and leaned back as he set down the brush and started messaging her shoulders. "I didn't want her to think I was warning her away from yet another Drake."

"I get your point," he said, remembering how irrationally Jasmine had reacted to Morgan's arrival. She'd been downright vampish. "Well, someone ought to say something to one of them," he looked around, out the window at the soft lights coming from Jasmine's apartment, "and soon, given the way they were eyeing one another earlier tonight."

"You don't think…?"

"Not yet," he looked at his gorgeous wife in the mirror, "but if he's affected one-tenth as much as I was, it won't be long."

Morgan turned and let her lips brush across his hand. "I know. There's no hope for them."

****

Jasmine pushed him away. She felt all tingly inside, like a fire was starting that she couldn't put out. It wasn't fear she felt. She just didn't know him well enough, yet.

Eryk sat up. Somehow, they'd slid down onto the cushions of the couch and her sweater was hiked up, exposing the smooth flesh above the low-rise pants. Every inch of him ached to touch her, to taste her, to bury himself in her. He jumped up and walked to the window, trying to put as much distance as he could between them and still be in the same room.

"I'm sorry." Her voice came out breathy.

"I told you it was okay. I won't push you." He turned around. Jasmine was sitting up and adjusting her sweater. He blinked. Her aura swirled and pulsed. He closed his eyes. That was *not* going to help. "If you're all right, I better go."

She moved her wrist. It didn't hurt at all. "Yes. I'm fine. Thank you for coming," she said perfunctorily.

They looked at one another and laughed. This was a fine situation. They couldn't keep their hands off each other, yet...there was something keeping them apart. She followed him to the door, not too closely, and waited until he stepped on the landing. "Thanks again." She held up her wrist.

Eryk stopped in front of the bed and breakfast and looked back down Main Street. All the shops were dark now, including The Shoppe of Spells. A single soft light glowed from Jasmine's apartment.

What a day! He was exhausted. He couldn't remember when he'd ever been exhausted. Of course, he couldn't remember when such a delicate woman—or anyone for that matter—had drained energy off him like she did. And, in such a stimulating way. He smiled to himself as he opened the front door, gently closed it behind him, and headed up the steps to his room. His room door stood open, just as he'd left it. Given what he'd learned today, he doubted this town had too many petty thieves.

Eryk stripped off his clothes and took a hot shower, briskly rubbing off the water. He winced as the towel ran over his hip and glanced down. The birthmark, a circle in a circle shape he'd had all of this life, looked darker and raised, almost like a welt. That had never happened before. Maybe he ran into something. He blinked and looked at his own aura in the mirror. It seemed closer to his body but still glowed in his customary colors. Except, he noted, there seemed to be more violet in the colors. He shrugged, flipped off the bathroom light and slipped into bed, hoping to capture a few hours of sleep. On most nights, his mind raced and sleep eluded him. Tonight, his eyes closed and he slipped into a warm dream about a soft woman with black eyes.

Chapter Seven

Sandra poured Eryk a second cup of coffee while he waited for Jasmine. He hadn't spoken with Jasmine since their rather awkward parting last night, but he knew she would come. The coffee was fresh, strong, and black and he was letting the aroma of it fill his senses when he noticed the pert little waitress was still standing there, coffee pot in hand.

He lowered the half-raised cup. "What can I do for you?" He smiled at the nervousness in her light blue eyes.

"I know this isn't proper," she said and glanced over her shoulder and lowered her voice just above a whisper, "you being a guest and all. But, I googled you last night. I thought you looked familiar—besides the fact that you look like Dorian." She set the coffee pot on the table and pulled an old folded program from her apron. It was from a show of his three years earlier. It was faded and worn, but she handled it reverently. "Would you mind? I mean signing it."

"Not at all." He took the pen she held out and scribbled across the front, *To my friend, Sandra. May all your days have magic! Eryk Vreeland*. He gently folded it over and handed it back to her. When she opened it, a small red rose lay in the middle.

"Oh, wow!" She beamed at him.

"Sandra," Teresa called from the kitchen. "Would you run a tray upstairs for me?"

"Oops," Sandra whispered and turned to leave.

"It's okay," Eryk reassured her. "It was my pleasure."

"Oh, there's Miss Jasmine now. Hi, Miss Jasmine. Would you like your coffee now?"

"Sure, Sandra. I'd love some."

Jasmine glided across the room. That's all Eryk could think of as he watched her approach. Could she get more beautiful? She sure as hell seemed to. She was wearing chocolate brown pants with a burnt orange sweater skimming her hips. It cut in just enough to accentuate her curves. He took a drink of coffee and felt it scald his tongue. "Damn." He put down the cup and grabbed the ice water.

"You okay?" Concern creased Jasmine's brow as she sat across from him.

"You made me burn my tongue." He let a piece of ice slip into his mouth and felt it melt.

He watched the mirth bubble in her eyes.

She tossed her head slightly, letting her wooden earrings swing. "I'm sorry—I guess."

Sandra came to the table and poured Jasmine's coffee. "Be careful, it's hot."

Jasmine and Eryk broke out laughing. "Never mind," Jasmine said when she saw the young girl's confusion. "Hey, do you think Bill will make me one of those special omelets?"

Sandra smiled. "You mean the one with spinach and mushrooms with sautéed tomatoes and that secret cheese sauce?"

"The very one." Jasmine nodded. "I'd kill for one of those."

"Make that two," Eryk interjected.

"Coming right up."

They watched her march into the kitchen, her blonde ponytail swinging. It seemed as though the door had just swung closed when she was back through it with a basket of hot muffins and creamed butter. "Bill says these ought to tide you over while he works his magic." She flushed as she looked at Eryk.

"There are all sorts of magic," Eryk supplied. "I have a feeling Bill's is one of a kind."

Sandra beamed. "You got that right. He's been teaching me some recipes. I hope to help in the kitchen soon."

"That's great," Jasmine added. "I can't wait to try out one of your creations."

"Really?"

"Really." Jasmine nodded.

"Oh, I wanted to let you know—Bonnie and Claire are doing a great job. Mom let me use my birthday money to buy an outfit from the Flair." She leaned over in a conspiratorial whisper, "that's what we call it now. It looks so hot—the outfit, I mean. Bob—that's my boyfriend—is taking me to Atlanta for a show...a stage show."

Just then, Teresa's voice carried from the kitchen, "Sandra..."

"Gotta run." She wiggled her fingers and ran toward the kitchen.

"I can't believe I used to babysit her. Gosh, it makes me feel old."

Eryk tilted his head and studied her. "Yep, I see the crow's feet forming as we speak. You are so old. Cougar."

Jasmine narrowed her eyes into slits. "Keep it up, bub."

This time Teresa appeared with a tray. "Figured I better bring these or they'd be cold before you got a mouthful." She set the steaming plates before them. "Sandra does love to talk."

"She's grown so much." Jasmine commented. "She's turning into a beautiful young woman."

"Yes, she is. And she's almost as much a handful as you were." Teresa smiled. "Enjoy," she added as she swung around. They could hear her laugh as she pushed the door open to the kitchen.

"Handful, huh?" Eryk asked and took a bite of the omelet. His eyes slid shut. "Sandra's right, he's a master magician."

"Good, isn't it," Jasmine said and joined him in sampling the fluffy masterpiece. "I wish I could do this. I can't. Lord knows I tried. I spent many a Saturday morning trying…and failing. Cooking isn't one of my gifts."

"I do okay. I don't starve. We're on the road so much." He picked up another muffin and broke it open, letting the steam rise. "I love lemon poppy seed."

He held a piece in front of Jasmine. Looking from under her lashes, she took a nibble, then grabbed the rest of the muffin. "Me, too." The words thrummed from deep inside. Eryk's blood raced.

For half a second all he wanted to do was drag her off to his room, pull her into his arms and devour her as she was doing to the rest of that muffin. He'd actually laid the linen napkin on the table and begun to rise when his phone gave a quick tone.

He sat back down and pulled it from his pocket. Without looking, he said. "What can I do for you, Dad?"

Jasmine stopped eating at the tone he placed on the last word. She could hear a very clipped, deep voice respond.

"Let's see. What excuse shall I use to NOT show up at her birthday party this year?" Eryk said.

Jasmine wiped her mouth and made no pretense of not paying attention. She looked right at him, watching the color of his eyes deepen.

"Hey, *DAD*, why don't we try something different this year. Tell her the truth—that I'm out of town visiting my *BROTHER*."

There was silence from the other end of the phone.

"Oh, you might throw in something to really make her birthday," he added through clinched teeth, "—that she finally got her wish, I'm not her son!"

The phone crackled. He pulled it away from his ear and stared at it. "Damn, fried another one." He casually tossed it onto the table and drank some water. "Now, where were we?"

Having heard most of the exchange and feeling the charged air around them, Jasmine knew things couldn't go back to what they had been before the phone call. She had to control a desire to reach up and feel if her hair was standing on end. She watched as he tried to smile across the table at her, but that twinkle that had existed only moments before was gone.

"Let's get out of here," she said softly and pushed back her chair.

"But you aren't done," he nodded to the half-eaten omelet on her plate.

"Bill always makes too much for one person." Then she noticed his empty plate. "Well, almost," she added. "How about we go for a walk before we head over to The Shoppe?"

"I'd like that." He threw down a tip and followed Jasmine. As they passed through the lobby, he stopped. "I hope Teresa will charge the meal on my room."

"She will or she won't. Depends on her mood."

They stepped out onto the porch and he took her hand. A faint tingle coursed between them—not entirely unpleasant. After a second, it was gone and their two warm hands intertwined naturally.

"Damn." Jasmine stopped at the top of the steps.

He followed her gaze to the black Lincoln parked in front of The Shoppe of Spells and looked back at her. "Let me guess. That man you keep mentioning, Bass?"

"Bask," she corrected. "What do you want to do?"

He shrugged. "How bad could it be?"

Jasmine closed her eyes and let out a deep breath. "Not something you want to say where Bask is concerned. You never know."

Eryk took a step forward, stopped, turning back to her. "How about you? Is this something you want to do right now?"

She rolled her eyes. "Devil's in the details. Might as well find out what they are."

He laughed. "I like your style, Miss Monroe."

Neither of them hurried as they made their way toward The Shoppe of Spells, not that they could have had they wanted to. As they crossed the street, a short, roundish, but very pretty, older woman stepped out of the small Victorian post office. As soon as she saw Jasmine, a smile appeared and her eyes crinkled.

"Miss Brenda," Jasmine called and threw her arms around her. Jasmine drew back and introduced Eryk to the postmistress.

Brenda didn't seem taken aback in the least by his similarity to Dorian. "You're the famous magician," she said, her eyes sparkling. "I saw you in Atlanta. It's so strange…," she tilted her head and looked him over, "I never noticed the likeness before."

He couldn't tell if she was joking or not, until Jasmine started laughing. "Right. They don't look alike at all."

Brenda twittered, trying to act bemused. "Well, now that you mention it…." She reached out and patted his arm.

"Welcome to Ruthorford," she said. "I need to run. Only have a half-hour to do my errands. Nice meeting you, Eryk." She called back as she rounded the corner.

They paused in front of the bookstore, Chapters, to view a display of books. Eryk noticed one by David Copperfield, graced the display. "I have a feeling that was done in your honor," Jasmine said, pointing to the magician's book.

"Did everyone know I was coming, except me?"

"No, but news travels fast in this town," she said. "And secrets are held close," she added quietly.

He turned and looked down the street. The small town lay before him like a picture post card. The median boasted benches, trees and brick paths that wandered out from a large fountain. The sidewalks in front of the shops were wide, adorned with Victorian lampposts and trees. The town fairly sparkled in the fall sunlight, an invitation to walk and window shop, or visit. He watched as people did just that. They'd wave or cross the street to chat. Several teenage girls walked down the street, pointing and laughing at a boy with a skateboard. The girls stopped in front of Jasmine's shop, then turned, wiggled tentative fingers at the boy, and went inside. The boy, paying more attention to the girls than where he was going, almost ran into a lamppost, barely swerving in time.

"I see you don't have any regulations about skateboards."

"Why? They don't hurt anyone and we'd rather they be here than somewhere where we can't see them. It's not like we have much crime." She laughed. "I put a chip in one of the benches myself, trying to show off."

"What happened?"

"I had to paint the bench," she chuckled, addressing the punishment and not the crime. "That was penalty enough.

"Oh, look." She pointed across the street to the small art gallery. "Kateri Chance—I guess it's still Chance," she amended, "is having a showing. It was in the Crosstown Gazette. I hope we're here when it opens."

"You know her?"

"I knew her when she was here a long time ago. Sad story. I'll tell you some day."

"I saw her work in Washington, D.C. She does incredible sculptures. Is she from here?"

"Part of that long story I need to tell you."

They had reached The Shoppe of Spells and, although the sign said closed, Jasmine turned the handle and opened the door. "Yoo hoo," she called.

"In the kitchen," Morgan called back. "Lock the door, please."

Eryk shut and locked the door before turning around to follow Jasmine back into the large kitchen.

Morgan, Dorian, and a man Eryk didn't know sat around the large round table. As they approached, the older, very distinguished man—he reminded Eryk of an English barrister he knew—looked straight at him, his steel-gray eyes briefly reflecting the shock of Eryk's similarity to Dorian before they became guarded once again. He'd taken off his suit jacket, which now hung from the back of the chair, and folded back his sleeves. He rose and stretched out a strong, sinewy arm. They clasped hands and Eryk caught sight of a circle tattoo on the inside of the man's wrist, not dissimilar to the birthmark on Eryk's hip.

"Mr. Bask, I presume." Eryk waited for a spark of energy but felt none and dropped his hand.

"Mr. Vreeland," Bask acknowledged but turned his attention to Jasmine.

She stood, almost shy and hesitant.

Bask stepped around the table and gave her a stern expression, eyeing her. "You scared the crap out of me, young lady," he said, his voice softening with every word.

She flung herself into his arms and Eryk saw the tears she was trying to hold back. "I missed you too, you old coot."

He lifted her off the floor in an embrace, surprising Eryk with his natural strength. "Well, hell, you aged me ten years."

She slid down and took a step back, still holding his arms. "What's that make you? A hundred and five?"

"Damn near." He laughed and pulled the chair out for her.

She turned to Eryk. "Ole Bask here and I go way back. He let me intern at the Abbott House one summer."

Bask laughed, a full body, rich sound that came from deep within. "Yeah. That little venture took three years to correct."

Jasmine's face reddened slightly. "I didn't know they weren't supposed to be alphabetical."

Bask patted her hand and turned his attention to Eryk, now sitting next to Dorian. "It's uncanny." He shook his head.

"Not really," Dorian said and slid a piece of paper in front of Eryk.

He scanned the paper. It looked like some sort of hospital release form. Mother: Patrice Drake. Father: Unknown. Birth: Natural, male, identical twins: Derrick Drake; Dorian Drake.

"Derrick." Eryk commented to no one in particular.

Under comments, it read: Infant reacted to silver nitrate application to eyes, causing clouding. Flushed with mild saline. Condition improving. Mother refused removal of membranous material covering eyes.

Eryk couldn't help but look at Morgan. She fluttered her lashes and smiled. "*We* are special. It's a damn good thing they didn't remove that. Yancy said something about a double lens when he treated me after Jasmine...." She let the words trail off.

Jasmine sat us straighter. "I shot wasp spray in her eyes—purely by accident, mind you. Really," she added for emphasis.

Morgan reached across the table and patted her hand. "I know that."

Eryk looked back at the document. *First child deceased, day two, crib death.*

"It says here we were born on August 16, 1980. It looks like I'm still your big brother, even if I am deceased," Eryk grinned, directing his jest at Dorian. "Anything on our mother? Or father."

As soon as he said it, Eryk's mind reeled. Was it possible that Donald Vreeland really was their father? Hadn't someone said the mother OD'd? Somehow, he couldn't picture dear old dad getting it on with a druggy. He could barely think of his father getting it on at all.

He realized how quiet the table had become. They were watching him.

"Sorry," he apologized. "Wool gathering."

"It's okay," Bask commented, "all this is a lot to take in." He looked over at Morgan and she gave him a slight nod, remembering how badly she'd handled the information about her adoption and Ruthorford.

She spoke, "I got a summons from Bask to come to Atlanta, where he unceremoniously informed me that my parents were dead. In his defense, he didn't know my adoptive parents hadn't told me I was adopted. After almost passing out, I up and fled back to Virginia. Luckily, I returned a short time later and...well, all's well that ends well." She took Dorian's hand and laid it on her large belly.

Bask couldn't help but look at Eryk and Jasmine, both of whom showed completely new combinations of traits, and wonder just what was happening to the line of the descendants.

Putting aside his musings, he turned to Eryk. "Years ago, one of my associates was in Washington, DC and passed your mother on the street. The eyes were a dead giveaway, being the Ruthorford green. He followed her to a hole-in-the-wall apartment and tried to find out something about her, pretending that she looked like his cousin, a runaway. She managed to get twenty bucks out of him, asking for formula money for her child. There was only one child in that rattrap—Dorian."

His expression saddened. "Unfortunately, by the time my associate got back to me and returned to the apartment, she'd overdosed on whatever she bought with that money. Dorian was bawling like a banshee. We brought him to Ruthorford and the Kilravens took him in and raised him. We tried to find something on the father, but never did. This," he pointed to the piece of paper, "was all we could dig up."

Morgan poured Bask some more tea and set it in front of him. This was the most she'd ever heard him say. A man of few words, he was more of a delegator. For him to come to Ruthorford meant something, but she wasn't sure what.

Bask nodded his thanks and took a deep drink. "Eryk...Derrick—"

"I'll stick with Eryk," Eryk said.

"Eryk, I'm sorry. We assumed the records were correct and one child had died. I don't know how the Vreelands obtained you. That's something you'll have to ask them. I am sure you will." Bask, still dealing with the fact that they'd somehow failed this man, tried to comfort. "Listen, son, it's obvious that they wanted you. They must have gone to a great deal of trouble to get you and keep all of this from you." He saw the look of disdain pass over Eryk's face before he masked it and wondered just what kind of life he'd actually had.

Bask had started the research the moment Jasmine has first called him from the fair. The society pages had read like a fifties family show. Photos of Donald Vreeland contributing large sums of money to the charities for which Eryk performed filled the pages. Come to think of it, he hadn't seen the "family" photos he would have expected of such a socially prominent family. There were pictures of the husband and wife together and plenty of pictures of Eryk, just not of the three of them together, unless they were on stage.

Bask glanced around the table at the foursome talking among themselves. Things would change for Eryk from this day forth. Ruthorford's descendants were a fiercely loyal bunch—to each other and their families. If Eryk hadn't had it before, he would now—if he knew how to accept and appreciate it.

"I would like for you and Jasmine to come up to Abbott House, fill out some surveys, take some tests. It'll give me a chance to show you around, help you get grounded before I send you two into the field."

"Field?" Eryk asked. They sure treated all this *stuff* matter-of-factly.

"Dorian can teach you what you'll need to know. That can be done before or after Atlanta, it doesn't matter."

Jasmine broke in, "He wants to poke us with needles and test our skills, both apart and together." She caught the looks going back and forth between Dorian and Morgan. "What is it with you two? You need some alone time?" she teased.

"Not exactly," Dorian said. He looked at Bask.

Bask stood, causing the chair to wobble on two legs. With lightning speed, Jasmine reached out and stopped it, brushing her hand against Bask's leg in the process.

He reached down and rubbed the spot. "You've got quite a spark," he said.

"Sorry. I'm still figuring this out...as you well know."

"Eryk," Dorian said, "you can stay here with us. Any time, for as long as you like. It will make the training go quicker."

Eryk gave a slight smile, but it didn't reach his eyes.

Morgan nodded, throwing in her support. "If you don't want to stay in The Shoppe with the soon to be squalling babies, the cottage is right there and it's yours."

"Babies?" Bask interrupted. "I thought there was only one."

Morgan turned to Bask, a glint in her eyes. "What? You thought I was becoming a beached whale with one baby? What did you think I was having, a hippo?"

He had the foresight to blush. "I wasn't going to say anything...,"

Morgan rubbed her huge belly and laughed until the stomach tightened and she winced. At Bask's concerned look, Dorian, Jasmine and Eryk all announced, "Braxton-Hicks," and laughed.

Dorian let the laughter settle down but grabbed the lightness of the moment to pin down Bask. "Eryk might not know you, but we do. It took more than these papers to make you come all the way to Ruthorford. And don't give me the 'I wanted to see for myself' routine. We know you better than that. Plus, all this insistence on training. Add in a visit to Abbott House and I smell a rat. Or to be more precise, a Gulatega."

Still standing, the older man pulled some more paperwork from his brief case before he closed it, setting in the chair. "It's not much, be there have been some reports of activity at Meadow's Keep." He laid the papers in the center of the table.

Morgan blanched.

"Gulatega? Ian?" Dorian asked, his words measured.

Eryk could feel a protective cloak emanate from Dorian to surround Morgan. He automatically responded by encircling Jasmine, whose hair suddenly stood on end.

"Hey!" she squeaked. "What was that for?"

"Not sure." The green of his eyes swirled.

"I didn't mean to start something," Bask said. "The reports we're getting are vague. Possible movement around the grounds. Some lights. All from outside spotters. Nothing official. But we need a couple to check it out."

"Not Morgan," Dorian stated firmly.

"No. I was thinking—" He looked at Eryk and Jasmine.

Dorian balked. "No. It's too dangerous. Neither one of them knows what to look for, or what to do if they find it."

Bask seemed unconcerned and waved it off. "Just a look-see. How long before you can get them ready?"

Dorian ran a hand through his black hair. "I don't know. A couple of weeks, maybe."

"Well, you've got days," Bask corrected.

"...there's no—" Dorian started to say.

"Hey...don't forget I'm sitting right here," Jasmine interrupted. Her energy heightened, sparking from her fingertips. "I can do whatever has to be done. I watched enough of Dorian's lessons with Thom." She jerked a thumb toward Eryk. "This greenhorn, here, I don't know about. I can guide him, I suppose."

Almost glaring at her, Eryk spoke, his voice low, "I'm a quick study."

"What about that meeting you said you want to have with your father?" Bask asked.

"It'll have to wait." Whatever was going on affected the safety of the people sitting around him. If he was in, he was all in. The man who'd ignored him all of his life would just have to wait. "What about Morgan's delivery?" He knew he and Jasmine couldn't be in two places at the same time.

"It'll be a short trip. I just want you to have a look. If you need help, I have a couple I can send in from West Virginia. You'll be back here in plenty of time to cover for Dorian and Morgan."

Bask grabbed his coat and slung it over his shoulder, not bothering to put it on, and picked up his briefcase. "I need to get back to Atlanta." By now they were all standing. "Why don't you and Jasmine come up in a couple of days?"

Eryk took the proffered hand. "Okay." He glanced at Jasmine, who gave a slight nod.

Bask studied Eryk. "Hopefully, I'll have some more information for you by then. We're still looking into things. I'm sorry. I wished I'd known."

"Well, if Donald Vreeland is involved, plan to look deep. He's damn good at covering things up," Eryk said.

Jasmine spoke. "Yeah, well Abbott House is damn good at uncovering," she said with pride.

Bask smiled at her. "I'm glad you're all right. Be careful," he added.

"I will," Jasmine rose on tiptoe and kissed him on his cheek. "Promise. We'll see you in a couple of days."

"Look over those reports," he said, walking toward the front door.

"I'll see him to the car," Dorian said. "Morgan, sit."

"I'm not Meesha," she snapped back, but sat anyway. "Jasmine, would you bring those rolls over...and some milk, if you don't mind?"

Eryk helped Jasmine get some plates, the rolls—which turned out to be hot cross buns from the B & B—a pitcher of milk, and a glass for Morgan. He noticed Dorian kept the closed sign up when came back inside and locked the door. *What now?*

Dorian grabbed a bun off the plate and took a huge bite.

"You're gonna gain as much as Morgan and it's not going to come off you so easily," Jasmine teased him, poking him in his still hard abs.

"I know, but I've been starving ever since she got pregnant."

Jasmine set aside her drink. "Okay, spill. What is it that you two have been hedging around and that caused Bask to run out of here like we were a bunch of hungry mosquitoes?"

"I guess there's no way to do this delicately." He finished off the bun, wiped his mouth, and took a drink from Morgan's glass, then reached over to fill refill the glass.

"Have you two slept together?" Dorian asked without looking at them.

"What?" Jasmine squeaked, her body shifting in her chair. "That is *none* of your business."

"I know that," he defended, still not meeting her gaze. "Unfortunately, it's Ruthorford business."

"How so?" she asked, although she knew the answer, or at least part of it. She was, after all, a descendant.

Eryk watched Dorian and Jasmine avoiding eye contact. Jasmine was obviously being defensive with Dorian. Her eyes flashed. When she squirmed, he wondered if it was because of the closeness she and Dorian had once shared. Or, was

Jasmine feeling a little guilty about the attraction that was building between them.

He watched as Dorian and Jasmine finally looked at one another and some sort of silent communication passed between them. Eryk looked away. The very idea of Jasmine with Dorian set his blood boiling. He turned his attention to Morgan, whose beautiful green eyes, which looked so different from his, being offset by her complexion and auburn hair, showed only love and concern.

"No," Eryk said, ending the rising turmoil.

Jasmine threw a frown at him. Dorian however, looked relieved.

"Good," Dorian said.

"Dory." Jasmine gripped Dorian's arm, mistaking his statement for possessiveness. His muscle flexed under her touch. Just muscle and sinew, not tingles and permeating warmth. She looked at her hand still resting on Dorian's arm. It was nothing like when she touched Eryk. When she touched Eryk, it was as though she touched his very soul.

Dorian patted her hand. "Let me explain. I put Morgan through hell, since I was determined to save her the anguish and not tell her. All it did was make things impossible. And then we did and shouldn't have and when she left—"

"TMI, sweetheart," Morgan interrupted, trying to rescue Dorian before he became a blithering idiot, "way too much information. Let me try." She turned to Jasmine and Eryk. "What my husband is failing miserably to impart is that once you sleep together you are match-mated, which, Jasmine, you should know. Bound forever. What you might not know—" she stopped at Jasmine's frown. "Let me try again. What you know intellectually, but not in experience, is that, once you are mated, and then separated, even for a little while, it can be devastating. When together..." she let the words soften into silence and got a dreamy look on her face.

Dorian coughed. "Now who's imparting too much information? All we're saying is to know what you are getting into. I did, sort of. But she didn't at all. I caved and we did it before we'd discussed the implications." He pushed his hand through his hair. "I'm not explaining this very well. You have to understand, the attraction between you will only get stronger, become an obsession, until you have no choice."

Jasmine's looked at Eryk, saw what looked like panic and, at that moment, wanted to be any place but here— someplace far away, like Virginia, safe in her room. She rose and, when Eryk rose as well, she held up a hand. "Please. I just need to be alone for a while." Without waiting for an answer, she turned and left The Shoppe, closing the door behind her.

Morgan caught Eryk's arm as he started past, shaking her head. "Let her go. She has some things to think through. I'm going to let Dorian give you the male perspective of the descendants' match-mating compulsion while I go take a nap." Morgan rose, waved Dorian to stay as well, and slowly made her way up the stairs.

None too happy, Eryk returned to his seat, looking out the window every now and again, hoping Jasmine would come back and rescue him from the birds and bees lecture.

****

Her mind on the mortification she felt seeing Eryk's panic at the idea of being bound to her, Jasmine pulled open the alley gate to slink inside, when she heard her name called. She closed her eyes and silently wished to be invisible, knew that wasn't going to happen, and plastered a smile on her face before turning to face Miss Alice. The round little woman

looked the same as she had all of Jasmine's life, beautifully
ancient. She bent and enfolded the old woman in a gentle
hug, careful not to crush the package she was carrying—
probably for the bed and breakfast. Miss Alice smelled of
lavender and lilac, that special blend Dorian still concocted
for her, even after Melissa's death. She was glad some things
never changed.

Miss Alice held out the package. "I was going to leave
this in the Flair for you, dear. I didn't want to disturb you and
that young man who's been courting you." The woman's eyes
twinkled.

"He's not…" she stopped when she saw the glint form in
Miss Alice's amber eyes. Never could lie to the woman. She'd
get that look and the truth would just spill right out. "His
name is Eryk Vreeland," she said and took the package.

"Oh, my," she said, fluttering her hands. "You mean the
magician?"

Jasmine couldn't help but smile at the old woman's
excitement.

"The one and only."

"He's so handsome. We saw him once." Then she leaned
in conspiratorially. "And he looks an awful lot like our sweet
Dorian."

Jasmine forced her lips together and nodded. It was
Dorian's and Eryk's place to disclose their relationship so,
even under Miss Alice's *truth spell,* as generations of kids had
called it, she kept her mouth shut. Instead, she opened the
bag and let the aroma waft out.

"Mmmm," she said and let her eyes close in
appreciation. "Muscadine scones?"

Miss Alice grinned from ear to ear, clearly thrilled. "Miss
Grace said she just had to make those for you, since they were
always your favorite."

Jasmine gave her another hug. "Tell Miss Grace thank you. You know how I love your treats. I've missed them so much. In fact, I was just heading in now. I'll make some tea to go with the scones."

"Be sure and add lemon. It enhances the flavor," Miss Alice said, pleased.

"I will. You take care." She kissed the woman's soft cheek, turned, and headed down the alley, letting the smile fade as she walked. Even an interruption by Miss Alice couldn't keep her mind off Eryk. He'd looked as though the last thing he wanted was a commitment to her. She pulled up her shoulders in defiance. Well, maybe it was she who didn't want a commitment. They didn't have to have sex to do Bask's bidding. Her conviction strengthened with each step she took until she was stomping up the steps.

She heard the bird call as she unlocked the door and grabbed the handle, just in case. However, her vision remained the same. She slowly turned and saw a hawk flying overhead. "No way," she breathed, feeling a familiar pull. It couldn't be. It circled twice, called loudly, and flew off. She watched until it was out of sight. Glancing around, Jasmine made sure her sight didn't shift, then headed inside, setting the scones, unopened on the table.

She walked over and lifted one of the slats of the blinds, looking across the street at The Shoppe of Spells. She couldn't see any movement inside and chided herself for even wondering. Still, she did. Like some starry-eyed schoolgirl, she wondered what they were discussing. She let go of the blinds. Well, it wasn't an adolescent game and this wasn't a crush. This was serious business. They were talking match-mated. She'd grown up in Ruthorford and she knew damn well what that meant. It was forever. It was no one else, ever. It was never wanting to be apart.

She walked back over and plopped down on the couch. Why hadn't she realized what was going on? The instant attraction. The irresistible pull. Probably, because it hadn't been that way with her and Dorian. Or with her and anyone else, for that matter. She'd had sex, good sex, before Eryk. Before the attack by Rob.

She shuddered. Rob. That's what it had been with Rob—an attack. She'd been assaulted. She'd come to terms with it. Moreover, with her abilities, it was highly unlikely anyone *normal* could assault her again and get away with it. Jasmine felt the energy tingle in her fingertips.

The thing was, Eryk wasn't normal. He was like her. No, he was like Dorian and Morgan combined, which was a hell of a lot stronger than she was. That should put the fear of God in her, but it didn't. She felt safe around him. When she backed away, it was because she wanted to take her time, give him time. Jasmine rolled her eyes at her own babble. The real problem was that, when she was around him, all she wanted to do was get as close as possible and put her hands and mouth all over him.

Jasmine jumped up from the couch. Geez, just thinking about the man skewed her brain. She walked back over to the window and looked out. Why hadn't he followed her? Probably one of them told him to give her some space.

Good! She'd take the time and a hot shower. That would make her feel better. More in control. Then she'd figure out just what she was going to do about Mr. Magician. She started stripping on the way to the bedroom, hoping Eryk sensed that she was just across the street, naked as a jaybird.

****

"Come on. Concentrate." Dorian called as the third ball of energy went wild, hitting the side of the cottage.

"I'm trying," Eryk called back. That was a lie. He knew damn well he could send that ball careening back at Dorian and flatten him. One more snide remark and he would, too.

"Stop groping Jasmine in your mind and concentrate." Dorian yelled.

That did it. Eryk's green eyes became slits and he threw up his hand. The sparkling ball of energy stopped right in the middle between him and Dorian, hovered a second or two, and then flew back at Dorian, like a flash of lightning.

Dorian ducked, the energy ball missing him by an inch. The ball stopped right behind him, hovered, swung a bit, until it was over his head and burst, allowing sparkling bits of sizzling energy to rain down on his twin.

"Damn," Dorian called and dodged away from the tiny bits of fire zapping his skin.

Morgan stood on the porch, hands on hips, staring at them. "If you boys are finished playing, I want you to try the portal. See if there's a male/female necessity."

The two men turned sheepish grins on her and spoke over one another, pointing, "He started it."

Morgan shook her head and headed back inside, letting the screen door slam behind her.

Dorian looked at his brother and let out a laugh. "Probably a good thing we weren't raised together."

Eryk followed him to the cottage. "Yeah, probably." He followed Dorian inside and stepped on the rug. "Are we gonna have to hold hands?"

"Let's try a more manly hold." He clasped Eryk's wrist. Eryk, in turn, clasped his.

"Now what?" Eryk had no idea what to do. "Before, Jasmine did the mojo."

"Let me try. Since I'm only energy and you have the aura energy like Morgan, see if you can pick up mine and latch on."

Eryk felt power surge up his arm. His first instinct was to repel it, not join with it. He had to dampen his own energy. The energy coursing through his body seemed to seek a different level. It stung like crazy. He tried to heighten his aura energy. He could feel the energy from Dorian try to weave with that. The crystals about the room started to glow, as did the rug, just like before with Jasmine. Unfortunately, it was damn uncomfortable, like thousands of bees stinging. He held on, waiting for the portal. The violet glow flickered, burst into the room between them, catapulting them apart. Dorian landed none too gently on the bed behind him and Eryk slammed into the edge of the couch, falling over it. "Crap," he yelped as his head hit the coffee table.

"You okay?" Dorian stepped back into room and offered his brother a hand up. Eryk just looked at Dorian's hand and pushed himself up, dropping down onto the couch he just fallen over, rubbed his head, and look about the room. The rocks and rug looked just like they had before they'd started. The burst of violet light had totally dissipated.

Dorian sat down beside him. "I'd say that was a yea and a nay." He wiggled his hand back and forth, his fingers splayed. "We'd have to work at it, but I think we could do it."

"Did it sting you?"

"No, but I only have one type of energy to deal with."

"Good. I was worried I had hurt Jasmine."

"Doubt it. If she's like me, then she only feels the energy ebbing and flowing."

"Hey," he said, studying Eryk, "want to try it by yourself. You do have both energies." Then he gave Eryk a croaked grin, "Maybe I'm just too much for you."

"As much as I'd like to wipe that stupid-ass grin off your face, I don't think I want to feel that again for a while. It hurt like hell, like I'd been tasered."

Dorian's cell phone rang. With it to his ear, he was on his feet in an instant, running for the door. "Something's happened to Bill," he called over his shoulder as he ran around the side of the shop. Eryk followed, close on his heels.

Jasmine was at the window staring across the street for the third time when she saw Dorian and Eryk fly out of the gate and race toward the bed and breakfast. She flung down the brush she was holding and ran out the door. *Please don't let it be Teresa,* she sent up a silent plea and realized in all likelihood it was Bill. *God, add Bill to that,* she amended as she ran down the narrow lane behind the shops to the side of the B & B. She ran through the open door to the lobby and up the wide staircase to their third floor apartment. The door gaped open.

Bill lay sprawled on the floor, on his back, unconscious, his face and lips a matching pale gray. Dorian and Eryk knelt on either side. Teresa knelt at his head. When she looked up at Jasmine, there were tears in her eyes.

"I came up to check on him." She dashed away the tears. "He'd said he was tired and wanted to take a short nap." She dropped her gaze to Dorian. "He's been doing that a lot more recently."

Dorian checked his pulse and his breathing. "Thready and shallow," he said. "Did you call Yancy?" He asked without even looking at her.

"Yes. Right before I called Morgan."

"Back away, Dorian," Eryk said, his voice resonated through the room, carrying a vibration. "I've only done this a couple of times but, I'm afraid if I don't, he might not make it for the doctor."

Dorian sat back, much like Teresa. Jasmine watched, gripping the doorframe, feeling the tears course down her face.

Eryk rubbed the palms of this hands together, as if trying to warm them, then reached out and grabbed hold of Bill's upper arms. Bill visibly jerked on the floor and his face went from ashen to flushed in seconds. Eryk eased the pressure on the man's arms and, while still having his hands firmly touching Bills arms, moved them down to the wrists.

Jasmine's gaze moved from Bill to Eryk. It looked as though the very air around Eryk shimmered. Bill moaned and Eryk released the older man. When Eryk tried to stand, he wobbled and Jasmine was there in an instant, grabbing his arm. She felt her own energy surge and pulse into him. This time, instead of it flowing back from him with a hum, hers slowed down. She led him over to a chair and let Dorian and Teresa help Bill onto the bed.

"What happened?" Bill asked as Teresa propped the pillows up behind his head.

"You tell us. You said you were going to take a nap and then I found you on the floor."

He took Teresa's hand. "I don't remember."

Still holding onto Jasmine's hand, Eryk closed his eyes. When he opened them, Bill and Teresa both came into view as pulsing auras of light. Bill's aura was still close around him but had less violet color and was completely filled in. There were no breaks at all. What he'd seen when he'd arrived was very different. Had he done that? Would it last? And for how long?

Teresa's aura was more pink, delicate, almost fae, except around her abdomen. There it dulled, flattened, became almost bluish. Maybe that was normal with an older woman, he thought, before he let the concern take hold.

He heard Jasmine's intake of breath and the tightening of her hand in his and swung his head until his gaze rested on her. She was magnificent. Her aura was like bursts of fireworks, bright and flashy, jutting out from her body much further than he'd ever seen. He realized she was watching Bill and Teresa and closed his eyes. He smiled at her when he opened them and met her questioning look, squeezing her hand and sending a push of energy.

"What's *he* doing here?" Bill asked from the bed.

Thinking the question was directed at him, Eryk started to answer, but stopped when he heard a melodious voice flow from the door. "Teresa called me. Get over it."

A tall, lean man stood at the door, his gaze on Teresa. Without acknowledging anyone else, he lifted his medical bag, which looked as though it had come through several centuries of use, set it on the bed, and pulled out his stethoscope.

"Now, if we can have some privacy," he said over his shoulder. When Bill didn't exclude Teresa from Dr. Yancy request, the doctor looked at her. "I could use a cup of coffee, if you don't mind."

Teresa looked from Bill to Mike Yancy, but made her way to the door with the rest of them. Jasmine slipped her arm around her cousin's waist, led her to a sofa in the hallway, and eased her down onto the cushions. "Why don't you wait here and I'll go down and get some coffee for all of us. You want anything else?"

Teresa lifted pleading eyes to her young cousin, not saying anything. Jasmine patted her shoulder and headed toward the stairs, giving Eryk and Dorian a brief smile and a silent command to stay with her cousin.

As Teresa lifted her hand to brush back the hair from her face, her hand trembled. Without a word, Eryk stepped over and placed his hand on her shoulder, giving a small surge of energy.

"Thanks," Teresa said softly and patted his hand. And thanks for what you did for Bill."

"No problem."

He noticed she refrained from asking what he'd seen. Maybe she already knew.

****

"What the hell's that for?" Bill scooched up against the pillows and watched the doctor pull several empty vials from this bag, a needle packet, and a band.

"You know damn well what." Mike said. "And I'll remind you that I'm the one drawing the blood so you might want to hold your tongue until I'm done."

Bill harrumphed but said nothing as Mike found the vein and drew several vials of blood, marked them, and stored them.

He finished his exam and pulled a chair next to the bed. "Want to tell me what's going on?"

"When hell freezes over," Bill grumbled, making Mike laugh.

"It's been decades, you old coot. I've gotten over it, why can't you?"

Bill tugged the blanket Mike had tossed over him a little higher and glared at the good doctor. "She loved you."

"Yup. That she did." Mike said, then added. "Then she loved you. She married you. She's not my concern, Bill. You are. When was the last time you went to a doctor?"

"You know the answer to that," Bill said.

"There are other doctors that can see you."

Bill didn't comment.

"So, what happened today?" From the set of Bill's jaw, Dr. Yancy knew it was like pulling quills out of a porcupine. He had a feeling when the big man finally let go, it would all come out at once.

"I guess I passed out." Bill mumbled.

"And?"

"I'm dying."

That got Yancy's attention. He studied the man lying in the bed. His color was good. He was thin, which, from what he could see from the sagging flesh, was a recent thing. Blood pressure was slightly low, a common trait among descendants. No fever. He'd have to wait for the blood tests.

"Why do you think that?"

"I just know. The only reason I'm alive right now it because that young magician came in and gave me one hell of a boost. I don't want to talk about me. I want to talk about Teresa."

Mike Yancy could do his best to look professional, but when it came to Teresa, his insides were anything but. He didn't say anything; he just let Bill talk.

"I know you still love her. I don't know about her. She'd never admit it to me, even if she did. I just want to make sure she's taken care of when I'm gone."

"You aren't gone, yet." There was harshness in Mike's voice.

"Damn it, Yancy. Can't you do this one thing for me?"

"And that would be?"

"Take care of her. Love her. Let her enjoy the rest of her life."

Mike wanted to rub his hand over his face in frustration. The man hadn't changed in years. He thought about grinning. Hell, it might stir Bill out of this mood. He didn't.

"Mike, just promise me and let's drop it. I promise to stay around as long as I can and you promise to help me do that. Then, it's your turn."

"If I weren't a doctor, I'd slug you a good one. Teresa's not something to be handed around, you fool. But, sure, I'll promise you, then I'll make you live a nice long, miserable life. If I thought I could take her away from you, I'd grab her and be gone. But, that's not the way this is going to play out, is it? For now, I'm going to place you on bed rest until I get the blood-work back. Make sure you don't have something that will infect your guests, then release you with the promise that you will come see me in two weeks. Agreed?"

"Agreed," Bill said quietly and Mike watched him.

He'd put a stat on that blood-work and go by and talk to Dorian and Morgan before he left. Eryk, too. Seeing the sadness in Bill's eyes, he patted the man's arm before he rose to call in Teresa.

"Come on in." He opened the door, knowing she'd be on the other side, waiting.

She walked past him without as much as a glance and went straight to her husband. Bill smiled up at her. It was then that Teresa turned to Mike Yancy, the worry etching lines in her still beautiful face.

"He seems fine, now. I've taken some blood. He's on bed rest until I call you with the results. Keep him away from the kitchen and the guests until then."

She nodded solemnly.

"I want to see him in my office in two weeks. If he has another episode, take him to the clinic or call the ambulance." Mike stuffed the stethoscope back in his bag, closed it and faced Bill. "Do as I say."

Bill nodded.

Teresa led the doctor to the door, standing with it open, in plain view of Bill. "Thank you for coming. I'll have him there in two weeks." Her face was a careful mask of politeness. Her eyes were worried. Mike wanted to reach out and stroke her soft cheek. Instead, he nodded and turned away, listening to the door close behind him.

Jasmine handed him a mug of hot coffee. "Let me take one in to Teresa and I'll meet you all downstairs." She walked over and tapped lightly on the door. When Teresa opened it, Jasmine didn't mention the tears she saw in her eyes. She simply handed her the coffee. "We'll be at The Shoppe."

They were waiting for Jasmine in the lobby, talking quietly. Dorian had a sack of food and his coffee. "I don't dare go back empty handed," he said.

No one spoke as they walked back to The Shoppe where Morgan was waiting at the door.

"He's okay, for the time being," the doctor informed her. "How are you?" His professional gaze took in the roundness and height of her belly.

"Ready to pop." She stepped back to let everyone file into the kitchen, listening to the chairs scrape across the floor as they were pulled away from the table. Morgan blinked and let her aura scan them each in turn. The only one that concerned her was Eryk, whose aura was close to his body and almost pastel, not the vibrant autumn-ish colors she'd seen the day they'd met.

Morgan waited until everyone was seated, coffee replenished, and the goodies plated and set in the middle of the table before taking a bite of an herb biscuit. She felt like a garbage disposal. She wiped her mouth and turned to Eryk. "You gave him one hell of a boost, didn't you?"

The response was a nod as he finished off the first biscuit and grabbed a second. "Sorry, I'm starved."

Yancy coughed. "Since I am a mere mortal, I need you guys to tell me what you saw." He had a legal pad on the table and was ready to take notes.

Morgan spoke first. "I saw him a couple of weeks ago. I noticed chinks in his aura. It flashed sporadically, not solid like it used to be. Bill's aura—and I think this is in your notes somewhere—was very strong and very healthy when I first met him. It's been since I got here, about a year ago, that he started changing."

Eryk furrowed his brow, trying to remember exactly what he saw. He looked at Morgan. "Did you notice a concentration of one color more than another?" he asked Morgan. Eryk noticed that her lip quivered slightly.

"What color?" Her voice cracked.

"Violet." Eryk said.

Morgan blanched. Dorian reached over and took her hand. Eryk instinctive reached over and took Jasmine's hand, linking his fingers with hers.

Morgan looked at Jasmine, trying to figure out a way to say what she was about to say without scaring the hell out of her. Bill was, in all ways but biological, Jasmine's father. She turned to her husband in hopes of some assistance. But, he couldn't see auras or creatures. He had to rely on her.

"Jasmine, I want to start this by emphasizing that what I'm about to say probably has no correlation to Bill. It's just an observation." She waited for Jasmine's nod before continuing. She could see Jasmine steel herself for the worst, whatever it was.

"When I saw Ian last year, his aura had a violet glow." She quickly held up her hand when she saw the furrow in Jasmine's brow. However, he was also surrounded by the Gulatega. That could have had an effect. There could be many reasons for the color. We are different from most people.

Maybe when we are sick, it probably shows up. I don't know a whole lot about that sort of thing. You should check with Bask when you go to Atlanta."

Eryk could feel Jasmine's hand tremble in his and he held tight.

"It didn't look like the other colors. It was almost a hue overlaying them," Jasmine said.

"You saw his aura?" Morgan and Dorian asked at the same time.

"Yes, when I was holding Eryk's hand." She felt uneasy all of a sudden, "Dory, don't you?"

"Even when I'm touching Morgan, I can't see auras. Just what did you see?"

They seemed to be leaning in toward her. She swallowed hard, feeling even more freakish. She concentrated on Bill, hoping what she said might help. Seeing him helpless like that scared her to death. He'd always been reclusive with everyone it seemed, except her. She was his little girl. Since she'd arrived this time, he'd seemed more standoffish. She'd thought he didn't want her worrying.

Jasmine tried to remember. "Well, his aura was close to his body and had breaks in it. The colors looked dull. Since I've never seen an aura before, I'm not sure what they are supposed to look like."

Morgan looked at Eryk and stood. He grinned and closed his eyes, knowing when he opened them, Jasmine would see Morgan's aura. When he opened his eyes, Jasmine was the one who spoke.

"Oh my God! You're so vibrant." She looked at Morgan's belly. "They're so bright. More shine than color, like starlight." Then she looked at Dorian. "Damn," she laughed. "Even your aura is hunky." She leaned back and turned to Eryk and held tight when he tried to pull away. "I just want to see how alike or different your auras are." She let her eyes move up and down his body, then swung back to look at Dorian.

"Remember," Morgan interrupted, "Eryk just boosted Bill. His aura may appear weak." She closed and opened her eyes. Eryk's aura had returned to normal. She sighed in relief.

"Eryk's has more colors and his spikes shoot out farther, but there's a similar rhythm to the pulse." Jasmine blinked, let go of Eryk's hand and fell forward, resting her head on her hand.

"You okay?" Eryk ran his hand up and down her back.

"Yeah. I got dizzy. Kinda queasy."

Morgan spoke. "You'll be okay in a moment." She moved to the sink and dampened a dishtowel under cold water. "Here, put this against the back of her neck." She handed the towel to Eryk, who folded it and laid it against her slender neck, letting his fingers trail across her skin.

Jasmine let the coolness of the cloth and the slight sizzle from Eryk's touch travel from her neck down her back.

"It did the same thing to me the first time. You'll probably need to eat something."

Jasmine raised her head with a twinkle in her black eyes. "Your answer to everything lately is to eat something."

Morgan patted her belly. "I won't deny that, but it's true. Eryk is more than likely still starving." She nodded to the man who'd just finished off the last biscuit. "Any expenditure of energy seems to need refueling." She opened the commercial size refrigerator and brought out a truffle bowl. Dorian got up and passed out bowls and spoons. "Eat up, guilt free. It's a yogurt, bran, nut, and fruit compote." Morgan heaped the parfait into bowls and passed them around.

Jasmine made a face as she took the proffered bowl. "I've never been a big fan of yogurt." She sniffed at it.

"Just try it. I promise, if you don't like it, you don't have to eat it." Morgan took a large spoonful. "And I won't mention how good it is for you."

Jasmine dipped the edge of her spoon in, pulling out a thin coating, and watched Eryk shovel another spoonful into his mouth. She let her tongue touch the back of the spoon.

She heard Eryk cough and looked up to see his focus riveted on her mouth. Unable to resist, she ran her tongue over the back of her spoon, watching the spoon in Eryk's hand dangle before hitting the table, splattering yogurt.

"Hey. It's not so bad." She tried to keep a straight face.

"All right. I think I have enough information." Mike Yancy, who'd been making copious notes, said and rose.

Jasmine's eyes widened. Busy teasing Eryk, she'd forgotten Dr. Yancy was on the other side of her. She felt the blood rush to her face and slunk down in the chair.

Mike leaned over, patted her on the shoulder, and said in a soft voice, "It's okay. I was young once myself."

Jasmine groaned while everyone laughed.

Dorian followed Mike to the door, where they stood talking quietly.

"One of your tricks *is* super-hearing," Jasmine said under her breath to Eryk and nodded toward the door.

"I try not to eavesdrop," he whispered back. "Besides, they're talking about Morgan."

"Gotcha."

Dorian came back to the table all smiles, bent, and planted a kiss atop Morgan's head. "The clinic is all set for the babies' arrival. Mike says he's going to swing by the Inn once more and check on Bill before he heads back."

He turned back to Eryk and Jasmine, "What are your plans? You're welcome to hang around."

Jasmine spoke up. "Actually, I want to go over to the Flair for a little while."

"And I really need to talk to my people. I left them in a bit of a lurch." Eryk rose, checked his phone. "How about I call you later?" He directed the question to Jasmine.

"When is your next show?" Morgan asked.

"Honestly, I'm not sure. That's one of the things I need to check on. "I would love for you two to come."

"We'd love to, but I'm afraid it depends on these guys," Morgan laughed, answering for both of them.

"I'll check our schedule and see what's going on. I'll be in my room, if you need me. Be sure and let Teresa and Bill know that, too. I don't want to intrude."

"Don't get up," Jasmine said to Dorian and Morgan as she stood. "I'm headed out as well. Unlocked or locked?" she asked, referring to the door.

"I have some prescriptions to fill, so I guess we're open for business," Dorian said.

Jasmine turned the sign over before she closed the door.

They were by the fountain before Eryk spoke. "We really need to talk. But you know that."

"And we will. I promise. Just not right now." She turned toward the shop, hurrying off before he could say anything.

A frown creased Eryk's brow as he watched her disappear inside the Fashion Flair. He didn't know her that well but something was bothering her and he planned to find out what it was. For now, he'd let her do whatever it was she needed to do. But later….

****

"Morgan's fine," Jasmine repeated into the phone. "I know you've talked with her, probably five or six times since I arrived…." She made a loud sigh, hoping that Jenn would catch the hint. "She looks fine and Eryk and I promised to come babysit The Shoppe while she pops out perfect babies. So, how is Lily adjusting?" she asked, changing the topic.

"She's doing very well. She loves the younger kids and has been helping out in the nursery and playroom every chance she gets. She's smart as a whip, too. Since we do the online school here, she had to test. Jasmine, she's can easily do college work. She won't fess up to a high school diploma since that would give us a lead, so she's facing a GED. Didn't seem to bother her at all. So far, she's been pretty quiet with Dr. Browne, as well. We just need to give her some time. Oh, and she wants to know if the fashion show was a scam?"

"Tell her I'm getting the clothes from my shop, which isn't a lie. I'll have them shipped before I head out. I guess we're heading up to Atlanta the day after tomorrow. Bask wants to see us, then on to Virginia Beach, then home. I'd give it a week at the most."

An idea struck. "Jenn, tell Lily she's officially my assistant, since I'm out of town, and I want her to go around the house and pick five girls, two women, and some younger kids as models. First, she has to get their permission, then she can find out sizes, and work up model sheets for each one so we can plan the wardrobe. That'll keep her hopping until I get back."

"That sounds great. I guess we *are* having a fashion show." Jenn's laughter spilled through the phone.

"Looks like. I'll talk with you later. I've got a call."

She didn't but she didn't want to go into detail about Eryk with Jenn. She'd fielded all the questions she could at this point and knew what was coming. She just wanted time to get her head on straight where he was concerned, before she tried to answer Jenn's questions. Jenn had a way of getting right to the heart of the matter. Of course, that's what made her so damn good at what she did.

Jasmine called downstairs and set Bonnie and Claire to the task of organizing a wardrobe from the sale items and items in storage, so she wouldn't deplete the shop's stock. She'd been thrilled with the girls' business savvy. They'd helped out in the store since they were younger, always wanting to hang around. Jasmine hadn't realized just how much attention they'd been giving it. She let them know either she or Lily would be calling them back with more details about what to ship up to Virginia and where. Jenn used several shipping businesses where she regularly received goods. That way, she had total control over what deliveries came onto the grounds. Most of the time she sent someone from Safe Harbor to do the pick-up, eliminating that risk completely. Jenn had the place more secure than Fort Knox.

A light tap on the door drew her attention as she shut off the phone. She could see Eryk standing on the landing and felt a warm thrill move through her. The smile was genuine when she opened the door.

"Wow. You look great," he said. He didn't know what it was, but she glowed. He watched her as she moved back into the apartment. "You really love what you do, don't you?"

She whipped around, a confused looked on her face.

He tapped his ear.

Jasmine let out a sigh. "Oh, yeah...that. How much did you hear?"

"Part of a conversation with Jenn and then the girls downstairs."

Damn it. He knew how to ruin a good mood. "I thought you didn't eavesdrop."

Now the energy was bouncing off of her. He held up his hands in supplication. "I don't. I caught the conversation right as I left the bed and breakfast." He held up a bag. "I tried to call. It went to your voicemail and I didn't want this to get cold." He walked over and set the bag on the table. "It looks like Sandra has stepped up from understudy, at least for the moment, and she sent this to us." Miffed, he walked back to the door.

He turned to her. "Listen. For some reason, I seem to be tuned in to you. I will try to block it from now on. Sorry to bother you." He yanked open the door.

"Stop! Please."

Eryk felt the tension move out of her in a breath. He stopped.

"You didn't. Not really. It just felt a little invasive." He was under her skin. Sometimes it was thrilling and sometimes it was annoying. She either wanted to rub up against him or put distance between them—a great deal of distance. Yet, she'd brought him to Ruthorford. She needed to stop being rude. Her guess was she wasn't the only one having issues.

Eryk stepped back around the table, took her hand, and let her to the couch. "The food can wait. Let's talk."

He sat next to her. "I know we don't know each other very well. All this has happened fast—for both of us. I don't care what anyone says. What happens between us is just that, between us."

Obviously, he didn't know Ruthorford. Jasmine looked down and toyed with the short nails of her hand, remembering when Dr. Yancy had clipped them, seeking the DNA of the man sitting next to her. It really hadn't been very long. Her nails hadn't even grown.

He'd stopped talking and was watching her. When she looked up, his green eyes seemed darker. Just looking at him warmed her blood and she felt tingly and feminine and wanted to concentrate on the fact that their legs were resting against one another's and the heat of his leg was warming hers.

When a tap sounded at the door, Jasmine jumped as though she'd been caught doing something she oughtn't. Eryk laughed, a low warm sound from deep inside.

As she got up, she looked back at him, "You jumped, too. Don't deny it."

She let Teresa in the door and took her into her arms. Her cousin felt thin and fragile in her arms. Stepping back, she saw worry lines etching her face. "You okay?"

Teresa nodded and saw the bag on the table. "I see Sandra sent you guys something to eat."

"I haven't even opened it, yet." Jasmine apologized and stepped toward the bag.

Teresa grabbed her arm and stopped her. "That's not why I'm here...well...not entirely. Sandra did want to know how you liked what she sent." Teresa gave a soft laugh. "That girl has really stepped in. She has taken over the kitchen like it was her own. I guess she was paying more attention than Bill gave her credit for. Believe me, that's not resting so well with his high and mighty, right now," she added. "I suppose he needs to feel indispensable."

Thinking of the girls downstairs, Jasmine smiled. "He's not the only one."

"Bonnie and Claire." Teresa said. "They really are good. You don't have to worry."

Jasmine led Teresa over to a chair. "You want something to drink?" she asked.

"No, thank you."

"How is he?" Eryk asked.

"Doing well. Driving me crazy, which speaks volumes. That's why I'm here," she said and waited for Jasmine to join Eryk on the couch. "Bill wants to make sure a confrontation doesn't happen in public."

She looked at Eryk. "He thanks you for your help." She took a steadying breath. "But he doesn't want you to do that again."

Jasmine was the one that spoke. "Why not? It saved his life."

The gaze Teresa cast on her cousin was full of love. "He knows that. He just feels, and I have to agree with him, that he could turn Eryk here into nothing more than an IV bag full of energy. What he did for Bill depleted Eryk a great deal. Bill saw that."

Teresa turned back to Eryk. "We don't know what's wrong with Bill. But, whatever it is, it's been progressing for some time. We don't want you to feel it's your responsibility to keep him going."

"I don't m—"

Teresa lifted her hand. "I know you don't." Her eyes glistened with unshed tears. "I'm relaying a message." She swallowed before she added, "I think you need to leave."

Jasmine's intake of breath came as a gasp. "You're asking him to leave Ruthorford?" Her voice was tight.

"For now. I think it's for the best." Teresa rose, holding the back of the chair to steady herself. "I'll let Sandra know you loved her gift." She turned to Eryk , who'd seen her wobble and moved quickly to her side. "I'm fine." She kissed him on the cheek. "You take care of Jasmine…and yourself." With that, and before Jasmine could say anything, she hugged her younger cousin and walked out, closing the door behind her.

Jasmine tried to hold back tears. When Eryk took her in his arms, she didn't resist. "You don't understand." She spoke with a sob. "Teresa would never tell anyone to leave Ruthorford. It just isn't…." She couldn't finish.

"She's right, though. I came over here to suggest we get out of here, too." He held onto her arms as she struggled to pushed away from him. "Jasmine," he said, making sure she was looking at him, "you haven't been yourself since we got here. I may not know you well, but the person I met—and the person I overheard talking with Jenn and the girls downstairs just moments ago—is not the person I've seen since we stepped foot in this town." He pulled her back into his arms. "It's like it swallows you up and you become something you think they expect you to be. You aren't that person anymore."

Every instinct Jasmine had yelled at her to deny what he was saying. Except, he was right. Almost with relief, she swiped at the tears and nodded. He seemed to know better than she did what she was feeling. It had been driving her crazy, as though she'd regressed into someone who watched everyone else before she spoke. It felt like they were watching her, expecting her to become the girl she'd been before. She wasn't that girl. She'd never be that girl again.

"Let's put our stuff in the car and go to Atlanta. I'll get us a suite someplace swanky with two bedrooms—I promise to stay in mine until we figure all this other stuff out—and we'll go see Bask tomorrow. Then, we'll take that plane back to Virginia where you belong."

"What about Dorian and Morgan?"

"We'll come and take care of it. Maybe, by then, we'll feel a little more settled about things."

She didn't ask what things he meant. Instead, she asked, "What about Meadow's Keep?"

"I don't see why we can't check that out. It's in Virginia, right? Not in Ruthorford."

Jasmine felt the pressure ease. This was the first time she'd ever looked forward to leaving Ruthorford.

Getting out of Ruthorford wasn't quite as simple as throwing stuff in the car and heading out of town. There was Morgan and Dorian, who worried that they'd driven them away. Eryk and Jasmine both promised it wasn't them, that they just wanted some time in Atlanta before going to Abbott House. Jasmine even threw in a little white lie about going shopping, letting her fashion-diva reputation help persuade them. She wasn't sure if they bought it or not, but they didn't argue. Numbers were exchanged and promises made with extra hugs all around.

Unlike Jasmine, leaving The Shoppe of Spells with Morgan and Dorian waving goodbye made Eryk feel like there was someone happily awaiting his return, a feeling he couldn't remember ever experiencing. It made him smile and take Jasmine's hand as they walked to the Land Rover. They drove down Main Street, did the U-turn, waved at Miss Alice walking down the street, and headed back up to the Abbott Bed & Breakfast to grab his clothes and check out.

They decided it would be better for Jasmine to say her farewells alone.

Chapter Eight

Teresa was sitting next to Bill when Jasmine stepped into their room. Bill was detailing orders for Sandra while Teresa was writing as fast as she could, rolling her eyes every now and again, just out of Bill's vision. Bill didn't stop when Jasmine walked in, but kept on shouting directions, corrections, and making a general nuisance of himself. Teresa just wrote and nodded, added, "Yes, Bill" or "I've got it, Bill" or "I will make sure she does it, Bill." Jasmine was sure Teresa was thinking, "Get off your high horse, Bill" or something far more crass—which Teresa would never say.

Finally, he wound down and smiled at Jasmine.

Teresa hopped up as soon as she had a chance. "I'll leave you two alone for a moment," she kissed Jasmine on the cheek. Jasmine knew she had "the watch" while Teresa delivered orders and snuck a chance to do a few things for their guests.

Jasmine leaned over, took his hand and brushed a kiss on his forehead, as he'd done with her so many times. She closed her eyes and tried to summon the feeling she felt when the aura appeared. It didn't come. *Damn.* She needed Eryk for that. So, she stepped back and did it the old fashioned way, studying him.

"Well, do I pass muster?"

She sat down on the edge of the bed. "Stop giving everyone such a hard time. You scared the hell out of us."

"Just overworked."

She made a face at him.

"Don't you get impertinent with me, young lady," he scolded as laughter filled his eyes. "My, you're a sight for these old eyes. How are you doing?" His voice gentled.

She couldn't help but look down, the initial embarrassment flooding through her. She straightened her spine and looked him in the eye. It had taken a few sessions with Dr. Browne to accomplish this—not to be ashamed for something that wasn't her fault. "I'm doing well. Safe Harbor has helped. Dr. Browne has helped. Jenn definitely helped."

He squeezed her hand. "You are a strong woman. I knew you would come through this. How about physically?" he asked haltingly.

"Healed. No lasting injuries."

Bill's eyes changed momentarily, filled with something akin to hatred. "I'd kill the son-of-a—"

She gripped his hand tight, not letting him finish. "I know you would and I love you for that, but you need to understand, Rob was as much a victim as I was."

Bill's eyes widened. "I'll grant you that, at some point, those damn Guls drove him insane, but before that, Ian managed to entice him to leave the university and go to work for him."

Jasmine had thought about this more than she wanted to admit. Now, she chose to defend him. "There's nothing wrong with wanting a better paying and more exciting job. It had to be incredible to think he was on the verge of such a discovery—a dimensional portal. I can see where he'd be lured." Seeing his expression, she added, "Don't get me wrong, I haven't seen him, have no intention of seeing him, and won't forgive him." She tried to hold back the shudder that passed through her body remembering his cruelty and violence. "I'm just saying vengeance is not an option."

His lips drew together tight. "All right," he conceded, then changed the subject, raising his brows. "Tell me about the magician."

Jasmine let out a laugh. "Talk about frying pans and fires," she said. "There's nothing to tell. Met him at a state fair, brought him here at Bask's request."

He slowly shook his head. "There's more to this story, though I doubt it's been written. He seems like a nice young man. Saved my boney ass. You be happy, young lady. That's all I want for you. You know that. And for you to know that I love you." Bills cheeks heightened slightly. He'd never been one for being "mushy" as he called it. He always said actions spoke louder than words. In fact, this was probably one of the longest conversations Jasmine had ever had with him.

"I know." She leaned over and rested her head against his chest, listening to the slow steady heartbeat as she had after her parents had died. The sound of his heartbeat had soothed and comforted her. She felt his hand stroke her hair and the rumble of his voice in his chest when he spoke.

"I've missed our Yahtzee games. You owe me."

She sat us, smiling. "Is that a challenge I hear?" It seemed to be the only game with enough chance that neither of them felt the other had an unfair advantage. When they were young, Dorian would join them, but he began getting too many Yahtzees and, although they would never accuse him of cheating, they wondered if his "charge" could be influencing his rolls somehow.

"Any time, little girl. Any time."

Teresa stepped in. "Eryk's waiting downstairs."

Jasmine gave Bill a resounding kiss on the cheek. "I love you," she said and turned before he could see the tears in her eyes.

"Don't forget our game!" he called and she heard the hoarseness in his voice. All she could do was nod and get out of the room before she completely broke down.

Teresa followed her and took Jasmine in a tight hug. "Go on, now. You have things to do."

"Take care of yourself and him. I love you." Jasmine's voice broke.

"I love you, too. By the way...," she halted for just a second, as if weighing her next words, "...I really like Eryk. He's very different from Dorian, even if he looks like him."

Jasmine whispered, knowing Eryk could probably hear them, "You know, I barely notice that he looks like Dorian anymore."

Teresa just smiled and put her arm around Jasmine's waist and led her down the steps, through the lobby to the front porch where Eryk was standing, looking down Main Street.

He turned when he heard them on the porch, saw the remnant of tears in Jasmines eyes and took a step forward. She gave a slight shake of her head and hugged Teresa one last time. "Call me. Call us, if you need us. Promise."

Teresa's smile didn't reach her eyes this time. "I will. Go on, now."

****

A few quick calls and everything was set. Jasmine watched with awe the efficiency with which Eryk arranged everything. There seemed to be new sides to Eryk's personality every time she turned around. She listened to the consummate businessman take command of the conversation and, in a most cordial manner, get exactly what he wanted.

Jasmine leaned back in the seat and watched the rolling scenery pass by. She'd missed the lushness of the mountains of Georgia and those sloping pastures encircled by black—the favorite fence color of late, except for one purple fence on a small goat farm. It seemed like mile after mile afforded glimpses of horse farms and luxury. Trees stood tall and swept long limbs over the road, dripping color in front of them. She was glad he'd opted to take the back roads to Atlanta. He drove with confidence, appearing to know where he was going. Thank goodness for GPS.

Jasmine watched his profile. She wanted to say something but didn't know what or how. He probably hadn't felt the sting she had when Teresa had asked them to leave. To ask a descendant to leave was unheard of and for Teresa to do so was monumental. Granted, the circumstances were unusual. It wasn't done because of him but because of Bill. Jasmine wondered why it bothered her so much. Except for that, everyone had welcomed him, accepted him. There would probably be several discussions about it before they returned for Morgan's delivery. Jasmine knew that, no matter what restrictions they placed on him, Eryk would offer his help if there was a need.

She must have drifted off. It felt like they were in downtown Atlanta, pulling in front of the St. Regis, in no time at all. Eryk handed over the keys and led her inside.

"Good evening, Mr. Vreeland," the Concierge greeted Eryk. "Everything is ready." He handed Eryk a keycard.

"Thank you, Martin. It's good to see you again."

"You, too. How are your parents? We haven't seen them in some time."

"Doing very well. I'll tell them you asked about them." Only Jasmine heard the tightness in his voice. With his hand barely touching her back, he guided Jasmine to the elevators.

They stepped into the quiet elevator and waited until the door closed.

"I take it you've been here before," she spoke softly.

"I've done shows for the Children's Hospital Gala a number of times. They always go out of their way to accommodate us."

"Money talks."

When she stepped into the suite, Jasmine let out a low whistle. "Boy, does it talk."

"I specified two bedrooms." He escorted her through the living room and opened a door to her suite.

She glanced around and down at her black jeans. "I feel positively heathen."

His eyes darkened to a forest green. "You look positively delicious." He took a step toward her and stopped when there was a knock on the door.

As the valet brought in their bags and hanging clothes and put them in the separate bedrooms, Jasmine took the time to look at the luxurious bathroom. She stepped back into the living room and saw the fireplace and piano for the first time. A large dining room sat off to the side.

"Would you like me to unpack your bags, Miss?" the valet offered.

"No," Jasmine said. "I don't think so." She felt as if she should have packed something a bit more elegant from her boutique, if she was going to let him unpack it. Now, that was a twist, packing for the valet.

Eryk walked over and handed her a glass of deep red wine, setting his aside, as he tipped the valet, and turned back to her with a toast. "To an evening where *nothing* happens."

"Cheers," she agreed and tapped her glass to his.

"They have excellent room service, if you prefer to eat in. Or, we can go downstairs."

"I have a feeling they dress for dinner here and I didn't bring anything—"

His raised brow stopped her.

"Okay, maybe I did," she admitted. "Can we stay in, anyway?"

From the look in his eyes, she wasn't sure what she'd suggested was the safest idea. Their eyes locked and the air in the room warmed.

She jumped when her phone went off. Scanning the message, she looked at Eryk. "Is there some place I can get a printout?"

He walked across the room and pulled open what she thought were a pair of closet doors. Tucked neatly inside was a fully functional office. Computer, all-in-one printer/fax, phone, and a shredder. She looked at the card on the desk, punched the number into her phone, and sent it. In a flash, several pages printed out. She picked them up and moved over to the couch, took a sip of wine, and scanned the sheets.

Eryk sat across from her, watching. When her eyes met his, her heartbeat did a staccato thrum. She couldn't seem to move. Then it was gone. "Are we going to be able to do this?" She set the wine glass down.

"Yes." He set his own glass down and moved over to the couch, sitting next to her. "May I kiss you, before I put my desire under lock and key? I promise it will go no further."

She swallowed. Had a hint of an accent crept into his voice or was she imagining it? She sat perfectly still as his warm hands eased under her jaw and around her neck, his thumbs tilting her head ever so slightly. She closed her eyes.

"Look at me, Jasmine."

Her eyes opened and she watched the color in his eyes change and began to swirl. He stayed a breath away for a long time, looking into her eyes. The energy was low and eased into her body. She felt his warm breath on her lips. Soon their hearts picked up the other's rhythm and beat as one. Finally, his mouth moved down to hers, fitting as though they'd come from a matching mold. His tongue barely touched the seam of her lips and they opened, welcoming him. He kissed her thoroughly but never forced her.

It was the most sensual thing she'd ever experienced. Jasmine thought she'd go crazy. She wanted to grab him and pull him closer—or push him back and fling herself across him.

Gently, he ended the kiss. She felt bereft. He turned, picked up his glass, took a huge swallow of wine and moved to the chair across from her.

"What did you get, if I might ask?" He nodded to the papers lying crumpled in her lap.

"Huh?" Her lips still tingled. It took her a moment to figure out what he was talking about. "Oh," she said, shaking off the feeling and looked down, quickly straightening the papers.

She briefly told him about Lily, sparing him a lot of detail. "I told Jenn to have her choose people for the fashion show and send me particulars. Jenn opened up the clothes closet for her. I was scanning this report on the phone and wanted to get a better look at it." She looked down and became lost in thought for a moment, then looked up at him. "She knows clothes...and style." She slapped the papers on his leg. "I'd bet odds she comes from money."

"May I?" he reached out for the papers.

She frowned but handed them to Eryk, watching as he scanned them.

"Here." He pointed at the paper. "She makes references to some labels my family uses. Accessories from a shop in Washington, DC." He got up and moved next to her. "See where she recommends you might order this bag and scarf from Gromman's. That's in Washington. My mother always insists we buy her presents from there."

Jasmine called Jenn. They talked for a few moments, hung up, and Jasmine turned back to Eryk. "Jenn says for now she'll hold that information close. Until we know exactly how she got those injuries and why she doesn't want us calling her family, Jenn thinks the fewer people that know, the better."

"It won't come from me," Eryk said. He glanced at his watch. "I can't believe I'm saying this, but I'm hungry."

Jasmine laughed. "It did seem we were eating the entire time we were in Ruthorford."

"Why don't you give ol' Bask a call and set up our meeting tomorrow, while I order dinner."

She made the call and headed to her room to freshen up. Bask couldn't understand why they hadn't opted to stay at Abbott House. It had a staff and guest rooms always available for visitors. Jasmine knew the old man too well. He just wanted more time to delve into Eryk's past and her newly discovered abilities. No matter how graciously he offered…in fact, the more gracious he was, the more she suspected his motives. Bask was, if nothing else, one hundred percent Abbott House. She often wondered about his past. No one mentioned it. Except that he came from a long line of people that served the good of Ruthorford.

Jasmine laughed when he suggested staying at the St. Regis was a waste of money. This from the man who would send a plane on a moment's notice. Or authorize an endowment to Safe Harbor in what was probably, she wasn't sure since she hadn't asked, an astronomical amount. However, she did promise to be front and center no later than 10 o'clock in the morning. He emphasized they were only about twenty minutes away, depending on traffic.

When she came out of the bedroom, Eryk was talking to a thin woman, wearing the crisp service uniform of the hotel, while she set the table. "Don't leave, Tina," he said and disappeared into his room.

Eryk walked back in smiling and handed the woman a small wooden case. "This is for Brian," he said. "It has a book and some supplies for beginners. I think he'll enjoy it."

"Oh, Mr. Vreeland, you shouldn't have," Tina gushed.

"It's a small thing, compared to what he's doing. Tell him he holds the magic within him to get better." He put his arm around her shoulders and hugged her.

Jasmine felt a slight crackle in the air.

"Tell Brian I expect him to get well and come to my show. You call me when he can do that and I will send my plane for him and you."

There were tears in her eyes. "All he does is talk about your visit to the hospital. He's doing very well. It looks like they got the tumor and he is almost done with the chemo. He's still weak but he gets stronger every day. He'll love this."

Tina turned to answer the tap on the door and direct the server with the dinner cart. With a last smile, she left and quietly closed the door behind her. Eryk escorted Jasmine to the exquisitely set table and held her chair. Once he was seated, the server showed him the wine, which he approved, and finished setting the table with silver containers and from those, he served their plates. Eryk had order a surf and turf dinner. A plump, medium rare fillet rested next to a succulent lobster tail. The server picked up a foiled potato, running it back and forth in his white-gloved hands before removing the foil, setting it on a side plate and, with a quick stab and press, it popped open to emit steam and presenting a fluffy, white interior.

"Butter? Sour cream?"

"Yes to both, please."

Herbed asparagus, long and thin, completed the presentation.

Hot rolls rested in a basket.

She waited until he was finished with Eryk's plate.

"Please call when you are ready for dessert."

"We will, Carl. Thank you."

Carl gave a quick nod of his head and left.

"Do you know everyone?" Jasmine asked as she dipped a piece of lobster into the drawn butter, held it as a few drop fell back into the cup, and then popped the morsel into her mouth.

He took a bite of steak, chewed, and swallowed. "Everything okay?" he asked nodding to the food.

"Wonderful."

"It's my business to know people," he answered her question. "Honestly, I've gotten to know these people over some years. Tina's grandson has cancer. I met him when I visited the Children's Hospital. She happened to be there that day. He was still recovering from surgery but insisted he be allowed to see the show, so they wheeled him down on a gurney. I went to up to his room later and found out how much he likes magic, so I got the kit."

Jasmine sipped her wine and watched him, purposefully bringing an image of Dorian to mind. A wave of Eryk's black hair had fallen over a brow, in a similar way Dorian's had a tendency to do. Eryk had more creases beside his eyes, probably a result of squinting into the sun. Although the men had very similar DNA, they were very different. She buttered a roll and handed it to him, then took one for herself. "I bet *visit* wasn't all you did, was it?"

"What do you mean?" He took a bite of the roll.

"I'll wager you gave the kid a little push of energy." She nibbled on the bread and offered him a big grin. "Just like you did Tina when you hugged her."

"Maybe a little one." He held up his fingers indicating a pinch.

She raised one brow.

He widened the space.

Jasmine leaned back, studied him before speaking. "You can't tell me you only treated one child."

He swirled the wine in his glass, lost in thought. "No. I won't tell you that. But, I've learned I have to be careful."

"How so?"

"It was my first show at one of the hospitals in Atlanta, in fact. I had already figured out that I could aid. Not heal, mind you. I'd tried that on some injured wildlife." He pulled his sweater away from his neck. A scar, long, thin and whiter than the rest of his skin, ran from the back of his ear, down and around, disappearing under the hand that held the sweater away.

Jasmine leaned forward, her hand reaching forward to touch the pulse she sensed next to his scar, caught herself and clasped her wine glass instead. She took a gulp of wine and choked.

"You all right?" he asked, yet his eyes held a smile. He'd seen the subtle movement and it had his pulse race just a shade faster.

"Fine," she coughed.

"Anyway. When I saw all those kids, I just couldn't help myself. I went to everyone they would let me near."

"What happened?"

"Carl found me passed out when he came to check the room. God knows how he knew, but he ordered coffee and food. I spent that night and the next eating and resting. I couldn't do the show the next night. It took almost a week for the headache to go away."

He rose. "Speaking of coffee, do you want some?"

"No. I'm fine."

Eryk poured himself a cup and returned to the table. "I've learned to pace myself. I still make it through the wards, but I do it in days, not hours."

Jasmine got a faraway look, staring into her wine. When she looked back up at him, her eyes twinkled. He could feel the sudden rise in energy coming off her. "Eryk, do you ever do a one man show?"

"My shows are one man," he defended.

"No," she waved her hand. "I mean without props or a crew."

"In the children's pods at the hospital, sometimes. Some sleight-of-hand. Why?"

"I really should discuss this with Jenn first, but, if she okays it, do you think you might do one for the kids at Safe Harbor. I know she'd never go for the crew, but maybe a one man show?"

He leaned forward, unaware that her energy was pulling at him, an instant turn-on.

"Eryk, these kids have been through so much, seen so much. They come to Safe Harbor, leaving whatever life they had behind and they are pretty cloistered for a long time. They aren't ill. Well, most aren't—at least not physically—"

He reached across the table and took her hand. "I would love to do it. You work it out and I'll come." Energy sparked between them and he released her hand.

She didn't seem to notice. "Would you? It would mean so much to them. I just know it would." She pulled out her phone, remembered they were at dinner, and set it on the table. "I'll call her after dinner," she tried to sound calm as she cut a piece of steak and popped it in her mouth.

Eryk sat back, chuckling. "I love it when you get excited. Your eyes dance."

Jasmine offered him a coy smile and tried not to rush through dinner.

****

Her swollen tongue tasted the coppery metallic tang of her own blood as it eased across her cut lip. She couldn't close her mouth. The last blow had misaligned her bottom jaw. A tooth moved when her tongue pressed on it. Son-of-a-bitch!

She smelled his fetid breath as the spittle hit her face. She turned her head away, but he snapped it back with his fist.

"You're gonna do it, bitch," he snarled. "I know you can. If you don't, Morgan will."

She no longer felt the pain in her arm as he tore the rest of her sleeve off. She had ceased to feel the pain after he'd pulled her arm out of her shoulder socket. It lay dead beside her.

His body was heavy as he pummeled into her, his sweat sticky and rank.

Tiny bursts of energy tingled in her fingertips. She had it. She stopped fighting him and reached for the energy, letting it move through her body to her good hand. With every ounce of determination she possessed, she thrust the energy out from her. His weight left her body. She concentrated and tried to produce more, shooting into the dark. He was somewhere. Jasmine let the energy surge through her and explode from her in rapid bursts, along with her screams.

****

The scream cut through him like a jagged knife, tearing into his soul. Eryk shot up, tossing the sheet on the floor, and hit the door on a run. He could see flashes strobing from the space beneath her closed door. As he gripped the doorknob, another scream tore through the night and he threw the door open, only to be slammed by a bolt of energy, knocking him back.

Jasmine twisted on the bed, one arm under her back, the other flailing, throwing balls and jagged bolts of energy in rapid succession around the room. Her black eyes were open, staring blindly at the horror from the abyss of a nightmare.

"Jasmine," he called, trying not to yell. The fear he heard and saw made it difficult for him not to rush the bed. He blinked. She came into view, shimmering like a lightning bolt, her whole being afire with energy.

"Shit," he cursed and blinked while diving to the floor to avoid another bolt. The last one had burned like hell.

He crawled toward the bed like a marine breaching a moonlit beach and came up on the other side of the bed. Just as he called her name, she let out another scream. He leapt onto the bed, grabbed her and rolled onto his side, getting her off that arm.

"Jasmine...," he called, feeling the pulse of energy burn through him, "...it's me, Eryk...," he tried to push against it, only to have it charge back. "Damn." He felt his body jerk as the energy gushed through him. He tried to take a deep breath and open his senses, accepting it instead of fighting it. Like tendrils, it slithered around his own threads of energy and grabbed hold, squeezing.

"Jasmine," he modulated his tone as best he could, "it's Eryk. You're having a dream."

She stilled. Another pulse went through him. He took it, letting his body adjust to her erratic rhythm, wondering how long before he lost consciousness. It felt like he was being defibrillated. Then, his heartbeat found hers and matched, beating wildly. He concentrated and slowed the beats. It seemed to take forever, concentrating while holding a wild woman, bent on destroying him. Finally, with one last jerk, her rigid body went limp against his.

He shifted, gently easing her onto the mattress. The sweat-drenched T-shirt she wore molded every line and the boy shorts had hiked up to reveal a gorgeous hip. When his eyes moved back to her face, she was watching him.

"Welcome back, luv," he said softly.

The fog began to clear and Jasmine stared at him, confused, waiting for understanding to unfold. Her eyes grew wide as she remembered the dream. She hadn't had one this bad since the first week after the attack and then she hadn't had the means to fight.

"Eryk," her voice wavered. She bolted upright. "Oh, God, Eryk!" She reached a hand toward him and stopped, drawing it back. "Did I hurt you?"

"I'm okay," he lied and swung his legs over the edge of the bed, sitting up.

Jasmine touched his side and he winced. She reached around him and turned on the light. His shirtless chest looked as though he'd been stung by a hundred jellyfish.

She tentatively reached out and tenderly touched a welt. "Oh, Eryk. I'm so sorry."

He took a deep breath. "I said I'm okay. I'll be fine. Are you all right?"

She took a deep breath and released it, also releasing the last bit of tension. "I'm think so. I don't know what happened."

He was trying not to look at her breasts, the wet T-shirt plastered against perfect mounds. "I think you somehow got your arm caught under you. When I came in, you were flailing." He looked away.

She rubbed the arm that tingled from the lack of blood flow and tried to put order to her world. Realizing how she was dressed—or wasn't—she grabbed at the sheet.

He shook his head and chuckled, but shifted so she could cover up. "I do believe that particular horse has left the barn."

Chapter Nine

As Jasmine let the hot spray of the shower pound on her back, she wondered if it had been just a nightmare. Or, had she suffered a flashback to what had happened in that mine a year ago. No matter what it was, she wondered how long it would have gone on had Eryk not intervened. Unknown triggers kept propelling her back into that hell without warning. At the moment, Jasmine wasn't as confident of her recovery as she had been a few weeks ago. Her fingers trembled with that realization.

The short shower and fresh clothes helped chase away the vestiges of what remained of the trauma. However, she still needed to face Eryk.

Jasmine emerged from the bedroom running her fingers through her still damp hair into a light-flooded living room. He'd turned on every available lamp for her. The aroma of hot coffee led her to the kitchen. As she passed the front door, it clicked and Eryk stepped in, his dark green sweater enhancing the emerald green color of his eyes. Her reaction was animalistic. She tried to smile and felt embarrassment heat her face.

"Coffee?" she asked and turned to the kitchen hoping he hadn't caught the lust shining in her eyes, particularly right after the horrid scene in the bedroom.

"Sure." He followed her and let the newspaper drop on the table as he passed.

She handed him a mug of black coffee, stirred sugar into her own, and watched the swirls. The sugar was another recent change. Now, she liked the sweet offsetting the bite of the coffee. In the last year, it seemed she'd wanted everything to be softer, smoother, or sweeter. Was it her compensating or was it physiological changes in her? She took a sip and embraced the hot and sweet flavor running down her throat.

Without looking at him directly, she murmured over the coffee, "About the damages…."

"Already taken care of," he said and followed her over to the table. "I told them you found a wasp in your room last night and, being allergic, went a little crazy."

Remembering how she'd shot Morgan in the face with wasp spray, she commented, "You aren't far wrong."

He saw the blush move up the slender neck emerging from the black angora sweater and followed the soft drapes as it flowed over even softer curves. He swallowed and looked away, moving the chair to sit down at the table.

"The hotel is extremely sorry and hopes you're okay," he explained. "There will be no charges to our room and they asked if you wanted them to change our accommodations. I assured them that the beast had been dealt with and you are fine. They will send someone up today while we're gone to straighten the room." He smiled at her. "I set the pieces of the broken lamp in the front closet."

Her face reddened. Eryk reached out and laid his hand over hers. She felt the tingle, almost imperceptible now.

"Want to talk about it?" he asked.

At first, Jasmine shook her head, then changed her mind. She leaned back in her chair, pulling her hand from under his. "Being raised in Ruthorford gives one a great sense of security. It's a small town and most of the people in town and on the farms surrounding the town have known each other all of their lives. Yes, we have some odd happenstances, but for us, it's all normal."

A tap on the door halted her next words. Eryk went to answer it and returned with a platter of piping hot pastries, compliments of the house. "They really hope you are okay."

At the smell of the pastry, Jasmine realized she was ravenous and thought back to what Morgan had said. She grabbed a bear claw and bit into it and, wiping the sugar from her lips and looked at the platter. "Good thing I'm not a diabetic," she said.

Eryk brought the coffee pot over, filled her cup, and topped his off. "Go on," he encouraged.

"Needless to say, I grew up trusting just about—no, not just about—everyone, with no exceptions. I knew a dating line when I heard one, of course. But, when I ran into Rob while I was on vacation, I thought nothing of it, other than coincidence. When he drugged me, I didn't understand. I was chained to a timber, lying on the cold ground. He was ranting and raving. He would unhook me, drag me down the shaft of the mine and demand that I tell him where the veins were. At first, I told him I didn't know what he was talking about. He'd hit me, drag me back up, chain me back to the timber and rant and rave some more. I tried reasoning with him."

She shuddered at the memory. "The look in his eyes told me he didn't believe me. I think he was delusional. He thought all women in Ruthorford were like Morgan." She looked into Eryk's eyes. "Or you. At first, I was ashamed that I wasn't. When I finally told him I didn't have any abilities, he beat me up, yelling at me that I was lying. Then something happened. I'll never forget the look on his face. It was like he'd gone completely crazy." Her brow furrowed as she thought back. "Suddenly, he started talking about going to get Morgan. I panicked. I didn't want him to do to her what he was doing to me. I tried to make him think that it was him, not me, who was the problem." She stopped to compose herself.

Eryk took her hand. "You don't have to go on."

"You asked. After last night, you deserve—" she stopped when his hand tightened on hers and amended her statement. "I want you to know…everything," she stared into her cup.

"I'm not sure what happened at that point. He drugged me again. When I came to, my clothes were torn. I told him the drug was having a dampening effect and I couldn't do anything with my arms tied. So, he unchained me and dragged me to the cavern, saying he remembered that we had to have sex to make it happen. He tore off the rest of my clothes. I fought like a banshee. I kicked him in the groin. He threw the chain around my neck and yanked me to the ground. I lost consciousness. When I came to he was raping me. Then, he beat me again. This went on over and over. I passed out. Or, I think I did. When I came to, he was on me. Spittle was dripping from his mouth, like a rabid dog. He seemed disoriented, like he was trying to remember what to do. He seemed almost shocked to see me underneath him. That's when he dragged me back up and chained me to the timber. At some point, he dislocated my arm and I passed out again. When I regained consciousness, he was gone. Dorian almost didn't find me because I was afraid it was Rob returning." Tears fell onto the table.

Eryk didn't say anything. He couldn't. Every fiber of his being wanted to kill the man that had done that to her. He could feel the energy pulsing through his body. He got up and walked to the window, looking out across the cityscape, willing himself to calm down. He felt her hand on his back.

"Eryk," she said, her voice trembling. "I'd understand if—"

He spun around so fast she jumped, stumbling. He grabbed her arms. "Don't you even say...." He looked into her shadowed black eyes. "Jasmine," his voice softened and he eased her forward, bringing her as close as possible, until his arms enfolded her. "I moved away because I didn't want to frighten you, not because I'm repulsed." Eryk stroked her soft hair until her head rested against his chest. He felt her arms go around him, tentatively at first, then tightening, until she was holding him as tightly as he was her. They stood there, holding on. He felt their heartbeats catch and hold and he felt himself reacting to her in a way he couldn't help, silently cursing the "match-mate" thing happening between them.

Eryk eased away from her, putting her at arm's length. As he stepped back, he saw the tears shimmering in her eyes. He kissed her forehead, took her hand, and led her back to the table. "It's a good thing I don't know where this Rob is," he muttered, more to himself than her and held her chair as she sat.

"He's in a rehabilitation facility," she offered, she voice soft, but still throaty from their closeness. "He has no memory of what happened. He doesn't even know who I am." She took his hand across the table. "I was pretty messed up when I arrived at Safe Harbor. However, I healed quickly and, as I healed, I changed. The thing is, I did heal. He hasn't."

"You're lucky you didn't get...," his words faltered.

"Pregnant? Or worse?" she asked, tilting her head. "I'm lucky I was given the morning after pill at the hospital. I don't know how I would have handled that, to be honest with you."

Jasmine absently picked up a pastry, broke off a piece, and took a bite before continuing "What I've seen at Safe Harbor shows me every day how lucky I was...and am. Believe me when I tell you, this was nothing compared to what others have been through—for years. Both adults and children. Not just physically, but mentally. And then, in order to be safe, they have to give up everything they have and everything they were." She let out a sound. "It's a shame we can't remove the offender—permanently—and give them some semblance of normalcy. We can't. Therefore, we do the best we can. You don't know how often I've wished I could give them just a little of the power I now have. Just enough so that they'd feel less afraid. Like I do." She raised her hand, flattened it, and a ball of energy danced on her palm, before vanishing into thin air.

"Well, you weren't helpless last night, that's for sure. I'm just sorry you went through that." He tried to smile, rubbing his jaw. "At least I know you can take care of yourself."

"John Davis, who takes care of the security at Safe Harbor and happens to be a descendant of Ruthorford—a Native American descendant—is teaching self-defense to Safe Harbor's residents, adults and children alike. I've taken several of his classes, myself. If nothing else, it helps rebuild confidence."

The sun broke over the tops of the buildings, sending a pink glow into the living room. "I think I'll take some coffee out on the balcony, if you don't mind. You're welcome to join me." Jasmine's voice was soft, her mind far away.

Wanting to give her some time, he picked up the plate of remaining pastries. "If you're done with these, I think I'll finish them off while I get some work done before we have to go. I need to rearrange a few things on my schedule." He saw her smile as he took a big bite. "I'm famished."

Jasmine rose and, topping off the mug, went out on the balcony and sat at the table nestled in the corner, away from the wind and, for her, the height. She set her mug on the table, enjoying the early morning.

She'd done it. She'd shared what had happened to her. Of course, Eryk Vreeland couldn't be counted as just anyone. As to what happened the night before, it was as though he'd absorbed her energy and fed it back to her in a different form, a form so warm and loving, Jasmine knew it would be a long time before that memory dimmed, if ever.

A shadow swept over the edge of the balcony. She held her breath. As it passed once more, she got the oddest sensation. She gripped the edge of the chair until the slight wave of nausea passed. She squinted and saw the wind catch a leaf in the *gutter* on the road below, sending it dancing along, until it disappeared into the storm grate. How was that possible? She blinked, realized she was still in the chair, gripping its arms, and tried to steady her nerves. In front of her, sitting on the balcony rail, watching the street below, was a large falcon. Jasmine had no idea how long she sat there, studying the gray-brown feathers ruffling in the cool breeze, afraid to move or even breathe, not wanting it to leave. Its head twisted and it looked her in the eye, gave a screech, and took off, its wings spreading to catch an updraft.

Jasmine leapt from the chair, grabbed the door and ran straight into Eryk. She squeaked, "Did you see?"

"I've been standing back a little, so I wouldn't disturb it. I was afraid it might…no, that's not right…you were so motionless…just staring." He pulled her away from the door and closed it. "Just in case it comes back." He chuckled. "A wasp is one thing, a hawk another."

"Oh, Eryk. It was amazing." She ran her hands through her short hair. "I think I've figured it out." Jasmine started pacing and looked at her watch. Too early to leave. "I've got to talk to Bask."

"Give me a minute and we'll go. I have a strange feeling that man is already there, if he doesn't live there."

"He doesn't," she called to Eryk's back as he disappeared into his room. "But he lives damn close," she added to the closed door.

****

The drive to Abbott House took closer to forty minutes than ten, after "Mildred," as they began calling the vehicle's GPS, wound them in and around town and got them stuck in two traffic jams. Fortunately, at the last intersection—where they'd been sitting for damn near five minutes—Jasmine recognized a side street and had Eryk cut across three lanes of traffic onto the narrow street, which wasn't as harrowing as it could have been since the oncoming traffic was also at a stand-still. Eryk shut down "Mildred" after her fourth "make a U-turn."

Eryk asked question after question about Abbott House and Bask. Still not knowing exactly how vetted he was, Jasmine fed him the media version. The Ruthorford version she decided to leave to Bask. Eryk already knew more than most; plus, he *was* Dorian's twin. But, she hadn't been cleared on what she could and couldn't tell him so, until then, she decided to play it safe.

The sun disappeared and a cold drizzle helped slow the drive even further. Finally, Jasmine pointed and Eryk hit the brakes and swung up a short drive to a closed gate. Hesitantly, he slipped his hand through the ivy and pressed the speaker button Jasmine assured him was hidden among the vines. He announced them and watched as the high iron gates slid back. As he eased through, a palatial, deep red brick mansion, complete with clinging ivy, loomed at the top of the winding drive. The shroud of overcast gray added just the right touch of drama.

Eryk let out a low whistle. "What did you say the Abbott-Ruthorford connection was?"

"Kind of a chicken-egg thing. Pull on around," Jasmine pointed, indicating the front. There is a porte-cochere on either side. I use the one on the far side. Carport," she added when he looked at her.

"I know what a porte-cochere is. Just surprised you did," he teased.

Eryk eased the vehicle over the packed gravel and under the covering, pulling to the left, which would leave room for another car to pass through or stop beside him. Jasmine was already climbing out by the time he came around the car.

"Won't you at least let me *try* to be a gentleman?"

She just looked back at him with that come-hither grin of hers and opened the massive wooden door. They stepped into a wide side hallway. The wood floor gleamed even in the low light.

"Missy?" Jasmine called out.

They walked down the hall and stepped into a gigantic foyer. Even by Eryk's standards, having come from a family who thrived on *palatial*, this was huge. In the middle of the impressive room sat an ornately carved reception desk. An elegant woman looked over her shoulder and smiled at Jasmine. When she stood, she was easily five-foot-eleven and striking.

"Missy, this is Eryk. Eryk, this is *Miss* Gwynn."

Missy took Eryk's outstretched hand. "My name is Esmeralda, but Mr. Bask asks that I be Miss Gwynn or Ms. Gwynn. Jasmine couldn't stand it when she was interning and thus started the Missy. He's in the library, by the way. Do you want to wait in his office?"

"No. I want to show Eryk the library, if that's okay?" Jasmine waited for Missy's nod and led Eryk to the wide stone steps. They split on a landing before curving back and heading to another floor.

"Nice to meet you," Eryk said over his shoulder as he followed Jasmine. Out of the corner of his eye, he saw Missy punch a button, probably signaling Bask of their arrival.

Jasmine stopped on the first landing, looking out of the expanse of windows. Far below and stretching back quite a ways was a formal English garden with a tall hedge maze in the very back. Eryk knew immediately this was something for which his father would gladly commit larceny. The elder Vreeland had been paying landscape architects a fortune for as long as he could remember to emulate such a spread. The estate had actually grown quite impressive over the years, but compared to this, it was paltry.

Eryk's quick movement kept Jasmine from falling into the window glass. He held onto her arm, steadying her. "You okay?"

She blinked and looked from him to the window, frowning.

"What happened?" He wasn't letting go of her arm until he knew she was all right.

"It happened again," she said in a low tone, almost a whisper. "Let's find Bask."

He kept his hand on her back, walking one step down—just in case.

"I'm all right. Honest."

"Then humor me," he said and stayed close to her until they were on the large landing.

Jasmine nodded to a door. "That's his office. The library's this way." She turned and headed down a hallway until she came to a set of tall, arched mahogany doors. She opened the right one and stepped inside.

The scent of oiled leather filled the room. Long rows of mahogany bookcases, filled with leather-bound tomes, towered in neat rows. There were large chairs with side tables and lamps set about for casual reading. Huge mahogany library tables, the grandeur of which he'd never seen, offered places to study. On one side sat several glass cases, displaying special volumes.

"Hey, old man, where are you?" Jasmine called. She followed an "in the fourth row, second stack," winding her way around, obviously familiar with the huge facility until she came to an area with another library table. Bask stood, rolling down his sleeves. Books were scattered over the table, as were several legal pads. A laptop and a tablet computer were shoved aside in favor of pen and paper.

"Don't get dressed on our account," Jasmine teased, walked over, and planted a kiss on the weathered cheek.

Bask smiled at her, turned and offered Eryk his hand. "I've been doing some research."

"Isn't that what you have peons for? Like me." Jasmine quipped.

He rolled his eyes. "Not like you. Never like you. Lord help me if another *you* shows up." He turned to Eryk. "Would you prefer to talk here or in my office?"

"Here's fine. Wherever the information is," he added.

"Then, please, take a seat."

They walked around the table and sat across from Bask while he stacked some books in different piles and organized his notes. "I wish I had more information for you, Eryk. I don't. I started doing research on Dorian's parentage years ago and kept coming to a dead end. I have a feeling Donald Vreeland has more information than I do at this point."

Eryk stilled his nerves. He felt the anger and agitation moving through him, unchecked. Jasmine's hand moved slowly onto his leg and she gave a reassuring squeeze. He let his hand drop onto his leg and he entwined his fingers with hers. The energy drifted back and forth, forming a slower rhythm.

Bask watched the two people across from him. Their mutual support did not escape his attention—they were growing closer by the moment. He wanted a good relationship for Jasmine. But, he also wanted to make sure this was it, before he gave his approval.

"You have to remember," Bask said, "when you and Dorian were born, DNA matching wasn't available. And honestly, with all the evidence pointing to Dorian being the only living child, we didn't pursue...," he faltered, a grimace crossing his brow. He took a breath and went on, "You changed things." He pushed a couple of faxed sheets across the table toward Eryk. "We still don't have any DNA from your birth mother. The woman who died around the time Dorian was found, we believe, was cremated. We are still looking into it."

In the distance, a door opened and shut. They could hear footfalls and Miss Gwynn appeared with a tray laden with glasses and a pitcher of iced tea. She set down coasters, drinks and napkins, and set a plate of scones on the only empty spot on the table. Without a word, she turned and left.

Jasmine took a scone, placed it on a napkin and slid it in front of Eryk before grabbing one for herself, all the while keeping her other hand linked with his.

Bask watched, expressionless.

"The papers in front of you are what I have found from the hospitals around the time of your birth, searching for twin births during that time. It took some digging, since most records have long been archived." He tapped a highlighted section with his pen. "This one is of particular interest. A woman gave birth to a set of twins, one of which was stillborn. She gave her name as Jane Doe. The name of the surviving male child is listed as Dorian. Identification we found in the apartment listed the woman's name as Janice Drake. Some paperwork we found on the child from a health clinic listed her child as Dorian Drake. We aren't sure of anything at this point, other than the fact that you and Dorian have matching DNA."

"May I keep this? Or have a copy?" He was holding the papers Bask had pushed in front of him.

"That's a copy. It's yours." He handed a manila envelope to Eryk. "I'm sorry, Eryk. I wish I had more for you. It looks like someone went to a great deal of trouble to obliterate any records."

"Thanks."

Bask interrupted. "One more thing. I want you to stop by the lab. I need some blood and DNA samples. Also, I'd like a CAT scan and a MRI on both of you."

"Where?"

"Jasmine will show you."

Eryk nodded and looked at Jasmine. "Your turn."

She released his hand and rested both of her hands on top of the table, set a pensive look on her face, and waited to get Bask's full attention.

"Is there anything in all these journals," she let her eyes skim over the room, "about someone looking through the eyes of a bird?"

Bask grabbed a legal pad, pulled it in front of him, and began writing. "You know the drill," he said without looking up. "What happened? When? How many times?"

Jasmine gave an exaggerated roll of her eyes and a slow shake of her head. "I didn't take notes."

Bask glanced at her as if to say, "Why not?" but said nothing, waiting with pen poised.

She tried to think back. "Something happened at the fair. But, not like what happened on the plane. Yes, I believe the first time it happened was in the plane on the way here. I didn't know what it was, then. All I knew was that I was outside the plane and I could see the ground. Then—it was the other night—I was going up to my apartment. I heard an owl and turned. Suddenly, I was flying through the air, looking at the ground. I could see bugs in the dark." She turned to Eryk and smiled before finishing. "I'd opened the door, so when I lost my balance, I fell into my apartment, landing on my wrist. Eryk arrived, having heard me with his super hearing, came to my rescue and reset my wrist joint." She moved her hand around in circles, demonstrating its apparent good health.

Eryk narrowed his eyes at her. She sent him a cocky smile and lifted a singular brow, knowing what was coming next.

As if on cue, Bask asked, "What super hearing?"

Jasmine's smile turned into a full-blown grin.

"Hyperacusis. Since I was very young." Eryk watched the man flip a sheet and start scribbling like crazy. He decided to turn the attention back to Jasmine. "Jasmine's last episode occurred right before we came here. Oh, and that moment on the stairs." Eryk narrowed his emerald eyes and grinned right back at her.

Bask stopped writing and looked up. He appeared to weigh his thoughts, torn between which avenue to pursue. He glanced down at his previous notes before flipping the sheet of yellow legal paper back, poising his pen. "Okay, tell me what happened," he said to Jasmine.

"It was like in the airplane, except, I was sitting on the balcony, finishing my coffee when, out of nowhere, I was looking at a leaf blowing in a gutter. When I shifted—that's the only word for it—I was sitting in the chair. There was a hawk on the railing."

Bask started to say something and stopped when Jasmine held up her hand. "Then, it happened here, on the landing."

"Here?" Bask looked up at her.

"Yep. Right here in Abbott House. I was looking out the window over the grounds and felt the shift start. This time it didn't follow through. Eryk grabbed me before I fell into the window." Her color heightened. "I get kinda dizzy at first."

"I can understand that. What else?"

She sat straighter. "Isn't that enough?" She threw up her hands in frustration. "In the last year I've gained abilities I've never had before and now this."

Bask had the courtesy to look sheepish. "Sorry. Sometimes, I get carried away."

Jasmine smiled. "You think?"

He made another note and closed the legal pad. Moving several books on the table, he pulled out a copy of a drawing and put it in front of Eryk. "This is a sketch of a Gulatega."

Eryk looked at the black and white drawing. The drawing depicted a cross between a cat and a raccoon. The snout was very short and the eyes were large and long. No fur had been drawn in, but a shadow had been added around it.

He studied it and set it aside, running a hand through his jet black hair. That errant wave Jasmine found so beguiling, fell forward. "Okay. I know I'm different. But, there are many people who are different. People who absorb electricity and release it—people who attract lightning." He noticed Jasmines expression and added, "No, I've never been hit by lightning."

He waved his hand toward the sketch. "But this...first, a dimensional portal...then, these creatures. I just don't know. I am having trouble wrapping my mind around this."

"Wait here." Jasmine got up and disappeared down one of the isles. She reappeared with several large volumes in her arms. He rose to help but she dumped them on the table, grabbed one and started flipping through it.

He sat back down and waited. Bask didn't say a word. When she found what she was looking for, she slid it in front of him. It was another sketch of the cat-like creature, curled up. The next page was a watercolor. The creature was on all fours, the violet outline surrounding it appeared more opaque than the creature. Its eyes glowed with the same violet color.

Jasmine turned another page and Eryk was looking at what could have been a photograph of the garden between The Shoppe of Spells and its cottage. It wasn't quite like any photograph he'd seen before. The picture focused on the head of one of the creatures outlined in a violet color. Again, the eyes glowed.

Before he could comment, Jasmine pulled another volume from underneath and opened it, resting it on top of the previous one. She flipped through several pages, found what she was looking for, and tapped her finger on the page. A pale, emaciated man sat in a chair, a vacant look on his face. She turned the page back. A robust man was laughing, sitting by the fountain in front of The Shoppe of Spells. "That was before Morgan's parents died." She turned the page, once again, to the emaciated man. "This is the same person a month after they died."

Bask reached over and took the book, turned to the end, and pulled out a photograph. "And this is four months after Morgan and Dorian drove the Gulatega back through the portal." He handed the picture to Eryk.

Eryk studied the picture, comparing it to those in the book. "Damn" was his only comment.

Still studying the picture, he said, "You said a man went through the portal."

"Ian. Yes," Bask nodded. "Apparently he had taken on some of the Gulatega's qualities. In particular, the violet outline and an intensity to the eyes."

He hesitated before continuing. "Much like Bill."

Eryk's gaze settled on Jasmine as she looked at Bask, comprehension and sadness heavy in her expression. Without thinking, he reached toward her face, realized what he was doing and pulled back his hand. "The violet color, there has to be a connection."

"I've never seen them, but I'd know them anywhere. I grew up staring at them. Let's show him your desk," Jasmine said. Without meeting Eryk's gaze, she turned and headed toward the door.

Bask didn't need to be asked twice and Jasmine knew it. He loved that desk. It was his pride and joy. Bask stepped around them, leading them across the upper lobby, where he stopped, opened the door, and held it for them to enter.

The office was done in dark wood paneling. The gray day cast the room into shadow, yet Eryk could imagine light filtering through the stained glass, streaming jewel tones across the room. It was a fabulous room. A huge oriental carpet covered the hardwood floor and in the middle of the floor sat a magnificent desk. It looked to be hand carved. Burled wood, darkened, maybe.

Eryk stepped closer. The top appeared to be held up by four gargoyles. Except Eryk knew from what he'd just seen that they weren't gargoyles—but the Gulatega.

"Meet the Musketeers," Jasmine intoned. "Athos, Porthos, Aramis—"

"—and d'Artagnan," Eryk finished and walked over to examine the carved figures. He moved his hand across the soft wood finish. "Amazing."

"Aren't they?" Jasmine stepped over and rubbed the carved figure, almost as one would a Buddha for good luck.

Eryk turned to Bask. "How? Where?"

Bask walked around the desk and sat in the plush oxblood leather chair, smiling.

"Now you've done it," Jasmine said and plopped down in one of the two club chairs facing the desk, sitting sideways and letting a leg swing over the arm, very much at home with the austere man.

Bask narrowed his eyes at her but spoke with affection when he began. "We don't have any history on this desk. It was found at an estate in South Carolina in the twenties, bought, and brought to the Abbott House. The likenesses are remarkable—so I'm told. I've never seen them." He turned to Eryk "You, and those like you, don't see them as a solid entity, but as vague violet outlines. The eyes have more intense color. They are about the size of cats and move as quickly. We haven't seen any since Ian went through at Meadow's Keep, which brings us to that issue." He sat up straighter.

"I don't know how I feel about sending you two on this assignment, since both of you are novices. But, since I've never seen them attack anyone—"

"With the exception of the man who took Meadow—" Jasmine piped up.

"Yes. Well, there is that."

"Didn't they also go after Dorian?" Jasmine turned around in the chair.

"Yes." Bask nodded. "I think that was an unusual circumstance. They got confused while protecting Ian. As soon as Morgan connected with him, they scattered."

"You aren't making me feel warm and fuzzy over here." Eryk interrupted.

Bask turned to Eryk. "Ian had an unusual affinity for the creatures—or they, him," he corrected. "And, apparently, his daughter, Meadow. She called them his pets." He turned and looked at Jasmine. "He hasn't met Meadow, has he?" He asked but continued before either of them spoke. "Of course he hasn't. But, he will and I'll warrant he'll understand. She's a very special young woman."

Eryk looked to Jasmine for clarification.

Bask provided it. "Meadow is a very special blend of the direct Native American line and direct Scottish line. This combination hasn't been around in a long time."

Eryk pulled his phone out of his pocket, glanced at it, hit a button and shoved it back into the pocket again. He frowned at Bask. "Sorry. Are you saying all Scots—?"

"Not at all." Bask's brows furrowed. "Not...no, just those from Ian's clan. Ian claimed he was the last living member. We're looking into that."

"What about Jasmine and me? It's my understanding that each of us is rather unique...." He stopped, pulled the phone out of his pocket again and looked at Bask. "I'm sorry,

I really need to take this." He rose and was making some comment as he left the room, closing the door behind him.

Bask reached over and pressed a button on his desk phone. Eryk's voice came through the speaker. "...he's where?"

Jasmine leaned across the desk and pressed the same button. "Have you no shame?" she chided.

"Not where Ruthorford—or you—are concerned." He was silent for a moment, studying her. "Let me send in someone from West Virginia," he suggested.

She narrowed her eyes at him. It wasn't like Bask to *suggest* anything. He was more of the command/demand type. She felt her spine stiffen and she sat up straight, using her posture to confront him. Before she could get two words out, Eryk walked back into the room.

"You don't think we can handle it?" he asked and walked over to stand behind Jasmine.

At Bask's look of surprise, he laughed and pointed to his ear. "Hyperacusis, remember? *I* can't help eavesdropping." He raised a single brow.

Bask leaned back in his chair and observed the two before him. How many times had he seen that same raised brow directed at him from the woman sitting in front of Eryk. Damn if they weren't a handsome couple, he thought. But, he'd wanted more time for her to heal. Hell, he just wanted to protect her. He knew he felt more like a father to the little hellcat than he ever wanted to admit. She'd clawed her spitfire ways right into his heart from the time she could walk—and sass back. Then, when her parents had died, leaving her alone, he'd thought about adopting her himself. But, what would an old bachelor do with an almost teenager, already with too much mouth and more daring than sense.

When Teresa had stepped up, he'd slipped, once again, into the background.

But, he watched. When she'd been kidnapped, he'd almost gone mad. Luckily, Dorian found her and Morgan's friend, Jenn Davis, took her to Safe Harbor to help her recover. Naturally, Safe Harbor had received a healthy endowment. He let a faint glimmer of a smile show. They— no...Jasmine—had done a great job. She, once again, had the fire in her eyes and the confidence he'd been afraid was gone forever, after the attack. He needed to stop being overly protective. She was smart and talented, and together she and Eryk would make a valuable team.

Eryk spoke up. "I don't know if this will help. I need to go to Virginia Beach anyway. Some personal business. I understand Meadow's Keep is nearby."

When Jasmine turned her head and looked up at him, he couldn't resist and ran his hand over her soft, black hair. He received one of her dazzling smiles, almost as a reward. He felt the joy bubble up from his very core. Looking into her eyes, he said softly, "Dad's in Virginia Beach, and I've made arrangements for some materials to arrive in Williamsburg for that project we talked about. I don't see why a side trip to Meadow's Keep shouldn't fit right in."

Jasmine was thrilled that he remembered their conversation about a private performance at Safe Harbor. She had, in fact, cleared it through Jenn, who'd laughingly commented, "He'll have a *captive* audience, that's for sure."

Sometimes families didn't leave the safety of the grounds, even the building, for months. That's one of the reasons she tried so hard to give them something to make them smile. The make-overs helped. A fashion show would, too. But, a magic show with Eryk Vreeland. Now, that was something special. She'd tried to get his assistant, Brandy, okayed to assist him, but that had been nixed. It looked like Jasmine was going to be sawed in half.

Bask let out an exasperated sigh. "All right, you two. Go get checked out while I make arrangements. Oh, don't forget to stop by Miss Gwyn's desk and sign the paperwork." He was already messing with papers on his desk. "Come back up before you leave and I'll have things in place."

"Eryk," he called without looking up, "are you flying or do you want to use our plane?"

Eryk pulled the door open and stood back, letting Jasmine pass through, "I'll fly. I'll get clearance and we'll leave late morning."

Bask, writing on one of his ever-present legal pads, waved his hand at them, "Fine, fine. I'll have a car waiting at the Newport News International Airport."

As they closed the door, Bask waited a few seconds and pressed the button. He could hear them talking to Miss Gwinn. Feeling comfortable that Eryk was out of earshot, he hit speed-dial.

"John speaking."

"Did you do that background check I asked for?"

"Yes. He's pretty much what he appears. Well, except for the abilities. He's dedicated to his craft and is renowned in the field. Well respected by other illusionists, by the way. There's a bit of jealousy as well, since they can't figure out how he's perfected some of his illusions so far beyond them. He keeps to himself. Dates occasionally, but isn't known as a big lover-boy. He does a lot of charity work. His corporation is large and he has his fingers in many pies, including his father's holdings. I'm not sure his father is aware of the extent Eryk is involved. That's all I've got so far. Will that do for now?"

"How do you feel about him coming to Safe Harbor?"

"I'll be there. It shouldn't be a problem, if he comes alone. I don't want to have to deal with more than one intruder at a time."

"Understood," Bask said and hung up.

Chapter Ten

Jasmine led Eryk to the elevators tucked under the stone steps. One had to know they were there to think of looking for them, and then only if they got past Ms. Gwynn.

Eryk looked back and noticed the cameras discretely positioned in the crown molding. This place had better security than some of his father's sites, and they had Top Secret ratings. The elevator doors slid open so quietly that Jasmine had to tug on him to get his attention. Eryk found himself wondering how that had escaped his hearing.

The doors closed and she hit a button. In spite of the aged beauty of the polished mahogany paneling and the carved handrails, Eryk had no doubt the elevator was state of the art. It slid silently down one floor and stopped. Jasmine opened a small panel and punched in a code. The elevator moved downward again and stopped. When the door opened, Eryk stepped into a sterile hallway, easily resembling a hospital or a well-funded laboratory. Several people moved from room to room. All wore white lab coats and displayed digitized badges.

"Hey, Jasmine," a young woman called. "Good to see you."

Jasmine nodded as the woman disappeared behind the tinted glass in a heavy metal door. She turned to see Eryk sniffing the air. She, in turn, tilted her head and sniffed. "I don't smell anything."

"Self-contained," he stated. He looked down the corridor, counting doors. The corridor ended in a T. "Quite a set-up."

She led him down the corridor and stopped outside a door, tapping on the glass. A young man opened the door and pulled Jasmine into a bear hug. "It's been so long." He stepped back and looked at her. "You look wonderful. How are you?" His tone had turned serious on the last.

"I'm much better, thank you. Ralph, this is Eryk Vreeland."

Eryk stuck out his hand. Ralph took it, pumping it heartily. "I *knew* there was more to your act than just illusions."

"That's a first." Eryk chuckled. "I usually get just the opposite." He made his voice grave, mimicking a pompous patron. "'There's no such thing as magic; they're only illusions.' To which I usually respond with some spontaneous bit of *magic*." Eryk let a small spark travel into Ralph's hand.

Ralph could barely contain his excitement. "That's wonderful. However, I suppose that's why you're here." He turned and led his way into the lab. "We'll start with basic blood work, then on to the machines."

When Jasmine started to turn back toward the door, Ralph called out. "No, no! You are getting the same treatment."

"Why, it's not like you don't have a ton of my blood."

Ralph's cheeks showed a tinge of red. "Not since…ah…you developed…."

She smiled and teased, "I hope you're referring to my latent abilities."

Poor Ralph turned beet red. Jasmine continued teasing him as she followed him into the lab, "It's okay, Ralph, I've developed both."

Sitting with a rubber band now made way too tight by a flustered lab tech, Eryk winced. "Jasmine, stop teasing Ralph or I'll have more holes in my arm than I want."

"Oh," Ralph said, slapped the crook of Eryk's arm and opened a butterfly needle, "don't worry. I could do this in my sleep."

"Well, I, for one, would prefer you not." Eryk was eyeing the haphazard way Ralph was waving the needle around while smiling at Jasmine.

"You'll feel a little pinch," he said.

"I know. I know. Just do it."

Jasmine watched as Eryk's lips paled. "Crap," she hissed. "Ralph, he's gonna go."

Ralph watched Eryk's face and pulled the vial and needle and slapped a piece of cotton on place. "Too late to pass out." He shook the stiff arm. "I'm done."

Eryk shook his head. "Good. I didn't pass out. You are good, Ralph."

Jasmine sat down on a small physician's stool. "Do me here, Ralph. Let him get some blood back in his brain."

Ralph swung around and wrapped the band around her arm.

"Don't look," she commanded, seeing Eryk watching.

"Watching someone else doesn't bother me. Needles don't bother me. Just blood draws."

"Really?" She smiled at Eryk as Ralph finished a second vial and tidied up, making a show of the ease with which she did the same thing. "Is that a chink in my hero's armor?"

"There might be a foible—or two," Eryk answered.

"Welcome to my world," she muttered under her breath and remembered Eryk's hearing as he tilted his head.

Without looking at Eryk, she ask Ralph, "And just why did I get two vials drawn and he only got one."

Ralph shrugged at her question. If he knew, he wasn't telling. "Brad's waiting down the hall," he said instead. "Let Eryk start with the CAT and you take the MRI first. You've already had a CAT."

"I've already had an MRI, too," she reminded him.

"Just following orders."

****

By the time Eryk was finished, he'd been poked, prodded, and scanned over every inch of his body. Hair'd been clipped, nails cut, epitheliums scraped, eyes dilated, and hearing tested. He'd done sniff tests and taste tests. He'd shown his abilities with and without Jasmine. He'd noticed how nervous the demonstrations made her, so he'd given a little push, just to calm her. She'd smiled and pushed right back. He wondered what kind of recording that had produced. He'd worn electrode caps and chased dots across a screen. Where he'd finally drawn the line was when they asked for a semen sample. To him, that was going too far.

His last test was with Ralph and when he finished, Ralph told him that Jasmine had headed back upstairs. He offered to escort him.

"No, I've got it. Oh, by the way, the next time my show's in town, give this number a call and you and Brad have a set of tickets waiting for you."

"Thanks. Appreciate it." He stopped for a moment. "How'd you know?"

Eryk just pointed to his ear.

"Damn. Forgot that."

Eryk laughed and offered his hand.

He waved as he passed Ms. Gwynn and took the steps two at a time. He knew immediately Jasmine was in Bask's office because he could hear them and they were having one hell of an argument. He slowed his steps and listened.

"I'm only saying this because I care," Bask insisted.

That took some wind out of her sails. Jasmine was quieter when she responded. "You can't have it both ways. You can't use me and protect me the way you want. We have to act together to do this job. You knew that going in. Now, you're having second thoughts—"

"All right," he interrupted her, "I'm having second thoughts. And thirds and fourths. You've been through so much. We don't really know him."

"You didn't know Morgan," she countered. "But that didn't stop you."

"That's not true. We'd been following her since birth."

Eryk heard the exasperated hiss coming from her. "Well, now it's our turn. You need us and you know it."

Bask was quieter, barely audible, "It's not that."

"Then what is it? Oh, wait. It's the match-mate crap, isn't it?"

He could tell she was pacing back and forth. He took a quiet step forward.

"Yes." Bask voice wobbled slightly. "You're like a daughter...." He let the words drift off.

Jasmine spoke with a warm quality to her voice, "I know, old man. You're like the father I never wanted," she teased but he could hear the love in her voice. "But we are who we are. If not me, it will be someone like me. And if it isn't him, it will be someone," she stopped and pondered her words before adding, "well, probably not someone like him — I doubt there are any more. But, who knows. It's so damn frustrating." He heard the chair move as she dropped down in it.

Eryk decided he wanted to be a part of the remainder of this conversation instead of being the object of it. He opened the door and walked in.

Bask looked up at him, a tight smile plastered on his thin lips. Jasmine didn't even turn. "He heard" was all she said.

He nodded to Bask. "Okay, about this match-mate stuff...."

"It happens to descendants. They're drawn to their matches. They invariable mate. It's forever." Bask voice was clipped.

Well, the old man couldn't have made it more to the point than that. "Dorian went over it. And what if you don't want...?" The words were out before he could stop them. He saw Jasmine's body stiffen.

"If you mate, that's it," Bask said, looking at Jasmine. "Right now, you have choices. The longer you stay around one another, the stronger the pull will become. I've heard it becomes uncontrollable at some point." He ran his hand over his thinning hair. "Of course, you two have been together— not literally," he added, his voice rising to a croak. He cleared his throat and continued, "I assume you haven't or this conversation wouldn't be happening—and you seem to have more control over it than others. Maybe you aren't—" he stopped when Jasmine and Eryk looked at one another. "Forget I said that," he amended and shook his head.

Jasmine spoke very quietly, defensively, almost a whisper, "I don't like it any more than you do."

"I didn't say that."

"You didn't have to."

Eryk walked over and sat next to Jasmine, ignoring the man across the desk. "Do you realize that a week ago I didn't know you or about any of this. Nothing. I thought I was an anomaly. Then, this gorgeous black-haired vixen shoots my magic right back at me and the world changes. I think I've done pretty well, so far." He reached over and started to take her hand, but she pulled back.

Bask got up and walked out of the room, closing the door softly behind him.

"Did he really think we wouldn't notice," Eryk said in a stage whisper, directed at the closed door.

Jasmine turned to him, tears brimming in her black eyes.

He stood and pulled her resisting body up to his.

"Don't," her voice cracked.

He kissed her. His warm mouth touched her soft lips and he was lost. Her lips trembled ever so slightly under his, but parted as if she had no choice. Eryk pulled her to him and they met, hungry and wanting, until the power turned their hearts into a single beating connection.

Jasmine pulled back. Stepped back "This," she breathed, "are you ready for this? For me?"

"It doesn't look like I have much choice." He regretted the statement the moment he made it. "Not that I want one," he added quickly. "I want you more than I've ever wanted anything or anyone. I would kill to have you." There. That was the truth of it.

Jasmine shook her head, tears streaming from her beautiful obsidian eyes. "That's biology talking. Genetics. It isn't fair."

He stopped dead. "Jasmine, is there someone else? Is this so repugnant to you? Am I?"

"No. And no." Jasmine saw his expression, saw the confusion. "See. We're going through the same thing. We are only rational when we're apart."

She walked over to the window. As she moved away, Eryk felt their heartbeats shift, become separate again.

He started to go to her and stopped, keeping his distance. "I want to say that we can do this job and take it slowly, making sure it's what we want—what both of us want—and not be dictated to by genetics. We are both anomalies, anyway. Stronger, I think, than those before us."

She turned and looked back at him. "I was raised in Ruthorford. Other than vacations, I never spent any time anywhere else until I landed in Safe Harbor. The world is so different on the outside."

"Then keep that in mind. Let's go back to Virginia. We'll take a look at Meadow's Keep, I'll see my father, and we'll put on one hell of a show at Safe Harbor. After that," he lifted his shoulders, "we'll see."

She smiled. Her black eyes twinkled for the first time in days. "You mean it. No strings?"

"No strings."

She started to step forward and stopped. "You won't mind if we don't shake hands."

Eryk laughed as he held the door for her.

****

One of the nice things about a fancy hotel was the fact that, with just a few words, dinner was served around the myriad of papers strewn across one end of the dining room table. Little lamb riblets, grilled, with different dipping sauces and some sort of warm wrapped veggies were all plated as finger foods. There was also spicy hummus served with toasted pita points. A nice Merlot completed the picnic affair. The food was so good, in fact, it served to distract them rather than allow them to plan the magic show they'd been determined to get on paper.

Eryk's focus was glued on Jasmine. She sat across from him, leaning over several of the rough designs he'd sketched for possible illusions, nibbling on a riblet, her soft black hair shadowing her cheeks. Her obsidian eyes were narrowed in concentration. His insides clinched. She was the most gorgeously intense woman he'd ever met. Every movement was elegant—enticing.

Jasmine stopped mid-bite and let her gaze move up from the papers until it locked onto his. She slowly lowered the rib bone she'd been unconsciously chewing on to the plate, picked up a napkin and wiped her lips. She had to break the connection that was snaking between them, weaving its own magic.

"What? Did I smear sauce?" She choked the question, trying to make things light. It worked. The moment passed. They were doing their best. The agreement was going to be hell to keep. Close proximity and heightened awareness. She'd suggest a walk but the rain had increased to a steady downpour and they were stuck inside. The creeks were already jumping their banks and a flash flood warning had been issued for Atlanta and the surrounding area, including the county where Ruthorford lay. She'd never known Ruthorford to flood. The waters surrounding it would rise and creep up a couple of feet, but never threaten the town or the surrounding farms. It was as though it had some secret outlet. The water could run pretty fast in the creek, however, going from a slow meander to a torrent in no time.

She turned at the loud screech coming from the balcony. They both rose and moved toward the balcony door, Eryk grabbing her arm before she got too close. Apparently, the visiting hawk was back, this time seeking shelter from the downpour. It sat on the balcony rail, safely out of the cascading waterfall from the upper balcony, slowly lifting one wing, then the other.

"Poor thing," Jasmine whispered. "It's drenched."

"Let's move back and give it some space. I don't want to startle it. I'm not sure how well it can fly, as wet as it is." They turned and moved away from the balcony door.

"Want some coffee?" Jasmine asked, moving into the kitchen where a carafe sat waiting.

"Sure." Eryk agreed and looked at her. "Want to try an experiment?"

She stopped mid-pour. "Depends."

"The bird looks pretty comfortable out there." He nodded toward the window. The bird was grooming its beak, having shaken off much of the water. "Want to see if you can get the vision at will—your will?"

Jasmine set the carafe back on the counter and moved to Eryk's side. "I'll try but I'm not sure what to do. It always just happens."

Eryk let his hand move to her back, its warmth penetrating her skin. "Relax. Try to recall the feeling right before it happened and bring that up."

She stared at the bird on the balcony. She tried to remember the feeling. Nothing happened. She closed her eyes, as when doing the aura thing and blanked her mind. She opened her eyes to a very close-up view of the building across the street. Eryk caught her as she swayed, holding her in place. He whispered softly in her ear, "See if you can direct where it's looking."

She moved her eyes. Nothing. But the slightest movement of her head and eyes together seemed to have an effect. Her arms grabbed Eryk's arm. "Hang on to me. It's not what I'm used to and I'm disoriented."

He slipped his arms around her, encircling her. The rhythm of their hearts changed. Even though it was something they now expected, it still hit with a punch. Jasmine let her arms cross and grasp his forearms, steadying herself, focusing her concentration on the visual effects she was experiencing. As she looked around, her brain assimilated and began translating the imagery. Although distorted for her, she began to see. Scanning the building, she could see through the windows into the rooms, almost as if using a telescope. "Whoops," she whispered and moved on as she saw a rather hefty man in boxers reach for a remote control.

The room next to his appeared to be vacant. She let her gaze linger, adjusting the focus until she could read a notepad on the bedside table. "Holy—" A sudden pain shot through the back of her eyes and she gagged.

Eryk swung her in one swift motion over the sink.

"I'm okay." The wave had passed as suddenly as it had hit. She stepped away from him.

He poured some iced water and handed it to her. "Sip this."

They both looked toward the screech coming from the balcony. The hawk was flapping its wings, drying them. The rain had subsided. Without a backward glance, the hawk was gone.

Eryk led her to the couch. "Are you okay?" Her brows were furrowed and she kept rubbing her eyes.

Jasmine nodded. "I think it's like wearing someone else's glasses." The corner of her lips curved up. "Oh, I think it was far-sighted. When I tried to look close, it sort of blurred. Far away I could see the writing on a pad of paper." She hesitated a second, "Or, the stripes on an old man's boxers."

Eryk lifted a brow.

"Don't worry, I moved on." She had a thought and turned to him. "When you were holding me, like the aura scan, could you see what I was seeing?"

"No. I tried. I did pick up the birds heart rate and the fact that it didn't appear to be aware of what was happening."

He watched her as she shook her head slightly and opened and closed her eyes. His awareness of her was acute. He took a step back, further away from her.

"Are you up to practicing a couple of illusions?" he asked, trying to think of something to focus on.

"You know, I'm not at all sure about this."

"Don't worry, you're a natural. And, I promise you will get a gorgeous outfit to wear."

She narrowed her eyes at him. "I am not going to wear that frou-frou thing Brandy wears. You understand me?"

She could see the laughter in his eyes. "No? Well, I guess naked would make it less likely to snag something."

"In your dreams, buster. In your dreams." Bracing her hands on her hips, she smiled. "Okay, Houdini, do your worst."

Jasmine had to give Eryk his due. He knew magic. He walked her through several tricks, using her as a prop as much as anything else. On the ones where she got frustrated or lost, he would tweak it slightly until, after several hours, the act started coming together and Jasmine found she was actually having fun.

For several tricks, they enhanced everything by using their combined energies. They would toss a small ball back and forth a couple of times then it would come to a stop between them, suspended in air. Puzzled, they would look at it, approaching from opposite directions until they were standing right under it, and it would burst into a shower of petals reigning down on them. Eryk wanted it to be water but

Jasmine didn't like the idea of having to make a sudden costume change.

They both nixed the mentalist illusions, figuring the audience probably didn't want any information even hinted at about themselves. They would be performing for a group of people in hiding, after all. This show was to be all about escaping that stress for an afternoon.

One of the hardest tricks to perfect was the levitation. He had Jasmine lie down on a board propped between two chairs. On stage, the equipment would be much fancier but the trick was the same. At first, he tried using just his energy but found that, if she fought him, she dropped like a rock. However, combining his energy with hers, it worked beautifully. When their hearts synced, he could relax her and then control her energy as well, which was one tiny bit of information he wasn't ready to divulge just yet. Once he had her relaxed, he directed the energy underneath and her body rose slightly. Then he carefully removed the board, then the chairs. During the show, he would have kids do that. They'd love it.

They must have been growing tired because, after the third practice, with Jasmine floating in the air, something shifted and her arms started flailing. Using an extra burst of energy, it was all he could do to hold her up until he could move beneath her to break her fall. She dropped like a dead weight right into his arms and, unable to counter her weight, he fell forward, straining to soften the landing.

Suddenly, she was on the floor and he was on top of her. Her eyes locked with his. Their hearts, still beating as one, now pounded, drumming through their bodies. She could feel his body harden on top of her and her gaze moved to his mouth. She wanted his kiss. She wanted to move her hips against his. Panic gripped her. Her words came out in quick gasps. "Get. Off. Me." She squeezed her eyes shut. "Please," she whispered.

It seemed like an eternity passed before he lifted his body from hers. She lay there, trying to calm her heart. Jasmine opened her eyes as she heard the balcony door open and close. She rolled over and saw him leaning against the rail, his arms stretched out along the rail. The very air around him shimmered. She blinked, thinking, somehow, she was seeing his aura.

Knowing it wasn't the best idea, she, nevertheless, stepped out onto the balcony.

His energy pushed at her. Then, as if in recognition, it slipped around her and pulled her forward. He turned and stood there as she moved to him. She wasn't sure if she could have stopped if she wanted to. A force drew her, pushing and pulling at the same time. She didn't stop until she was pressed against his body and could feel the contours of his muscles and the hard length that pressed into her abdomen.

"You're—"

He let his hands come up her arms and rested his forehead against hers. "Yeah." He breathed softly. "I'm a healthy man. This seems to be my constant state when I'm around you."

"Well, it's not going to help...," she said, yet found her hands sliding up his chest to move around his neck.

He swallowed and buried his face in her soft neck, inhaling the scent that was all her. It was a scent that would be with him for the rest of his life. A scent he would crave until he died.

"God," he whispered against her throat, "you smell so damn good." He took a nip of her soft flesh and heard her gasp. Felt her melt into him. Before he lost all control, he lifted his head, slid his hands up her arms and gently pulled her hands from around his neck. Knowing it was a result of their working together, he resisted the very thing he wanted most. "I can't believe I'm saying this, but we are going to fight it. For now," he clarified.

Her eyes locked with his. "Thank you," she said and blushed when the words came out a throaty purr.

Letting a wicked grin form, he transformed the moment with a tease, "Anytime...any time at all."

"You!" Jasmine laughed, now released from the compulsion. She pushed away, still laughing, and walked back into the suite. "I think I'll call it a night." She turned and grinned at his exaggerated leer. "Alone."

****

On the flight back, Jasmine asked if she could sit back in the cabin. First and foremost, she had no desire to do another solo outside the jet. Once was enough for that experience. She'd barely kept it together even when she did have control over it, like the night before. It was just too damn soon to do it again. Since Eryk didn't insist on her playing "co-pilot," she figured he'd already assessed the situation. He handed her a set of headphones when he adjusted her seat belt, a move she figured was accomplished more for his pleasure than her safety.

The ride back to the airfield near Ruthorford had been pleasant enough, though a little tense. After they'd finished hashing over the act, awkwardness strained the quieter moments. He offered to take Jasmine by Ruthorford to see Teresa and Bill, but, when she'd called the night before, Teresa had insisted she go on and not worry—that everything was fine—and besides, she'd maintained, Ruthorford was out of the way. Jasmine damn well knew everything wasn't fine. She could hear the edge in Teresa's voice.

She was torn. Bask needed her. Jenn needed her. Eryk—she wasn't sure if Eryk needed anyone or anything. He seemed so in control of himself. Except, when he was kissing her. Yet, even then, he appeared to have control.

Not that she didn't want him in control. She did, didn't she? Jasmine leaned her head against the high back of the leather seat and looked forward. She studied his profile as he watched the instruments and talked to someone on the headset. She saw the slight tick in the muscle in his jaw. He was not happy. Yet, his voice was as smooth as silk, his movements precise. The tiny movement when he tightened his jaw was the only indication that something was not right.

She watched his hands, the way his sinewy arms flexed, and she wanted his hands on her body. Jasmine bolted up. Geesh, she felt like a rutting…something. She shifted around in the seat, trying not to feel the heat pooling in her womb. Slamming the headphones on her head, she tapped the button.

"What's our ETA?" She tried to sound professional.

He laughed. "About a half-hour? Why?"

"No reason. I was curious."

"Miss me?"

"Oh, get over yourself," she tried to sound stern as her lips curled into a smile.

"You're welcome to come up here and keep me company."

"No. I wonder if Jenn got my message." Jenn had been out of the office when she'd called. It was rare for Jenn to be out of the office, ever.

"Oh, I talked with John. He picked up the equipment and it's waiting for us at Safe Harbor. I'll drop you off there. I have an appointment. I'll come by in the morning to check out the equipment and we'll go to Meadow's Keep in the afternoon."

"You're not going to stay at Safe Harbor tonight?" She hated the way that came out, the way her voice sounded needy. It was like this thing that was happening to them was sending fine invisible tendrils out, linking them.

"No." He modulated his voice so it soothed, calmed. "I have something I have to do. I'll be there first thing in the morning."

"Whatever," she snapped. "Don't do that...that thing you do with your voice. It doesn't work with me."

"Oh, yeah? Then why are you so riled up?"

She took off the headset and tossed it in the seat next to her and glared at him when he looked up in the mirror he'd installed to see back into the cabin. He flashed a grin, showing his pearly whites and she could just imagine his eyes glowing green behind those sunglasses.

Jasmine leaned back in the seat and closed her eyes, trying to shut out his image, which was not the easiest thing to do. The unruly black waves, those green eyes, a mouth that could be firm and soft at the same time. There was a grace about him that intrigued her. His movements were fluid, yet precise. Jasmine figured that came from performing and having to choreograph his every action on stage. Yet, as handsome as he was, there didn't seem to be the arrogance that could easily have developed from all the adulation.

Of course, there was the fact that he looked like Dorian. Funny how she seldom, if ever, thought of Dorian when she was around Eryk. Was it the genetic attraction they had for one another that also gave him that distinctiveness? She peered through slitted eyes, wanting to study him undaunted. What was that old saying? "Be careful what you wish for. You might get it." All of her life she'd wanted to be like the other blended female descendants—like Morgan or Meadow. The fact that she didn't have the eyes or the healing capabilities had caused her years of torment. That was probably the reason she'd developed the spirited personality. In her defense, it was an "I don't give a damn. I'm unique all on my own" attitude and it had served her well. Then again, thinking of Rob, she admitted, it had also gotten her in trouble.

Now she had the descendancy she'd longed for all her life, even though it was packaged differently. Unfortunately, along with that came the mate-matching potential. She was so attracted to Eryk that sometimes she couldn't hold a single thought. When he was around, she just wanted to move closer. When he wasn't, she was miserable. And they hadn't had sex—yet.

The urge surged through her even in face of the brutal attack she was still getting over. Until she'd run into Eryk, Jasmine had believed she could live a very productive life without any male intimacy. Dr. Browne believed that would change as she healed.

The moment Eryk had stepped onto the stage at the State Fair, she'd felt the sudden pull. That pull had only grown stronger. Here they were faced with the fact that they didn't know if they were ready for a lifetime commitment, yet almost unable to avoid it.

She wondered if Morgan and Dorian ever thought about that or if they went about their happy little lives doing what nature intended—Ruthorford style. As soon as she thought that, Jasmine realized how catty that sounded. She seemed to have gone from being bitter because she wasn't like those she envied to being bitter because she was.

"Buckle up," Eryk called back to her, "we'll be landing soon."

****

Jasmine hadn't fully emerged from the SUV before she was caught in a tight hug. She laughed and threw her arms around Jenn, so glad to be back with her. She knew the moment she saw Safe Harbor come into view just how important this had become to her.

"I am so glad you're back. I've missed you so much!" Jenn's voice was rich and bubbly.

They moved to the back of the vehicle where Eryk was shaking hands with John Davis, Ruthorford's answer to the ultimate security expert.

He opened the back of the vehicle and took out her bags—all five of them. "I swear you didn't have this many when we left."

"Of course not." She smiled under her lashes at him. "I had a few things to bring back."

"I thought they were shipping that stuff back?" He sounded confused.

"Yes, but I had things I needed right away." She saw the young girl, Lily, standing at the top of the steps, by the door, almost out of view, taking in the scene.

"Lily," Jasmine called. "Come here, I have someone I want you to meet."

Lily approached slowly, her eyes widening as she approached Eryk.

He held out his hand. "Hi, Lily. I'm Eryk. It's nice to meet you."

Lily took his hand and murmured hello, keeping her eyes down.

Over her head, Eryk frowned at Jasmine.

"I have to get back," Lily whispered, turned, and ran inside.

"That's odd. She's really come out since she's been here. Must be your devastating good looks," Jenn teased Eryk.

Eryk looked at the retreating figure. "I don't recognize the name, but I swear I've seen her before."

Jenn swung around, putting her hand on his arm. "If you remember, please let me know. She's not talking about her past and I have a feeling...." She let the words trail off.

"Will do." He glanced at his watch. "I'm sorry to run off, but I've got an appointment. I'll be back in the morning. Eight o'clock okay?"

"Sure. Any time," Jenn said, shooting a questioning look to Jasmine, who just shrugged. "I'm sorry you can't stay for dinner. We'll talk tomorrow."

She hooked her arm through Jasmine's. "So, tonight, we'll have a girls' night."

Jasmine smiled at Jenn and looked at Eryk. The silence stretched between them.

Jenn dropped Jasmine's arm, grabbed a suitcase, and motioned to John with a nod of her head. "We'll just get these inside."

Eryk waited until they were on the porch before he turned to Jasmine. "I'll try to call you later."

Suddenly awkward, Jasmine wasn't sure what was expected of her, if anything. They'd spent so much time together and now...things were strained. She gave him a small smile. "Don't worry about it. I'll see you in the morning." She tried to sound casual.

Eryk started to move toward her and stopped. "You need help with this?"

"No," she said and picked up the suitcase.

"Then I'll be going." He walked to the side of the SUV, turned and looked back at her. She had turned and was walking toward the steps, her elegant back tall and straight, despite the weight of the suitcase. He let himself admire the curve of her hips and the sway of her rear as those long legs moved up the steps. He felt instant heat and, trying not to groan out loud, he got in the car and headed toward the beach.

As Jasmine walked into the foyer, she noticed Lily hanging back. "Are you busy?" Jasmine asked.

The young girl quietly shook her head, not retreating but not moving closer, either. Jasmine studied her. Why the sudden shyness? Especially since Jenn had said Lily had been so enthusiastic about putting together the information about the volunteer models and suggestions as to what would look good on them. She'd even gone so far as to suggest different styles that would be fun in the fashion show.

"I got your list and recommendations." Jasmine set the suitcase down and walked to Lily. "You have quite the eye." She smiled. "I've brought some things back with me for you to go through. I'll have John take them to the wardrobe room."

A glimmer of a smile appeared on the young face. Then, the hint of the chipped tooth appeared as Lily let the smile spread.

"John, would you please take these four suitcases to wardrobe? I'll take the other one to my room."

"Lily, if you want to go with John, you can unload the goods." Jasmine let her brows raise and her smile widen.

"The rest should be here tomorrow or the day after," she called to Lily's retreating back, as the girl followed closely behind John down the corridor, her attention focused on the suitcases. "I'll check in with you later," Jasmine shouted, laughing.

Jenn stepped out of her office. "I'll meet you in your room in a few minutes," she said and glanced at her watch. "And I'm bringing wine."

"Sounds good to me," Jasmine called over her shoulder as the elevator doors opened and she stepped in. She turned and pressed the third floor button, still musing about the change in Lily. It was obvious something had happened when she introduced her to Eryk. At first, she thought it was celebrity awe, but now, thinking on it, she wasn't so sure.

The elevator door opened and she stepped into the residents' hallway. The scent of lavender hugged her senses and she smiled. The gifts Morgan sent Jenn always had such a soothing effect. Walking to the end, she punched in her code and listened for the click. Jasmine grasped the knob and turned, swinging the door wide. When her powers had first shown up, she'd gone through about five keypads before she got it under control. She let out a little snort and let the door swing closed behind her. She carried the suitcase over and hefted it onto the bed, much like she'd done with the lock case, not so long ago. Looking down at her fingers, she rubbed them together, willing and dispelling a small current. In such a short time, she seemed to have changed so much.

She glanced up. The room was the same. It was just as Spartan as her apartment in Ruthorford, yet it seemed more alive. Maybe there was something to that old saying, "you can't go home again." Or, maybe it was because this is where she'd actually come alive, or come into her own. It felt like she'd been dormant in Ruthorford, waiting. What if Rob hadn't kidnapped her? How long would it have been before the change began? Would it have even happened?

A soft knock on the door broke her train of thought. She pulled the door open and watched as Jenn walked in, a bottle of Merlot in one hand, two wine glasses in the other, and a smile plastered on her face. The smile disappeared. "You okay?"

"Oh…yeah. Just thinking. Not the best thing to do when you're tired."

"Well, tired's okay. I'll have you sleeping like a baby in no time. John's downstairs, manning the office so we can have a girls' night." She set the glasses on the small dinette by the window and opened the bottle, pouring the deep red liquid liberally into each glass.

"I don't have any cheese and crackers." Jasmine walked to a small cabinet. "Will these do?" She pulled out a box of Cheezits.

"Perfect." Jenn held her glass up in a toast, "To friends."

"To friends."

"God, I've missed you." Jenn plopped down in one of the two overstuffed armchairs, Jasmine's concession to comfort. "Now, tell me everything."

Jasmine sat and slung one leg over the arm. "Morgan looks great. Big as a house, but great."

"Come on. I talk to her almost every day. You know damn well I want to know about the hunky magician."

"Well," Jasmine drawled in her best southern, "he is a rather nice hunk of maleness."

Jenn rolled her eyes. "More than I remembered. And that look he gave you when you were walking up the steps…" Jenn let out a low whistle. She expected Jasmine to laugh. When she didn't, she studied her friend. "You're blushing!" she exclaimed.

"It's complicated," Jasmine swirled the wine in her glass, not looking at Jenn.

"You're from Ruthorford. What isn't complicated? So are you and he…?"

"No." Jasmine said quickly.

"Why do I get the impression that it's not by choice?" She studied her own wine for a moment, until the thought struck. "That...that match thingy." She sat up straight. "You two are like Morgan and Dorian, aren't you." A frown creased her brows, moving her bangs, as she pondered her own statement. "Except reversed," she added, and smiled, proud of her conclusion.

Jasmine ran her fingers through her hair. "Yes. Except, neither of us are ready. Why is it when you're offered what you think you've wanted all your life, it's so complicated?"

"Oh, honey. I'm so sorry. This probably isn't something I should tease you about, huh?"

Jasmine gave Jenn a half-smile, took a deep drink of wine, and wished she could handle Eryk as well as she always handled wine.

Chapter Eleven

Eryk turned onto the side road that would take him down the narrow lane that stretched along Atlantic Avenue's "gold coast" in Virginia Beach. These were the summer beach houses of the very wealthy. A fine sprinkling of yellow-tan sand dusted the street, with heavier patches strewn about from a recent wind. He turned into the driveway of the multi-story building. The place hardly resembled the beach houses that dotted the road closer to Atlantic Avenue. This place was brick and concrete, a clean modern sweep of deck surrounding vast expanses of glass, sitting on a dune overlooking the Atlantic Ocean. As he stepped through the tall gate, security lights flashed on. He made his way up concrete steps and rang the bell beside the double teak doors.

He'd barely stepped back when the butler opened the door. "Mr. Eryk! It's good to see you. It's been a long time." The initial rise in voice was the only step out of character the older man allowed.

"Hello, Daniel," Eryk smiled and held out his hand. "It's good to see you, too." Daniel was tall and slim and had to be seventy, if he was a day. Ever loyal to the family, he'd spent his life always being where they were, generally leaving after they did and yet being there waiting for them when they arrived. Growing up, Daniel had been more father to Eryk than his own and the simple handshake spoke volumes.

"How's your mother?" Eryk stepped into the wide foyer.

Daniel smiled and shook his head. "She just got back from Colorado. I'm just grateful she didn't try skiing."

Eryk laughed. "Give her my best." He'd sent her beignets from New Orleans' famous Café Du Monde for her birthday—her 89th birthday. He adored Gloria. She was spry, brilliant and enjoyed life more than anyone he'd ever met. When he was in his teens, he'd gone to stay with her and she'd taken him to a ranch in Wyoming where he'd learned to ride a horse and lost his virginity to a neighboring rancher's daughter.

"I will," Daniel said. "She inquires after you all the time."

"Did she ever come to one of the shows?"

Daniel shook his head. "She said why should she pay money when she could see you *perform* any time she wanted." There was a twinkle in the old man's eyes. Daniel and his mother had always known about Eryk's *talents* and always treated him as though he was the most normal kid in the world. Eryk loved them for that.

"You're right, of course." He glanced around the great room, off the foyer. "Is my father around?"

"He's in his study. Will you be staying for dinner?"

"I doubt it, Daniel. I'm sorry."

"Another time, perhaps." There was a hint of sadness in the voice.

Eryk reached out and patted him on the arm. "Definitely. I have someone I'd like you to meet."

Daniel lifted a brow. "A woman, perhaps?"

"Yes. A woman," he said and found himself wishing he could sit in the kitchen with a cup of coffee and talk about Jasmine. "You'd like her."

"Then I look forward to it." With that, Daniel turned and made his way to the kitchen.

Eryk walked down a wide corridor off the great room and knocked once on the door before opening it. His father sat behind the massive mahogany desk, working. He was the only man Eryk knew that kept his suit jacket on at home. He could count on one hand the number of times he'd seen him in really casual clothes. Ironically, they didn't suit him at all.

"Daniel, I'll eat later," he said without looking up, his head bent over the papers.

"I'll let him know," Eryk said and stepped into the room.

The man's head jerked up. "What are you doing here?" He looked past his son at the door Eryk had left open.

"It's nice to see you, too," Eryk commented as he walked over to a narrow set of carved doors, pulled them open to reveal a fully stocked bar, poured a general splash of scotch into a short tumbler, walked back to his father's desk and set it in front of him.

"What the hell's that for?" the old man snapped.

"What? We're gonna have a meeting without you getting a drink first?"

"I don't have to put up with this crap from you." He pushed his chair back. "But since you're here, why don't you tell me what the hell you meant by your comment the other day."

Eryk sat in the chair across from his father, leaned back, studying him. He'd always figured he resembled someone on his mother's side and, since he'd never met them, he never worried about it. His father was shorter, stockier, with nondescript brown hair and brown eyes. His mother had blue eyes and black hair, a striking woman, and, although taller than her husband, carried herself with elegant grace. No one would ever suspect she'd come from the wrong side of the tracks—thus, her complete break with her family. Eryk had figured a long time ago that the two of them didn't have a single heart between them.

He'd thought hard about how he would approach his father. Now, it just seemed he wanted the truth. Eryk held up his hand and let a small ball of energy form—let it dance above the palm of his hand. He watched it, then shifted his gaze to the man across from him and watched the beads of sweat glisten on the old man's forehead and the hand tremble as he reached for the scotch. "Why don't you just tell me who I am?" Eryk asked.

Donald Vreeland took a long drink of scotch, took the handkerchief that he never used from his breast pocket and wiped the sweat from his brow. "I don't know what you mean."

Eryk let the ball disappear with a pop. Donald flinched. Eryk leaned forward, narrowing his eyes. "Well, I don't have your DNA and I do have a twin brother. Why don't we start there?"

"What?"

"You heard me."

Eryk watched the man who'd claimed to be his father visibly slump. The shoulders sagged and, for the first time in Eryk's memory, the man had no presence. The suit seemed to hang looser on his frame. He could almost feel sorry for him. Almost.

Donald finished the scotch and leaned forward, letting the glass rest between his hands. He stared at it as he spoke. "You know, I'd never had a drink until the night you were born."

Eryk said nothing, just waited.

"Your mother went into premature labor. Probably all that damn effort on her part to look like a debutante while pregnant. Anyway, the child—a boy—was stillborn. I was devastated. Someone approached me in the hallway. A woman had come into the charity ward and had given birth to twins. She was strung out on drugs but the babies seemed fine. For a price, she would switch our dead infant with one of the living babies. I stroked a check for $30,000.00, the switch was made, and no one was the wiser. Everyone acted like Martha had given birth to a healthy baby boy. She'd been unconscious so she had no idea what had transpired. I was so sure she'd know that I went out and got lit. Funny, she didn't appear to be aware of anything unusual."

Donald rolled the glass between the palms of his hands, watching the scotch move along the edge of the bottom. "I had no idea what happened to the charity case. I assumed she took her baby and went back to wherever she'd come from and spent her portion of the money on drugs. When your mother didn't show the natural affinity toward you, I figured she just wasn't maternal by nature. Then, you started doing...," he waved his hand in Eryk's direction, "...whatever that is and I drank." He raised his glass in salute and finished the last of it before lifting his gaze to Eryk. "I set up a trust," he said in self-defense. "I fed it faithfully so you'd never lack. I did everything I thought was right."

"Except be a father to me." The hardness in Eryk's voice put a chill in the room.

Donald didn't answer.

Eryk rose and walked to the door.

"Does the other boy...?"

"Yes." Eryk stated and walked out the door, not looking back.

Daniel was at the front door. Eryk stopped. "I'll call you." He took the older man in an embrace and felt the strong sinewy arms hug him back. He'd never once acted afraid of Eryk's powers.

"I can't wait to hear about the young woman."

He nodded and opened the door, stepping silently into the night.

****

"Okay, okay...I'm trying *not* to drop the damn thing. Maybe if we got some more help." John groaned under the weight of the equipment.

"No! The fewer the people that see the set-up, the better."

Jasmine stopped at the sound of the shouting and winced when she heard a crash and a few well-chosen expletives. She pulled open one of the heavy doors to the auditorium and stepped inside, watching Eryk dragging a large crate across the stage with John now shoving the other end, all the while mumbling.

"Boys. Boys." She tried to keep the laughter out of her voice. "Eryk, have you thought about trying to use your...you know...." She wiggled her fingers. "I mean, if you can levitate me or yourself, surely you can give an assist to John here." Both men turned and glared at her.

"Actually—" Eryk stared at the crate and, with what looked like it took very little effort, pulled the huge piece across the rest of the stage.

"Now you use it!" John moaned, rubbing his hand against his lower back.

"Don't be such a baby," Eryk hissed.

Jasmine stopped on the second step leading up to the stage. Talk about déjà vu. How many times had she watched Dorian and John go through the same motions over something inane. If she didn't know it was Eryk standing on that stage, she would have sworn it was Dorian. From the look on John's face, he'd just realized the same thing.

"Wow." John turned to her.

"I know." The spell broke as she approached.

"What?" Eryk was applying leverage to a crowbar, trying to open the crate. "Magic doesn't work on everything."

She decided comparing him to Dorian at this moment might not be her best option. He looked ragged. Dark shadows emphasized his green eyes, giving them an almost sinister gleam. His shirt was still damp from the sudden cold shower that had appeared out of nowhere, drenching him before he got inside. Jasmine could sense, and she wasn't sure how, that he was straining to maintain whatever little congeniality he possessed at the moment and that wasn't much.

"Jasmine...," Lily called from the door, stopped when she spied Eryk, turned, and without saying another word, fled back out the door.

Eryk stared after the girl.

"Okay. That leaves no doubt. What is it about you that sends her into hiding?" Jasmine approached Eryk, watching as his eyes narrowed in concentration.

"My guess is that she thinks I recognize her. And I do. I think. I just don't know from where."

"Really? You need to tell Jenn whatever you can. The girl is obviously scared. Try to remember." She turned and headed back down the steps.

"Wait," Eryk followed, taking her arm. "Let's not." He hurried on when he saw her expression. "I don't mean Jenn. I mean let's let Lily think I don't have any memory of her. Maybe if I can be around her a little, I'll remember." He walked with her up the aisle.

"Hey," John called. "What about all this stuff?"

With a wicked grin at Jasmine, Eryk called over his shoulder. "Oh, just put it anywhere."

They let the door close behind them, shutting out a few more expletives from John.

****

The plan had worked. As soon as Jenn had approached Lily, supposedly concerned that Eryk's eyes were the problem, letting her figure out for herself that he didn't know her, Lily was all over the stage, actually hinting that she wanted to be in the act. Jasmine put Lily in charge of costumes and, under Eryk's direction and a few quick sketches by Lily, she was off to wardrobe, a huge smile showing her chipped-tooth grin.

It took until midafternoon to get the stage set up just the way Eryk wanted it. Every piece had a precise place and he worked from the drawing and scene mark-ups he'd done earlier. Apparently, with such a small stage, placement was essential, not only for effect, but for ease of transition. He made her walk through the steps several times, once or twice rearranging part of the set. He finally called it quits—but only after Bask had called, telling them to get a move on—he wanted a report on Meadow's Keep sooner rather than later.

****

Eryk turned down Atlantic Avenue, heading toward Fort Story, before Jasmine realized he wasn't using the GPS. "You've been here before."

"I've never been to Meadow's Keep," he said and she watched as he glanced toward the ocean side, over and over.

"Know someone on the Gold Coast?"

He seemed distracted. "Huh? Oh, yeah. I do. My parents—the Vreelands, he corrected—have a place there."

"That's where you went last night, isn't it."

"Yes." The word was soft, like a balloon deflating.

She reached over and touched his arm, jerking back her hand as the current slammed into her. Her brows furrowed. That hadn't happened since Ruthorford.

He didn't look at her. "I guess I'm strung out. Sorry."

"I would have thought all that work on stage would have taken the edge off."

"I guess not."

"Want to talk about it?"

"Not really. What's the address?"

She tapped the GPS and he glanced at it and slowed into the left turn lane, the tires splashing through puddles of water. They turned and drove away from the shore. The sand and dunes were quickly replaced with a smattering of small homes, their frequency thinning as they moved inland. Out of nowhere, the road narrowed and ended at twin stone pillars. They moved through and, about a hundred feet in, a tall black iron gate loomed in front of them. It reminded Jasmine of the Abbott House in Atlanta.

Eryk pulled to a keypad and entered the code Bask had given them. They watched the gates pull back, not as quiet as Abbott House, but this place had been pretty much untended for over a year. They still didn't see Meadow's Keep. The road took a sharp right and wound around through heavy pines.

"This must back up to Seashore State Park," Jasmine stopped with an intake of breath. Before her rose an honest-to-God castle, albeit smaller, but with all the features she'd ever imagined for a castle: pediments, turrets, and stone. She leaned forward, staring through the late afternoon deep gray mist. "Boy, does the weather fit this place."

The drive wound around in front of the mansion. A stone and wood walkway crossed over what looked to be a moat surrounding the castle, leading to the entrance. "Holy cow," she said.

"My thoughts exactly," Eryk concurred. He got out of the SUV, grabbed the camera and took shots, backing up to get a better view. Jasmine waited by the vehicle, not quite willing to go up to the entrance alone.

"I bet this place would be a blast on Halloween," she found herself whispering.

"Yeah, can you imagine the fun we could have," he said from across the drive, tapped his ear, and smiled at her as she rolled her eyes. He took several more shots before heading to the front door.

Eryk punched in another code and the massive door lock released. He stepped in. The place smelled of dust and vacancy, its interior shrouded in shadow.

Jasmine hit the lights, startling him.

"What?" she asked. "Bask said the electricity was on. This is not going to be like one of those TV shows where the guys go into a dark room with flashlights when there's electricity available. Those things never end well." Having said that, she hit every switch on the wall panel. The place blazed with light. The enormous hallway stretched quite a distance toward the back. Massive stairs started about halfway down the corridor and went up to another floor, leaving an arch with a closed door in the back.

"That must be the way to the kitchen," he said.

When he started forward, she grabbed his arm. The shock wasn't as sharp but it was still there. "I'm not going back there until I'm sure there's no one up here."

"Good point." He grinned at her. "Got your gun?"

"Don't be snide," she retorted. "Besides, I have you." She let energy pulse between her fingers. "And me," she added and smiled. Not quite convinced that their combined abilities would be enough to stop whatever would threaten them, she squelched the sense of foreboding that wanted to wrap itself around her.

She stepped to the left through an arched doorway. A formal parlor, the room contained exquisite furniture from another century. A thin layer of dust had settled on the top of the mahogany pieces. She walked through the parlor to another side archway and into a dining room. The massive table had chairs to seat eighteen people. Heavy brocade drapes pooled beneath a massive window. Another door circled back into the hallway.

They walked across the hallway toward a pair of ornately carved doors that stood partially open. Jasmine halted. Eryk turned and looked at her, half expecting her to say she'd heard something, which confused him since he hadn't. Instead, she pointed to the wall. Deep black scorch marks marred the wall.

"That was either done with some hellacious energy—or a blowtorch," Eryk commented.

"Apparently, there was quite a battle between Dorian and Ian here in the hallway."

He stepped over and let his fingers run over the marks. "I'd say," he let out a low whistle. Then, seeing her expression, he turned and moved to another room.

They glanced into a small study in the front of the hall and then moved back to the partially closed doors. Eryk pushed them open, keeping Jasmine behind him. Before them lay a library the likes of which neither had ever seen. It was straight out of a historical novel with deep tapestries, heavy drapes over leaded windows, and ornately carved massive furniture. The scent of rich leather covering hundreds of books permeated the room.

Jasmine walked toward the window and stopped at the indentations in the carpet. "I bet this is where the case was that's now in the library at Abbott House."

Eryk remembered the huge book encased in glass and nodded. He ran his hand along the tooled leather back of the large master's chair. He wouldn't be surprised if this had come from some Scottish castle.

So far, they'd heard nothing. Felt nothing.

A quick tour of the upstairs revealed a child's lavishly appointed bedroom, easily befitting a little girl's fantasy of a fairy princess. A master suite connected by way of a bath to a smaller wife's bedroom. Two more huge guest rooms were on the other side of the hall, one of which was a replica of a turret room with tiny windows spiraling around and a cone shaped ceiling. Given the undisturbed dust, it didn't look like anyone had been in the rooms for some time.

They went back downstairs and stopped outside a small room at the bottom of the steps. Eryk heard Jasmine's intake of breath as he pushed open the door. He flipped on a single overhead light. The room was vacant except for a small cot positioned across from the door, a manacle dangling from the iron head-rail. A sink stood in one corner, another manacle hanging from the pipe. "What the hell?"

Jasmine spoke quietly, a slight quiver to her voice. "This is the room where Ian kept Morgan. Later they handcuffed Ian to the sink to ground his powers." She stepped backward from the room.

"You okay?" He asked and quickly turned off the light and closed the door.

She nodded, not quite willing to trust her voice. She wasn't the only one who deserved nightmares, she realized, and thought of Morgan's smiling face. Jasmine hoped she would reach that place one day, where nightmares were just memories. For now, it was one day at a time.

Careful to dampen his energy, Eryk reached for her hand and led her to the back, through the archway, opening a heavy door that led into the large kitchen. The island alone was stunning, its length easily covering eight feet and topped with black granite. The room had enough appliances to accommodate a large staff. They moved around the island and stopped at a small door in the back. Bask had said the lab was downstairs. "You ready?"

Jasmine nodded, swallowing her fear. "Let's get this over with."

He flipped on a light inside the door, revealing steep, narrow steps. At the bottom landing, a cold dank wall of stone faced them. They made two sharp turns before Eryk could find a switch embedded in the stone. He hit the switch and the room ahead flooded with fluorescent light. Dry erase boards sat against two walls and stainless steel tables stood in the middle, outfitted for experiments—he couldn't imagine what kind and wasn't sure he wanted to.

Jasmine stood at the door, not stepping into the room.

"Jas—"

"I'm okay. This was Rob's lab, from what I've been told." She was staring at formulas slashed in red across the boards, some ending with a hand smears and others with scribbling written right over the first.

Anger moved through him, surprising him with its intensity. "Then, why in the hell—"

She stopped him with a look. "I'm not that girl anymore. We have a job to do. Let's get on with it."

Eryk promised himself to have a discussion with Bask about sending her in here. He didn't care if she'd never been here before or not. That monster had been. Swearing under his breath, he walked over to heavily reinforced, arched doors. It looked as though the lock above the handle had been torched. *Dorian.* The handle moved easily in his hand.

They stepped into a cave. If they hadn't known it sat directly off the lab, they would have thought they'd traveled through an underground tunnel. He looked for a light and, finding none, pulled a small, wide-beam flashlight from his pocket. He knew, with his eyes, he could see easily in the dark, but he wasn't sure about Jasmine. His beam, with the light from the lab flooding in, brightened the place. The floor was mixtures of dirt, sand and stone. The walls, a mix of stone and concrete, sparkling as the beam of light moved across them, as though gems were embedded in them.

Jasmine pointed at the floor. A faint mark ran in a line about four feet long in the dirt. "I think that's where the fissure is."

Eryk knelt and shined his light, gingerly reaching out and pushing a finger into the line. It felt solid underneath. He stood and turned to Jasmine. Her nearness caused a tingle to race across his skin. "Do you think Bask expects us to give it a try?"

"I don't think so, but I'm not sure." She stepped back from him.

"You feel it, too?"

She rubbed her arms. "Ever since we entered the lab. I thought it was the eeriness at first. But every time I get close to you, I tingle—not that I don't..." she let the words die off.

He smiled at her. "I know. But, this is different. I wonder if it's intentional. If somehow they made it so that people with our traits would be drawn to one another." He shrugged and tried to smile. "Makes it easier."

She walked back into the lab. He followed and closed the door.

"I think we need to call Bask." Her voice seemed deeper.

He stepped up to her, his breath teasing her face.

Her eyes were black and heavy lidded, her mouth full and inviting.

She breathed him in. His scent was one she would never forget. Every time she smelled him she wanted to rub up against him like a cat. She looked up into his glowing green eyes and stepped back. "Your eyes," she whispered. "They're glowing."

He rubbed his hand across his face. "Upstairs. Now!"

She didn't have to be told twice. She fled up the narrow stairs. He followed close, through the kitchen and down the corridor, until they reached the front door. He yanked open the door and stepped into the cold heavy mist, taking several deep breaths. "Call Bask," he said, not looking at her.

She leaned back against the narrow stone sidewall that protected the entrance and pulled out her phone. Bask answered before the first ring stopped.

"What took you so long?"

"Geez, old man, it's a freakin' castle." She tried to sound nonchalant.

"Well?"

Jasmine swung away as Eryk's hand snaked out to grab the phone, barely keeping him from snatching it out of her hand. With the look she saw on his face, she had no intention of letting him talk to Bask until he calmed down.

"From the untouched dust, it looks like no one's been inside since your people closed it up." She hesitated before asking. "Where we supposed to try to open—"

"Good God, no!" Bask yelped into the phone. "Not without a lot of back-up."

"I'm really glad you said that," she spoke into the phone and shook her head at Eryk, who smirked and tapped his ear.

Seeing that his eyes had returned to normal, she stuck out her tongue, but stepped back when he stepped forward. She found herself against the wall.

"Then, we're outta here," she tried to sound chipper, expecting him to just hang up, as was his practice.

"Jasmine…are you all right?" he asked softly.

The sound of his concern was almost her undoing. "Yeah, I'm okay. But a small FYI. That downstairs is really creepy."

"I've heard. I know I shouldn't have sent you. But with Morgan—"

She interrupted him, "Hey, old man, you aren't going soft on me, are you?"

She heard a grumble and the phone disconnected.

Eryk saw her smile, really smile, for the first time since they'd arrived.

"We're good," she said. However, he wasn't smiling. He seemed deep in thought. "Shall we go back to Safe Harbor?" she asked. "We have a show tomorrow." She started toward the car.

"Wait." He took her arm. "I want to go back inside. I didn't look around."

"Yes, we did."

"No. I mean *look*."

Jasmine's face paled. She stood a little straighter. "Okay—"

"Alone." He cut her off. "You wait for me in the car. I'll lock up when I come back."

She swallowed. "No. I want to go back inside. I need to see if it's us or the place."

"You sure? You don't have to."

Her nerves steadied. His nearness was less painful. That was the closest she'd come to feeling out of control.

Downstairs, for an instant, she'd felt as though she were on fire and he was the only thing that could put out the flames. For a few moments, she hadn't been sure she wasn't going to attack him. Given what she'd been through, she was surprised at herself, and more than a bit frightened.

She moved around him and opened the door, pushed down her fear and stepped inside. Nothing. Eryk moved in behind her. She felt the heat of his body close to hers but not the firing of her nerves. "Do you think it's that cave downstairs?"

Eryk's movements were sure. He stepped up to her and put his hands on her arms. She felt a slight tingle, as she always did when he touched her. His nearness always made her want to move closer. She closed her eyes and focused. No, it wasn't more than usual.

"You all right?"

She opened her eyes and looked over her shoulder into his emerald green ones. There was no glow. She visibly exhaled. "I'm good. And your eyes are fine."

"I want you to go wait in the car. I'm going downstairs. I want to see if it's the room or if it's only when it's us together in the room. Plus, I want to look around. I'll do better if I'm not worrying about protecting you." He moved away from her.

Protect her from what? Panic seized her and she clutched at his arm. "Don't. I don't like it."

His voice was firm. "Jasmine, go get in the car. I'll be right back."

She turned and walked outside, pushed the car door wide open, and sat sideways in the vehicle, her feet firmly planted on the ground, her cell phone in her hand. Jasmine trained her eyes through the open door toward the back of the hall.

Minutes ticked past. What the hell was she thinking, letting him go back down there? What if something happened? She had her finger on her quick-dial when she saw him come out of the kitchen. He waved at her and proceeded to close doors and turn out lights as he moved down the corridor. Flipping off the hall lights, he pulled the door shut behind him and stepped over to her, looking in her eyes. His eyes always glowed slightly in the dark. She studied him. They weren't glowing any more than they normally did and she let out a sigh and smiled.

"It doesn't mean I don't want to kiss you."

On impulse, she jumped up and kissed him lightly on the lips before darting back into the car. She turned an impish smile to him. "There. You've been kissed."

Eryk let out a low laugh, closed her door, and walked around the SUV. He climbed in beside her. As he pulled away, he glanced back at the castle. In the fading light, it really did look like something found on the moors of Scotland. There was a sense of relief when he saw the gates close behind them. He hoped they wouldn't be back.

"I'm starving. How about we head down the beach for some dinner?"

"Dinner sounds good." She turned in her seat. "Did you see anything?"

"Nothing. No more than at the cottage." He waited a beat. "Plus, I didn't feel the way I did when we were together down there."

She nodded. There had been something there that pulled them together. She made a mental note to bring that up to Bask.

Jasmine saw him glance toward the ocean. "Where is your parents' house?" she asked.

Eryk drove down Atlantic Avenue a few blocks and turned left. He stopped on the road closest to the ocean and looked out his window. Jasmine leaned forward. The huge building looked as if it had been picked up from some urban complex and plunked down between older beach homes. Its coldness was a stark contrast with the shabby chic welcome of the houses on either side.

"It doesn't look like anyone's at home," she said.

"I'm sure he left this morning. Probably to get as far away from me as possible." The statement was said softly but she could hear the bitterness.

"I'm sorry," she said and let her hand rest on his arm. This time, the current eased between them, like silk sliding over skin. At a loss to figure it out, Jasmine stared at her hand on his arm. One minute the energy slammed into her; then in another instant, it was like a caress.

Not moving her hand, she spoke, "You confronted him last night, didn't you."

Eryk reached for the gears, letting her hand fall away. "Yes." He didn't say anymore until they were on Atlantic Avenue. "Ever been to the Raven Restaurant?"

"No."

"I haven't been in a long time. Let's give it a shot."

Atlantic Avenue's traffic was sparse, probably the time of year and the weather. By the time they'd driven the length of it, parked, and entered the restaurant, Jasmine was cold, damp, and starving. Seated in the atrium, Eryk suggested they sit on one side of the table with their backs to the live cam.

Jasmine swung around and waved for the camera. She nudged Eryk. "Come on, smile for the camera. It's good publicity." Eryk turned and flashed his million-dollar smile before turning back. They both ordered steaks and Ravenfries.

Jasmine toyed with her napkin. Sitting so close to him was making her aware of his every muscle. The hair on her arm rose.

Eryk stood. "Come on," he said, eyed the camera, and headed down the room and to the side. He held out a chair for her. "We ought to be okay here," he laughed.

"Thanks." She waited until he took the seat across from her. "You don't know what it's like. The tingling. I don't know what you feel, but it's—"

Eryk slight shake of his head silenced her. He raised his hand and caught the waitress' attention.

The waitress walked over carrying their plates. "Whew! I thought you'd left."

"No," he flashed that megawatt smile at her and Jasmine watched the woman's demeanor shift.

"I just wanted a different seat. I hope that's okay?" he asked.

"Oh, sure."

Jasmine quickly lifted her hands as the plate came down with a thud in front of her, the waitress never shifting her gaze from Eryk. With a much more precise movement, she lowered his plate, moving her hand away slowly, over his hand resting on the table, almost like a caress. Because Jasmine knew he could see her, even though he was looking at the woman, she crossed her eyes. His smile widened.

"If you need anything else?"

"I'm fine, thanks." He looked at Jasmine.

"Some Ketch—" Jasmine started to say and found it placed in front of her before she could finish. "Thanks," she said.

"Sure. Enjoy your meal." One last look at Eryk and the waitress headed over to check on another table.

"You are unreal," Jasmine shook her head, dipped a fry into some Ketchup, and took a bite.

"What?" He was laughing as he cut into the rare meat. He chewed for a moment. "This is really good."

His hair, tousled into unruly black waves by the damp, framed his chiseled features. The sharpness of his jaw was outlined by the shadowy beginnings of a beard. His green eyes glimmered with mischief. He looked like a complete rake—and totally irresistible. Jasmine put her attention on her steak for a moment.

"When she brushed your hand…" she hesitated.

"She didn't feel anything," he finished for her. "Well, except my incredible charm."

Jasmine's slow smile went straight to his gut. He could feel his blood warm and stir. Her short black hair, now damp, wisped around her face. Her eyes held depths of promises that he ached to explore.

"You don't feel it, either, do you?" she asked quietly.

He stopped, sat back and looked at her. "Honestly. I feel it on so many levels that sometimes I can barely breathe. All you have to do is be near me and my heart tumbles."

As they looked into one another's eyes, the air around them stirred. Their energies reached out, one to the other.

His voice was rough, low and edgy when he spoke. "I won't rush you. But, I don't want you to think I'm not affected. I fight it every moment. I just don't want to frighten you."

"I'm not frightened—of you." She pushed fries around with her fork. Not looking up at him, she finished. "It's this connection. The need. I don't know if it's you or the Ruthorford thing."

"Does it matter?" He waited for her answer.

Jasmine put the fork down and sat back, gathering her thoughts. "You know, when I became a teenager and the "thing"—she made air quotes—didn't happen between Dorian and me—and, believe me, I expected it to—we expected it to—I felt like a total failure."

She held up a hand when he started to speak. "Let me finish. It was so ingrained. It was like the whole town was waiting. We even tried to force the issue." She laughed at his not so subtle brow lift. Did she see jealousy flicker across his expressive green eyes for just a second?

"I would have been nice if Melissa and Thom—that's Morgan's biological parents and the people who raised Dorian—had told us the truth. I figure they knew. I mean with Morgan and all." She shrugged. "We'll never know now."

She took a sip of her soda and sadness filled her eyes. "I still miss them. Maybe they didn't know. I am, after all an anomaly. Given how I look, Dorian and I should have produced an offspring like Morgan."

He studied her for a moment before he spoke. "You make it sound so...so matter-of-fact."

"I grew up with it. Everything in its place, so to speak. I wanted desperately to be a part of that legacy. Or, I thought I did."

"You don't now?" he asked. She saw he was trying to keep emotion out of his voice.

"I don't know. Now that it's happening. I mean right there in front of me, with me...and you...I don't know how I feel. I know I feel bad for you."

"For me? Why do you feel bad for me?"

"Because you don't really understand. You have this incredible desire for me. And, if we let nature take its course, that's it. Now and forever. You and me." She snapped her fingers. "Kinda takes the romance out of it."

He reached across the table and took her hand. She felt his energy seeking hers. Eryk looked down at their hands and the energy softened. He lifted her hand.

"One. I was in on the conversation. Although I found it hard to believe at first, I've had some time to process it. Two. What makes you think I just want to have sex with you and be on my way? I'm not like that. I've never been like that. Oh, I'm no virgin. But, I'm no Casanova, either. I can shock the hell out of people. My eyes frighten them. So, no. I'm not.... And, three." He brought her hand to his mouth and nipped at her fingers. "I have never...and I mean never...wanted any woman as completely as I want you. Sure, I crave you. But, I can deal with that. I adore being around you. I love seeing you first thing in the morning, sleep in your black eyes, your hair all tousled, and the way you flow across a room. I love the way you come back at me when you don't agree. And the way you turn to me when you need me."

He watched her swallow. He felt the current zigzag down her arm, spiky, unsure. "What I'm saying is I'm on the path I want to be on. We can fight it, slow it down, and let our hearts and minds catch up. Or we won't." Then he smiled at her. "I'm happy either way."

A soft cough sounded from across the aisle. They broke apart. Obviously mistaking what she heard, the waitress was all grins. "Honey, if you don't want him, I'll take him."

Jasmine's face reddened. Eryk laughed. "See. You better hurry. The line's getting longer."

The waitress reached over and put her hand on Jasmine's shoulder, leaning in. "Seriously. You take your time. Marriage isn't something you rush into. Trust me. I'm on number three." She patted Jasmine's shoulder and set the check nearest Eryk. "No rush. I'll take that whenever you guys are ready."

"Could I have a doggy bag?" Jasmine asked the waitress. She knew she couldn't swallow another bite and not choke, and she wasn't sure it was the food.

Chapter Twelve

"Ut-uh. No way! There is no way you are getting me into that costume." Jasmine held the hanger away from her, eyeing the black leather-looking cat suit. Jenn had clapped her hand across her mouth, determined not to laugh and hurt Lily's feelings. Lily's whole expression had gone from excited expectation to letdown in light speed.

Jasmine let out a long breath. "Lily, honey. I just don't think—"

"You said you didn't want to wear a costume like his assistant's."

"You're right. No fishnet stockings for me."

"Well, I thought this would solve the problem. With the right hair and make-up you'll totally upstage him."

Jasmine narrowed her eyes and looked over at Lily. No two ways about it, the girl had shown a real talent for wardrobe. Maybe she wasn't wrong here. Jasmine held up the costume again, reached out and let her fingers run down the soft fabric. She looked at Lily. "I'll try it on."

Lily clapped.

"*Just* try it on," she emphasized.

An hour later, with the black suit hugging every curve, her hair gelled into cat ears, a fur tail belted around her waist, and a green sequined collar, the exact color of Eryk's eyes, secured around her long neck, Jasmine turned sideways and stuck one spike-heeled boot forward in a pose. "You know, this is almost obscene."

Jenn sipped the wine she'd supplied to encourage Jasmine into the costume. "Almost?" She choked, her blonde curls jostling, as she tried to contain her laughter.

Actually, the costume showed nothing, which was good, since the audience was made up of women and children. The teen boys and girls would definitely appreciate the fact that their wardrobe high priestess was wearing a cat suit.

Jasmine took a generous swallow of wine and stood pondering herself in the mirror. "Lily, would you please run downstairs and see if there's anything to munch on. I'm starved. Nothing too filling, mind you. I want to be able to zip this tomorrow."

"Do you want anything, Miss Jenn?"

"Sure, I think there's a veggie tray in the main fridge. Dip's on the shelf above it. If you want something else, go ahead and fix it."

"Tray sounds good. But, I'll look." Lily opened the door and looked back. "You look awesome," she told Jasmine.

Jasmine smiled at her. "It's your doing. Now, if you run into Eryk, don't say a word. I want to surprise him." With the show tomorrow, Jenn had insisted he stay in one of the guest rooms on the first floor, away from the clients and away from Jasmine. Which was a good thing, especially right now.

They heard Lily giggle as she closed the door.

Jasmine turned back to the mirror. The tail hung down, trailing softly on the floor. With a flick of her fingers, the tail lifted off the floor and moved out in front of her toward the mirror. The movement was jerky at first, then steadied. She made it dance around until it looked alive.

Jenn watched. "That's impressive. What are you up to?"

Jasmine turned and the tail slipped up over her shoulder and lay across it. "I need you to do me a favor. I need some thin wire and two of those flat, rollie eyes you use for the kids' crafts."

Jenn tilted her head. "I can see the eyes, but why the wire?"

"I can control the current better with a thin length of wire. Make it very thin, I can always double it if I need to. I hope this works." She shot Jenn a grin.

Jenn saluted and headed to the door. "I suppose you don't want to show Eryk?" Jenn voice had that teasing lift Jasmine had grown to love.

"NO!" she exclaimed. "Oh, we can't tell Lily. She doesn't know about the power thing."

"So, how are you going to keep it from her?"

"I'll think of something," Jasmine said, turning back to the mirror. She smiled. *Not bad. Not bad at all.*

****

The auditorium buzzed with voices. Although they hadn't made the show mandatory, having a celebrity putting on a show for them had all the residents piling into the auditorium.

Eryk, doing a last minute check on the equipment with John, who'd volunteer as a stagehand, waved at Jenn as she crossed the stage toward the curtain.

"Where's Jasmine?" Eryk looked beyond her toward the side entrance. They'd practiced when they'd gotten back from dinner. Jasmine knew the act but showed some nerves. Then, she disappeared upstairs and he hadn't seen her since. He would have loved to have gone over it one more time this morning.

"She's getting ready." Jenn said quietly. "She doesn't come on until you finish the sleight-of-hand stuff. She'll be here." She stopped and watched him. He was dressed in tight black pants tucked into high black boots, a flowing shirt open at the neck. He looked like a buccaneer. He glanced over toward the side again. Since she'd known him, she'd never seen him nervous. He was definitely showing some nervousness now. She glanced at her watch. "Are you ready?"

With one last look around, he nodded.

Jenn stepped through the curtain and everyone applauded. She had made sure the small stand was where Jasmine wanted it, close to the split in the curtain. After her effusive introduction, Eryk stepped through the curtain.

He had geared today's show for the kids, making sure that there were no tricks that hinted at violence or entrapment. He started with linking rings, did a cut and restore rope illusion, and had the audience amazed at the floating light bulb. He sent the lit bulb dancing in midair above the audience. He'd let it hover over someone, had them take it, exam it, then release it into the air again. The only thing he had to be careful of was not to let the person get shocked as he controlled the current. He had the kids hooting with laughter as he had a golf ball appear and disappear under a cup. Of course, much of the fun was the speed with which it was done and the flow of dialogue, which he kept heavily accented for his performances.

Eryk had asked for a dollar from someone in the audience and had her come on stage to sign the bill in bold letters with a heavy black marker. He had just made it disappear when giggles erupted from the front. He could tell by the current teasing the hairs on his arm that Jasmine was somewhere nearby. He pulled a lemon out of his pocket and the audience erupted in laughter. Then he felt it. Something on his shoulder. He turned. Nothing.

Pretending ignorance, he set the lemon on the small table, snapped his fingers and a small knife appeared in his hand. Again, laughter from the audience followed the slight tickle he felt on his other shoulder. What was she up to? Ignoring it, he cut the lemon and pulled out the dollar, the signature clearly visible. This time the whole auditorium erupted. He lifted his hands in confusion.

"Over your head," children called.

He looked up quickly. "Nothing."

"Behind you," they shouted.

He swung around and came face to face with what appeared to be a furry snake with two large bug eyes. He reached out and grabbed it, stepped to the side and let the audience see that it disappeared through the curtain.

Two can play this game. He lifted his hand and, with an illusionist flourish, pointed at the curtain. It eased apart to reveal Jasmine, her side to the audience and away from him, her hand to her mouth in a stage giggle. Dressed like a black cat from head to foot, every luscious curve of her body enhanced by the shiny black, his breath caught. He was holding the end of her tail. Posed in her stage stance, she turned her head toward the audience. Looking at the audience, she pointed over her shoulder.

The kids shouted. "He's behind you."

Eryk held the tail and, with an exaggerated motion, he pulled her toward him. She slowly stepped right into him and jumped, startled. She turned, looked at him, giving a loud purr into his hidden microphone, and rubbed up against his arm like a cat. He let his hand stroke down her back before he even realized what he was doing. Sparks flew from his fingers and the fur on the fake tail bristled to twice its size.

They performed the skit as though it was a part of the act and their antics had the whole auditorium filled with laughter. Finally, he took her hand and held it up.

"My lovely assistant, Jasmine Monroe."

She bowed.

The room burst into applause. He took this time to regain his composure. Jasmine turned and smiled at him and he almost lost it all over again.

The curtains slid opened to reveal the stage. John came on stage and took away the table, replacing it with two high black chairs. He positioned a black board between the two chairs.

Eryk led Jasmine to the chairs and helped her lie down atop the board, her tail draping over the side toward the audience.

"I'm going to need some help." He pointed to a young girl, a young boy about the same size, and a larger teenage boy. "You three." He motioned for them to come on stage.

They walked up the steps and Eryk positioned the two younger kids at Jasmine's head and feet and had the teenager stand to the side.

In practice, Eryk and Jasmine had made sure they were in close contact before the illusion. Just seeing her in that costume had already heightened his awareness of her. Her rubbing up against him has done the rest. Now, as he stood behind her, he let his hand run down her side from her hair to her foot. He could feel the moment when their hearts beat as one. In rehearsal, this had eased the stinging feeling she complained about when he levitated her. With their hearts in sync, she said it felt more of a warmth than a thousand fire-ants biting at her. Eryk explained to the audience that this illusion was like the floating light bulb, only bigger—to which Jasmine raised her head.

He pushed it back down. Her tail twitched. The audience laughed.

"Relax." He made a pretense of calming her, waving his hand over her face, as if to hypnotize her. The tail drooped and hung limply to the floor.

"Now," he said to the young boy, "remove the chair." He could see the child's eyes widen. "It's okay," he encouraged. The boy pulled the chair back.

He nodded to the young girl. She eased her chair as well.

Eryk turned to the teenager. "What's your name?"

"Allen."

"Allen, come stand in front of my assistant." As soon as the young man did so, he said, "Oh, would you please hand her tail to me." The audience laughed. When Allen lifted the tail, the tip twitched. He almost dropped it, but managed to hold it up so Eryk could take it and lay it on her legs.

"Now Allen," he said so everyone could hear him. "Do you see those handles on the side of the board?" When Allen nodded, he continued. "Grab them and, together, we're going to ease the board down slightly and then walk to your left.

They both took hold and when Allen started to move, Eryk said, "Your other left."

The audience roared. They pulled the board down and moved away from Jasmine, leaving her floating in the air—no board, no drape, just Jasmine. John appeared, took the board, and walked off stage.

The audience clapped. Eryk raised his finger to his lips. "We really don't want to wake her right now, do we?" The room fell silent.

He moved his hands and her body slowly drifted above his head. Concentrating, he pushed energy up and around her.

"I'd like you three to walk over here. Make sure there are no wires."

The three from the audience moved under Jasmine, walked around, and stepped back, nodding.

"Anything?"

"No," all three whispered, shaking their heads.

Making sure they were out of the way, he positioned himself under her, snapped his fingers, and caught Jasmine as she fell into his arms, setting her upright. She and Eryk took hold of the small children's hands. Jasmine smiled at Allen, who blushed, but took hold of the young girl's other hand and they all bowed. The audience went wild!

For the final illusion, Eryk walked to the back of the stage and pushed a long table forward, on top of which sat a long mirrored, topless box. He undid the hinges so the sides hung down over the sides of the table, and he had Jasmine lie down on top of the table. Eryk raised the sides, hooking them together, encircling Jasmine, hiding her from the view of the audience. The tail managed to pop out over the top several times, sending peals of laughter through the crowd. Once all the sides were up, he pushed the table around, showing all sides, with the tail peeking out one last time. As soon as he'd pushed the tail back in, he clapped his hands and the sides fell away. Jasmine was gone, only the tail remained. He picked it up and draped it around his neck. Applause erupted as Jasmine rose from a seat midway up the aisle. She came on stage and, holding hands, they took their bows.

From the expressions on the faces of those in the audience, the performance was a huge success. For a few moments, everyone in the audience had been able to suspend reality, enjoy themselves, and laugh. Knowing what she did about the tragic lives of those in the audience, Jasmine was thrilled to give them that freedom.

The curtain swung closed in front of them as she turned to Eryk. "How do you do this all the time? I'm beat."

Before he could answer, Jenn ran across the stage. "I'm afraid you're gonna have to do another kind of disappearing act. Sonya called. People are looking for Lily."

Jasmine watched Lily's face turn ashen and caught the slight movement she made toward the exit. Jasmine stepped forward and put her arm around the frightened girl—to calm her and to keep her from bolting.

"I've already been in touch with Bask. He suggested the *fortress*." Jenn said softly, glancing around as she emphasized the word.

"Got it," Jasmine said. "Clothes?" She pulled at the costume whose comfort level was lessening by the second.

"In the van," Jenn said. "*Eryk*'s going to leave here and go to the airport. You'll be in the back. From there you'll transfer to another vehicle. He'll supposedly fly off. The problem is how to keep them from seeing you transferring from one vehicle to the other, if they follow you."

Eryk spoke. "Not a problem. I'll handle it. It's what I do." He smiled at Lily. "We'll take care of you."

Lily didn't look all that confident. Her eyes kept darting toward the door.

Jasmine stepped closer and said in a whisper. "Don't think about it. Let us take care of you. We can. Trust me." With that, she held up her hand in front of Lily and let a ball of energy form. Lily's eyes widened. Jasmine closed her hand, dissipating the energy, and smiled at the frightened teen. "We won't let anything happen to you."

"Who *are* you?" Lily's voice cracked.

"How about we get you to a safe place and then I'll tell you and you'll tell me?"

Chapter Thirteen

Jasmine and Lily sat in the back of the van as Eryk pulled into the drive of Meadow's Keep. The transfer at the airport had gone well. They saw the men who'd followed them from outside Safe Harbor. Who knew that Eryk had a hidden talent? He could bend energy in such a way that, as he explained to them, made him, and anyone he touched, virtually invisible. She still wasn't sure how he did it. Somehow, he'd made it appear to those watching as though only he boarded the plane, although all three of them had. Then, all three of them left the plane, totally unseen, walked around the building to the plain paneled van waiting in the employee's parking lot.

They were barely on Interstate 64 when Jasmine began peeling off the cat suit, threatening bodily harm if Eryk as so much glanced in the rear view mirror. Not that there was much he hadn't seen already, she realized, remembering her nightmare at the posh hotel. It was just the idea. She saw his green eyes flash in the rear view mirror once before he turned the mirror away.

"Don't tempt the devil," he commented and Lily offered a weak smile.

Now, sitting in jeans and the loose navy cashmere sweater, Jasmine felt much more herself. Of course, she wasn't going to feel completely comfortable until she rid herself of the gelled cat ears. No matter how much she brushed, her black hair sprang back into two tufts.

They drove in silence, keeping a lookout for their pursuers. Lily sat wringing her hands, occasionally swiping at the tears that escaped.

Eryk swung off Atlantic Avenue from the center lane, not giving a signal, the van leaning, the tires squealing as they made the sharp turn. He didn't slow until he reached the tall iron gates. He punched in the code and watched the gates pull back. This was the last place he wanted to be.

"Whoa!" Lily leaned forward over the console as they pulled around and the motion lights came on. "That's a friggin' castle."

"Pretty much," Jasmine remembered her own reaction.

"Who has a castle in Virginia Beach?"

"I guess we do." Jasmine tried to sound nonchalant.

Lily dropped back on the seat. "First you do real magic. Now you tell me you have a castle. Who are you guys—some sort of superheroes?"

Jasmine caught Eryk's raised brow.

"I'm going to go check things out, just to be on the safe side. You guys wait here. And keep the doors locked," he said and got out of the van, clicked the remote locking them in, and looked back to make sure the gates had closed.

"He's really hunky," Lily announced to Jasmine.

"Umm-hmmm."

"Are you two sleeping together?"

Jasmine coughed. "What?"

"I said—"

"I heard what you said. I know you're a woman of the world, but that doesn't entitle you to ask that question." Jasmine said.

Lily looked down at her hands. "Sorry."

That van door slid open before Jasmine had to break the awkward silence. "Okay, ladies. Let's get settled." He grabbed the suitcases and waited for them to step out of the van. Jasmine took her suitcase from him. Lily, seeing Jasmine, reached for hers, which hit the ground from the weight. Jasmine figured she must have packed everything she had at Safe Harbor.

"Allow me," Eryk said, using that accent of his as he took the suitcase from her.

Jasmine could almost hear Lily sigh.

They stepped into the long corridor. "I'll move the van around back once we put our suitcases away. Okay, here are the rules, Lily. You have access to everything, except the two rooms that are locked. The one at the foot of the stairs," he nodded to the door where Morgan had been manacled. "And the locked room off the kitchen. There's nothing in the first room, but it has some wiring issues. And the one off the kitchen goes to the basement and the steps are unstable."

"Don't worry. That leaves plenty to explore," Lily tried to make her voice light, stepped forward, peering into the first room and letting out a low whistle.

Eryk shook his head and moved toward the stairs. Lily and Jasmine followed him up the stairs. As Lily went past Meadow's princess room she stopped so quickly Jasmine had to step around her to keep from running into her. "Do you think I can stay in here?" Lily whirled and faced Jasmine. Then, as though she realized she should be too old for this types of room, Lily's pretty face took on a rosy blush.

"I'll tell you what," Jasmine said. "I'll flip you for it."

"You…want to stay in here?"

"Who wouldn't?"

"Me," Eryk commented from the doorway to the master.

Jasmine turned to him. "Well, that's because you're a guy. But we'll let you toss the coin. I call heads." She hoped that Eryk knew how to control a coin toss, otherwise she'd be spending the night in more pink than she could stand in a lifetime.

Eryk pulled a quarter out of his pocket, showed it to both girls, and tossed it into the air. He watched it closely, caught it, slapped it on the back of his hand and uncovered it. "Tails. Sorry, Jasmine. Let's go find you another room."

Jasmine watched Lily step toward her and stop. For a moment, it looked as though she might have thrown her arms around Jasmine in a hug, but caught herself. Instead, she turned and began exploring the room. Hey, it was a start. A start Jasmine was afraid might end too soon. She needed to call Jenn and find out what was really going on.

"We'll meet downstairs in thirty minutes, okay?" Jasmine called from the hallway.

Lily nodded and sat on the frilly canopy bed, letting her hands move across the comforter.

Jasmine followed Eryk down the hall where he stopped, looking at her.

"I'll take the master," Eryk said. "You could take the adjoining *mistress* chamber."

"That's okay. I'll take the turret room." She moved to the room across the hall from the master. "I'm going to take a shower and get this gel out of my hair."

"Oh, I don't know. I kinda like the ears."

Jasmine purred as she shut the door in his face.

She let the shower spray flow over her body, easing the aches. Her muscles burned as though she'd been in a gym, preparing for the Olympics. Her respect for Eryk's real assistant increased tenfold. As soon as things calmed down, Jasmine planned to lobby Eryk for a raise on Brandy's behalf.

Jasmine was amazed at the ease with which Eryk performed. Because of the link between them needed for some of the illusions, she could feel when his heartbeat changed. No matter what they did, his heart rhythm had remained steady—except when he'd first seen her on stage. When he pushed that curtain back, his heart rate had skittered before it steadied out.

She smiled and wiped the steam off the mirror, revealing her lean, muscular body. She would never have the curves Jenn had—or the boobs—but what she had was taunt and firm. She turned to the side and stood straight. Yep, perky breasts tipped with tawny areoles, flat tummy, and a round butt. She glanced down at the white scar on her hip, which had almost obliterated the birthmark which identified her as one of Ruthorford's descendants. She grabbed the lotion sitting on the counter and rubbed it onto her flesh. Her hip wasn't the only scar remaining from Rob's attack. She had several, the most pronounced, however, were the one on her hip and one on her side, next to her breast. That one was fading. In time, she hoped, it and the memories it brought back would fade as well.

Her cell phone rang from the bedroom. Wrapping the towel around those high breasts, she stepped into the round room and picked up the phone. "You're not going to believe this room. It's like something straight out of a historical romance, tapestries and all," she said to Jenn without preamble.

Jenn's silence had Jasmine leaning against the high bed. "What? Talk to me," Jasmine encouraged.

"Sonya said a social worker, a private investigator, and a lawyer came to visit her."

"Oh, Jenn. I'm sorry." Jenn spent so much of her time protecting her wards.

"Not to worry, Mr. Bask has that covered. As far as they know, some runaway who vaguely matched Lily's description stayed here overnight. Somehow, the photo and paperwork got lost. Just watch your back. There's a lot of money behind the people looking for her."

"We had a tail to the airport. Eryk lost them, just like he said he would. As for the money issue, I'm not concerned about that. Abbott House can checkmate any money move. Who are they? Who is she?"

"Her name is Arabella Greeson. Her father is Porter Greeson, as in Greeson Industries."

"Greeson...why does that sound familiar?"

"How about Beverly Greeson?"

Jasmine stood up. "You mean the socialite. She's spends more on couture than a small country's budget." Jasmine had met the middle-aged diva on several buying trips. Beverly Greeson was the darling of every fashion house from New York and Paris. And, from what she remembered, the woman had a reputation as a snobby bitch. It was hard to believe that the friendly, helpful girl wanting the princess bed was a product of that woman. Of course, it did explain her incredible fashion sense.

"Bask says to lie low for a couple of days until he gets back to you. There should be plenty of food. If you need anything, give him a call."

"I'll talk to you later." Jasmine grabbed a fresh pair of jeans and sweater and headed back to the bathroom, still holding the phone.

"You gonna be okay?" There was concern in Jenn's voice.

"I'll be fine. Don't worry." She wished she were as confident as she sounded. Playing house with a ready-made family hadn't been on her immediate agenda. Now, it seems, it was.

"I'll call you when I can," Jenn said.

"Please. And give Morgan a call. See how she's doing. I don't want her worrying about this delay."

"Already have and she's good."

The sound of laughter floated out of the kitchen and made Jasmine smile as she came down the stairs. Jasmine really liked Lily—correction—Arabella. She hoped this wasn't the last laughter she heard from the young girl. It was her job, and Eryk's, to make sure that didn't happen. With renewed determination, she swung about the bottom of the steps and headed back to the kitchen.

"Again! Do it again," Lily urged Eryk. The voice was far different from the hard bitter sounds that emanated from her when she'd first arrived at Safe Harbor.

Jasmine stepped in to see the pancake fly high into the air. She saw Eryk glance her way, give her a smile of appreciation, and look back in time to catch the flipping pancake perfectly in the pan.

"Want some?" he asked Jasmine as he slid the plate-sized pancake onto the plate and placed it in front of their young companion.

"Sure." Jasmine circled around the island and took a seat next to Lily. She looked over at her. She really did like the name Lily better. Lily suited her. The sweetness, the freshness. The girl sitting next to her bore little resemblance to the one Sonya had brought to the shelter. Even with the impending threat, she sat next to Jasmine, scoffing down a giant pancake, as though she didn't have a worry in the world. Jasmine glanced over at Eryk, admired the lanky muscles and the blazing green eyes. Maybe she didn't have a worry. He had a way of making one feel safe.

Eryk slid a huge pancake on her plate. "Eat it while it's hot." He poured more batter into the pan and let his eyes lift to hers, almost like a caress.

That's when she felt the sizzle run up both of her arms at once. The room got warm and she could almost feel her pupils dilate in response. Jasmine immediately glanced over her shoulder at the locked door that led to the basement. She'd almost forgotten it—and their reaction to each other when they stepped inside.

"Sometimes a pancake is just a pancake," he said quietly. *Or, a reaction is us, reacting.*

"Huh?" Lily questioned.

"Nothing," they said simultaneously.

Jasmine's brows drew together in a frown. Had he said the last part or did she just think he had. She picked up the syrup bottles and examined them, choosing the butter pecan to add over the melting pat of butter he'd slipped atop her pancake. She cut into it and her fork eased through the fluffy disk. She slipped the hot bite, dripping with syrup, in to her mouth and closed her eyes. The hint of vanilla blended with the butter pecan and butter and she almost moaned.

"Good, huh?" Lily studied Jasmine's reaction.

"I'll say. Any coffee to go with this?"

He motioned with his head.

She stepped around him to the opposite counter. "Want some?" Jasmine asked and poured the steaming liquid in a mug.

"Already have some, thanks. Lily here's decided on chocolate milk for her breakfast-supper."

"With extra chocolate. You know there's a TV in my bedroom with a DVD player and lots of movies?"

"No. I didn't."

Eryk sat at the end of the island and ate a quarter of the pancake before he even looked up. "Performances make me hungry," he said between bites, careful not to make eye contact with her again.

Jasmine sipped the hot coffee. "I don't know how Brandy does it. I think every muscle I have is screaming."

"Well, she doesn't do it quite the way we..." he let the words trail off suddenly aware of Lily's rapt attention.

"And just how do you two do it different?" Lily asked, her eyes twinkling.

"Trade secret," he said and took another bite.

Lily lifted her hand and wiggled her fingers. "The zappy thing, maybe?"

Eryk's head shot up.

"I kinda showed her *my* secret," Jasmine said softly, not looking at Eryk.

Eryk set down his cup. He studied Lily and let his voice turn serious. "I suppose that lets you into the secret world of the magician, Lily. It's a very special place, where secrets are kept."

"I can do that." She crossed her heart. "I promise."

Now was as good a time as any, Jasmine realized. "As can we...Arabella." She set her coffee cup down and turned to the young girl.

Lily's eyes took on a look of panic and flitted from Jasmine to Eryk and back. "How?"

Without answering, Jasmine looked at Eryk. "Eryk," she said, "meet Arabella Greeson."

He tossed down his napkin. "I knew you looked familiar."

Lily eased to the edge of her seat, ready to flee.

Jasmine shook her head. "It's okay, Lily. I *can* call you Lily, can't I? I've grown rather fond of the name."

Lily didn't speak. She was looking at Eryk.

"Lily, stop worrying." Eryk said, casually taking another bite of pancake. "It doesn't change anything. We're going to protect you from whatever it is you're afraid of."

"But your Dad and my Dad."

"Are good friends. I know. Don't worry about that. Why don't you tell me what happened?"

It was Jasmine's turn to look surprised. "Your families?"

"No." Eryk got up and brought the coffee carafe to the island. "My *father*"—only Jasmine caught the slight emphasis on the word—"and Porter Greeson, Lily's father, went to college together. They've stayed in touch. Her family hired me to perform for her thirteenth birthday." He slapped his palm against his forehead. "Which happened to be in springtime."

"Okay, so I was off by a few months," Lily said quietly. She pushed the plate away. "I'm not very hungry, anymore."

"Sweetie, I meant what I said at Safe Harbor. Knowing your name doesn't change anything. We're going to take care of you. Aren't we, Eryk." She turned and looked at Eryk.

"Absolutely."

It was obvious she wasn't buying it at this point. "I think I'm going to go to bed." Lily got up from her chair and walked toward the door. Her demeanor had changed, her shoulders were slouched and her walk slow."

Jasmine started to go after her.

Eryk grabbed her arm and, when she looked back, he shook his head.

"I'll check on you later," Jasmine called to the retreating figure. She turned to Eryk. He raised his finger to his lips and waited, listening.

He spoke softly. "Give her a little time."

She sat back down, took a sip of her coffee and grimaced. It was cold.

"Want some fresh?"

"No. I'll never sleep tonight. What can you tell me about her family?"

"I really don't know a lot. Porter was one of those entrepreneurial kids who began his business before college. He went on to school with my father, went back to his business and it went worldwide, fast. He and my father stayed in touch." He was stirring sugar into his coffee, suddenly lost in thought.

She noticed his expression change every time he mentioned his father. "You want to tell me what happened between you and your father?"

"Nothing much. I confronted him. He told me he bought me. We parted." He still hadn't looked up from his mug.

"Bought you?" She choked out the words.

This time when he looked up there was bitterness in his expression. He told Jasmine what he'd learned the night before at the beach. "I can't say that I'm not grateful for him getting me out of a bad situation." He toyed with his coffee mug. "I guess it's the fact that he never even tried to be a father to me. Add to the mix the fact that, as soon as my abilities started to show, my mother deserted me as well. The sad part about that," he said, "is that she didn't even know that she wasn't my mother."

"Eryk, I'm so sorry." Jasmine reached out and laid her hand on his forearm and felt his current reach for her. She accepted it, let it blend with hers and return to him, giving comfort, she hoped.

He took a deep breath and let it out slowly. "Every time I have to refer to him, my throat closes up. I don't want to call him Dad. I don't even want to refer to him as my father."

"Then don't," she said simply. "Call him Donald. Mr. Vreeland. Asshole, whatever makes you happy."

He smiled for the first time.

She decided it was best to move away from that topic for now and she removed her hand. "What else can you tell me about Greeson?"

"Nothing, really. I wonder why she ran away?"

"You don't know why Sonya brought her to us, do you?" At the shake of his head, Jasmine related her first meeting with Lily and how different she was. "There were some old as well as recent injuries suggesting abuse."

She held up her hand when Eryk let out an expletive. "We have no way of knowing who did the abusing, but Eryk, there's a reason she ran away, and there's a reason she's so afraid."

"Son of a bitch," he hissed, shaking his head. "I just can't imagine it being Porter Greeson. He used to come to the house. I remember him talking about his wife and little girl. He was the epitome of the doting father and husband. It used to make me jealous as hell. He positively glowed with pride and love. He was devastated when his wife died suddenly."

"Beverly isn't Lily's mother?"

"No. Porter met Beverly about three years ago in Paris. They were married within three months. I don't think Da...Donald...," he tried the moniker, liked it and continued, "has seen him since. She has a grown daughter. I can't remember her name."

"Well, damn," Jasmine spoke so softly Eryk barely heard her, which was saying something. He took the plates to the sink, giving her a moment.

Poor kid. Memories of another time came flooding back. She hadn't been much younger than Lily when she lost her mother and father. In celebration of their fifteenth anniversary, her dad had taken her mom on a skiing trip. They loved to ski. It was to be the honeymoon they'd never had. Teresa was commandeered to take care of Jasmine. On their second day, an avalanche took a good portion of the mountainside, her parents along with it. It had taken years for her to accept the fact that their bodies might never be found. At times like this, the visceral ache would punch like a fist into her stomach.

Jasmine's hand slowly rubbed at the invisible ache. "I'll go talk with her. Maybe I can reach her." She rose from the bar stool.

Eryk was around the island in a step. His hands rested on her shoulders. He had felt the anguish wash over her as though it had been his. "Jasmine," he said quietly, looking into her exotic eyes. He couldn't continue. Instead, he drew her into his embrace, letting his energy softly encase her, sending a light pulse of comfort.

Her arms encircled him and she inhaled his scent as she rested her head against his chest briefly. Too briefly, for the pulse sharpened, sped up, skittering awareness through both of them. She stepped away offering him an apology with her eyes, turned away, and went in search of Lily.

She found her sitting in front of the dressing table in her room, staring into the mirror. Tears streaked her checks. Jasmine walked quietly up behind her, reached around her and picked up the brush. Only when Jasmine ran the brush through her hair, did Lily look up. Her eyes looked hopeless, almost devoid of color.

"When I was young, my mother used to brush my hair. It was a little longer then."

Lily's eyes shifted downward, away from the memories. Jasmine pulled the brush gently through Lily's hair once more. "My parents died when I was twelve. I still miss them," Jasmine said.

Lily's eyes sought hers in the mirror. "I miss her so much."

"I know." She felt the tears in her own eyes, the ache and emptiness they'd both experienced. "I know." Jasmine softly stroked the girl's hair. "Is there anything I can do?"

Lily slowly shook her head.

Jasmine set down the brush and put her hand on Lily's shoulder. "How about we talk in the morning?"

"Thanks. Tell Eryk I'm sorry."

"He understands. Get some sleep. You're safe with us. I promise." As Jasmine eased the door closed behind her, she heard the soft sobs through the door. It took every ounce of her willpower not to turn back. Tomorrow they would find out the truth.

It made her furious, this impotence she felt. She'd been at Safe Harbor a year and the anger still welled in her with each person that found Safe Harbor's sanctuary. They came— battered, beaten, and silent. It was the wounds on their souls that called out to her. She'd never known betrayal by a family member, or even a member of her community. When she'd been attacked, Teresa had been there to pick up her pieces before she had time to completely fall apart. One thing Rob hadn't been able to reach was her spirit—because Safe Harbor had been there. But, so had Ruthorford. As was their way, they'd extended their sense of community, surrounding her with love to help ease her through the worst of it.

One of her first calls had been from Bill—the man who'd set aside is own angst to become her father figure when her parents had died. He'd said he loved her and she was his little girl, letting her know there was nothing that could happen to change that. Even Bask had been there for her, though she doubted he'd admit it in this lifetime. She always knew she could go back to Ruthorford and pick up where she'd left off before Rob had attacked her. Or, she could stay on at Safe Harbor. It was her choice.

Where did the others at Safe Harbor end up? What choices did they have? What did they have to go back to? There'd been times, when the families were getting ready to leave, that she wanted to bundle them up and send them to Ruthorford. She wanted to erase the fear and trepidation she saw fleetingly in their expressions, before they attempted to hide it.

She was so lost in thought, she almost ran into Eryk. He'd stepped out of the library, two glasses of wine in his hands. "I was just coming to find you." He held out a glass. "How's Lily?"

"She sends her apologies."

He nodded, turned, and walked back into the library. Soft music filled the room and a fire crackled in the fireplace.

"Nice," she said, walked to the soft leather couch, and sunk into its richness.

"I figured you could use a moment to relax." Though tempted, he didn't sit next to her but took the deep leather chair next to the sofa. "What were you thinking about?"

Jasmine looked up. He was studying the fire. It burnished his features and made his eyes appear more crystalline than usual. If she hadn't known Morgan, those eyes could appear unearthly, even frightening. Instead, they compelled her.

"I was thinking about how lucky I've been to have Ruthorford and Teresa and Bill. Even Bask."

"Bask," he teased, knowing the older man's affection for Jasmine was genuine.

"His bark is worse—"

"I know. I can tell." He looked at her now, humor in those emerald eyes.

Jasmine felt the tug in her belly. A tightening. An awareness of the virility of the man across from her. She took a sip of wine and set it on the heavy coffee table between her and the fireplace, not wanting the wine pushing the warmth she felt any further.

She leaned back into the soft leather and studied the flickering flames, listening to the hiss of the sap before it popped, and the smell of wood. "I love a real fireplace."

"I saw the wood stacked under the porte-cochere when I pulled the car around. I couldn't resist. Tell me more about your thoughts." He didn't want to tell her he felt like he could almost read them. As though, for a moment, he'd shared them.

She shrugged. "I suppose I was thinking about the people who come to Safe Harbor." She took a deep breath. "More about when they leave. When they come, it is all we can do to get them out of the nightmare mode they've been living in before they got to us. They jump at the slightest sounds. They apologize repeatedly for the most inane things. And the kids. The wariness. They're like scared rabbits. You can almost feel their little hearts beating out of their chests. The physical wounds go away long before the emotional ones do, if they ever do. Then, they get thrust back on the street. Oh," she looked at him, her eyes intense, before she continued, "we do everything we can to make sure they're safe. We try to find them work, a place to live." She looked down and took measure of her perfectly manicured nails. "But, it just isn't enough. They aren't ready, really. But we have no choice." She was quiet for a moment. "Sometimes they come back. Sometimes they don't make it back." Her voice cracked.

He saw the pain in her eyes, saw the muscles in her throat constrict as she swallowed. He saw her try to push it away and smile at him. "The music's nice." She changed the subject.

****

Lily stood at the top of the stairs, listening to the murmur of their voices as they drifted from the library. She'd started down thinking maybe a Coke would help the jitters she felt in her stomach. She'd had them since they'd left Safe Harbor. Hearing the concern in Jasmine's voice eased her own fears a little.

She'd taken the first step down when she heard a soft tone coming from the master bedroom. By the time she reached the bedside table, it had stopped. The light on his cell phone went black. He must have left it when he'd taken his shower.

She picked it up to take it to him. As she reached the hallway, she stopped, then rushed into her room, softly shutting the door before she hit some numbers.

"Carol," she whispered, "is that you?" Lily turned on the tub faucet and closed the bathroom door.

"Bell? I can barely hear you? Where are you? Everyone's frantic!"

"I can't talk any louder." She tiptoed over to the vanity and sat down. "I took off, okay. Had to."

"Then you don't know."

"Know what?"

"Beverly," Carol whispered back, referring to Lily's stepmother, "called me. She asked if I'd heard from you. I told her I hadn't, 'cause I hadn't. She told me to call her when I heard from you. Your dad was in the hospital."

"Where? When?" Panic surged through her, first at the mention of Beverly, then the news about her dad.

"I don't know. She called this afternoon. Said they were taking him to the lodge to recover."

"Thanks, Carol."

"Where are you?"

"Can't talk now." She hesitate a moment. "Do me a favor, will you?"

"Anything. You know that."

"Don't call Beverly. I've got to go." She hung up before Carol responded, turned off the tub, and snuck back into Eryk's room to replace the phone. She could hear them talking downstairs, quietly. She had to go. She had to get to her dad.

She set the phone back on the table and saw the keys lying next to it. Holding the keys in a tight fist to keep them from jingling, she tiptoed back to her room, nearly jumping out of her skin when Jasmine's phone shrilled from the library.

****

"Hey, old man." Jasmine smiled, ready to tease Bask.

Eryk watched the smile and the warmth in her eyes change in a second. She sat up straight. "When?" She listened for a moment. "He doesn't want me to come?" She repeated the words, her voice breaking. "Well, I don't care what he wants. Bask, Teresa's on the other line." She clicked accept. "Teresa, when did it happen?"

"Jasmine, honey, he's been going downhill since you left. I called Dr. Yancy this morning, against Bill's insistence. He's at the clinic." Her voice softened, grew a little hoarse. "Bill doesn't want you to see him this way. He said to tell you he loves you more than he ever dreamed possible...," she paused when her voice cracked. "There's nothing they can do for him, sweetie," Teresa's voice came out in a sob.

"I'm coming. Bask will get me there." Tears fell from Jasmine's eyes.

Eryk moved to the couch and put his arm around her. At first, her energy battled with his. He persisted and his heart beat softened hers. Her breathing eased.

"No," Teresa's voice was firm. "Please do as he wishes. This is hard enough. He won't let them treat him."

"Why the hell not?" Jasmine let anger replace sadness.

"Because it's his wish. I don't know. Morgan wanted to try. I begged him to let Eryk come. But he says it's only temporary and he won't deplete either one of them."

"I'm coming." Jasmine disconnected the call and hit speed-dial.

Eryk straightened, cocked his head and listened. The sound of an engine. Eryk was off the couch and running toward the front door, only to hear the gate moving. "Shit," he cursed and flew up the stairs, taking them two at a time. "Lily," he shouted toward the bedroom and at Jasmine at the same time. The door stood open. Lily was gone.

Jasmine was on the phone with Bask. "Lily's gone," she all but yelled. She stepped into the hallway and looked up to see Eryk walk in from the side door in the kitchen, shaking his head at Jasmine.

"She took the damn van. Dammit. We're stuck. I don't know, Bask. Just get someone here with a car." Jasmine felt her throat tight. She hung up on Bask.

Eryk walked over and put his arms around her. "I'm so sorry. About Bill. I don't know why I didn't hear her leave." He said, lying. He knew damn well. He'd been concentrating so intently on Jasmine and controlling her pain that he'd let his guard down.

"We'll get you to Ruthorford, somehow." He reached into his pocket for his phone. It wasn't there. Without a word, he ran back out of the room and up the steps. Jasmine followed him. He reappeared from his room studying his phone. "She made a call." When he started to dial, she put her hand on his, stopping him.

"Give me the number," she said as she dialed Bask. She repeated the number to Bask and told him that was all she had.

"Don't beat yourself up. She's been on the street. She's good at disappearing. But we're better," Bask tried to reassure her before he ended the call.

Eryk slammed his hand against the bannister. "I want to get you to Ruthorford."

It wasn't two minutes before Bask called back. "It's her best friend, Carol. I talked to her. She told me that the stepmother called and said her father was in the hospital and they were moving him to their lodge to recover. She has no idea where the lodge is. Stay put. A car's on its way."

"Not funny," Jasmine said into a dead line. As *if* they had any way to go anywhere.

She dialed Jenn. Without preamble, she asked the question that kept nagging at her. "Who actually approached Sonya?"

Jenn gave it some thought. "Lawyer, private detective. I don't know for sure."

"Was the father with them?"

"Let me check. What's wrong?"

"She gone. Her best friend told her that her dad was sick."

"Damn. I'll call Sonya."

Eryk was on his phone. "Listen. Sorry to bother you. When was the last time you talked to Porter Greeson?"

Donald Vreeland's voice was clip. "Probably a couple of years ago. Why?"

"Have you heard anything about him being sick, recently?"

There was silence. "No. I don't think so. Wait. I did hear he was in a hospital in Belgium a while back."

"Dad," Eryk almost choked on the word but hoped it would get results, "do you remember where their lodge is? The one in Virginia."

It had done the trick. Of course, throwing a little suggestion into his voice hadn't hurt either. His father's voice eased. "You remember. We used to go up there before Sarah died."

No. He didn't remember. That's because he hadn't been invited. They'd gone without him. They'd always gone without him. When he was young, a governess took care of him. Then, when he was older, he was sent away to school. His father's words brought him back. "Pretty place. It's a shame about Sarah. I went to his wedding to that socialite, Beverly—"

"Dad...," he snapped, then modulated his tone. He had to get that address. "Do you remember the address?"

Silence.

"Dad?"

"Hold on, I'm looking." The banter was gone. He'd lost whatever control he had over his father.

"I don't have an address. But, I can tell you about where it is."

Eryk held his impatience in check. Pushing his father at this point was not going to get him the information he needed.

"I have some notes on the computer."

"Send them to my phone, please, Dad."

"Okay. Done."

"Thanks."

"Eryk...." His father hesitated.

Eryk didn't give him a chance to continue. "I've got to run." He broke the connection.

Jasmine was sitting in front of the fire, staring at the flames. She didn't turn but kept staring, as though she was held captive by the hypnotic flicker. Her voice was soft when she spoke. "We don't know if she was trying to get to her father or running away." She forced her eyes up to his. "What if we're wrong?"

"I'll take that into consideration. You're going to Ruthorford."

Jasmine shook her head, the sadness like a weight, pushing her shoulders down. "No. There's nothing I can do for Bill. There might be something I can do for Lily." She heard her own voice hitch and took a deep breath.

"You don't have to." Eryk knelt in front of her, letting his hand cup the back of her neck. As soon as he did, their rhythms began to sync. He could feel her determination, her sadness.

"You didn't see her. You didn't read the notes on her physical abuse. I promised I would protect her—"

He brought his hand around and let his thumb stroke her jawline. "*We* promised." He amended quietly.

Her lips curved slightly as she nodded. "We promised." She let his touch sooth her.

Eryk's demeanor changed. "Let me borrow your phone."

The phone still cupped in her hand, Jasmine held it out. "Sure."

Eryk stood, looked through the numbers and hit one. "No," he laughed into the phone, "this isn't brat."

Jasmine knew Bask would have been trying to make her feel better, teasing her. Now she was embarrassed for Bask and maybe a little jealous. Bask only teased her. Hearing Eryk's laugh had tripped some sort of switch. She pushed the rising emotion down.

His voice turned serious. "Wouldn't that vehicle have some sort of tracking device?" He asked. He was silent for a moment, glanced at Jasmine before he spoke. "I should have realized you already had that covered. Okay. She's right here." He held out the phone to Jasmine.

"Sorry." She waited for him to read her the riot act for letting someone use her phone to call him. When it didn't come, she felt her nerves bunch. "Bask?"

There was a tightness in his voice she didn't recognize. Her insides shifted, waiting.

"He's gone, princess." Bask's voice was soft, gentle.

"No," she whispered and felt the tears fill her eyes. "But I just talked with Teresa."

"Dr. Yancy just phoned me. He just passed. Quietly."

"Teresa?" she asked with a broken voice.

"Mike's taking care of her. She'll be okay." He hesitated for a moment. "Jasmine, I want you to know something."

"What?"

"Bill asked for me to figure out what was going on with him. I'm sending a team to retrieve the body—" he stopped, tried again, "I'm sending a team to bring Bill back here to Abbott House."

Jasmine had visions of Bill being dissected, studied. She squeezed her eyes shut, forcing away the image. "If that's what he wants," she said flatly. Her stomach lurched; she felt the bile in her throat." She unconsciously took the glass of water Eryk held out to her and sipped.

"He was worried about whatever he has spreading throughout the descendants."

"I understand." Part of her brain didn't. It was Bill. Big gruff, loveable Bill. Not some experiment. "Here." She shoved the phone at Eryk, set the glass down, spilling some onto the table, and ran from the room.

Eryk heard the sobs coming from the deepest part of her being. "Bask, I need to go." He was already walking after her when he heard the bedroom door slam.

"I'll call you back about Lily. Go to her." The connection ended.

Eryk pushed the phone into his pocket and went up the stairs, listening for her sobs. It was quiet. He opened the door. She lay on the bed, curled into a fetal position, her face buried in the pillow she hugged. There was no sound, just the quivering her body made.

He slipped around the other side and eased onto the bed, curling his body around her, pulling her to him. He wrapped his arm around her waist and rested his head against hers, letting his energy flow into her, but not stopping the grief. She needed to release some of the anguish and the pain.

One thing he knew about himself, and surmised it to be true about her, was that, because of the way they were, they felt more intensely than others. It was as if the energy fed the emotions, be it happiness or sorrow, joy or grief. Or lust. With Jasmine being new to her abilities, it was unlikely that she'd learned to dissipate the energy that surged when her emotions surged. The best he could do now was level it off a little, let her grieve without being overcome.

Her body began to relax. He felt her muscles unbunch, one at a time. He was hoping maybe she'd drift off. She didn't. Her energy began to tangle with his, her silken cords snaking around his strands, sending a warm current up his arm and through his body. He tried to ease away from around her, but she turned with the movement of his arm, like a long lanky cat, her limber body curved toward him. He felt her inside of him, her energy calling to him, pulsing with his, a dance that wouldn't be denied. He tried to swallow but found his breath coming quicker as he looked into the watery black depths of her eyes.

Jasmine didn't know when the comfort had shifted to desire, when her body became hot and restless, wanting to be touched, stroked. She couldn't get close enough. She lifted her gaze to his and found herself staring into swirling deep emerald pools. Looking into his eyes sent her heart racing, the blood pounding through her veins, to pool deep inside, spreading outward, exciting nerve endings as it went. She licked her lips.

His eyes riveted on her mouth. Slightly swollen from her crying, it pouted, begging to be kissed. He felt her breath tease his mouth as her eyelids drifted half closed in invitation. He gently pulled her to him as his mouth took hers. He heard the sigh, then the soft moan as the kiss deepened.

Their energies swirled about them, wrapping them in a hot cocoon of desire. She became pliant in his arms, arching against the hand that stroked her. The heat of her body called to him. He felt her arm move around him, kneading the muscles of his back, pulling him closer to her. She arched against his hard length, moving her hips against him. The blood pounded in his ears.

He came out of this daze of desire. The pounding wasn't in his ears. It was the front door. He jerked back and stared into her gorgeous face, filled with desire. She blinked, seemed to become aware of her body pressed against his, and pulled her hips back as her face flushed a delightful pink.

"The...," his voice broke, "...the door."

Jasmine took a deep breath and looked around, trying to orient herself. She swung around and sat up on the side of the bed. The pillow she'd held fell to the floor, its case still damp from her tears. She pushed her hands through her hair, leaving it sexily disheveled.

"I better get that," he said and walked around the bed. Before she could react, he leaned in and pressed a hard kiss on her mouth, turned and strode from the room, shouting, "Hang on. I'll get there."

She smiled, hearing his voice crack again. Good. It wasn't just her. What the hell had come over her? Had someone not pounded on the door, she was sure she wouldn't have stopped before she'd had her way with him. All she wanted was to make love to him. It wasn't a "want," it was a "need." She needed to become one with him. Almost as if it were her right. No guilt. No shame. Just need.

She looked around. Was it this place? Like what happened in the lab. Was this whole place triggering their attraction? No, it was more than attraction. It felt different from anything she'd ever felt with any man in her life. Even Dorian. The scary part was that this was one itch that, once scratched, would bind her forever to one man. Was this what she really wanted? Was she ready? She pictured Eryk in her mind and a smile formed on her lips. He'd been so kind, so gentle with her. So receptive. Jasmine shook her head trying to clear it.

The voices she heard downstairs helped. So did the sound of her phone ringing in the distance. Glancing in the mirror, she ran her fingers through her hair, swiped at the smudges under her eyes, and adjusted her more than slightly wrinkled sweater before heading to the first floor. She found Eryk in the library talking to a man and a woman she didn't recognize.

"Martin and Stacy brought two vehicles, one for us. They'll hang out here for a while, in case Lily returns."

She nodded, but knew Lily wasn't coming back here. His eyes burning into hers, Eryk handed her the phone.

"You okay?" Bask's voice was gentle.

"Yeah. I'll be okay." Her voice sounded deeper, throaty.

If Bask noticed, he ignored it. "We've got a bead on her. She's heading toward Richmond. I figure she's going toward those coordinates Eryk gave me. Can't be certain until she gets there. She could turn off any time."

"Why aren't you having her stopped? Brought back?" She had an uneasy feeling building in her gut.

"Because something's going on. Porter Greeson hasn't been heard from for a couple of weeks. I don't know who called her best friend. I had assumed it was Porter's wife, but she denies it. She said her husband's been in Europe and is in the hospital in Belgium—for food poisoning. That he was fine last she heard. She didn't sound all that concerned. She sure as hell hadn't rushed to his side." There was disdain in his normally unemotional delivery.

"The weather's getting worse." Bask cleared his throat and his voice was once again clip, directive. "Plane's grounded. Can't send a chopper. You two need to get on the road. I'll keep you posted."

With each word, Bask was back to his controlling self. Jasmine was more comfortable with that. As long as he was strong, she could be strong.

"Martin and Stacy will keep a lookout," he said.

"The lab?" Jasmine asked. "Are they going to…?" Afraid of being overheard, she didn't finish.

"No. They work for John Davis. He sent them over."

"I've never seen them at Safe Harbor."

"Princess, Safe Harbor is only one of John's concerns. You take care." He hung up.

Eryk was coming down the stairs. "I threw some things in an overnighter. Yours, too," he added when she started to speak. "Let's get going."

Jasmine grew reflective as soon as they got on the road. The deep gray mist didn't help. She knew this was the right decision, but the idea of leaving Teresa alone at a time like this tore at her soul. She called Dorian only to find out that he and Morgan were already with Teresa. She was glad, but it should have been her. Teresa and Bill had gotten her through her grief. Now, she should be doing that for Teresa. She could just see Teresa, even in her pain, pushing it aside to make sure those staying at the bed and breakfast weren't affected. As if her thoughts traversed time and space, she got a text message from her cousin. *I found this attached to some documents. I scanned it, knowing you'd want to read it. I'm fine. I promise. You take care of that girl. I love you. T*

Jasmine opened the attachment and blinked, read the first words and had to clear the tears from her eyes.

To My Darling Daughter (because that's what you've been since the day you slipped your small hand into mine at your parents' funeral)—

I know I wasn't always the best father. Sometimes my fear of people overrode my good sense, but I tried to be there for you, the best I could.

I want you to know how proud I am of you. You grew into a beautiful, smart, savvy, and loving woman, a true descendant. As I can attest, being a descendant isn't always the easiest course to navigate, but in the end, it is a worthwhile endeavor. I know you were late coming into your own and it seemed to take the act of a mad man to bring it out, but that's not true. We all come into our own when the time is right and not before. I didn't come to my maturity until I returned to Ruthorford. It took Teresa to bring it out. Would that I could have done right by her…but I was obsessed with her from the time we were kids. It is only now that I can release her to be who she is and, with your encouragement, find the happiness she so rightly deserves.

I want you to know that you're exactly what you're supposed to be. You are the bravest woman I've ever known and I'm proud to have been allowed to share a part of your life. Take your steps as YOU see fit, be it slow and cautious, or fast, throwing that caution to the wind. Know that I love you and want only for you and Teresa to have long and happy lives.

Do not mourn me, for I'm doing what I must.

Uncle Bill

(p.s. Don't worry about furthering your talent in the kitchen. Although you can cook better than you think, that isn't where your talent lies. I love you.)

With tears flowing and a smile on her lips, Jasmine saved the document and put the phone away.

****

"Come on, honey. We're gonna be late." Teresa's voice was soft, yet held a note of urgency.

"It's not like they're going to start without me," Jasmine said with a bit more vinegar than was necessary. It wasn't Teresa's fault that all the people were standing around in the cold, waiting for a twelve-year-old. It wasn't like her parents were even in the damn graves. Why they bothered to dig up the dirt and make mounds in front of the granite markers was beyond her. So, if they were going to have the service, and she was going to be there, she was going to wear things her parents would have liked. She turned to Teresa, standing patiently in the doorway. "You go on. I want to put on the blue sweater my dad gave me and the boots mom bought. I'll meet you there."

Teresa didn't move—just frowned. "I can wait."

"It's next door. I promise I'll be right there." She walked over to Teresa and put her arms around her, kissing her on the cheek. Even at twelve, Jasmine was already taller than Teresa. Still all legs and arms, she hated the fact that she didn't have enough curves to fill out clothes the way she wanted.

Not waiting for an answer, she unzipped the dark brown dress she said she'd wear. It wasn't right. It was ugly and not what her parents would have wanted to see her in, even if it was their funeral. Especially, if it was their funeral. When she turned around Teresa was gone.

She let herself sink onto the side of the bed. This wasn't happening. They hadn't been found. Presumed dead wasn't dead dead. They weren't even having a ceremony at the second, private cemetery. Because there weren't any bodies. She tightened her hands into fists.

All descendants got two graves—one in the pretty cemetery next to the Chapel and one in the private cemetery in the woods behind The Shoppe of Spells. That's where the bodies were, in the private cemetery. Except her parents—their bodies wouldn't be anywhere—except under tons of snow and ice that would never melt.

She stood and pulled on the black skirt and the periwinkle sweater that made her skin glow. She slipped on the kid boots that had been a present from her mom and zipped them up. Standing, she slipped on a beret over her long black hair, cocking it just so, and put the blue tartan plaid around her shoulder, her fathers. Now, she was ready.

She slipped out of the side door of the B & B and made her way around the back of the Chapel to the side. She could see people gathered around, but couldn't see the headstones. Her stomach lurched. The nausea spread. Then she saw him. Bill. Standing off the side, under an old pecan tree, apart from the crowd, but just close enough. She took a deep breath, swallowed the bile rising in her throat and walked over to him. Tall and large, like the tree, he never turned. She stood beside him, slipped her hand into his, and felt the warmth course through her body, giving her strength.

****

Looking over at her, Eryk wasn't sure he wanted to wake her. But, she was frowning and he felt the sadness rolling off of her in waves. He didn't need a repeat of what had happened at the hotel, not in a moving vehicle. Eryk saw a sign and pulled up to a drive-through. "Jasmine," he said softly, "do you want something?"

She started. Blinking at the glare of the harsh lights, she tried to focus, straightening in the seat. "Diet Coke. Thanks."

"You want anything to eat?"

Not sure if the nausea was just a memory, she shook her head. "No. I'm fine."

They drove in silence for a time, until Eryk felt Jasmine's focus had returned to him. Only then did he ask her about her life with Bill and Teresa. She started slow, haltingly, but as the memories surfaced, she began reminiscing, even laughing. He let her express her grief in her own way. She finally mentioned the letter and the funeral. She left out the part about the dual cemeteries. Bask could explain that one.

Jasmine was relieved that Eryk hadn't mentioned what had happened in the bedroom at Meadow's Keep. She sure wasn't going to bring it up. Just being in the car with him took effort. Her body seemed to call out to his. It was beginning to annoy her. She caught him shifting in his seat. It was obvious she wasn't the only one suffering.

They were near Richmond when Bask called. The van Lily'd taken had stopped about an hour out to the northwest. From what Bask could gather, the area was very rural. He linked the GPS instructions to their car.

"By the way," she asked Bask, "did you ever get someone to take a look at Lily's medical records or the x-rays?"

"Mike did. The reports indicated her injuries were a result of a vehicular accident and some falls. Apparently the kid is clumsy."

"Like hell she is," Jasmine hissed. "She didn't have one incident the whole time she was at Safe Harbor. Something's not right," she added under her breath.

"I'll keep looking. Although, one of her teacher's did ask social services to look into it. On a couple of occasions, she was completely alone when the accidents happened. Everyone was elsewhere, corroborated by others."

Jasmine let the words sink in, not ready to put in her two cents. Something just didn't feel right. She let the phone rest in her lap and looked up to see Eryk glancing over at her. In the dark, with just the light from the dashboard illuminating his features, he looked so damn rugged, so dangerous. His eyes glowed faintly in the dark, sending shivers down her spine—not altogether unpleasant shivers. She was glad it was dark so he couldn't see the direction her thoughts had turned and the way her body betrayed her.

The drizzle turned into more of a mist and the fog lay low against the ground as they turned down an old gravel road. Tires crunched and bumped as they maneuvered down the unkempt lane. It would do them no good to meet someone coming the other way because there was no place to pull off. Trees grew close to the road, with the road carved out in a meandering fashion through them. When the lane suddenly widened, a huge dark shape rose out of the fog. Eryk switched his lights off, turning on only the parking lights. They were almost upon the van before they saw it. He hit the brakes and took a slight skid to the left, just missing the bumper. Pulling further in, he turned the car around so they were facing out, and stopped.

Jasmine looked out the window and gave an involuntary shudder. A large building loomed against a moonless sky, more apparition than wood and stone. She climbed out and closed the door, the sound much louder than she expected. Eryk walked over to the other vehicle and put his hand on the hood.

"Cold," he whispered.

"Well, if anyone's here," she whispered back, "I'd be real surprised. Unless they're in a basement."

Eryk took her hand and led her around to the back. He stopped and motioned for her to wait. Like hell, she thought, glancing around at the blackness behind her. Eryk was peering through windows, then came back to the door, tried it, did his energy thing, and turned the knob. Nothing like a little B & E, she thought to herself, trying to force down the nerves.

She followed him in, staying on his heels, while her eyes adjusted to the dark. He stopped, listening.

"There's no one here," he whispered in her ear. "I'd hear them."

"Like you did at Meadow's Keep?" she jibed, her voice low.

"I was distracted. I'm not now."

He opened and closed doors down the hallway. A pantry, utility room, broom closet, and half bath. No basement. They walked through the kitchen. Dishes cluttered the counter. It looked as though someone had been eating standing up. A coffee cup sat on a table near the window. He opened the refrigerator. Jasmine squinted into the blinding light.

"Looks like there's just enough food for several days. Not enough to house a convalescing patient."

"Do you think they took him back to the hospital?"

They'd walked into the great room. Magazines were tossed on the couch.

"Stay here." Eryk said and headed to the stairs.

When Jasmine started to follow him, he stopped. "I'm serious. If anything happens, get the hell out," he said and handed her the car keys.

She didn't like it but nodded and let her energy flow to her fingertips. Jasmine positioned herself behind the door, at the foot of the stairs, where she could see someone coming from any direction.

As the moments ticked by, Jasmine's nerves began to vibrate. The place was too damn quiet. Her pulse pounded in her ears, making it impossible to hear anything else. Hell of a time to have a panic attack. She breathed in through her nose, exhaled slowly out of her mouth. As quickly as it had increased, her heart steadied and slowed. Her breathing evened.

Eryk. The thought slipped into her mind. She looked up the stairs to see him staring down at her, his eyes glowing. He moved fast and was in front of her in an instant, placing his hands on her arms. She inhaled that clean scent that had become so familiar.

"I know I keep asking this but, are you okay?"

"I'd love to say, 'You know me too well,' but you cheat. You look at my aura or feel my energy…or read my mind, for all I know. However, I appreciate the thought," she said softly and looked at his hand, "and the energy manipulation." She stepped back, just out of his reach—into safer territory.

"No one's here," he said in a normal tone. "But they were."

Chapter Fourteen

As they headed further west, being directed by the accented voice of the GPS device in the vehicle and the directions download by Bask, Eryk wondered just how in the hell he'd managed to get in the situation he found himself. Not a month ago, his life had been nice and tidy. Orderly. Hell, it was planned out for the next couple of years. Now, he found himself sitting next to a gorgeous brunette he couldn't seem to get out of his friggin' mind for even a moment, driving God knows where in order to rescue a girl he wasn't even sure needed rescuing. Scratch that...he was pretty sure Lily needed rescuing...he just wasn't sure from what.

His business manager had called again. He'd put him off. However, when Brandy had called, he'd paid attention. It wasn't as if he could ignore them. He was a corporation, after all, with employees depending on him. So, as of now, the show was on hiatus. Fortunately, for him, this time of year was slow anyway—for the performances. It was a busy time for him development-wise. This was when new shows were planned, illusions created, sets designed, and schedules secured. If he wanted to be ready for the summer kickoff, he'd better get back damn soon.

Funny, that wasn't the way his career had started. It had started as an act of defiance against his father. Oh, he'd played with magic and illusions from the first time the current leapt from his fingers. Daniel, more father than butler, had known, right from the onset. He figured Daniel probably knew even before he had. Eryk smiled to himself, remembering how often he had zapped Daniel inadvertently. Daniel had shown him some tapes and given him some books. The magic was a way to corral his power, keep it in check. Then, he did a show for the children's hospital when his best friend developed leukemia. Then another...and so forth, until he found himself with a corporation, a manager, and people that depended on him. He didn't mind that. They were good people and understood more about him than most. They knew when his moods threatened and to leave him alone. Anger had been the hardest to learn to control and with it, the energy flow. Knowing how well controlled he was now, that seemed eons ago.

Then Jasmine came along. Just being around her had his mind in a twist. He'd never felt anything like it. He craved her, like a parched man in the desert craved water. When she was near, he wanted to be closer. Touching her. Inhaling her. When she wasn't, he thought he would go mad. Dorian had made it damn clear just what the ramifications were of their being intimate. Sex. One act of sex, pure and simple, and he was bound to this woman for life. That was something that was hard to wrap his mind around. Yet, he still wanted her. He should be running for the hills. The truth was, he doubted he would ever want anyone other than her, even if she chose to go on without him.

"What?" she responded to the look he gave her.

"Nothing. Just thinking." He pulled his mind back to the problem at hand. "Any idea what we're going to do when we get there? Wherever *there* is."

"Bask did a search and found one property that belongs to Greeson within a 200-mile radius. There are others, out of state, but this seems the most likely. It's a wild shot, at best. But we have to start somewhere."

"It's obvious that Lily went to the lodge. Someone had to be waiting for her. We didn't see any indication that a sick man had been cared for there. So, we need to assume that she went with them—willingly or unwillingly. I didn't see any sign of a struggle."

Eryk watched Jasmine squirm to retrieve her phone.

She jiggled her phone out of her pants' pocket and answered. "I don't know where we are," she started the conversation. *God*, she moaned inwardly, she was picking up Bask's bad habit of answering the phone in the middle of a conversation.

"Keep with the GPS. I just wanted to let you know that we located Porter Greeson." Bask didn't seem at all perturbed with her comment.

"He's not where we're headed, is he?" Jasmine's stomach did a flip-flop as apprehension surged.

"No. He's in a private sanitarium in Sweden."

Jasmine mind swung to visions of Rob, the man who'd attacked and raped her, residing in the privately funded—the majority of which came from Abbott House—convalescent facility in Virginia. She didn't say anything, just waited for Bask to continue.

"Jasmine. Whoever is doing this, is *not* Porter Greeson. I talked to the girl's—"

"Lily," Jasmine injected. She didn't like Lily being referred to as 'the girl.' "Her name is Lily."

"What? Oh. Yes. Lily," Bask slipped in the correction. "Her friend said she was very close to her father and was upset when she told her he'd been ill. All she knew was that *Lily* had ended their conversation abruptly. She figured she was heading up to the lodge."

"As I told you, it was obvious that Mr. Greeson, especially if he was ill, hadn't been there. However, someone had been staying there and made a hasty departure, apparently with Lily in tow. Where's the stepmother?" Jasmine's tension sent tiny shots of energy through her body. The phone crackled.

"Calm down, Jasmine, you're breaking up." Bask admonished. He was tired of replacing her phones. At least now he know why. "Beverly Greeson is at their house in Arlington. That's the number I called and she—I assume it was her—talked with me. I found some pictures of her, but none of the daughter. I'll keep looking."

"Thanks."

"By the way, Teresa says they will plan a memorial for when you come down."

Jasmine felt her throat constrict. She was doing her best not to think about Bill. "Thanks," she whispered.

She laid the phone in her lap and looked at Eryk.

"I heard."

"Oh, yeah. I guess that's convenient. Am I too loud, when I'm next to you?"

"No. I find your voice very soothing, actually."

They were interrupted by the lilting voice of the GPS. "Turn left 300 feet."

He slowed and turned off the country road.

"What do we do if she isn't here?" Jasmine hated considering that possibility.

"I don't know. Get some rest and regroup, I suppose. I don't know about you, but I'm getting tired."

"I just hate not knowing. I don't want to leave her out there, alone…facing God knows what."

He reached over and let his hand cover hers. The current that passed between them was low but steady. She looked up and smiled. Jasmine realized she was getting used to the feel of his energy seeking hers. She was more than getting used to it, she sought his in return.

Jasmine wasn't sure where they were headed in this relationship or if it was a relationship, even now. It embarrassed her to think about how assertive she'd been in the bedroom at Meadow's Keep. There was no doubt in her mind that she would have had her way with him given half a chance. This "match-mate" thing was stronger than she'd ever suspected. Teresa had warned her years ago. One just doesn't take heed without need.

After what happened with Rob, and even knowing what had happened between Teresa and Bill, then Morgan and Dorian, she'd still doubted its ability to override her fear. Yet, there she'd been, acting like a cat in heat, not thinking, just wanting. And here she sat, rationalizing her irrational behavior. Behavior as old as the descendants.

The jingle of her phone made her jump. She slipped her hand from under Eryk's and picked up the phone.

"...sending you a picture. You need to look at it," Bask voice streamed in like he was in an ongoing conversation. Half the time, Jasmine wondered if he just kept right on talking after they disconnected. She smiled at the image in her head.

The smile left her face as the picture popped up on her screen of her phone. "Who the hell...?" she didn't finish but turned the phone for Eryk to see. It was a picture of a woman, several years older than Jasmine, she surmised, around Eryk and Dorian's age. She was stunning. Thin, tall, short brown hair, rich, the color of mink, and emerald green eyes. The same eyes looking at her now from the other side of the vehicle.

"Who is that?" Eryk asked, his voice taking on a weary quality.

Jasmine put the phone on speaker. "I don't recognize her. I know there are more of us out there, but I don't recognize the face. I do, however, know those eyes. Who is she?"

Bask's voice broke up.

"Damn it, Bask. You're breaking up. What?"

"You need to calm down, then, Jasmine. You're spiking. That's Arabella Greeson's step-sister. I've been looking all over the place. I found it in a press release about the time her mother married Porter Greeson. There was a side note. Her name's Morna Monroe." He let the news sink in.

"Don't tell me she's my damn cousin?" Jasmine hissed.

"She has her mother's maiden name. All I can find out is that Beverly Monroe arrived in Paris about thirty years ago...from Scotland...with a small child. Claimed her husband was dead. Nobody cared because she had plenty of money to throw around. Everyone assumed Monroe was the married name. Apparently, she had an "in" to the elite, set down her roots, and stayed there. Claimed to be a very private person, allowing no pictures to be taken of her daughter. The one at Beverly's wedding is all I could scrounge up."

"And you are such a good scrounger," Jasmine noted.

As she talked to Bask, Eryk turned off the headlights and eased forward into a dark gravel circle. No lights were on. There were no cars parked in front. The place looked deserted. Of course, Jasmine learned this from Eryk, since she didn't have the night vision he did. Curious, she reached over and laid her hand on his arm and blinked. Though dim, she could begin to make out details of the building in front of her. When she turned to Eryk, he was watching her. She pulled her hand away. "Sorry," she whispered and hoped he didn't see her blushing.

"Bask. I don't think anyone's here. It looks closed up. No cars. We'll take a look around and get back to you."

"Be careful, you two. Now, particularly—be very careful."

Jasmine slipped the phone in her pocket and opened the door. With the interior lights off, even with her eyes adjusting, she stepped into the blackness. Eryk came around the car and reached for her hand.

"Do you want to stay here?" he asked softly, misinterpreting the tremor that went through her, causing her hand to shake slightly.

"No. I can see when I'm touching you. Probably not as well as you, but some."

He gave her hand a squeeze. "Then, by all means, touch me." There was a lilt in his teasing whisper.

She reached out and pinched his side, though there wasn't much to pinch of the tightly fitting flesh.

"Ow. I owe you." He pulled her along with him and walked around the house to the back.

He stopped, turned to her, putting his finger to his lips. The tension surged, as did the energy. Eryk dropped her hand and cocked his head, listening.

"There's no one here," he said after a moment. "We'll take a look around. I hear an animal foraging and the hoot of an owl in the distance. No human sounds." He put his hand on the knob and Jasmine watched purple-blue sparks shoot from beneath his grip.

"Let me try next time."

"Sure." He eased open the door. "Have you noticed anything odd?"

"Like what?" She followed closely behind him as they stepped directly into a large great room.

"No security. Silent or otherwise."

"Not having much experience with breaking and entering, I'd have to say, no, I didn't notice."

He took her hand. Immediately the area seemed brighter. He pulled her back outside, threw the lock and pulled the door shut. "Here, before you grasp the knob, hold your hand around it, but don't touch it."

She did as he asked. "And?" She looked at her hand encircling the door knob.

"If it were armed you would feel a slight buzz. Not enough to set it off but enough for you to know it's there. It won't tell you if it's set or not, just that it's there. That's when you have to make the decision if you want to really do it and risk having the cops on your ass."

Before she could comment, he continued. "Now, grasp the knob. Let the current move quickly through your hand. Too slow and it won't disengage. Too fast and you'll pop it."

Jasmine applied her deadbolt technique, turned the knob, and opened the door.

"You're a natural." He smiled at her and followed her back into the great room.

She wasn't about to tell him how much practice she'd had, opening locks. He was right. The wrong amount and it could actually fuse the lock. That's why she had a bolt cutter.

A slight smell of dust and disuse assailed her senses. No one had been here for some time. Eryk flicked on a table lamp and the warm glow swept over an oxblood leather sofa. A large stone fireplace, flanked by high picture windows overlooked the back. She stepped around the couch and noticed that a fairly heavy layer of dust, undisturbed, covered the narrow table butted up against the back of the couch.

"No one's been here for at least six months," she mused. "Wonder why they keep the electricity on?"

"Because they can." Eryk mumbled. He'd grown up rich. Electricity to run a closed up cabin cost but a pittance, making the place available on a moment's notice. This structure wasn't that different from his father's in Massanutten, Virginia.

He went into the kitchen, flicked on some lights, and opened the fridge. Bottled water, Coke, Light Beer, Ginger ale. An unopened block of cheese. Couple of cans of tuna. V-8.

The pantry revealed soups, crackers, just slightly out of date, pasta, jars of sauce. An easy and quick dinner.

Part of the pantry housed bottles of wine resting on their sides. He picked up one, looked at it, brought it out to the kitchen, and set it on the counter.

"Let's finish our tour and then I'll fix us a bite to eat. I'm starving."

"Here?" Jasmine asked.

"Why not? No one's here. I'd hear someone long before they got here." He shrugged and made his way up the steps to the second floor.

They found five bedrooms, all with their own baths, cleaned but unused. Clothes hung in four of the five closets, but not enough to indicate year-round inhabitance. One looked to contain clothing that Jasmine guessed belonged to Lily. She slid the hangers across the rod, examining the clothes with a critical eye. *Not bad*. She contemplated taking a few things back with her for Lily. No. Something had spooked her enough to cause her to flee her own family. Until she knew what that was, she didn't want to push anything on her, even clothes.

They walked back into the kitchen and Eryk immediately started pulling out pans. "We're having pasta. Nothing fancy. But the wine is excellent." He smiled over his shoulder at her.

Jasmine opened several cabinets until she found the wine glasses and, setting them on the counter, reached for the bottle.

"I've got it." Eryk took the bottle from her, rummaged through some draws and came up with an opener.

"You don't have a problem doing this, do you?" She settled on one of the bar stools on the other side of the large island. It looked like hand rubbed teak and was warm to the touch. She found herself absently stroking it as she watched him.

"What? Availing myself of their hospitality? Not a bit."

He set the bottle aside to let it breathe and worked on the sauce. He found some garlic, slightly aged but still okay, dried herbs, a package of dried mushrooms, black olives, and canned Roma tomatoes. He poured water and oil over the dried mushrooms and set them aside, started the garlic simmering in oil, opened the cans, a jar of sauce, and filled a large pot with water from the tap over the stove.

"I'd like one of these," Eryk said, indicating the tap as he shut off the water. "If I ever settle down, I think I want one."

"Where do you live?"

"Here and there. I'm on the road a lot, although I do have a place in Mississippi, where we winter over."

"Don't you worry about hurricanes?"

"Not really. We're far enough inland to be okay. So far. Knock wood." He knocked on the teak wood of the island. "My buildings were built to withstand storms: heavy chain walls, hurricane strapping and the like. Hell, we'd be safer in the equipment rooms than in the apartments. I have an apartment building for all of us."

"How about the families?" she asked, thinking of Brandy.

"Brandy's husband's an engineer," he said. "Her parents live in one of the apartments and take care of their twin boys." His mind flashed quickly to the two laughing redheads, their curls glinting in the sun as they roughhoused around the workshop. The crew had built them one hell of a play area with a fort, spiral slide, and all sorts of contraptions to keep them entertained, nearby, and out from underfoot. Sadness singed his heart. He and Dorian could have been like those little boys, not a care in the world, except seeing what trouble the two of them could get into. He knew his childhood had come nowhere near that kind of rough and tumble joy. He wondered if Dorian's had.

Jasmine watched him stir the sauce as he spoke and knew the moment a troubled thought took hold. She could sense it as well as read it in his expression. She absently rubbed at her heart.

She retrieved the bottle of deep red wine and poured each of them a glass, quietly setting his next to the stove where he worked. As she stepped back, her fingers brushed across his arm and she felt the surge of energy smack into her.

Instantly, his fingers curled around her wrist and he turned, took the glass from her hand, and pulled her into an embrace, his mouth crushing down on hers, searing her soul. She let the feel of him rush through her. It was at once hot and sizzling, cold and tingling. Her lips parted and she accepted his heat as his tongue stroked and teased.

Her phone broke them apart like two guilt-ridden teenagers, their faces flushed, their nerves on edge. Her voice broke when she answered the phone.

"You aren't getting sick, are you?" Bask demanded.

She wanted to cough, to clear her throat but didn't dare. She took the glass Eryk held out and took a gulp of wine instead, felt it hit the wrong pipe, and the coughing spasm start. She shoved the phone at Eryk.

"Something went down the wrong way," Eryk said and tried to steady his own voice. He hit speaker.

Bask, as usual, began in the middle of a thought. "...did some checking. The next closest location is down in southern Virginia. It belongs to Porter's wife, Beverly. Why don't you two stay where you are, get some sleep. I'll load some coordinates in the GPS, or I can meet you somewhere with the helicopter and have a car waiting."

"I'm not leaving her stranded...," Jasmine tried to choke out, thinking of the mine where she'd been shackled, naked and hurt.

"And you won't be doing her any good exhausted. Your powers dampen when you're tired. You might not know that, so I'm telling you. We don't know what you're facing—or who, for that matter."

"Who?" Jasmine's voice quieted.

"I don't like the feel of this." Bask supplied. "I don't like it at all. I can't trace Beverly Monroe to Scotland. Morna doesn't exist until that picture at the wedding, except for anecdotal quotes." Bask hesitated a second. "The only reference I have to Scotland, at this point, other than the original descendants, is Ian and he said he was the last. No. I don't like this at all." He hung up.

Jasmine looked at the dead phone. "God, that man drives me crazy." She set it down on the island and found herself edgy and nervous and definitely not wanting to look at Eryk. "I think I'll get my bag and freshen up, if that's all right?"

"Need some help?" Eryk asked, trying to keep his tone serious, as he stood with his back to her, drained the mushrooms, and added them to the simmering oil.

"No." She let out a laugh. "I don't think so."

"I'll finish this and set it to simmer. Take your time."

Jasmine slipped out the back door and headed to the vehicle. She reached for the door handle when she realized how well she could see. Glancing up, the saw the moon peeking through the trees. An earsplitting screech pierced the night and she fell back against the door, dizziness spiraling through her as her vision shifted. Thrusting out her hands, she felt for the frame of the door, held on, and blinked. She was above the trees, looking down. Something scurried across the ground, a small length of fur. Bright lights broke over the trail of the animal. The bird circled and she could see the building, the car, and her body leaning against the door. She could also see the lights filtering through the kitchen. She blinked and took a deep breath, slammed the door and ran to the back door. As an afterthought, she hit the remote, locking the vehicle.

"Hit the lights," she yelled, "someone's coming."

Eryk had already hit the switch. She saw her phone on the island just before the lights went out. She grabbed it and dialed through to Bask. "Someone's coming up the road." She yelled into the phone before Eryk grabbed her hand and pulled her into the hallway. She could see the lights of the car flash across the windows as the car pulled up.

Eryk thrust her behind him. "Stay behind me. They won't see you."

"What about you?"

"I can bend the light. They won't see me either," he waited a beat, "unless they come inside."

Jasmine pulled her arms up tight, grabbed fists of his shirt, and tucked her head, resting it against his back. She felt the energy spread into her and back out through him. Although they were down the hall, she felt like they were totally exposed. She prayed Bask wouldn't call her back.

Eryk stood still, a statue, pushing with his mind. *The house is empty. There is no vehicle. Leave.*

Two men walked toward the front of the house, flashlights shining. As they stepped on the porch, one of their phones went off. "Yeah, Sarge. Nobody here. Quiet as a mouse." He listened for a moment. "Sure. We'll swing by and pick up the pizzas." They began to move away. Eryk kept concentrating until the vehicle had circled around and left. Finally, he relaxed and shook his shoulders, releasing the tension.

"How come they didn't see the car?"

"Not sure. I tried to put thoughts in their heads that it wasn't there. I really have no idea if it worked."

Jasmine stepped back. "That's a neat trick. You think I can learn it?"

"Haven't a clue. We'll try some time. But right now, I'm starving." He stumbled as he turned and Jasmine put her arm around his waist steadying him.

"If it's that much of a drain, maybe I don't want to know how to do it," she teased.

Eryk's energy could drain, yet be instantly replenished. The weakness would only last a couple of minutes. He didn't bother to tell Jasmine that since he was enjoying the feel of her arms around his waist.

"You want me to finish up?" She hesitated next to him.

"No. I've got it. You call Bask and let him know we're okay. I have a feeling the old man is chewing his nails."

Jasmine moved around the island and hit redial, watching Eryk turn the stove back on and wait for the water to boil. Her conversation was quick and he promised to call and wake them up in a couple of hours.

Eryk set the plates on the island. Steam rose and the aroma of Italian herbs and garlic mingled with the rich sauce and smelled liked someone had slaved for hours over a stove. He toasted her with the wine and they dug in, hunger replacing conversation.

Jasmine hadn't realized how much he'd put on her plate until she sighed and pushed it back, leaving more than half of the plate still covered with food. Her head felt a little light and the wine was coursing through her veins. "I think I'm more exhausted than I realized. If you don't mind, I'm heading on up. I'll take the room at the top of the stairs. I'll shower later. Alone," she added.

"I'm right behind you once I clean this up."

By the time she reached the room, she could barely keep her eyes open. She pushed off her shoes, one foot at a time and crawled across the bed, dragging the cover over her. She blinked once and was fast asleep.

The heat in the room was stifling. She could smell lavender. Not light, but heavy. Cloying. She pushed back the covers and the scent lightened. She rolled over on her back and opened her eyes. The swirls in the plaster ceiling undulated, moving to a rhythm. Jasmine smiled. The dream felt familiar. The air shifted and moved around her, caressing her body. She let her hands move across her body, following the caress of the air. She inhaled the lavender, no longer heavy but enticing.

Her body ached for him. She could smell him—that scent that was Eryk—mingling with the lavender. She was free to have her dream lover. She let her hands move up his chest and slip around his neck, opening her eyes to gaze into the swirling deep green of his mystical ones.

His mouth crushed down on hers, taking what was his. Their tongues battled, stroked, cajoled. The room grew hotter and they pulled at their clothes, wanting the freedom from their weight and the magic of their bodies touching, sliding together, seeking.

The energy clashed, fought, and merged until two hearts beat as one. The energy found a voice and hummed around them as they sought and explored and fed. The ache was too much. With arms and legs entwined they became one, riding the waves of energy until their cores exploded and they fell to earth, sated.

God, what a dream. Jasmine took a deep breath and threw out her arm—across Eryk's solid chest. She shot up like a rocket, turned and watched his green eyes focus. She followed his gaze to her naked breasts.

"Shit!" She tried to grab the sheet tangled beneath their two bodies. "What in the hell are you doing in my room?"

A smile played across his lips and he looked toward the door. She frowned. The door was on the wrong wall. The sheet slipped away and her arm fell. She was in *his* room. She had come to *his* room.

She looked back at him, panic in her eyes.

He sat up on the side of the bed and ran his hands up and down her arms, letting his energy soothe. But, it didn't, it pulsed and the urge to slip into each other's arms and a heated kiss was overwhelming. He stood and, as his mouth moved over hers once more, sanity slapped at her, and she leapt back, nearly tripping over a pile of clothing.

Jasmine shook her hands as if to dissipate the energy or fling it away from her. "Oh," she muttered. Oh, no." She reached down, grabbed some clothes, and fled.

Eryk watched the svelte, naked shape retreat across the hall. Just watching her move made his pulse pound in his veins. He couldn't get enough of her. Okay, sure, so part of it was that match-mate thing. When she came in his room earlier, his very being reached out for her. Looking back, he wasn't sure if he'd ever had a choice. From the time she appeared at the fairgrounds, her soul called to him. Now he'd answered. He smiled, And it felt damn good. He stretched, arched his back, felt his muscles lengthen and relax. The power flowed through his body, every fiber carrying energy.

Then he felt it—gut wrenching anguish. It coursed through his body like molten lava, sluggishly tugging at his heart. He reached for his jeans, rubbing at his chest where the ache was, and yanked the denim up his legs. He had leapt two steps forward as the anguish clawed at him. He slammed open the door across the hall and ran through the empty room.

In the bathroom, she was slumped against the large marble tub, her arms wrapped around her naked waist, tears falling unchecked to the floor. Not a sound emerged from her lips. With her head down, he couldn't see her face. But, he could feel her, as though his soul rested next to hers.

Eryk sat next to her and gathered her cold, naked, quivering body into his lap. "Jasmine…honey…it'll be all right. We'll make it all right—"

A soft whimper escaped as she curled deeper against him.

"It's not so bad. I'm really a nice guy," he encircled her with his arms and rocked.

"Oooooh—" The sound came out half moan, half hiccup.

He brushed her hair back, tilting her head back and looked into the deep black pools of her eyes, filled with tears. Eryk gently kissed her brow. "There's no one in this world I'd rather be tied—" He realized, at her louder wail, that that particular word shouldn't have come from his lips and decided silence was best. So he held her and rocked her, until the weeping passed.

Once she quieted, he shifted her and managed to stand, holding her to his side. "Let's get you into a warm shower." He turned on the water and waited, holding her up.

Jasmine let him hold her. It was all she could do. The sadness had encompassed her. She knew Eryk was right. He wasn't a bad guy. Hell, she'd been the one to come to him. She couldn't seem to control the pain and anguish that drained her of any thought. She let him take control and lead her under the warm spray of water. It soothed the ache. As he took the bottle of body wash and poured it into his palm, she opened her eyes and her heart melted. Eryk was standing under the spray with her, still wearing his jeans, the v of the unzipped front having slipped down to show a trail of dark hair that thickened and disappeared beneath the soaked denim. Her breath quickened as her eyes moved up his abdomen and over the taut muscles.

Eryk took the soap and spread it across both palms, then ran his hands up her arms. All he could think of was to soothe her ache. The contact with her flesh sent a flash of energy through him, straight to his gut and his eyes focused on her tawny brown areolas as they hardened and puckered before his gaze. He swallowed and raised his gaze to her face. Her eyes had darkened and she parted her full lips and let her tongue slip out, licking the bottom one. Her hands took his wrists and slid them around until his hands were cupping her breasts. Then she slid her now soapy hands up his chest to ease around his neck. She pulled his mouth down to hers.

They were lost in passion. His mouth took hers and she began to rub herself against him, moaning, begging. He pushed her back against the wall, his mouth nipping at her neck, his hands luxuriating in the heat of her body.

"Please," she whimpered.

Eryk shoved his jeans down, and lifting her, eased her down until he was deep inside her swollen body. Jasmine wrapped her long legs around his waist and began to move as he cupped the cheeks of her bottom.

As they moved together, the energy built between them, flowing back and forth, as though they shared one system. Their hearts, pounding furiously, beat out the same rhythm. She called his name in her mind and he answered, as if they'd spoken. Higher, they reached yet higher, and their bodies seemed to meld together. When their climaxes exploded from them, so did the energy, sending sparks of light dancing around the shower.

Still breathing heavily, Eryk held her in place against the wall and let the shower ease his galloping heart. "I'm so sorry, Jasmine," he panted out. "This was not what I intended."

Her voice came out as breathy, "Me, either." She unwrapped her legs and slid down his body. Then she looked up at him. "I do feel better," she added with a half-smile.

"Well...uh...glad I could be of help...," he said but didn't smile.

Jasmine reached up and placed her hand on his face. "I really am better. I don't know what happened."

Eryk stepped out of his jeans and kicked them aside. "Shall we try this shower thing again?"

The double-headed shower made for double efficient showering and Eryk stepped out as Jasmine rinsed her hair. He was waiting for her with two towels, one for her head and one for her body. Eryk watched as she wrapped the oversized towel about her body, neatly tucking the ends over her breasts.

She walked over to the tub and, briskly rubbing the towel over her short black hair, sat right above where she'd been leaning earlier. Her hands abruptly stopped their motion. "Oooh." The moan was low and keening.

Eryk swung around at the sound to see Jasmine grab her middle and lean forward. In one step he pulled her up into his arms. Jasmine stiffened and stood rigid against him. Seconds passed as neither budged—her assessing and him waiting.

Jasmine stepped away from him and looked up into his green eyes that had instantly grown darker. "Did you feel that?"

Cautiously, he studied her. "When I pulled you to me, it was the same anguish as earlier. Are you okay?"

She frowned. "Yeah," she responded and stopped, seeming to take some sort of mental inventory. "Yeah," she repeated, her voice stronger. "I'm fine."

"Then what the hell just happened?"

"I don't know, but we're gonna find out." She walked back to the tub and sat in the same spot. Prepared this time, the anguish wasn't as sharp, but it was still pervasive.

Jasmine reached out her hand to Eryk.

Eryk had watched her take the two steps to the tub, her body tall and sure. As soon as she'd lowered herself to the edge, a frown creased her brow and she reached out for him. The moment their hands touched, he felt that sapping ache, the sadness oozing through him like lava. He pulled her to him and away from the tub. The ache lessened until it dissipated. He found himself taking a deep breath.

Jasmine ran her hand through her short hair, setting it into soft spikes.

Eryk smiled. She was the only woman he'd ever seen that was beautiful any way he saw her, whether coiffed and dressed in her designer couture or still damp from a shower, scrubbed, with her hair in total disarray. He felt a warmth in the region of his heart and let it settle, enjoying the intimacy of it.

"I can't think of the damn word," she said, bringing his thoughts back to her pacing back and forth. She waved her hands in the air, giving them a little shake. Tiny sparks flew from her fingers. "Damn," she uttered and tucked her hands under her arms.

"You okay?"

As if she had just realized he was there, she turned and focused on him. "That psychic phenomenon—the one where an object keeps an image—or something like that." She resumed pacing. "I need to call Bask. But I don't want to call Bask."

"Why don't you want to call Bask?"

She stopped and confronted him. "Because he'll know," she hissed.

"I have a feeling he suspects anyway. We really need to talk to him. What happened was strange, even by Ruthorford standards, I suspect."

"Well, don't look at me. I wouldn't know." Her voice rose and each word became clipped.

Eryk threw up his hands. "Hey. I'm on your side. Remember me, your mate."

If looks could injure, he was sure the one she gave him was meant to do harm.

"I was just trying to throw a little levity on the situation," he added.

Her narrowed eyes shut him up. He grabbed his jeans and wrung them out. "Well, these have to go in a dryer or you need to go get me some jeans from the car."

"Why me?"

"Because this is all I've got." He whipped off the towel and plastered a big grin on his face.

Jasmine felt her breath hitch. He was magnificent. *And he's mine.* Now, where in the hell had that thought come from. "Put the towel back on, I'm going." She marched out of the bathroom and halfway across the hall when she stopped, pivoted on her heel, and stepped up to him to grab her clothes out of his hand. His laughter followed her into the bedroom where she took pleasure in slamming the door.

Jasmine slipped on the jeans and sweater she'd worn the day before. She was really getting tired of being so haphazard in her appearance. It wasn't that she was vain. It gave her a sense of control. She cursed herself for not at least bringing in her bag when she ran from the car. She was straightening her sweater when she heard the chirp of her phone coming from the pile of items still on the floor.

She grabbed it up and dropped down on the edge of the bed. It was Bask. She inhaled deeply and answered the call. "Hey, old man." She tried to sound nonchalant.

As usual, he picked up right where he'd left off. "I can't find anything else. Morna's a mystery. I don't like mysteries."

"Then you work for the wrong organization, wouldn't you say?" She couldn't help herself.

"Watch your mouth, young lady," Bask admonished, but she could hear the jest in his tone. "Okay, now for something serious. Teresa called. She's worried because she hasn't heard from you."

At the thought of her cousin, Jasmine felt the flush creep up her neck. She should have called more and been there for the woman who'd loved her like a mother. "I'll call her when I hang up. Promise." She hesitated then hurried on before he could hang up. "I have a question. What is it when you can sense something from an object?"

She glanced up and saw Eryk leaning against the doorjamb, his arms crossed over his muscular torso. At least the towel was back in place. Still, just the sight of him sent her heart racing.

"You mean psychometry? Why? Has Eryk—"

"No," she interrupted. "It's me."

"You? When did this star...." His words trailed off.

Jasmine shut her eyes and rushed on, avoiding his questions. "I felt something in the bathroom. Severe anguish. It was almost painful. I don't know if the person was upset or in pain—or both."

"Can Eryk feel it?"

"I think so, I don't know."

Suddenly, he was excited. His words came out in a rush. "Okay, go around, separately. Or together, if you must. Pick up objects. Maybe we can get a reading. The strongest would be the most recent. Damn," he added, almost to himself, "I need to do some research. I'll get back to you." He hung up.

Jasmine rolled her eyes as she put the phone away.

"Do you think you can get me some clothes before he calls back?"

Having just started to call Teresa, she ended it and tucked the phone in her pocket. "Sure. I'll be right back." She retrieved her boots from across the hall and headed downstairs, careful not to inadvertently touch anything. At the back door, as she grabbed the doorknob, she got a swift push of frustration and anger. She released the knob as if it had burned her and headed out to the car.

The night seemed brighter. Maybe it was getting closer to dawn. Jasmine slammed her palms against her ears as a cacophony of night noises seemed to explode around her. She winced and ran for the car. She hit the remote, only to have the headlights flash, momentarily blinding her. She should let him go naked.

As she grabbed the door lever the feeling of caution and tension and caring coursed through her. Eryk? Still musing on the sensations, she grabbed his gym bag and released the strap just as quickly. Damn. She was going to have to get a handle on all these sensations flooding through her. Concentrating on calm—on herself, she grabbed both her bag and his and headed back inside.

Eryk waited at the top of the stairs, backlit by the light coming from the rooms behind him. The green of his eyes almost pulsed.

"You okay?" She asked as she came toward the stairs.

"Yeah. Just every damn thing I touch freaks me out."

"Me, too." She didn't go into detail. She trod up the stairs and handed him his bag.

Eryk walked to the bathroom and stopped at the door. "You might want to let Bask know he needs to budget in a new shower for the owners."

"What are you talking about?" Jasmine walked up behind him.

He pointed to the shower. She stepped around him. "Oh, no," she moaned. The glass walls of the shower stall had tiny star-shaped pings randomly splattered throughout. She stepped over and touched the outside. It was smooth. However, on the inside, each starburst was a tiny chip with cracks radiating outward.

When she turned to him, her eyes were wide, resembling the overlarge black eyes of a surprised kitten. "You want me to tell Bask."

He tried to keep his expression solemn, but watching her, found it impossible. Obviously, this wasn't the time to start teasing her. He leaned over and kissed her on the forehead. "Don't worry. I'll take care of it. I helped break it, after all."

"Thanks. I can't believe we did that." When her phone vibrated in her pocket, she stepped around him and, with one look back at the cracked shower, moved to the room she'd originally had. She had to get out of the clothes she'd worn for two days. She began stripping as she talked.

"Teresa," she said into the phone and pulled on fresh jeans, wrangling the sweater over her head and quickly thrusting her arm and the phone through a sleeve. "I meant to call you. Just so much has happened." That sounded lame even to her own ears. Teresa had to be going through hell, yet the voice that responded seemed calm and composed.

"Bask called me. He indicated you were exhibiting signs of psychoscopic abilities."

"Is that psychometry?" Jasmine asked.

"Token-object reading...whatever you want to call it. Maybe I can help."

"You—?"

"It's been a long time. Running a B & B with it would have driven me nuts. I've learned to, sort of, disable it."

"I never knew. I sure could use the ability to disable it right about now," Jasmine laughed into the phone. "Between me and Eryk—" she said and stopped, realizing how much she was giving away.

"You're mated, then," Teresa commented, saying it quietly as a statement rather than a question. Silence followed.

Jasmine closed her eyes. There was no going back. She felt tears well in her eyes and tried not to let it show in her voice. "We don't know what happened," she defended. "We had dinner. I was suddenly tired and went on up to bed. *In my own room*," She emphasized. "I swear I was asleep before my head hit the pillow. I woke up in Eryk's room. The deed was done. I swear to you, I don't remember...," she hesitated. "I thought I was dreaming."

"Are you okay now?"

"Other than the fact that, if we get within two feet of one another, we can't seem to control ourselves, we're just dandy," she said, the sarcasm belying her anxiety.

Teresa tried to ignore the anguish she heard. "What did you have for dinner?"

"What?" That was not the question Jasmine expected. "I don't know. Jarred spaghetti sauce," she finished fastening her jeans, holding the cell phone against her shoulder. "Actually, it was pretty good once he finished doctoring it."

"Jasmine, I want you to go in the kitchen and tell me everything he put in that sauce," Teresa commanded.

"Sure, but I don't understand." Eryk stepped out of his room as she stepped onto the landing. A charcoal gray sweater topped a pair of black jeans that hugs his lean hips. Jasmine tried to ignore the fact that she'd actually salivated and had to swallow. "Teresa needs to know what you put in the sauce."

When he came up behind her, Jasmine felt her body quake and her heart thump. She spun on the steps and held up her hand. He stopped two steps up. "Just stay back," she whispered in a hiss.

"What?" Teresa asked.

"Nothing."

When they got to the bottom of the stairs, Eryk moved around her and led the way into the kitchen. Dawn was breaking through the windows, giving a faint trail of light across the island. He assembled the ingredients, adding the packaging for the mushrooms and pasta from the trash. He stepped back and leaned against the sink counter, at least five feet from her.

Jasmine moved to the island, picked each item up in turn, rattling off the list. "A jar of Ragu sauce, traditional. Oregano, garlic, dehydrated onion, parsley, marjoram, sage, thyme, dried mushrooms, canola oil, truffle oil, Barilla thin spaghetti—"

"Stop," Teresa snapped. "Did you say truffle oil?"

Jasmine reached over and picked up the small bottle. "Yeah. I think he used that with the canola to reconstitute the mushrooms." She glanced at Eryk who nodded.

"That's it."

"What's it? What are you talking about?" Jasmine put the phone on speaker, to which Eryk tapped his ear. She hit the speaker button again.

"Oh, God," Teresa murmured, then said louder, "It's the truffle oil."

"I only used a small amount," Eryk said stepping forward. As he neared, Jasmine narrowed her eyes 'til he rolled his and stepped back.

"It doesn't matter. Descendants are allergic to truffles. The glutamic acid, a natural ingredient in truffles, changes in the descendant's unique system. Although the amino acid is found in many other things, when it's truffles, descendants react—big time. Combine that with truffles replicating a male pheromone, which is why you became the aggressor, and, well, it's history repeating itself." Jasmine could hear Teresa's sigh. "I'm so sorry."

Jasmine was trying to get her mind around what she'd just heard—she'd basically attacked Eryk. That seemed to be the gist of it. All because of a damn mushroom. And Teresa was apologizing.

"Drink water. And coffee. The water will flush it out of his system. And for some reason the caffeine will...how shall I say this...dampen the effect."

Eryk began scrounging around for coffee and found some beans in the freezer. He filled two large glasses with water and set Jasmine's on the island, carefully stepping back to fix the coffee. But not before Jasmine saw the smile and the glint in his eye. Oh, yeah, she was going to have trouble living this down. And, since they were pretty much bonded for life—it was going to be one long humiliation. With that thought gnawing at her gut, she asked, "What do you mean about history repeating itself?"

There was only a second of hesitation, but Jasmine sensed there was a lot of turmoil on the other end of the line. "Truffles are the reason Bill and I...."

Anger rose in Jasmine's throat. "And you didn't bother to say anything. Does Bask know about this? Why in the hell isn't there some sort of "Descendants' Handbook?" She stopped and took a second to collect herself.

"Truffles are so rare, we didn't think anyone else...."

"Hey, it would have been simple—like 'Don't eat mushrooms!'" Jasmine regretted the words the moment they left her mouth. She heard the hitch in her cousin's voice and said, "I'm sorry."

"No," Teresa said, "it's all right. I should have said something. Well...it's just that...with you not showing any traits...."

Jasmine closed her eyes. They'd thought her aberrant. Moreover, she was, just not in the way they'd expected. She saw Eryk take a step toward her, concern in his eyes. She felt him before he even moved and shook her head slightly. He stopped, but reached out and put another glass of water in front of her, along with a cup of black coffee.

Remembering Bill, Jasmine said, "Teresa, you don't have to go on. If this is too painful...."

"No. Just give me a second."

She imagined Teresa wiping her eyes with the lace-edged handkerchief she kept tucked in her waistband. Jasmine didn't even know when that had started, but Teresa always had a beautiful hand embellished handkerchief on her. Guests would see it and send her one as a thank-you gift. She had accrued quite a collection. Normally, it was just an ornament.

"I'm okay now. As you know, when I was young, I was rather enamored of Mike Yancy."

"The three of you were the talk of the town for years...," Jasmine said without thinking. She suddenly regretted reminding her of the rumors that had circulated when Bill had suddenly shown back up in town after having been gone for years. It astounded everyone that suddenly she and Bill were together and Mike had been pushed aside.

"Yes, I suppose we were. Bill and I had been close as children. When he went away, I was torn apart. I lost one of my best friends and yet I knew the only way he would fulfill his dreams was to leave. He became one of the top chefs in Europe. When he returned, and he really hadn't meant to stay, he brought with him some very rare truffles. They'd never bothered him. One night he fixed me a gourmet dinner, using them as a garnish. To make a long story short, the next morning I woke in his bed. The deed had been done." Her voice was softened by sadness.

"He didn't know?"

"No one did."

"Oh, Teresa, I am so sorry." Jasmine realized for the first time that Teresa and Bill hadn't been a love match. No wonder Dr. Yancy stayed away.

"Don't be. I had a good life with Bill. The one I felt sorry for was Mike. It was difficult for him. He was just starting out with the Abbott Foundation, a position he took because of me. Anyway, the only reason I know what happened is because of Mike. He did years of research. Even looked for an antidote." Teresa's voice had almost a forlorn quality. "I'm so sorry, Jasmine. He never did find one." There was a finality to her statement.

Jasmine glanced over at Eryk, who was on his third glass of water and smiled. Maybe it was the truffle oil, maybe it was the descendant match-mate compulsion, but her heart felt warm and loving as she watched him, not laden with the sadness she expected.

He turned and caught her smiling. "What? She said I needed to get it out of my system." His eyes widened. "I think that's about to happen." He set down the glass and left the kitchen at her chuckle.

"What's so funny?" Teresa asked.

"Eryk just fled the room after his third glass of water."

Teresa's slight laugh sounded good. Having heard her so forlorn had tore at Jasmine's heart. She'd always been the upbeat one. She had a way about her. People loved being around her. People listened to her. Jasmine always suspected that was her gift, a sort of compulsion. That's why she was Ruthorford's so-called Mayor. Teresa's tone was lighter when she spoke. "You know, you and Eryk had chemistry from the get-go. Don't let this get you down. Things could work out for the best, you know."

It was just like Teresa to look for the silver lining. Jasmine watched Eryk step back into the kitchen and her mind flashed back to the shower. "You know, you could be right, Teresa. Now, tell me about the psychometry."

"Oh, yes. Well, I don't know if you and Eryk are stronger together or separate. I never had anyone other than myself to work with. You touch an object and wait. The most recent contact someone has had with the object, the stronger the impression. Mostly, I feel emotions. I've heard some people will get visions. I never did. If it's muddled or very faint, the person hasn't touched it in a long time or was weak, like from an illness."

"How long?" Jasmine interjected.

"Can't really tell. Depends on the strength of the individual. Tell me what you've got."

Jasmine relayed what had happened in the bathroom, sitting on the tub, including the fact that Eryk had come running when he felt the emotions coming from her, without touching either her or the tub. She also mentioned the door, the car and the bags.

"Well, Eryk's feeling what you feel is the match-mate connection getting stronger. But the fact that he was feeling what you were honing in on makes me believe that together you might be able to get visions. The car is a good example of length of time. That handle had been touched by many, but Eryk's impression was the strongest and the most current. The door knob, I guess was someone who'd left there recently, even if it appears no one has been there. Trust your gut. Physical appearances can be deceiving. Our descendants' instincts are spot-on." She waited before continuing. "I hope I was of some help."

"Yes. Very much." She stopped long enough to take a sip of the black coffee Eryk had set in front of her. "About everything," she added.

"Are you all right?" Teresa's question edged toward the less talked about.

Jasmine knew what she meant. She looked at Eryk and knowing how attuned his hearing was, there was no way, no matter where she sent him, that he wouldn't hear her. "I'm fine. I think Eryk thought my problem when I was crouched next to the tub was a flashback from the attack by Rob or what had just happened between us. To be honest with you, other than right at the beginning—and I really think that was more my expecting it than it happening—I haven't had any problems separating the attack and rape from what's going on with Eryk." She used the words rape and attack because Dr. Browne had told her that using the word rape, not just attack, vocalized it. At first, it had been difficult. This time it came out as a word, without the anger. She turned the question around. "How are you doing? Really."

"I'm sad. Bill and I spent a lot of years together. You completed our little family. He was a good husband and father. A little strange, mind you, but a good man." She laughed at her own joke—a descendant calling another descendant strange.

His reclusiveness had become more and more difficult in the last few years. Jasmine now wondered if he might have known things about himself that he wasn't willing to share, even with family.

"We'll have a big memorial as soon as I make sure Lily is safe," Jasmine promised.

"You do what you must. I'm fine. Your next priority, of course, will be Morgan and Dorian. She's big as a house and about ready to pop. Don't tell her I said that," she chuckled.

"I won't. Thanks, Teresa. I love you."

"I love you, too, we'an." Teresa threw in a bit of brogue around her Scottish endearment. "I just want to make sure Eryk takes good care of my girl."

Before she could answer, Eryk called out, "I will. Count on it."

Chapter Fifteen

Slipping the phone back in her pocket, Jasmine took a large gulp of lukewarm coffee before turning to Eryk. When she did, he was within arm's length and looked so hot she felt her own temperature rise. The shower had left his black hair with an errant wave that hung just above his brow, giving him a devil-may-care look. His green eyes moved from her eyes to her mouth and remained fixed there. She couldn't help but lick her lips. In one swift motion, he had her by her arms and pulled her forward, his mouth crushing down on hers. She thought she would drown in the taste of him. Parting her lips, she invited him to share his intensity, which sent them both into overdrive. Mouths and hands moved all over one another. The air sizzled with their lust. He was yanking her sweater up when her phone went off.

Jasmine leapt back and pulled down her sweater, then pulled the offending instrument from her jeans pocket. She glanced at it. Bask. She answered and watched Eryk stick his head under the running faucet, at first taking a drink, then just letting the water splash over his head.

"Yeah," she tried to sound sedate, but the sight of Eryk put a chuckle in her voice.

"I just got off the phone with Teresa," he began. "Look, if this is too difficult for you, I can send in another team."

Jasmine frowned. Just how long had she and Eryk been going at each other. "No." She waited, hoping he would give her a hint.

"I know you've never done this sort of thing. Teresa said it could be damn intense."

"Yeah…." *To say the least.* She felt the drops of water hit her as Eryk shook his hair, having dried it with a paper towel.

"We don't have a lot on psychometry—"

"Ohhhh…" Jasmine laughed. He wasn't talking about their sex drive, thank God. "No. We'll be fine. We really haven't had a chance to go through the entire place, yet." She felt her face flush. They hadn't gotten out of the kitchen.

"Okay. Call me when you have." He hung up.

"Does that man ever sleep?"

"I woke him once. That may be the only time I've ever known him to actually be asleep."

When he took a step forward, she held up her hand. "Apparently, you still reek of truffle. Stay away or we won't get anything done. I'm going to guzzle coffee. You go in the great room and see if you can pick up anything. Take one side and I'll take the other. If we get something, the other person can try. THEN," she almost shouted the word, "and only then, we'll try touching it together."

"How long does this last?" He said as he walked toward the great room.

"A lifetime." She replied to his back.

He stopped dead in his tracks and laughed. "S-w-eet!"

They went around the room twice. Nothing affected them like in the bathroom upstairs, or the back door knob. She grew impatient as frustration seeped in. Lily was somewhere but they didn't have a clue where. She didn't know if what she'd felt upstairs what Lily or someone else.

"I have an idea. There are some clothes upstairs that I would bet are Lily's. Let's go see what we get off them. Then we'll have something to judge other readings by."

"Sounds good to me. How are you feeling?"

"Better. I have a terrible headache but I don't feel nearly as horny."

"Darn. Remind me to buy some truffles down the road."

Jasmine smirked. "Yeah, right." She brushed past him, letting her body touch his as she passed, just to let him know she could. She didn't let it show that the current that flashed through her was so intense it almost made her stumble.

Upstairs, Jasmine pulled open the closet doors. "These look like her style and about her size." She ran her hand over one of the tops. The sensation was very faint. "I need to find something that she liked to wear. Try to find something worn looking."

Eryk moved to the dresser while Jasmine kept going through the closet. "Hey," he called, removing the lid to a wicker basket. Think I found a laundry hamper." He reached in and pulled out an oversized KISS t-shirt. "Got something."

Jasmine moved over to him and reached for the t-shirt. With him still holding it, the moment she touched it, the sensation was immediate and strong. Although she hadn't experienced this ability when she worked with Lily, she knew instinctively it was Lily. That sweet teenage enthusiasm filled her body. She pulled the garment away from Eryk and hugged it to her. The feelings weakened, until it was just a faint sensation.

"Damn, I'm gonna need you to do this."

"Hey, I love you, too." He said it as a joke but it stopped them both. He put everything he had into dampening his energy, having no idea if it would work for this, and cupped her face in his hands. "Listen," he said softly, looking into her eyes. "Once we've got Lily, we'll talk. I care about you. Really care. Not just the sex—which, by the way is beyond great—but the connection. It's going to be all right." He saw the worry sweep across her obsidian eyes and disappear. "Stop worrying. Trust me." He leaned in and placed a soft kiss on her mouth, then moved back. It took everything he had to move back that one step.

"What say you we rummage through some dirty laundry?" With that, he lifted up the hamper and dumped the small pile of clothing on the floor.

She was still smiling as the both knelt and felt each piece, making sure they touched each garment together. A big, fuzzy robe held the most energy. The turmoil set Jasmine back on her heels. There was anger and pain and sadness all rolled into one big glob of energy. It *had* been Lily sitting on the side of that tub. Jasmine felt tears well in her eyes and brushed them away. Someone had physically hurt her. She might not have been wearing the robe when it happened but she'd had it on shortly afterward. There was no energy other than Lily's on the garment.

Jasmine threw everything back into the hamper. "We need to search the other rooms." Angry now, she headed to the master bedroom. If Lily's father had caused the injuries she'd seen….

They went through Porter Greeson's closet and chest of drawers. There was nothing of his in the hamper. They didn't get anything except sadness and confusion. He'd definitely been ill, but he wasn't violent.

They assumed the other closet held Beverly Greeson's clothes. Jasmine recognized the couture immediately—Chanel, Dior, Lauren, Givenchy. Only faint sensations, even with Eryk holding the same piece. There was sadness, frustration, and fear.

They moved on to the one other room that held anything. This had to be Morna's room—the elusive stepsister. Jasmine threw open the closet and took a cursory glance. The clothing was expensive but erratic. Where Beverly's was top couture and reserved, Lily's had been fresh and young, and as expected, experimental. Here was chaos. Wild colors, or gray and brown. Expensive, then something from Walmart. She reached in and grabbed a funky sweater. It was all she could do to hold on. Vibrations ran up her arm, manically slamming a myriad of emotions into her. When Eryk touched the same garment, everything intensified. She would have fallen had Eryk not caught her.

"Shit!" The force of her unexpected fall shoved him back until they were on the bed with Jasmine sitting between his legs.

"I know this isn't the time, but you smell really good," he said into her neck.

For an instant, she leaned back into him. His arm came around her and he brushed the sweater. The same violent chaos rushed through them.

"Damn," he whispered.

Jasmine started to get up.

"No." He held her in place. "Don't move. I'm getting an image."

Jasmine froze and held onto the sweater, trying not the feel the heat from his groin against her butt. She took a deep breath and closed her eyes. All she got was chaos. "What do you see?"

He stood, nearly dumping her from his lap and grabbed her arm, looking around the room. Still holding Jasmine, he moved to the dresser and stooped over the side. Leaning against the side of the dresser was a riding crop. He picked it up and put part of it in Jasmine's hand. The anger and hatred took her breath away.

"The woman who owns this beat the crap out of Lily, using the wrong end."

"You can see it? How?"

"I don't know. It's like I'm looking through her eyes. I can see the whip and Lily in the doorway, her arms crossed in front of her face in defense. The person with the whip has an issue with uncontrolled fury."

Jasmine broke the contact. She ran her hand through her hair. "How are we going to find Lily? There has to be something here that will give us a clue." She rushed to the desk sitting in front of the window. It had papers piled all over the top and crammed in the drawers. She took one side and Eryk took the other. He stood, staring at a piece of paper.

"Didn't Bask say Porter Greeson was in a place in Sweden?"

"Yeah. What have you got?"

"I'm not sure. But it's got a place listed and two phone numbers, one scratched through."

Jasmine grabbed the piece of paper and pulled out her phone. This time she pulled a "Bask." Barely waiting until he answered, she started feeding him the information.

"Anything else?"

"I don't know. Eryk had a vision of a woman beating Lily with the wrong end of a riding crop."

"I'll look into this. You keep looking." He hung up.

"Did you see a computer anywhere?" Eryk asked.

"In the office downstairs." They both headed downstairs. This time she got sensations from the handrail, but they were confused, mussed together. Still, she was getting more and more. Maybe there was a learning curve. She ran into the office and turned on the desktop tower.

Waiting for it to come up, they looked through the desk drawers. They were neat, with not much in them. This was not the office Greeson used for business.

Eryk sat in front of the screen, his fingers flying. Screen after screen popped up. "No good," he said, "she's wiped all her history."

Behind him, Jasmine turned on the printer. It came to life and shot out a page, blank except with a line of printed information at the bottom. The date was four days ago. She handed it to Eryk.

"Call Bask. Have him contact the ISP. She was looking for something."

Jasmine had him on the phone before Eryk finished and hung up almost as quickly. "He'll get back to us." She started pacing, nibbling on her thumbnail. "I don't think she had Lily here. But you get visions of her." She paced some more, stopped and turned to him.

Eryk watched as she moved back and forth. He could almost see the wheels turning in her mind. Even distracted, worrying her nail as she did, she was a study in fluid grace. He could feel the energy pouring off her—the anguish for Lily and the natural sensuality that was Jasmine. Just watching her made his jeans tighten uncomfortably.

"What?" She cocked her head and studied his face. Her eyes focused on his. "Oh. Concentrate, will you?"

"Trust me, I am." He smiled at her.

"On the task at hand." Then she narrowed her eyes, daring him to comment. "Let's try the control thing for the garage door. Or, the back door again. I want to see if we can…you can see something more."

"Good idea."

The door to the garage was off the kitchen and, sure enough, there was a box on the wall. They stood close to one another, fighting the current racing through them as they both put fingers on the button. Jasmine watched Eryk close his eyes and weave slightly. Sensation after sensation rushed through her. Anger, determination, joy. The last one baffled her. It didn't fit with the others, yet it did.

"What do you see?"

"There's some sort of perverse happiness going on. She—I'm assuming it's Morna—has a piece of paper in her hand and a backpack or something." He moved his hand to the door knob. Jasmine followed. "She opened the door. I can see the garage door going up. I'm looking at a silver SUV."

"Can you see the license plate?"

"No. She moved too fast. She's tossing the backpack in the back. Getting in the vehicle and getting ready to leave. I think she's headed to the first place we went. But, that's just a feeling. She's excited. Whatever it is, she's definitely chosen a course of action and I don't like what I'm feeling. I think she's mad. As in crazy mad."

Jasmine pulled back her hand. Her gut twisted. All she could think of was Rob and the madness that had overcome him, precipitating the attack on her. Yet, Rob wasn't connected to Ruthorford, except that he'd been hired by a descendant to study the portal. His madness came from contact with the Gulatega. Descendants weren't affected by them. From the picture she'd seen, Morna was a descendant, with abilities. A mad descendant? She suddenly questioned whether Ian had been crazy. Morgan and Dorian had said he was dying and desperate when he'd kidnapped Morgan. They also said that the illness that took Bill had similar symptoms. Was there a connection? Would Bill have gone mad?

Jasmine put her arms around herself, pushing off the cold fear trying to take hold. When Eryk pulled her into his arms, she didn't resist but took comfort in his strength and closeness. She felt his energy flow through her and back to him. It warmed and comforted. She stepped away when it began to change to something more sensual.

"Now that we're connected, I can sense your feelings. You sure you're all right?" His voice was soft and soothing.

"Just letting my mind go places it shouldn't." She tried to smile up at him.

"You do understand that, given what you've been through, you have every right to be wary of what's going on. Why don't I call Bask and go on my own, or get someone else?"

Jasmine stiffened. "No. One—we don't have time. Lily's life is in danger. I can promise you that. I'm not letting anything happen to her if I can help it. And, two—whatever I'm dealing with I'll just deal with. Later, if I have to, I'll have Dr. Browne help me sort it out. One thing I learned from her is not to be afraid to accept help."

"You also have me," Eryk said and, rubbing his hands up her arms, he kissed her on the forehead.

"I know." In her mind she added *for better or worse*, then chastised herself for the sarcasm and instantly wondered if he'd read her mind. A slight flush warmed her face. Damn, she'd blushed more around him than she had in her entire life.

"I like the glow that gives your cheeks," he said, a twinkle in his eye.

Had he read her mind?

Jasmine figured they'd have plenty of time to figure things out once Lily was safe and sound.

Surprised she hadn't heard from Bask, she pulled out the phone. It chirped in her hand. "I was just going to call you."

She told him what they'd found. She had a mental image of Bask brushing it off, deeming his more significant.

"ISP was a good idea. She made several searches for 'getaway' locations. I'm betting on the one she went to several times. It's not too far from the first place you were. I've downloaded the coordinates into your GPS. John Davis is on his way now. He'll meet you there."

Knowing John was going to meet them made Jasmine feel better. Although he was a descendant from the Native American side, he didn't seem to have "traits," as far as she knew. However, he was in charge of Ruthorford's security and now had a license in Virginia, since becoming affiliated with Safe Harbor. Abbott House was very careful to keep law enforcement connections current wherever they needed to be.

"Eryk had a vision of the vehicle Morna might be driving. Here. Talk to Eryk. I'll go get our stuff together so we can leave." She handed the phone to Eryk and headed upstairs.

After throwing her few things back into her bag, and careful not to touch anything, she took a last look around, and went to put together Eryk's bag. It was sitting at the foot of the bed, packed and closed. She smiled. He was definitely going to be the neater of the two of them in this relationship. Allowing only a moment to let the long term implications settle in her mind again, she looked around and, grabbing the bags, headed downstairs.

Eryk was leaning with his back against the island. "Thanks. I appreciate it. We'll get back to you." He saw her holding the bags. "I'll trade you. You take the phone and the two coffees I nuked from this morning, and I'll take the bags. Oh, and grab that box of Nilla Wafers. I'm hungry. I figure those are probably the safest thing we can eat at this point."

Jasmine was dying to know what he was thanking Bask for but didn't want to sound that snoopy. It was probably something to do with his business. She stuffed the box of cookies under her arm, grabbed her purse and the two coffees and followed Eryk out to the vehicle.

She heard a loud screech and watched as a large bird circled above. *Please, not now.* When her vision didn't shift, she sent of a whisper of thanks and joined Eryk in the vehicle.

They'd gone a good twenty miles when Eryk glanced over at her. "Penny for your thoughts."

"You mean you can't read them. Dorian and Morgan can read each other."

"Do you want me to try?"

"Not particularly." She looked out the window.

"Okay...for now...I'll stay out of your head and you stay out of mine."

"I don't think I can get into your head." Jasmine pushed down the urge to try. "I can sense some things when we're touching...."

"...hmmm...," he mumbled, then added, "So, what were you looking so pensive about?"

"I was thinking about Lily. I don't know what shape her father is in or what's wrong with him. I don't feel comfortable sending her back to the stepmother, even if the stepsister is out of the picture. She's still underage, so the authorities could get involved..."

"Bask is working on it." Eryk said simply.

Jasmine smiled. That must have been what he was talking to the old man about. "Thanks."

"Don't thank me yet. I don't know what he can do, if anything. I don't know if she can stay at Safe Harbor. I hope Bask can have something worked out by the time we get her back. I mentioned Brandy to Bask. Maybe she could stay with her."

Eryk's phone rang. "Hi, John. We're about thirty minutes out." He listened for a few moments. "We'll figure something out when we get there." He laid the phone on the console.

"It's a secure compound. John's about a mile away at a diner. We'll meet him there."

****

John rose from the back booth as they walked into the long diner. Jasmine couldn't help but smile at the gorgeous man that had been her friend for as long as she could remember. His warm brown eyes twinkled as he pulled her up off the ground in a bear hug. "You are lookin' good."

Once again, Jasmine felt her cheeks tinge. This blushing thing was definitely becoming a nuisance. John looked over Jasmine's head at Eryk. "You better take damn good care of her or you'll have me to answer to."

"John…," Jasmine moaned.

"What? It's Ruthorford. You're descendants. 'Nuf said."

Jasmine looked at the floor and rubbed her fingers over her brows before she slipped into the booth. Eryk slipped in next to her. As his leg settled against hers, she felt the rush of longing and, as inconspicuously as possible, put her hand down and pushed his leg away. He shifted slightly, giving her a few inches between them. Not nearly enough.

"Think we can eat while we plan?" Eryk reached across Jasmine and pulled out a menu.

"You ate almost the entire box of cookies."

"Meat, woman. I need meat."

John just shook his head and laughed.

They ordered burgers and fries all around and coffee. As much as Jasmine longed for something other than coffee, she remembered Teresa's suggestion and kept her mouth shut. The edge was off, as long as they didn't touch. However, there was still this rumbling she felt inside, as well as this desire to lick his body from one end to the other. Jasmine grabbed the coffee the waitress had set in front of her and downed it, scalding her tongue. She followed with ice water and asked for more coffee.

"Sure, honey," the waitress said, "but you look pretty edgy as it is."

Eryk choked on his coffee.

Jasmine closed her eyes and took a deep breath before forcing herself to be polite and smile at the waitress.

John waved his hand over a map of the compound he laid before them. "It's as secure as Safe Harbor. I'm not sure how we're going to get in. I have Bask working on it."

"Doesn't he delegate?" Eryk asked. Bask seemed to have his hand in everything and he'd swear he was handling it all personally.

"Oh, yeah. He has legions of little Baskettes running around." John laughed.

"Good, cause I can't figure out when or if the man sleeps."

John stopped laughing and turned serious eyes to Eryk. "Bask *is* Abbott House which *is* Ruthorford. I can't remember him not being in charge. And he does a damn good job."

Eryk nodded. There was so much he didn't know about the place and the people he was suddenly a part of. He'd figure it out. He looked over at Jasmine, who was attacking her cheeseburger like she hadn't eaten in weeks and felt a sudden surge of protectiveness. She, too, had become a part of him and God help anyone who tried to hurt her.

John answered his phone. He listened for a moment. "I'm sure that will work. It has to." He hung up and turned his attention to the couple across from him. "You two just eloped. Eryk, being famous, wanted his honeymoon to be private. Bask made reservations for you to arrive in about an hour. I'm the bodyguard who's going make sure it stays private. Apparently, the compound is set up with individual residences, set away from one another. He took one as far in the back as possible. They said they had one other residence a little more secluded but it's currently occupied." He ate a French fry. "I'll bet my lunch that's Morna's. I don't have any idea where the two places are in relation to one another."

"Here's the deal," John continued. "I'll lead the way in. You follow me to check-in but I'll do the checking in. The less they see of you the better. I've got Eryk's business card. Let's get this show on the road."

They waited in the car while John checked them in. He walked over and handed them a key card. Apparently, this place has a small cabin behind it for *the help*," he laughed. "I guess that's me. Bask went out of his way to make our story plausible. Gotta love a detail man."

The compound was gorgeous. Trails meandered off from the small road that wound around through large trees. A small post with a number indicated their drive. Their building was not visible from the road. They pulled in front of a large log building set among a stand of trees. As Jasmine stepped out of the car, she could smell pine and the faint odor of a fireplace being used somewhere in the distance. They stepped inside to a cozy great room with a large fireplace to the right and a kitchen and dining area on the left. Straight back a hallway led to the bedrooms and a cut-log stairway led up to a loft/library. She walked back down the hall. "I'll take the room under the steps. You two can decide which of the other two you want."

"You sure you don't want me to take the cabin and give you *honeymooners* some privacy?" John teased.

Jasmine glared at him before slamming the bedroom door. Her head was still pounding and her nerves were taut. She dropped onto the bed and put an arm over her eyes, trying to shield out thoughts of Lily being tortured. She felt like she was transferring what had happened to her, but she couldn't be certain, and that was scaring her to death.

Someone knocked lightly on her door.

"Go away."

The door cracked. Eryk stepped over to the bed. "You forget that I can feel you."

She pulled her arm down and glared at him.

"I'm not reading your damn thoughts but I feel the pain and uncertainty coursing through your body." He sat down on the edge of the bed.

Like it was the most natural action in the world, Jasmine rolled to her side and curled her body around his, seeking comfort.

Eryk ran his hands through her soft black hair. He was always amazed at the feel of it. Like ebony mink. He moved his hand down to her back, sent a soothing push, and felt her inhale.

"Why don't you rest?" It was more than just a vocal suggestion; it was a command, low and compelling. He followed it with, "John's driving around to see if he can find out anything. I promise I'll wake you when he returns." He felt her head shift as she nodded and he started to rise from the bed.

Her hand touched his leg. "Thank you." Her voice came in a soft whisper, slurred slightly by the lull of sleep.

He patted her hand and eased it back onto the bed. For an instant, he stood above her, looking down and he felt his heart swell with emotion. Worried that she would sense him, he pushed away the feeling and walked out of the room, pulling the door shut.

As sleep overtook her, Jasmine's lips curved in a slight smile. She had felt the swelling of emotion and liked it. She liked it very much.

Chapter Sixteen

Jasmine walked into the great room as the sun sank low in the sky. She felt rested, albeit a bit rumpled, but at least the headache had lifted. Eryk and John were sitting at the dining table sipping coffee.

"Want a cup?" John asked.

She nodded yes, although, she doubted, when this was over, that she'd ever want it again. She took a seat at the end of the table and John placed the cup in front of her. Her stomach constricted at the strong smell. "Any chance we have some milk and sugar?"

John turned and pulled some cream out of the refrigerator and set a spoon in front of her. Eryk eased the sugar bowl in her direction with a smile. "Later, we'll try tea."

As she slowly stirred the sugar into the lightened brew, John filled her in. "They have cameras around the entrances of all the residences. Moreover, they have their own security cruising the area. Twice I had to explain that I was doing the same thing as your private bodyguard. They didn't like it."

"Do you think we could go on foot?"

"I don't see any choice, but be advised, this is one large complex."

She took a sip of the sweetened coffee and found she liked it. A faint sound caught her attention. She rose as she set the cup down, almost spilling its contents. "I just might have a solution." Jasmine moved to the side door and opened it. The screech sounded again. *Could it be?* She stepped onto the deck that wrapped around the cabin and looked toward the sky. Her view diminished by the foliage and the darkening sky, she could, just barely, make out the shape of a large bird circling above. She could feel its heart fluttering in its chest and she held out her arm.

"Are you crazy?" Eryk rushed forward to pull down her arm.

"Stay back. I mean it," she ordered.

He stepped back. Either she knew what she was doing or she'd be torn to shreds. John joined him and placed his hand on Eryk's shoulder. "We have our legends. I think I'm about to see one come to life," he said in a low voice, barely audible.

As they watched, a flutter of massive wings beat the air and a large falcon took its place on her arm. Talking softly to the bird, she eased it onto the railing of the deck. Very slowly, she ran her fingers down the soft feathers of the falcon's breast. When she spoke, it was soft, "This is Bryn. We met at the fair." She switched back to the bird, her voice quiet and melodic, "What are you doing here? Aren't you far from home?"

The bird proceeded to clean its beak on the wooden rail, acting as if it were totally at home with the three humans on the deck. Jasmine glanced around and, seeing a chair nearby, stepped over to it, sitting down. "Now let's see if Bryn will give us a hand." She closed her eyes. The bird stopped, took a few slow blinks, turned, and took flight.

Jasmine gripped the arms of the chair, fighting off the dizziness. They rushed through the trees to open water.

"It seems we butt up to a lake of some sort." Her voice was jerky, her breathing shallow and quick.

The bird circled higher and Jasmine tried to acclimate to the movement. Remembering the experience at the hotel, she moved her eyes to the left. The urge to open her eyes to look was immense, but when she tried, the vision doubled and became blurry. She kept her eyes closed. They flew past several cabins, set further back in the woods. Although she could barely see them, they all appeared to have a lot of windows facing the water. She tried to urge the bird closer. At that moment, they flew past a two-story building sitting right on the lake. She could see movement inside. As she urged the bird to circle higher, she spotted a vehicle on the other side of the cabin that looked just like the one in Eryk's vision. "I think I've got something," she whispered, afraid her voice would break the connection.

The bird circled up and over the water, too high to look in the windows. However, she could see light and movement. Suddenly, the bird focused on something moving on the ground and circled closer. Not wanting to be part of the bird's dining rituals, she opened her eyes and broke the link. Almost in protest, a loud screech came from the sky.

"Another time, Bryn. Another time."

Jasmine would have leapt from the chair, except her equilibrium was off. Instead, she leaned forward and hung her head between her knees, letting the nausea pass. She felt Eryk's hand on the back of her neck and the nausea was gone. Taking a deep breath, she let it out slowly. "Thanks," she said before sitting up.

It was a few more seconds before she turned to her companions. "It's not much but it's more than we had a few moments ago. I think I saw the silver SUV in front of one of the cabins. She jumped up and leapt off the deck, racing through the trees in the dark. Eryk grabbed her hand and her surroundings brightened.

"You are becoming convenient to have around," she said with a chuckle.

"Hey, guys. I can't see in the dark."

Eryk smiled at her and they stopped, waiting for John to catch up.

"Besides, I have the gun," he added.

Eryk and Jasmine held up their unlinked hands and sparks jumped from the fingertip.

John shook his head. "Oh, yeah. I forgot. I'm with the human Taser team."

Eryk laughed and slapped John on the back. "Don't worry. I have a feeling you'll come in handy yet."

Jasmine linked hands with both men and they made their way through the trees, finally stepping into the clearing along the lake bank. There was about a three-foot drop to the water. Jasmine wondered why she thought they'd be walking down a beach. She looked to her right. Because there was a beach, four houses down. "That's it, she said, pointing."

"That's quite a ways from here. We have to get past at least three places. We can't go by way of the road. Too much security. The moon's too bright to take a boat—even if we had one. Looks like we're on foot," John commented.

The three started walking along the river's edge until they came to a small clearing that ran from the next house down to the water.

John spoke in a whisper. "We might want to turn off the phones."

"Good thinking," Eryk pulled his out and hit the button.

"Last thing I want is Bask calling to check on us and waking the neighborhood." Jasmine switched hers off as well.

"Yeah, he does have some impressive timing...," Eryk said, laughter in his tone.

There were no lights on in the cabin next to theirs, but they crossed the yard one at a time to play it safe. The moment Eryk let go of Jasmine's hand, the world darkened. Damn, she liked having his night vision. John went first, then Jasmine, then Eryk.

As they got to the third lawn, Jasmine grabbed Eryk's arm. "Why don't you just use that invisible thing?"

"What invisible thing?" They had John's attention now. "You two are getting more interesting by the moment."

"It's not an invisible anything. My energy can shift light energy." He said in a hushed whisper, then turned to Jasmine. "Operative word—light. We don't have enough."

"Oh," she replied and shrugged her shoulders.

"Shhhh," Eryk hissed and put his finger to his lips. When he spoke it was very soft, barely audible. "I think I hear an animal approaching."

Jasmine turned to John. "Looks like you're up."

"What?" Eryk asked.

"Shhh." Jasmine repeated his gesture and pointed to John stepping away from them into the trees.

Eryk tuned his hearing toward John. He listened as the animal moved through the brush and John moved to intercept it. He heard what sounded like a cooing sound, but with a deep resonance to it, then the shuffle of feet as the animal moved off.

Jasmine said in a voice she knew Eryk would hear but was barely audible, even to herself. "He's sort of an animal whisperer."

John stepped back up. "Guard dog. They have several running at night. Shouldn't be a problem." He led them out into the clearing and crossed it.

Eryk was amazed at how quietly a man of John's size moved. He motioned them to stay behind him as he went on ahead. When they joined him on the other side, Jasmine spoke. "Next house is it. Do we have a plan?"

"We'll play it by ear," John said. "First, we locate Lily and assess the situation. How many people. Weapons—type and number. They we'll move back here and see what we want to do. Eryk, since you have the most acute vision and hearing, you go first. Jasmine and I will check the perimeter from here."

Eryk moved off without another word. Between the tension pouring off Jasmine and John and the energy from Jasmine bombarding his senses, he was glad to step away from them for a few moments. He listened. He could hear John and Jasmine moving down the property line toward the front. He stepped closer to the house, behind a small group of trees in the back. It gave him a good view of the windows. Light shone from the downstairs. Someone was moving around in the kitchen, mumbling.

"Why do I have to do all the work? If she'd gotten rid of her like I told her to do at the lake last summer, we wouldn't be having these problems. But, nooooo, she lost her nerve. Shit. Do I have to do everything for her?"

The rest became garbled. It was a woman's voice and it sounded edgy and tight, like a violin string pulled too taut. It had to be Morna and she was obviously planning to dispose of someone. His guess would be Lily.

She came into view, crossing the room with a tray. He watched her as she mounted the stairs. Blinking he looked at the aura. Pitted and jagged there was a lot of red in deep purple. He blinked again watched as she crossed the loft, stopping to open the door. That's where Lily had to be. He listened again. She'd left the door open so he faintly heard her speaking.

"I've brought you some dinner, little sister. If you'll behave, I'll take off the tape and feed you." The voice got harsher. *"Don't try to fool me, you little bitch. I know you're not asleep."* He heard a moan and a muffled scream. *"You made me spill it. Now I have to make some more. Don't go anywhere."* The last was singsong.

He watched her rush down the steps and cross back into the kitchen. They needed to get to Lily now. He ran back to the side and met John and Jasmine.

"No other cars. The front of the house is dark. I don't see anyone else. I think it's the woman and Lily." Jasmine's voice was rushed.

"We have to go now. Morna's up to something. Front door will be the best."

They stepped up to the front door. Eryk held his hand over the knob. "It's got a sensor, damn it. When you go in, go to the back stairs. At the top, Lily's room is across the loft on the right. I'll head to the kitchen. We'll have to move fast. This thing could be silent or raise all kinds of hell." With that, he let his energy flow through the knob. He heard a ping and the door opened under his grip. He pointed them to the back stairs and he turned left toward the kitchen.

Cutting through the dining room, he listened and didn't hear anything. He stepped into the kitchen. Contents of cabinets, food, and chemicals were scattered all over the island. Whatever the woman had fixed, it was probably lethal. She wasn't there.

He ran back out and raced up the stairs, taking them two at a time. The door stood open and John's frame filled it, his weapon aimed inside.

"Put it down and step away from her," John's voice came out in a command.

Eryk stepped up behind Jasmine, whose energy was spiking like an aura around her body. Across the room,

Morna had yanked Lily in front of her by her hair and had a knife against her throat. Her green eyes swirled, wide and skittish, as she watched the people in the doorway.

"You back off or I cut her," she yelled. Spittle flew from her mouth.

Lily's mouth was covered in duct tape and her hands were behind her, probably also taped. Eryk could hear her moaning against the pain. Her face was swollen, one eye a mere slit.

Eryk could feel the energy pouring off Morna, erratic, frantic and mad. When she spied him, her eyes stopped roving and focused on him, staring hard.

He stepped around Jasmine, putting her behind him. He looked Morna in the eye, sending out a push.

"You. You're like me." The voice, at first amazed, took on a warbling sound. She looked to John and back to Eryk. Her eyes grew darker, filled with heat.

Jasmine could feel the energy pulsing off Eryk. He was trying to compel a madwoman.

Morna's eyes softened and she glanced down at Lily, almost as an afterthought. "Let me tidy up here…."

Then, everything happened at once. She moved her hand forward with the knife and John's gun went off. A neat hole appeared in Morna's forehead and a splash of red hit the wall behind her. Lily fell off the side of the bed with the knife.

Jasmine's shoved passed Eryk and John with a force neither man expected. She bounded around the bed. Morna was slumped on the floor, wedged between the wall and a dresser, her body having smeared blood and gray matter in its wake.

Jasmine knelt beside Lily who lay on her side, the knife beside her. Blood was running across her leg. "Get me a towel. Call 9-1-1," Jasmine yelled.

John was issuing directions into the phone as Eryk handed Jasmine a towel. Jasmine was working to get the duct tape from around Lily's wrist. Lily's mouth had pink welts where the tape had been on her mouth. Eryk handed Jasmine his knife to cut the tape and watched Lily wince at the sight of it.

"We're not going to hurt you. Let me get this off. Lie still, sweetie."

"Get me out of here," Lily screamed.

"The paramedics will be here in a moment. No! Don't look back there."

Jasmine positioned herself between Lily and Morna's dead body.

"She tried to kill me," Lily cried.

"You're safe now. I promise."

Two paramedics stepped into the room following by a policeman. John stopped the policeman and they stepped to the other side. Jasmine eased herself back, still blocking Lily's view, but let a paramedic near her.

Lily grabbed Jasmine's ankle, "Don't leave me," the young girl begged.

"I'm not going anywhere," Jasmine promised.

Lily winced as the paramedic pushed around Lily's leg, talking into a headset at the same time. They placed a tourniquet above the gash, and injected something to numb the area. He reached over and placed the knife in a plastic bag. They applied something to the wound and slowly loosened the tourniquet. Blood seeped but didn't run. He bound the wound and, with the other EMT, they lifted her onto a gurney. Jasmine followed them out, glancing back once at the dead woman, whose dull green eyes stared vacantly into hell.

Eryk caught Jasmine's gaze as she passed him. It was one he couldn't fathom. Yet, he hoped it was one that was not long lasting. It tore at his soul.

Even with all that Rob had done, Jasmine hadn't felt the hatred and vehemence that she'd felt when she saw Morna holding Lily by the hair, her body beaten, her eyes full of fear. At that moment, she wanted to send every ounce of energy she possessed into the woman, wiping her from the face of the earth. In fact, the only thing that had stopped her was Lily, and knowing that residual energy would travel into her as well.

Then Eryk had stepped forward and when Jasmine saw the look change in Morna's eyes, Jasmine felt the rage of jealousy whip through her. She'd seen that look—the one that changed Morna's green facets into swirls—in the man who stood between her and that bitch. That was a mating look. *Well, tough shit. He's mine.* She knew those words had to have gone through her mind at least once or she wouldn't be remembering them now.

"Jasmine," a weak voice brought her back, "are you all right?" Lily's hand clasped her arm.

"I'm fine. Put that oxygen back on. I was just wool gathering." She gave Lily a smile and brushed the soft brown hair away from her face as the ambulance sped to the hospital.

"I'm sorry."

"No. Don't say that. You have nothing to be sorry about. You did nothing wrong." She repeated the very words Dorian had said to her a year ago, outside a deserted mine shaft.

****

With Jasmine heading to the hospital and John directing, or misdirecting, the crime scene, Eryk felt a bit at odds. He knew they'd passed some major milestone, but he'd be damned if he could figure out what it was. The look he saw on Jasmine's face kept nagging at him. He hadn't been able to read it. Not like her other ones.

"Bask wants to talk to you." John held out the phone that had been plastered to his ear since the police arrived.

Once again, the man seemed to be in mid-sentence when he put the phone to his ear. Eryk listened, trying to catch up. "...did what you asked. Talked with your attorney. He said he'll take care of everything."

Eryk smiled. "Thanks. That means a lot to me."

"Means something to me, too." Bask said. "Give Jasmine my love."

Was that a lilt he heard in the old man's voice? "I sure will. We're heading to the hospital as soon as things here are squared away."

Bask actually laughed. "Son, you will discover, where descendants are involved, nothing's ever squared away."

Eryk handed John the disconnected phone.

One of the police officers gave the two men a ride back to the cabin, hemmed and hawed before asking Eryk for his autograph. Eryk pulled out one of his business cards wrote on the back and handed it to the officer.

The man read it and grinned, his eyes crinkling. "Hey, thanks. My wife and kids will love it."

"Free pass?" John asked as they walked into the dark cabin.

"The least I could do," he said and went about gathering their bags.

John popped the top on a Coke and handed it to Eryk, opening one for himself as well. "They stopped Beverly Greeson at the airport. Seems she suddenly had an urge to travel to Argentina. Interpol is also interested in her.

Apparently, they've been tossing a "black widow" theory around for some time. Three dead men. Suddenly, she's singing like a canary and letting her daughter take the rap. There'll be some tree shaking, that's for sure. With the daughter dead, we might never know. Bask is working on getting the body released to Abbott House. That could get sticky. There are a lot of agencies wanting those remains."

They walked out to the vehicles. John threw his bag into the back. "I'm sure I'll hear more about it later. I'll keep you informed."

"Thanks."

"I'll check out. You go on to the hospital. I'm assuming that's where you're headed. I'm heading back to Safe Harbor."

Eryk stuck out his hand. "Thanks. For everything."

"Not a problem. Welcome to the family." His eyes crinkled. "Never a dull moment."

****

Why was it all hospitals felt the same? Jasmine shoved the bill and coins into the vending machine and pulled out a Coke. The walls here were the same off-shade of green as the one she'd been in after the attack on her. Same florescent lights. Same antiseptic smell. She popped the top and headed back to the ER where the nurse had to buzz her in.

She walked down the hall to the cubicle where Lily lay on the bed. Luckily, the leg wound was minimal. The bruises on her face would heal, as would the cracked rib. The woman who'd inflicted those, and probably others, was dead. Part of Jasmine wished she was alive so she could have the satisfaction of killing Morna herself. No, neither Bask nor Dr. Browne would approve of that. Well, Dr. Browne definitely wouldn't. Bask might understand. At least she was being honest. Dr. Browne would approve of the honesty.

She plastered a smile on her face and stepped into the cubicle. The fragility of the young woman lying on the bed startled her. The face was bright blotches of purple and one eye was swollen shut. But, it was the far away, almost vacant look that worried Jasmine. She reached over and pulled the straw out of the water cup and slipped it into the can. Easing up Lily's head, she put the straw to her lips. Lily had trouble closing her swollen lips around the straw, but managed a small sip.

"How ya doing?" Jasmine eased her back onto her pillow and made a pretense of looking at the monitors beeping in the background and the fluid dripping into the IV.

"Been better." The voice was flat.

Jasmine reached down and took hold of the hand not stuck with a needle. She looked deep into Lily's eyes. "I'm going to try to give you a little help with the healing. Mind you, I'm still new at this, but I'd like to give it a try."

Lily's eyes widened.

"I can wait for Eryk. He's probably better at it."

"He's definitely cuter." The chipped tooth grin appeared when she lifted the one side of her lips that wasn't split.

"Hmmm. So you prefer beauty over brains." As she said it, she let her energy flow, trying to not push too much.

"Male beauty—that male beauty, definitely. Ow!"

"Oops." Jasmine laughed and squeezed Lily's hand before letting go.

"I think you did that on purpose because you're jealous." Lily's eyes twinkled. "You like him, don't you?" She asked, teasing in her tone.

Jasmine felt her face flush.

"Like who?" Eryk said, smiling that megawatt showman smile as he stepped into the cubicle.

Lily took down at her hands. "Nobody...," she whispered.

"She finds me irresistible." He walked over and put his arm around Jasmine's waist and gave a tug.

"In your dreams." But the sarcasm failed when her black eyes twinkled and she smiled at him.

Eryk turned his attention to Lily. "How's my other best girl doing?"

Lily blushed and played with the lightweight blanket they'd covered her with. She spoke without looking up, "I'm sorry I ran away."

"And heisted my car," Eryk said jokingly and felt Jasmine's elbow impact sharply with his side. He let out an oomph.

"I'm sorry about that, too." Her voice was barely audible.

"Lily," Eryk reached over and gently lifted her chin, until she was looking in his brilliant green eyes. "I'm teasing you." At the same time, he gave a gentle push and felt his energy flow softly into the wounded girl. Her eyes did a slow blink. Her mouth slackened. "Why don't you rest now, sweetie? We aren't going anywhere. We'll be right here when you wake up." He maintained contact until her eyes closed completely.

"Did you...?" Jasmine whispered and stopped when he put his finger to his lips.

"...and he did it better..." Lily's voice was a teasing whisper as she drifted off.

Eryk took Jasmine's arm and led her outside the cubicle. Once outside, he looked into her eyes, studying her. "Are you all right?" He could feel the tension.

Jasmine pulled her arm away. "Don't."

"I can relieve some of that tension."

"Maybe I don't want you to. Did that ever occur to you?" Jasmine could feel the agitation moving through her and knew he was just a convenient target. "You walk a fine line between helping and controlling."

"Okay. Point taken." He stepped back one step and his voice became modulated and even. "I talked with Bask on the way over here. Arrangements are being made for Lily to return to Safe Harbor. Her father is being transferred to a facility not too far from there."

Jasmine's body froze. Yet, she tried not to show any emotion. She knew, just by the feeling in her gut, that Lily's father was being taken to the same facility that housed Rob. Her gaze slid back to the young girl in the bed. If she wants to go see her father, she'd go with her. It's a large facility. There'd be no reason for her to run into Rob at all.

Eryk knew the moment Jasmine's attention was no longer on him. He didn't know what was distracting her, but he'd figure it out.

"Jasmine...," the voice was plaintive, coming from the bed.

Jasmine put her smile back in place and moved to Lily's bedside.

"Are you hungry? I know they've approved food."

Lily slowly shook her head. "Not really. Have you heard anything about my dad?"

"Yes. In fact, he's on his way to a place near Safe Harbor. You are going back with us when they release you. You'll get to see him before you know it." She had no clue as to his condition so, for right now, she'd keep everything positive.

"The police said they arrested Beverly. Is Morna dead?"

Jasmine sat on the side of the bed and wished with every fiber of her being that Dr. Browne was here instead of her. With all the insight Jenn had given her about handling new clients, she wasn't sure what to say or do at this moment. She settled on the truth.

"Yes. Morna's dead. I'm sorry."

"Why?" she asked and pushed herself up on the hard mattress. "She was going to kill me. She was really crazy, you know."

"I kind of figured she was."

Eryk stepped up to the bed. "Lily, had Morna hurt you before?" He'd talked with the police downstairs. They'd said Lily hadn't said much to them, or was unable to. They were concerned that without something, Beverly would be released and, at this point, they didn't know if she was the mastermind, a conspirator, or just another victim.

Lily looked down at the bed, then up at Jasmine. "Miss Jenn said you'd been hurt before."

Jasmine nodded. "That's true."

Lily seemed to take that as encouragement. "Morna didn't like me much. At first, she would get irritated if I was in the room when she would come in. She'd say, 'I need to talk to *my* mother,' and I would leave. She always called Beverly Mother, never Mom. I called Beverly *Beverly*. She didn't seem to mind. Mostly, she ignored me. And, she was pretty nice to Dad. Beverly, I mean, not Morna. Morna used to narrow her eyes at Dad when she didn't think he was looking. But, he started traveling a lot and I didn't see him as much." She stopped to take a deep breath and sip the Coke Jasmine had brought. With her swollen lip, Lily was having a hard time, even with the straw.

Watching the girl struggle, anger shot through Jasmine. She wished she could share her newly acquired abilities, not only with the girl in the bed, but with most of the residents at Safe Harbor. *Boy, would that cut down on the need for a Safe Harbor.* She felt the tingle in her finger tips and turned back to Lily. She saw Eryk turn his eyes to her from the other side of the bed and saw just the smallest crinkle in the corners, as though he'd heard her thoughts. She tried to ignore the way her pulse sped up.

"Go on, Lily," she encouraged.

Lily looked down at the blanket, not meeting their eyes. "The first time, I'd come home from school. When I got to the landing—our bedrooms were on the second floor—Morna came flying out of her room, screaming, 'You've been in my room, you little bitch!' She shoved me. I tried to tell her I hadn't, but she shoved me again…and I went down the stairs. I still had my backpack on. I guess it knocked me out because, when I came to, Beverly and Morna were standing over me and Morna was saying how I'd slipped. Beverly told me to get up, but I couldn't. She seemed upset, but called 9-1-1. I'd dislocated my shoulder and twisted my ankle."

Jasmine tried to swallow by her mouth had gone dry. She knew that had been the beginning of what had to have been a horrendous change for Lily. "Is that why you ran away?"

Lily nodded. "I knew something was wrong. Dad hadn't been home for months and Morna had been gone, too." She suddenly looked up at Jasmine and smiled. "Beverly and I were really beginning to get along. With Morna gone, Beverly would ask me questions about school and everything. I had a dance coming up and she took me shopping. I got the coolest dress. She has really good taste—almost as good as you, Jasmine."

Jasmine smiled. It took so little to win the child's heart.

"Anyway, Morna returned and I overheard her say something about taking care of it. He won't be back." Lily's eyes lifted, the panic plain. "I knew it was my dad she was talking about. I went to my room and tried to call him. I tried all his numbers. I couldn't get him. Morna came to my room and started hitting on me. I was scared. She had this look in her eyes. I started fighting back. I don't know how I did it, but I got away. That's when the cops got me."

"Lily, it's none of my business, but I want to know. When we found you, you were pretty beat up and the clothes you were wearing…." Jasmine didn't know how to finish the question.

Lily's eyes widened. "No!" she squeaked. "It wasn't what you think. When I left I went to a friend's house, but her mom was friends with Beverly. Well, not exactly friends, but she wanted to be. I knew I couldn't stay there. My friend called a friend of her brother's who drove me to Norfolk. He took me to one of his friend's house who gave me some clothes cause mine were all dirty and messed up. She dressed kinda cheap. I wasn't hooking. I was asking for money so I could get a phone to find my dad."

Eryk jumped in. "You were panhandling," he said, obviously relieved.

"I guess that's what you call it. I guess from what I was wearing and all…." She let her voice trail off.

Jasmine smiled at her. "Hey, it got you to us, which is a good thing. We'll have to get something pretty for Detective Sonya, as a thank you gift, don't you think?"

Lily's eyes lit up. "Yeah. That would be great." Her eyes sparkled. "If they ever let me out of here," she called toward the nurse walking by.

****

Jasmine's ass was dragging. She felt like she hadn't slept in a month. From the moment they'd released Lily to return to Safe Harbor, it felt like the girl had gone into overdrive. Immediately, they had to stop and the first available fast food place and fill up on more grease than Jasmine figured she'd had in a year. Then, Lily had talked nonstop, even with a swollen mouth, for the entire two-hour ride back. Not the kind of talk she could sit back and nod, yet ignore, but the kind that required her active involvement. Clothing. Wardrobe lines. Designers. As if that wasn't enough, the dynamo herself, Jenn, had met them at the door and everyone seemed to be talking at once.

She pulled off her jacket and let it drop on the floor, on her way to bed. The light rap on the door came just and she was crawling onto the big, soft bed.

"Go away." She could only get a mutter.

"You sure about that?" Eryk's warm voice washed over her and her body responded, despite her exhaustion.

Lying on her stomach, she turned her head and opened one eye to see him standing next to the bed. "How did—"

He just smiled at her. Jasmine moaned and turned her head away, but scooched over to make room on the bed.

The moment he eased his body down beside her, Jasmine's body came alive. As much as she wanted sleep, her very skin seemed to tingle. He was touching her and she felt the blood pulse through her veins to settle in her core. Her breasts felt heavy and achy. Her loins throbbed.

She turned on her side he see him facing her, watching. His emerald green eyes had darkened and had that molten look. Her breath caught. He reached over and ran his finger over the curve of her cheek.

When he spoke, his voice was deep and husky. "I have to leave soon."

"Now? But…"

He cut off her words with his mouth and she found herself drinking him in, wanting so much more. She ran her hand up his chest and around his neck to sink her fingers in the thick black waves that she loved to touch. She pulled his mouth tighter and opened her lips, seeking the intoxication of his tongue. She moved her body against his in a silent plea.

That was all it took. Eryk reached for her with a passion he had known only with her. When he was near her he became insatiable, wanting to meld their bodies, their beings. He arm dragged her closer until his hardness pushed against her and she, in turn, moved against him. At once they were tearing at clothing, trying to get closer. His mouth and his hands took her, spreading fire in their wake. He took the hardened peak of her breast in his mouth and laved his tongue in a pushing circle, feeling it harden more until he suckled and she moaned. His hand dipped and his fingers spread through her black curls until he found her moisture and eased his finger in, spreading the heat.

Jasmine moved, leaning toward him, begging. She couldn't wait. She needed him to fill her. As he eased himself between her legs, his hands clasped her arms and he stared into her eyes. With their eyes locked, he sank deep within her and let the energy flow. She felt the rhythm of their pounding hearts shift, converge into a single beat. Current flowed through her and back to him, encasing her body in a vibrating heat. Her hands grabbed the sculpted muscles of his back, molding them. She moved, meeting his thrusts until there was nothing but him and sensations flooding her. The sensations built until she thought she would die and then their nerves exploded and pulsed in waves of completion.

Their bodies crashed onto the bed.

"What the hell?" she gasped. Their bodies still connected, she felt him tense above her.

"Uh...did we just?"

Jasmine giggled. "It sure felt like it."

"Wow," he said and buried his face in her neck. A chuckle escaped.

She punched him lightly in the back. "Stop that. That's not funny." But her voice betrayed her.

He lifted his head and looked into her eyes. "That, my love, was some magic." He reached down, kissed her on the nose, and eased his body to her side. "I really did just come by to tell you I was leaving." He let his fingers trail down her damp abdomen. "And, if I don't get up, I'm still not going to make my plane."

She stilled. "You aren't flying? You haven't had any sleep." She propped herself up on her elbows and studied his face. His face was shadowed in several days-worth of beard, giving him a rakish look. She wanted to push him back on the bed and straddle him. The thought had her blink twice, trying to clear her sex-fogged brain.

He caught the look and let his eyes slowly gaze down her long body, memorizing the lush fullness of her breasts, the curve of her waist and the legs that went on forever. She wore a thin silver chain around her ankle and that had the blood rushing to his groin. God, he would never get enough of this woman. But, he had places to be and people to see. He leaned over and placed a kiss just below her naval, glanced up and saw her eyes darken. Mustering more control than he felt he had, he kissed her on her love-swollen mouth and eased off the bed.

"Bask has someone meeting me at the plane. They're going to fly while I catch some sleep. How he'd found someone who would fly to Mississippi on a moment's notice...." He didn't finish, but pulled on his jeans and buttoned his shirt.

"Don't even ask. He won't answer." Jasmine was slipping her clothes on as well.

"Go back to bed. I'll call you tonight."

Already somewhat dressed she followed him to the door. She wanted to say something, but waited, not letting the words come. Instead, she nodded. One more quick kiss and he was gone. She closed the door and leaned against it.

****

A light tap on her door brought her awake. She didn't remembered lying down.

"Eryk..." She pulled open the door.

"Sorry," Jenn said, grinned, and lifted the tray she was holding. "I thought some tea and scones might be just about the right thing."

Jasmine ran her hand through her hair. "Let me rinse out my mouth...or something...." She pointed to the bed. "What time is it?"

"Ten-thirty," Jenn call out to her.

"Damn," Jasmine responded and closed the bathroom door.

In minutes, they were propped in her bed with the tray between them, sipping Earl Grey tea and munching on cinnamon scones.

Jasmine let the cinnamon melt on her tongue. "God, don't tell Teresa, but these are as good as hers."

"They ought to be, they are hers."

Jasmine stopped in mid chew.

"She overnighted a care package." She handed Jasmine a note.

Jasmine recognized the Abbott Bed & Breakfast stationery with a pang of homesickness. Teresa's neat scrawl slanted across the notepaper:

Hey, Sweetie—

You've certainly had a time of it, haven't you? I figured some goodies waiting for you would make things a little better. Just picture me sitting across from you and Jenn, chatting away.

I just want to let you know I'm so very proud of you. You are an amazing woman and I love you with all my heart. I know things haven't gone like you might have liked but, trust me, these things have a way of working out.

I'm doing fine. We'll talk more when you and Eryk come down to help Morgan and Dorian. She's big as a barn now. Both of them are happy as larks.

Enjoy the treats.

Love you,

Teresa

"You okay?"

Jasmine nodded and wiped away the stray tear. She sighed a deep sigh. "I feel bad that I haven't been there for her."

"If I know Teresa, she'd want you to be exactly where you are—with Lily."

"How is Lily?"

"She slept until about nine o'clock and made a beeline to wardrobe."

Jasmine shook her head and smiled. "She a resilient girl, isn't she."

"Most of them are," Jenn added.

Jasmine looked at her friend. Jenn would know. She'd been saving them for years.

"She agreed to meet with Dr. Browne this afternoon."

"That's good. I think Dr. Browne can help her get through this."

"I talked to Bask this morning, by the way." Jenn topped off their cups and handed Jasmine the honey.

Jasmine stirred the honey into the tea and sipped the sweet liquid. The light filtered in through the window and played across the comforter on her bed. The warm serenity of sitting in bed with a good friend, sharing tea and talk, slipped into her mind like a hug and she relished the feeling. Eryk's image stole into the scene and she felt complete.

"Uncle Mike had a conference call with the facility in Sweden. It was on the up and up," Jenn said. "He's at the facility here now and will examine Mr. Greeson when he arrives this afternoon."

Sometimes a small world was very small indeed. Mike Yancy, Ruthorford's doctor as long as Jasmine could remember, and Teresa's ex-boyfriend, had turned out to be Jenn's uncle.

She saw Jenn staring at her. "Tell me about Greeson, because I know Bask had more to say than Dr. Yancy was coming." She smiled at Jenn.

"Boy, do you know Bask," Jenn laughed. "He emphasized that he was speculating—like three times—but that didn't stop him at all."

"Yeah. Sometimes I wonder, if he weren't doing all this in an official—," she air quoted official, "—capacity, he'd just be a gossip. Go on."

"His theory is, with Morna being like Morgan, she attracts the Gulatega...which, he suspects led her to craziness. Well, not exactly. He thinks she was crazy to start with. However, without knowing anything about them and the fact that only she could see them probably made her think she was hallucinating." Jenn rushed on, "You know, vicious cycle." She twirled her hands. Jasmine doubted Jenn could talk without using her hands.

"Somehow, Morna locked up Greeson with some Gulatega." Her expression took on one of sadness.

"Not food poisoning?" Jasmine asked.

"No. One of his people found him almost dead from starvation. His mental capacity was so diminished, he couldn't feed himself. They sent him to the sanitarium. As soon as Bask heard this, he sent people into the facility in Sweden, but they didn't find any of the creatures there. However, Greeson's condition is not good. That's why Bask sent Uncle Mike."

Jasmine closed her eyes. Somewhere downstairs, Lily was going about her morning with no idea her dad might never be the same. She prayed that wasn't the case. Lily'd been through so much already.

"She wants to go see him as soon as he gets here," Jenn added. She looked at Jasmine. The same sadness had slipped into Jenn's normally vibrant expression.

"I'll go with her," Jasmine said softly.

Jenn reached out and touched her arm. "I hate for you to go there, but Lily trusts you."

Jasmine gave her a half smile. "I know; otherwise, you couldn't get me within ten miles of that place."

"It's a big place." Jenn tried to comfort her friend.

Jasmine nodded, drank her tea, and stared out the window as the sun disappeared behind clouds.

Chapter Seventeen

The day broke bright and warm, a total juxtaposition to Jasmine's mood. The last couple of days had been a whirlwind of activity, trying to get back into the routine of Safe Harbor, while keeping reigns on Lily. The girl was a bouncing ball of energy. She talked a mile a minute and, even with the wonderful ideas she added, she seemed almost to suffer from attention deficit disorder. It wasn't until Lily asked her for the fifth time in fifteen minutes when they could go see her father that Jasmine realized she was scared silly and trying to compensate.

Her own unease had escalated with each passing day. She knew the cause. That damn match-mate thing. She slammed the door to the wardrobe and caught it before it closed and shattered the mirror screwed to the back of it. Her reflection showed a woman, dressed in the height of fashion, with dark shadows under her eyes. Lack of sleep. Of course, it would help if Eryk's phone calls weren't short and rather stilted. Troop this. Brandy that. Jasmine threw the top she held in the hand on the chair, rather than rip it to shreds, her jealousy pouring out of her in waves.

"Are you ready, yet?" Lily's head popped around the door.

Jasmine let out the breath she'd been holding and forced herself to smile. "Sure am. Let's head out."

Jenn was by the front door. "Sure you don't want me to tag along?" Her eyes showed the concern only Jasmine read.

Lily spoke up. "I'm sorry. I didn't think to ask you. I was too excited. Jasmine said we'd have lunch in Williamsburg on the way home after seeing Dad."

"It's okay. I couldn't be gone that long, anyway," Jenn lied. "I've got a lot of work to do. You two take your time. And, if you stop by the Trellis, bring me some Death by Chocolate." She gave Lily a quick hug.

Dr. Browne had talked to Lily about her father, taking the tack that he most likely had had a stroke and they didn't know what the prognosis was right now. When they brought him in, he seemed to be in a catatonic state. Everyone hoped there'd been some improvement since he'd arrived. Jasmine had tried to prepare Lily. She had no idea if she'd succeeded.

The medical facility was much larger than Jasmine had thought. It sat far back and had a huge main building encircled by a road with many outbuildings. Some looked like houses, some condos.

When they pulled into the parking lot in front of the main building, Jasmine turned to the suddenly quiet young woman next to her. "You ready?"

"I don't know." Lily turned pleading eyes to Jasmine. "What if he doesn't know me?"

Jasmine took her hand, stared into her eyes and let a small amount of energy flow. "Remember, we talked about this. We won't know until we see him. I'll be with you. And, no matter how he is now, tomorrow holds promise."

Lily smiled and let go of Jasmine's hand. "You're right. At least I got him back." With that, she opened the door and hopped out.

They were expecting them. Jenn had made sure of that. A nurse led them down the hall to a private room. The curtains were open and sun poured into the room. Flowers sat on a table near the window. A single hospital bed sat in center of the room. Porter Greeson lay in the bed, the head raised, staring at the wall. His sky blue pajamas gave a tint of blue to his silver hair. He'd been shaved and prepped for Lily, Jasmine was sure.

The nurse stepped over to the bed and leaned in front of him. "Mr. Greeson. You have a visitor. Your daughter, Arabella, is here."

Realization hit Jasmine. This man didn't know her as Lily.

"Daddy," Lily's tremulous voice broke. "It's me, Bella."

The older man blinked and shifted his eyes toward his daughter. The corner of his mouth lifted in a strained smile and a tear slid out of the corner of his eye.

Lily turned to Jasmine, her eyes overflowing with tears. "He knows me. He knows me."

Jasmine felt her own eyes fill as she nodded and watched Lily lay her head on his chest.

Porter Greeson slowly moved his hand until it rested on his daughter's head. He made no other movement and the slight shake of Lily's shoulders let Jasmine know she was crying.

Moments passed before Lily stood. She reached to the bedside table and, taking a Kleenex, dabbed at the tears on his face, then her own. "It's okay, now, Daddy. I'll take care of you."

Jasmine thought she would burst into sobs if she didn't get out of the room. "I'm going to step out for a little bit, if that's okay." Her voice sounded husky. "There's someone here I want to see."

Lily nodded, not turning away from her father. "I'll be right here." Her voice sounded upbeat.

Jasmine walked over to the nurses' station and grabbed a tissue from the box on the counter. The nurse that had led them in smiled at her. "I am so happy. There was a huge improvement in him since yesterday. We've been telling him his daughter was coming since we found out. At first, it seemed to cause him some distress, but once we specified Arabella, he changed. We bathed him and got him all fixed up. He had a feeding tube until this morning. It was obvious he wanted it out. After seeing her and their closeness, I can see why." The nurse's eyes' pinkened. "Damn," she muttered and grabbed a tissue herself.

"Can you tell me where to find Rob Milineaux?"

The nurse checked her computer. "He's in room 444. But, right now he's down in the cafeteria. Go back to the lobby and turn left. It's at the end of the hall."

"Thanks. Please let Lily...I mean Arabella know I'll be back in a few moments."

"I will."

Jasmine moved down the hall, measuring her steps as if she were on automatic. This probably wasn't the best idea she'd ever had, but not knowing was driving her crazy. She stopped outside the door to the cafeteria and took a calming breath. She stepped into a yellow, cheerful room. Round tables with flowers on each table were scattered about the room. Along the back wall were several stations. She could smell bacon and figured they were still serving breakfast. Trying to act nonchalant, she stepped over to one of the stations, picked up a tray, and moved down the line, asking for a biscuit and butter, although she knew she'd choke on the smallest bite. She fixed a mug of coffee and, lifting the tray, turned and faced the room.

She saw him immediately. He was sitting at a nearby table with a couple of male nurses, or attendants. His once gold blond hair was threaded with gray and he was heavier and softer than she remembered. He was talking with one of the men, his voice animated and light. He turned his head, saw her, and stopped talking. His head tilted and a frown formed between his faded blue eyes. Then, a slight smile formed on his lips. "Do I know you?" he called to her.

Her stomach lurched. She couldn't utter a word. She tried to smile and shook her head.

Glancing around the otherwise empty room, he indicated the chair across from him. "Please join us. No one should eat alone."

Jasmine looked to the male attendants for some sort of guidance. One of them rose. "Well, my break's over, Rob. She can have my chair." He turned and smiled at Jasmine. The other attendant smiled as well but didn't leave.

Forcing one foot in front of the other, Jasmine crossed the short distance and prayed the tray wouldn't slip from her sweating hands. She set the tray down and the coffee jiggled, spilling some over the side. In a flash, Rob lifted the cup and dabbed up the spilled coffee with some napkins.

"There. That's better. Is that all you're eating?" he asked, eyeing the lone biscuit.

She managed to find her voice. "I'm not very hungry. I just wanted something to nibble on."

He pushed a small container her way. "Try this on it. It's homemade preserves from one of the nurses. She's so sweet to bring them. Are you sure we don't know one another?"

Jasmine swallowed. "I do believe we have a mutual friend. Morgan Drake...I mean Briscoe."

Rob screwed up his face as he searched his memory. "The name sounds familiar. I've been ill," he informed her. "Sometimes my memory isn't what it used to be." Then, his eyes brightened. "Yes. I remember Morgana. I think we dated a couple of times in college."

Jasmine didn't correct him, although she knew both of them had been out of college for quite a while when they'd met.

"How is she?"

"She's fine."

He smiled and stuck out his hand. "I'm Rob Milineaux."

Jasmine stared at his hand, wiped the moisture from her own on the napkin in her lap, and eased her hand into his. His hand felt cool and soft, like a child's.

"I've been editing a tenth grade physics book for one of the local schools," he announced proudly.

"That's wonderful." She remembered someone telling her that, although his memory was spotty, he did recall his physics, but not the work he'd done on the portals. He had no memory of the time he'd spent in the lab in Meadow's Keep. She decided to test the theory.

"So, are you a professor?" She tried to sound casual.

He looked at the attendant and made the same face he had when he'd tried to remember Morgan. "I think I was." He leaned forward. "You see, I had some sort of stroke...I think. My memory is iffy at best, except for my academics. I have trouble with people and places and timelines." He brightened, "But show me a formula or an equation and I'm just dandy. I also grade papers for some of the local professors," he told her.

An idiot savant. Jasmine frowned.

"Oh, don't be sad. You seem sad," he said almost childlike. "What you don't remember can't hurt you." He laughed, finding himself witty.

Jasmine rose. Her knees wobbled. "Well, I need to get back upstairs."

"You didn't touch your biscuit." He looked hopeful.

She smiled at him, this brilliant man-child. "You may have it." She handed him the preserves. "Don't forget these."

He took the container. "Oh, I won't. It was nice meeting you. I think I've forgotten your name."

"Teresa," she lied.

"Well, it was nice meeting you, Teresa. I hope the person you came to see gets well soon."

"Thank you."

She turned, dropped off the tray and fled, not stopping until she was outside, leaning on the brick façade of the building, gulping in air. She couldn't seem to catch her breath. Jasmine dashed away the tears that rolled down her cheeks. The images that had haunted her for a year crumbled like dust. She hadn't been the only victim in that mine.

At least her injuries had healed.

She let the tears fall, unchecked, until there were no more. She closed her eyes and saw Eryk, tenderness in his eyes, and could have sworn she felt his fingers brush her cheek.

"Thanks," she whispered into the air, and made her way to the nearest lady's room to make herself presentable to Lily, who missed nothing.

****

Lily had been talking nonstop since they'd arrived at The Trellis for lunch. Less crowded than usual, they'd been seated right away and had their orders taken in record time. Jasmine toyed with the Chicken Pot Pie, which was one of her favorites, its savory aroma doing nothing to whet her appetite. Lily, on the other hand, was wolfing down her cheeseburger at an alarming speed. Orders for three Death by

Chocolate desserts—minus the ice cream—had already been given.

Lily's enthusiasm was contagious and Jasmine let herself be comforted by the girl's talk of the future, when she and her father would be together again. If Jasmine had ever wanted anything more than for that wish to come true, she couldn't think of it.

Jasmine made a mental note to call Bask and see if he could find out more about the situation. There was no telling what evil Morna and her mother had attempted with Greeson becoming increasingly incapacitated. If anyone could unravel that mess, Abbott House had the connections and the money to do so. It was times like this that she was happy to be part of Ruthorford and the Abbott House. Before she knew it, she'd consumed over half of her pot pie.

****

"Oh, my God!" Jenn bounded down the steps, her blonde curls bouncing, as Jasmine stepped out of the vehicle.

"What?" Jasmine's insides clinched.

"Morgan's gone into labor," Jenn's eyes were wide. She grabbed Jasmine's arm. Jasmine could feel her heart racing.

"Calm down, Jenn." Jasmine laughed. "She's okay, right?"

"Wow," Lily yelped. *What that child needs is more excitement,* Jasmine thought and rolled her eyes. It looked like both females were jumping up and down.

"You have to leave," Jenn ordered.

"Would it be okay if I pack first?"

"I took care of that," Jenn pointed to the front steps where Jasmine's bag sat upright.

Jasmine had visions of two weeks of jeans and sweaters, given Jenn's propensity toward that particular uniform.

As if reading her mind, Jenn supplied, "I actually think I did a good job. I know what you wear."

Jasmine smiled and handed her the bag with the desserts inside. "I guess I won't be needing these."

Jenn opened the bag and smiled. "I think I can take care of these just fine." She wiggled her brows at Jasmine.

"With my help," Lily injected.

Jasmine reached for her luggage and was grateful to see the makeup bag behind it. With the two bags in hand, she moved back to the vehicle. "I gather you're taking me to the airport."

Jenn dangled keys and handed Lily the goody bag. "No cheating. Wait until I get back."

"I can't go?"

"I need someone here to look after things while I'm out."

Lily wasn't buying it.

"Scoot," Jenn ordered with a laugh.

Jenn drove and Jasmine filled her in on Lily's father, warning her of Lily's possibly misjudged prognosis. Jenn promised to bring Dr. Browne up to speed. After a moment of silence, Jasmine told her she'd seen Rob. Jenn stared at her so long, she almost drove off the road.

"I'm fine. Really. Actually, I'm better than fine. Poor Rob isn't, however."

"Poor Rob!" There was another erratic movement of the wheel.

"Should we table this until you aren't driving?"

"I'm fine and we're almost there anyway. I can't believe you found sympathy for Rob."

"You didn't see him, Jenn. The only thing left of the man is his physics, his books." When Jenn didn't respond, she added. "You'd have to see him."

"Well, that's not going to happen," Jenn stated.

They pulled up to the private jet Bask had waiting for her. After handing the attendant Jasmine's bags, Jenn hugged her. "Eryk's meeting you there. Give Morgan and Dorian my love and, for God's sake, take pictures."

"Will do. You take care of Lily."

Jasmine sat back in the soft leather seat. She was the only passenger and alone in the large cabin. No matter how they timed it, it would be a good three hours before she'd be there. The twins would probably not arrive before she got there, but one never knew. Not that she was absolutely necessary for the birth, she reminded herself—but given Jenn's mania earlier, for a moment, she wasn't sure. She smiled. Jenn was a trip and a half, no matter what the circumstances. The woman's energy and life force never failed to amaze Jasmine. She felt lucky to count her as a friend.

Jasmine held her breath through the takeoff and settled back as the attendant arrived with a ginger ale over ice, her favorite. Leave it to Bask to make sure she was comfortable. There really was no need for an attendant, except, she mused, it gave someone a job, and since jobs were scarce, she liked that idea.

Bask. Jasmine realized she'd have to talk with him. Maybe Morgan and Dorian could give her some idea of how to handle that conversation. *Hey, Bask, now that Eryk and I have slept together...* She winced. Well, hopefully, she could put that off for a little while. Or, at least as long as she and Eryk were needed in Ruthorford.

What she and Eryk were needed for was to ensure nothing came through the portal while Morgan was incapacitated. She and Dorian were determined to have those babies in the same bed Morgan had been born in, above The Shoppe of Spells. She and Eryk would camp out in the cottage.

Then what? Who knew?

****

When the town car pulled in front of The Shoppe of Spells, Eryk was standing out front. He stepped over and opened the door, offering her his hand. The moment their fingers touched, the current surged through them, seeking and finding a rhythm, an equilibrium. Jasmine looked into the vibrant green eyes for a moment before they shifted and looked to the rear of the car, where the driver was unloading her suitcases.

Not quite the welcome Jasmine had expected, but the circumstances weren't exactly normal either. She refused to let it bother her. This wasn't her time, it was Morgan's and Dorian's, and she hoped she would get to see them before the big event.

"How's Morgan doing?" she asked.

"Walking the floor upstairs. Has been for hours. I'm a nervous wreck." Eryk's voice quivered.

Jasmine let the laughter bubble up. "Then imagine what Dorian's going through."

Eryk slowly shook his head as he held the door open for her. As she stepped inside, the whistle of a teakettle went off.

"Boiling water? Really?"

"There's my girl." Teresa's voice preceded her from the kitchen. Taking Jasmine into a tight hug, she laughed. "I was making tea."

Jasmine held the hug a few seconds longer, inhaling the wonderful scent that was Teresa. She wasn't sure, but thought Teresa felt lighter. She stepped back and looked at her cousin/mother. Her face glowed with the good health she'd always had, wisps of blonde, now streaked with silver, framing her face. Although Teresa had complained about its unruliness for years, Jasmine has always loved the fringe of soft curls.

"Can I?" Jasmine nodded her head toward the stairs.

"I don't see why not. I don't think anything's going to happen for another couple of hours."

Jasmine glanced over at Eryk, who was looking a little distracted. "You go ahead," he said, "I'll get some tea ready."

Teresa offered Jasmine a knowing smile and guided Eryk toward the kitchen while Jasmine made her way up the stairs.

"Why don't you go help Teresa?" Jasmine could hear Morgan moan through gritted teeth.

"I'm not leaving you," she heard Dorian respond.

She approached the bedroom to find Morgan holding her oversized belly and plodding across the floor, Dorian in her wake. From the look on Morgan's face, Dorian was not helping. From the look on Dorian's, he was at a complete loss and in a damned near panic.

"Hey guys," Jasmine stepped into the room.

Morgan gave a visible sigh of relief.

"Why don't I stay with Morgan for a few moments and you go down and get some tea," she offered.

"No. I don't want to leave her," Dorian snapped out.

"Please, Dorian," Morgan moaned. "Leave me." Seeing the dejection in his face, she quickly added. "Just for a few moments."

"If you're sure?"

Jasmine took his arm and led him to the door, planting a kiss on his bedraggled face. "Eryk doesn't look so good. Maybe you can ease his mind."

The two women listened for his footfalls on the stairs.

"Thank you," Morgan mouthed.

Jasmine gave her a hug and felt the belly tighten and Morgan lean into her. "Are we timing those?"

"Teresa says it'll be a couple more hours, yet. She sent Mike over to the clinic. Brenda cut herself and says only Mike can do the stitches."

"I bet she wouldn't have said that if she'd known you were in labor," Jasmine raised a brow, knowing how the postmistress loved being the first to know whatever was going on in Ruthorford.

"Yes," Morgan said and started pacing again. "If word got out, every person in town would be downstairs. I'm not sure I'm ready for that."

"Where are your parents?"

"They're out in the cottage, getting it ready for you and Eryk."

Jasmine felt her face redden.

"Oh, come on," Morgan moaned. "They had their trial by fire with us. Mom is so happy you and Eryk and going to be in the cottage…just in case. She wants you guys to be comfortable. Besides, if you think Dorian was bad, you haven't seen my Dad." Her steps faltered a little as the pain gripped her and she grabbed Jasmine's arm.

Flashes of their less than auspicious beginning wriggled into her memories as she led Morgan around the large Victorian bedroom. How she'd inadvertently hit Morgan eyes with wasp spray and Dorian didn't believe it was an accident. How she'd flirted with Rob at the Abbott Bed & Breakfast, thinking Morgan was playing one guy against the other. Finally, how she'd try to convince Rob, when he'd gone mad and kidnapped her, that she was like Morgan and he didn't need Morgan.

"Don't go there," Morgan said softly and squeezed Jasmine's arm. "We have become much more than the sum of our parts."

"Thank you." Jasmine placed her hand over Morgan's and gave a little push of energy, hoping to give her a little strength.

Morgan tried to smile, but it didn't reach her eyes. "I think I better lie down. And...," she hesitated as she hoisted herself up on the tester bed, still a struggle, even with the step, "I think you might use your ability to tell Eryk to send Dorian up. I'd do it, but I'm afraid he'd go into cardiac arrest."

Jasmine laughed. "Give me a moment, I'm still learning the craft."

Morgan smiled. "If all else fails, you can yell over the banister."

"There's that, too."

"I think it worked," Morgan squeaked at the sound of the cavalry storming up the stairs.

Jasmine was startled by the similarity of the two men. Except for the green eyes of one and the haggard look of the other, she was looking at identical men—at least in appearance. Then she saw the smile Dorian offered his wife and her heart melted.

"You might let the Briscoes know it's almost time," Jasmine said, stopped, and added, "wait, I'll come with you."

Jasmine turned back to Morgan, placed her hand gently on Morgan hard stomach. "Make it easy on your momma. I'll see you soon." Then she leaned over and kissed Morgan on the forehead. "Love you. I'll be downstairs."

"Love you, too." She squeezed Jasmine's hand. "Is Mike downstairs?"

Eryk answered. "He just got here." He could hear the good doctor talking softly to Teresa, affection in his voice.

Jasmine led the way. She stopped at the bottom of the steps and watched as Mike stood talking quietly to Teresa, his hand resting familiarly on her back as they stood facing the counter. "Morgan asked if you would come up now," she tried to keep any hint of judgment from her tone.

Teresa turned, looked straight into Jasmine's eyes, and smiled. "I'll go get the Briscoes." She didn't wait for a response, looked back at Mike, then walked out the back door. Jasmine moved over to the door and watched her cousin walk through the still lush garden to the Victorian cottage in the far back. Within seconds, she was holding the door open for Morgan's parents as they rushed past, their expressions a combination of anxiety, pride, and love.

Jasmine contemplated going out to the cottage. This was not the time. This was Dorian and Morgan's time. She turned and joined Eryk in the kitchen. He set a mug of tea in front of her and sat down across from her.

"You're looking good," she said.

"Thanks." He took a drink from his mug, not meeting her eyes.

He was acting strange. No. He was acting like a stranger. Which was odd, since they were mated. He could never be a stranger. Even if he wanted it, it wasn't going to happen. Maybe he'd had second thoughts and was trying to back off.

Teresa stepped back into the kitchen, made her own tea, and joined them at the table.

The silence lengthened.

Eryk cocked his head. "There's one," he said, continuing to listen intently.

They all seemed to hold their breaths. "And two," he smiled from ear to ear. The sound of wails drifted down from upstairs.

"We can all hear that," Jasmine commented, a twinkle in her eyes.

The three of them moved to the stairs but didn't go any further. Both Teresa and Jasmine watched Eryk, knowing he could hear what was going on upstairs. "Almost," he whispered.

As if by command, Dorian leaned over the mahogany railing, a grin splitting his face.

They rushed up the steps, stopping outside the door. Eryk and Jasmine stepped back, letting Teresa go first. They moved in behind her and stood at the foot of the bed.

For someone who'd just given birth, not to one, but two babies, Morgan looked radiant. A bit sweaty, but glowing. In each arm was nestled a red-faced baby, one swaddled in pink, one in blue. "May I present Melissa and Thomas Drake," Dorian announced. At the sound of his voice, the babies opened their eyes. Both had the emerald green eyes of their mother.

Jasmine looked over at Eryk. "Looks like you are no longer unique."

Morgan's parents stood on one side of the bed, their eyes red from tears. Talbot had his arm around Becky as they looked lovingly down at their grandchildren.

Tears of joy made Morgan's eyes glisten like emeralds as she spoke. "Dorian and I would like it if you, Jasmine, and you, Eryk, would consent to be our children's godparents. Eryk, you need to understand that, for Ruthorford descendants, it's a contract. You will agree to be a part of our children's lives forever. We understand if you need to think it over. But we wanted to ask the two of you formally, in front of all of our families." Sudden realization struck Morgan and she blushed, realizing that Eryk's parents weren't present. "Oh, Eryk...I didn't mean...." She shut up and looked at Dorian.

"It's all right. It's been some time since I was even a little bit close to the people that raised me. No offense taken." He looked at Jasmine.

Jasmine could feel his heart beating fast. Taking a chance, she reached out and slipped her hand into his, waiting for their hearts to acclimate. *I would love to, if you would.* She formed the words in her mind and willed him to hear her.

Eryk squeezed her hand. "We would be honored," he answered for both of them.

Mike Yancy stepped into the room, carrying a tray with glasses and a bottle of champagne. He popped the cork, filled the glasses, and passed them around, giving Morgan a small amount. He raised his glass. "To our newest descendants." The glasses were clinked and sips taken, followed by sounds of pleasure.

"Bask sent it," Mike confessed. "You don't want to know how much it costs."

****

Jasmine was holding little Thomas when she looked over at the bed. Morgan was sound asleep. Becky was sitting beside the bed rocking Melissa, while Talbot looked on, the movement of the rocker beating out a slow rhythm. Dorian and Eryk stood to the side whispering. The doctor reached over and eased Thomas from her arms. "I want to have a last look before I head home."

From the doorway came Teresa's voice, barely above a whisper. "Why don't you stay at the Bed & Breakfast tonight? That way you can check in on them in the morning. There's plenty of room at the Inn," she joked.

She turned to Jasmine and spoke softly, watching Eryk as he paid attention to all conversations. "Food's set up downstairs. Be sure and get something to eat before you head over to the cottage. Oh, I put some things in the fridge over there for tomorrow, in case you don't want to come over here first thing. Becky and Talbot are planning to stay in the guest room to help out for a few days." Eryk nodded slightly to acknowledge Teresa without turning away from Dorian.

The room had quieted and the stress of the day finally took its toll on Jasmine. She swayed slightly, grabbing the bedframe. In a heartbeat, Eryk was by her side, holding her arm. "Let's get you over to the cottage. I'll come back for some food. If I remember correctly, there's a great looking claw-foot tub over there calling your name."

"I'd like that. Thank you."

Dorian stepped over and kissed her on the cheek. He was still grinning like a fool.

"Congratulations, old man," Eryk whispered. "Give Morgan our love. If you need us, call. We can manage the shop for you."

"I just might do that. Thanks for being here with us and thanks for consenting to help us raise our children." He turned and embraced his brother.

Jasmine felt the tears well and turned toward the door.

Chapter Eighteen

The light filtered in through lead paned windows, casting an early morning glow across the quilt. She'd always loved the cottage, even though it contained the ever-present threat of the portal. She'd never felt threatened. Jasmine stretched out her cramped muscles. She'd nearly fallen asleep in the tub when Eryk helped her out, dried her with the lavender scented towel and slipped the nightshirt over her head. The last thing she remembered was him pulling the quilt up as she slipped into lavender scented dreams.

Now the smell of coffee teased her senses and she looked toward the open French doors. Eryk stood watching her, holding two mugs of coffee.

He stepped into the room. "Feel better?"

She pushed the pillows back and sat up. "Much. Thank you."

He handed her a mug of coffee and sat on the edge of the bed facing her. "Jenn called on your phone after you went to sleep. I hope you don't mind, she told me about your day. Considering all you dealt with, I suppose running interference with my bullshit didn't help."

Jasmine's first thought was to say she didn't know what he was talking about. But she knew for a fact that more bullshit wouldn't make things easier. "I'm better now."

"We need to talk."

Jasmine set her mug on the bedside table. It was always better not to have scalding liquid in your hands when you got bad news. Likewise, Eryk put his on the table beside hers.

"There was a reason I was acting so weird yesterday. I got here in the morning. I'd spent the entire day with Dorian and Morgan, watching them prepare for the birth of their children, watching them loving one another."

Her gut clinched. *It was too much for him. He wants out. Oh God…there was no out.*

Eryk grabbed her shoulders. "No! Don't do that. Let me have my say."

"How come you can read me so well and I can't read you?" She knew she sounded childish but, suddenly all her defenses were flying up. And…he looked so gorgeous. His hair was still damp from his shower and he wore a teal colored sweater that threw blue lights into his eyes. He'd even shaved. She felt the lust start moving through her veins and she closed her eyes.

She felt Eryk lean his forehead against hers and felt his breath upon her face. *Please don't give up, yet, she prayed.*

"I'm not giving up, you little fool. I'm trying to tell you I love you." He whispered the words.

Her eyes flew open. "You don't want to leave? But, yesterday — it felt like you were backing off."

"I was. I'd realized how much I loved you and was afraid you'd sense it and rebuff me."

"Rebuff? Who says that anymore?" She laughed and laced her fingers together behind his head, pulling him to her as she scooted down in the bed. "Rebuff — my ass." She pulled his mouth to hers and let all the passion she had stored rush from her and encompass him. Slowly the passion eased and she found she was making love to him, sharing her being and her soul. With every touch and taste, she gave of herself. She traced and memorized the hard grooves of his muscles and the texture of his skin. She inhaled the scent of him and stroked his velvet hardness. She moved on top of him and eased him into her body, making him her own. When the world exploded around them, they truly became one. "Eryk, I love you," she whispered.

"Look," he whispered, with gentle fingers, turned her head toward the great room.

All the stones in the cottage glowed in a soft iridescence, as though faeries had sprinkled their world with faerie dust. She smiled and nestled closer. They were one.

****

"Are you sure it's okay?" Jasmine asked as Eryk helped her into the Jeep. The day was sunny and the wind light. A perfect "Jeep" day, meant to be spent riding through the country with the top down.

"It's fine. Morgan's up and about. Becky and Talbot are still here and Teresa's on call, should anything happen. Relax. We'll only be gone a couple of hours at most."

"But where are we going?" She turned to him.

He smiled. She sat next to him wearing brown pants topped with a rust colored cowl-neck sweater, slipping off one beautiful shoulder. Gold loops hung from her small ears. He leaned over and kissed her full mouth. God, he would never get enough of her. "It wouldn't be a surprise if I told you, now would it."

She shrugged and decided to enjoy the day and the ride with the man that continued to amaze her. Jasmine leaned back and glanced at the canopy of trees stretching over the country road. The colors were vibrant, having come to their fullest when the cold snuck in several days ago, right after the babies' births. It was even cool enough to have a fire in the fireplace.

She almost felt guilty. Everything was going so well, they were barely needed. Well, except to take pictures. They must have downloaded hundreds and, with every phone call, Jenn wanted more. Lily had a million questions and had decided, like it or not, she was Aunt Lily and was awaiting, none too patiently, for an invitation to visit. Soon, they promised. Very soon.

Eryk stopped at a railroad crossing, easing over the rusted tracks. Farther in, he passed through an old covered bridge to emerge into a small, deserted town. The center of town was cobblestone, heading off in four directions; each intersection had a handmade stop sign, now faded. Long forgotten overhead lines dripped with vines. He pulled the Jeep to the side and helped her out.

She looked around. An old brick building stood on one corner, its double wooden doors closed. Next to it sat a squat log structure, proudly proclaiming itself the library. Across the narrow street was a row of shops, a hodgepodge of various designs, some cottages, a couple of brick, another log. Tall trees lined the streets for as far as she could see, their branches reaching toward one another to form a canopy. A smattering of buildings dotted the distance.

She turned to Eryk. "What a marvelous place. How did you find it?"

"Bask," he said simply.

She stepped into the middle of the intersection, looking first one direction, than another, and heard the screech of a hawk. Looking upward, she watched the bird circle and dip before disappearing into the trees. Smiling, Jasmine turned to Eryk. Her smile faded as she picked up the hammering of his heart. Tilting her head, she waited, suddenly unsure.

"When we were at Meadow's Keep," he began, his voice cracking ever so slightly, you talked about wishing there was a place where people could go to start over. Somewhere, other than a halfway place. You talked of what people needed and about second chances. I looked into some things. I pulled some strings. I took a chance with you as you took a chance with me. Let's give it to others."

Smiling, hope in his eyes, he held out a large, old-fashioned key. "Welcome to your own Meadow's Keep."

She looked from him to the key and back to his smiling eyes. In two strides, she was in his arms, laughing, crying, and loving the man who had become her other half.

To Second Chances

Coming in 2014

from Shanon Grey

Second Chances

The GateKeepers, Book Three

"The body's gone."

"What'd you mean, 'the body's gone'?"

"Did I sound like I stuttered?"

No. Definitely not. Kristoff Bask wasn't one to stutter. Or mince words, for that matter. Mike Yancy squinted, his thumb and forefinger pinching the bridge of his nose, and tried to focus on the old wind-up clock sitting on the bedside table, atop a mound of dusty medical journals. 4:47 in the friggin' morning. Well, at least it wasn't 3, like the last time Bask had deemed whatever it was an emergency. Mike couldn't remember what that was for the life of him and it'd been last week.

Bask was talking, as was his bent, never waiting for the other person to catch up.

"...when Jim left at 11 last night, it was still..."

"You had Jim work 'til 11?"

"I did not...not exactly...I just thought it would be better to get the autopsy done as soon as possible."

Was that hesitancy Mike heard in the old man's voice? Couldn't be he was getting soft. "I'll be there as soon as I get some clothes on."

The line went dead. No goodbye, kiss my ass, nothing. Mike pulled his aching body up from the side of the bed. God, what possessed him to up the weights last night? He rubbed the small of his back as he grabbed his khakis off the back of the chair. For a man in his fifties, he considered himself in good shape, especially for a doctor who had no life of his own. Why on God's green earth he'd decided to beef up his workout.... Who was he kidding? It was because Teresa Abbott Ruthorford was a free woman. Well, almost. Once they recovered Bill's body—again.

STAY TUNED FOR A RELEASE DATE IN EARLY 2014!

ABOUT THE AUTHOR

 **SHANON GREY** weaves romance and suspense with threads of the paranormal. THE SHOPPE OF SPELLS was the first in her series, THE GATEKEEPERS, about the quaint town of Ruthorford, Georgia and its very special inhabitants. PENNYROYAL CHRISTMAS ~A Ruthorford Holiday Story~ gives another insight to Ruthorford's special descendants. Under contract with Crossroads Publishing House, her books are available in e-format and print at most booksellers.

Shanon spent her life on coasts, both the beautiful Atlantic and the balmy Gulf. Hurricane Katrina taught her the fragility of life and the strength of friendship, family, and starting over.

She just found out that her son salvaged notes and pages of her original novel, Capricorn's Child, which she thought had been destroyed with everything else. (Ironically, a neighbor found her marriage certificate in a tree.) She plans to resurrect her original novel one day.

She currently lives in Coweta County, Georgia, trading the familiarity of the coast for the lush beauty and wonder of the mountains, where her husband fulfilled her lifelong dream—to live in a cottage in the woods, where inspiration abounds.

Stay up to date on other Shanon Grey books and events by visiting her website at:

www.ShanonGrey.com

You can also visit Shanon on Facebook and Twitter @ShanonGrey. She would love to hear from you. You can write her at shanongreybooks@yahoo.com.

<u>SHANON GREY's BOOK LIST</u>

The Shoppe of Spells ~ Book One ~ The GateKeepers

Meadow's Keep ~ Book Two ~ The GateKeepers

Pennyroyal Christmas ~ A Ruthorford Holiday Novella

Coming Soon

Second Chances ~ Book Three ~ The GateKeepers

Nancy Naigle
Out of Focus
COMING NOV 2013 – The Granny Series – IN FOR A PENNY

Johnson Naigle
inkBLOT

Sam Phillips
BATTLE OF MIAMI
and the
Rick Cunningham Suspense Novels
Deadly Voyage
Deadly Friendship

Made in the USA
Middletown, DE
12 May 2016